DEAD STREETS

"If vampires with a romantic penchant for ordinary human girls have been done to death, a zombie with a heart of gold might just be the Next Big Thing."
Death Ray

"A terrific melding of the horror and private detective genres. Waggoner's writing is visually led, and the *Blade Runner/Dark City* atmosphere is well drawn. A great start to what is hopefully an ongoing series."
Total SciFi

"It's a *classic*. If you're a fan of Simon R Green, you'll especially enjoy Nekropolis. It's a horror spoof done with a sense of wit and pulp detective done tongue-in-cheek. Sam Spade, watch out. There's a slow-footed zombie creeping up on you!"
Bewildering Stories

"Tim Waggoner is well on his way to being proclaimed horror fiction's leading surrealist… His descriptive powers lend a cinematic quality to his prose that plays out spectacularly in the mind's eye."
Cemetery Dance

"Tim Waggoner has created a credible world of horror, inhabited by every kind of misbegotten creature... But it's a great plot, too, with convincing, if arcane, detective work. Just plain amusing, witty and incredibly cleverly conceived."
Aurealis Xpress

D0816300

To Linda —

TIM WAGGONER

*Come with me for
a stroll down*

Dead Streets!

A MATT RICHTER NOVEL

Tim Waggoner

**ANGRY
ROBOT**

ANGRY ROBOT
A member of the Osprey Group

Lace Market House,
54-56 High Pavement,
Nottingham
NG1 1HW, UK

www.angryrobotbooks.com
Dying for it

Originally published in the UK by Angry Robot 2010
First American paperback printing 2011

Copyright © 2010 by Tim Waggoner
Cover by Vincent Chong

Distributed in the United States by Random House, Inc., New York.

All rights reserved.

Angry Robot is a registered trademark and the Angry Robot icon is a
trademark of Angry Robot Ltd.

This is a work of fiction. Names, characters, places, and incidents are the
products of the author's imagination or are used fictitiously. Any
resemblance to actual events, locales, organizations or persons, living or
dead, is entirely coincidental.

Sales of this book without a front cover may be unauthorized. If this book is
coverless, it may have been reported to the publisher as "unsold and
destroyed" and neither the author nor the publisher may have received
payment for it.

ISBN 978-0-85766-046-6

Printed in the United States of America

9 8 7 6 5 4 3 2 1

DEAD STREETS

ONE

That night, working security at Sinsation, I learned something new. Just because you're dead doesn't mean you can't hurt.

I'm not talking physical pain. I hadn't experienced any of that since the day I died and was resurrected – through means I still don't quite understand – as a self-willed zombie. And I'm not talking mental and emotional pain. My body may be dead, but my brain is still very much alive – or at least functional – so I still experience those kinds of pain on an all-too-frequent basis. I'm talking about an entirely different sort of pain, one that up to this point I hadn't given very much thought to: aesthetic pain.

I was making my way through the thrashing, gyrating crowd that choked Sinsation's dance floor, doing my best to shut out the noise blasting from the stage, but it was impossible. Kakophonie was simply too damned loud. The band's lead singer went by the sobriquet of Scream Queen, and considering that she was a banshee, the name fit. She looked like an emaciated human woman in her early twenties, with long, stringy black hair, a bone white complexion, eyes set in dark hollows, lips snail belly gray, and a stylish touch of grave mold at her temples and the nape of her neck. She wore a tattered white shroud made from sheer fabric that left little about her too-skinny body to the imagination. Her nails were black, overlong, and sharp, and I wondered if they were fashion statements or weapons. Both, I decided. In Nekropolis almost everything – and every*one* – is a weapon in one way or another.

The rest of the band's lineup was an eclectic mix of Darkfolk. A lean male vampire with cyberimplants played guitar, his technological enhancements allowing him to act as his own amplifier. A short boar-faced, beetle-bodied demon, gender unknown and perhaps inapplicable, played bass, while a huge werebear with a truly impressive set of shaggy dreads pounded away on drums that had been specially reinforced with titanium to stand up to whatever punishment the lyke could dish out. I wasn't sure how he managed to hold on to the drumsticks with those paws of his, though. It's hard to describe the sort of music Kakophonie played, mostly because it was so deafeningly loud that it sounded more like a solid wall of noise than anything else. Darkfolk's senses are different than humans', and I suppose it's possible that to the assembled vampires, werebeasts, demons, and assorted other creatures, the band's music was pleasing, even soothing, but to my zombie ears, it sounded like a dozen vehicles colliding head-on at a hundred miles an hour... over and over and over.

But as bad as the band was, the lead singer was worse. There was a reason she called herself Scream Queen and it wasn't an ironic reference to the term for a horror movie starlet, or at least not only. The Queen's idea of singing was to open her mouth as wide as she possibly could – which, given that she wasn't human, was disturbingly wide indeed – and shriek at the top of her lungs for the entire length of a song without ever pausing for an intake of breath. To be fair, her tone did vary, rising higher, falling lower and with a vague sense that there was some sort of rhythm to the sounds she produced. But there was no way anyone even remotely in their right mind would consider what the Scream Queen did as singing.

I was starting to consider tearing off my own ears and destroying my eardrums with a couple well-placed finger jabs – I could always get my ears repaired later – when a man on the far side of the dance floor signaled to me. He was tall and handsome, with rusty-red hair and a beard that contained enough gray to be considered distinguished. He dressed entirely in black – black jacket over a black T-shirt, black slacks, black shoes – the only variance in the color scheme being the golden medallion he wore around his neck. I'd seen the medallion close up many times, and its face was emblazoned by a circular series of runes that I couldn't translate, but which looked appropriately grim and mysterious. The hand signal meant *All clear on my end,* and I nodded to the warlock and tried to keep from scowling as I returned the message.

I decided to check on the rest of the team, each of whom was stationed at a different position in the club. Scorch was on the opposite side of the dance floor from Bogdan, and she was dancing wildly to Kakophonie's music, though how anyone could find enough rhythm in the bizarre sounds the band produced to inspire any movement other than severe convulsions was beyond me. Scorch appeared to be a young woman just entering her teens and she wore her blonde hair in a long ponytail that fell down to the middle of her back. She usually dressed in a riot of color, in counterpoint to Bogdan's more severe style, and tonight was no exception. Her sleeveless blouse had been sewn together from patches of bright colors and though her skirt was denim, her knee-high socks were rainbow striped. Though Scorch appeared to be just another fan of Kakophonie's out to have a good time, her gaze was focused and intense, taking in everything around her. I caught her eye and she gave me the all-clear signal, accompanied by a wink and a grin to let me know that just because she was working didn't mean she couldn't have fun too.

Tavi was hanging out by the bar, nursing a mug of aqua sanguis and grimacing whenever he took a sip. The synthetic blood substitute might taste like the real thing – or close to it – but it provides little nourishment. It's kind of like Nekropolis's version of non-alcoholic beer. It's cheaper than the real stuff and easier to come

by, and any number of the city's Darkfolk drink it –
vampires, demons and lykes, especially. Tavi was one
of the latter, though he usually chose to go about in his
human form. Many lykes never bothered to don their
human shapes in Nekropolis as they saw no reason to
hide their true natures here. After all, if you live in a
city of monsters and you *are* a monster, you might as
well look the part twenty-four seven. But others still
availed themselves of the camouflage of appearing
human whenever they wished and Tavi was one of
them. Right now he appeared to be a middle-aged man
of East Indian descent, lean and wiry, with short black
hair, wearing a tan Nehru jacket and matching pants. I
once asked him if the jacket wasn't something of an
ethnic cliché. In reply, Tavi asked me if my gray suit was
any less of a cliché, considering it was the same sort of
outfit I'd worn when I was alive back on Earth.

Your suit screams "cop," he'd said.

I couldn't deny it. *At least I don't wear a trenchcoat,* I
had replied.

Tavi gave me the all-clear sign, I returned it, and I then
trained my attention on the last member of our team.
Even if I hadn't known where she'd be, I wouldn't have
had any trouble finding her. Devona and I shared a psychic bond that had gotten stronger over the months we'd
been together and we could sense each other's presence
within a thousand-foot radius or so. A slender, petite
blonde who wore her hair short, Devona wore a won-
derfully form-fitting black leather outfit that, given the
temperature in the club, would've caused her to suffer

heat prostration if she'd been human. But she was only half-human, on her mother's side. Her father was a vampire – one of the city's five Darklords, in fact – and while she physically appeared to be in her late twenties, chronologically, she was in her seventies. What can I say? I always did have a thing for older women.

Devona stood at the edge of the stage, gazing up at Scream Queen as if she were the banshee's biggest fan, when in truth she couldn't stand the woman's so-called singing anymore than I could. In reality, Devona was telepathically scanning the area surrounding the stage for any strong negative thoughts or emotions that might indicate someone wished Scream Queen harm. Vampires have a great many abilities, but half-vampires tend to be more psychically gifted than their full-blooded brothers and sisters, which is one of the reasons why vampires mate with humans from time to time: to add those psychic abilities to the sum total of power in their clan. For the first seven decades of her life Devona had used her powers to help safeguard her father's collection of mystic artifacts, but she and Lord Galm had experienced a recent falling out, resulting in her being cast out of the Darklord's home. I was sorry for that, especially since I'd helped cause that falling out, but considering that Devona had moved in with me soon after, I wasn't too sorry.

Devona must've sensed my watching her, for she turned to look at me and smiled, and I felt the feather-gentle touch of her thoughts brushing my mind.

All's well so far, love.

I smiled back, nodded, and we both refocused our attention on our work.

Sinsation's own security was pretty lax, consisting primarily of a single bouncer, though I had to admit he looked appropriately intimidating. A hulking man in a black pullover sweater and gray pants, he stood just inside the club's entrance, leaning against the wall, tree trunk-thick arms crossed over his massive chest, glowering at everyone from beneath a prominent Neanderthal brow. His skin was greenish-gray and his bald head had a line of scar tissue around the circumference, showing he'd had brainwork done.

The bouncer was a Frankenstein monster, constructed to be massively strong and near impossible to kill. His kind were common in Nekropolis, created by Victor Baron – the original Frankenstein monster – to fill those jobs that required brute force and plenty of it. And there was no shortage of such positions that needed to be filled in Nekropolis. Baron creates all sorts of fleshtech for the city, but these monsters – often referred to as the "repurposed dead" – weren't objects to be owned. They were individuals in their own right, hired to perform a task and paid for it like anyone else. The difference was that they were created to perform specific functions and that bothered me. I wondered how much choice they really had about what they do. Could someone like Sinsation's bouncer wake up one morning and suddenly say to himself, "You know, I'm tired of crushing skulls for a living. I think I'll take up waterpainting landscapes instead."

But the Frankenstein monsters I'd encountered seemed content enough with their lot, so who was I to judge?

Kakophonie was one of the most popular bands in Nekropolis and their fans packed the club that night. Sinsation's theme was based on the classic seven deadly sins: greed, sloth, gluttony, hate, lust, envy, and pride. Greed was represented by the precious metals and gems worked into the floors, walls, ceiling, and furniture. Cheap imitations, most likely, since none of the club's patrons seemed especially interested in absconding with a platinum coated chair or prying off a diamond studded wall panel to take home as a souvenir. The servers brought you copious amounts of whatever food or drink you ordered – gluttony in action – and diners reclined on couches in the style of the ancient Romans as a nod to sloth. Lust was represented by several private rooms in the back of the club where any patron could retire to do anything with and to anyone who was willing, and as for hate... well, it wasn't uncommon for several good sized brawls to break out in the club during the course of an evening. Pride and envy were easily taken care of, for Sinsation was one of *the* places to be seen in the city and not just anyone was granted admittance. I recognized a number of Nekropolis's more notable citizens. Fade, gossip columnist for the *Daily Atrocity*, was there, of course. The reality-challenged woman is always on the scene of any happening where she can be seen by a sizeable crowd who can help keep her existence reinforced. Darius the Sideways

Man was in attendance, which was a bit surprising since he travels between alternate versions of Nekropolis, and I hadn't seen him in our dimension for a while. And the Jade Enigma stood at the back of the crowd, hidden within his, her, or its voluminous green robes and looking appropriately enigmatic.

The only reason the owners of Sinsation would allow the likes of me to shamble across their threshold was because I was with the band – or more specifically, with Scream Queen.

After leaving her father's employ, Devona had helped me on a few cases, but she'd soon become restless. She'd spent all of her life living in her father's shadow, most of it residing inside the Cathedral, Lord Galm's stronghold. She wanted to do more than work at my side as an unofficial private investigator. She wanted to explore her newfound independence and make her own way in the world. I understood. After all, I've always been something of an independent sort myself. So Devona decided to use her knowledge of security systems and procedures, both mystic and mundane, that she'd gained working for her father to start her own security business. Being the daughter of a Darklord – even a half-human, banished daughter – had helped her quickly establish a reputation and her business had gotten off to a good start and was doing quite well. So well, in fact, that she'd been able to bring Bogdan, Scorch and Tavi onto the staff, and I helped out when I wasn't busy with my own work. Which meant that this night Devona was my boss. When I was a kid back on

Earth I had a folksy uncle who was fond of saying, "Life sure is a funny old possum sometimes, ain't she?" I know just what he meant.

Scream Queen had hired Devona because during Kakophonie's last two gigs someone had attempted to abduct the singer. Her own security – a pair of two-headed mansters – had managed to foil both attempts, but only barely, and not without a significant amount of injury on their part. Among other indignities they'd suffered they were now a pair of one-headed mansters. Both had quit before their service to Scream Queen could prove fatal. Left without security the Queen had turned to Devona. The details of the two abduction attempts we'd gotten were a bit sketchy, but then mansters aren't exactly Mensa material. Each attempt had occurred at a different time – one before a gig, one after – and the assailant had been cloaked by an illusion spell that faltered when he, she, or it was attacked, revealing a masked figure encased in black body armor which concealed not only the gender but also the species of the kidnapper. One thing the mansters agreed on was that whoever it was knew how to fight and use weapons, both the standard fare – knives, guns, swords – and those of a more esoteric variety – spells, charms, enchanted objects – which meant we were probably looking for a professional hired to do a job as opposed to an obsessed fan who wanted to take home more than just a T-shirt with Scream Queen's face on the front, but otherwise, as we say in the private detecting business, we didn't have a goddamned clue.

Enemies? According to Scream Queen, she didn't have any.

"Everyone loves the Queen, darlings," she'd said when we'd asked.

Did she owe anyone money? "Certainly not! I have more darkgems that I can ever possibly spend"

What about the band members? "If they had any enemies, I'd know about it, and if they needed darkgems, they could always come to me. We're one happy family, darlings."

We'd questioned the individual band members, of course, but they'd told us the same thing. So our strategy tonight was a simple one: never take our eyes off Scream Queen and keep watch for anyone suspicious in attendance. Unfortunately, this being Nekropolis, everyone looked suspicious.

Vermen servers scuttled back and forth through the club, taking orders and delivering food and drink with characteristic speed. The humanoid rodents moved swiftly, constantly shaking with a nervous energy that most people found annoying. That, coupled with a musky body odor reminiscent of wet skunk, made their species one of the lowest regarded in the city. But there was no denying their speed and efficiency, at least when it came to completing simple tasks, so vermen were widely employed as servants throughout Nekropolis. The sight of them always made me uncomfortable, though. Their position in the city's social order struck me as a sort of racism – or maybe the right term would be species-ism – and I had to remind myself that this wasn't Earth and while the vermen resembled humans to a point, they weren't human. So I told myself to take a "When in Rome" attitude and tried not to think about the situation, but I never felt very good about doing so.

As a rule, vermen tend to be short – between four and five feet tall – with rat heads, lean bodies covered with brown, black, or gray fur, and long hairless tails. They tend to walk hunched over with a shuffling gate, though they can move damned fast when they wish to. The creatures avoid clothing for the most part, though sometimes they'll wear vests, mostly just to have pockets to carry things. The vermen employed at Sinsation, male and female, wore black vests with gold buttons and matching bow ties. I suppose the club's management was hoping the vests would make the vermen look classy and formal, but the overall effect struck me as rather silly.

"Pardon me, sir. Can I get you anything?"

I barely heard the voice over the music and I turned to see a verman server quivering before me. When I first came to Nekropolis I thought vermen trembled like that because they were always afraid. I'd soon learned that they shook due to their rapid metabolic rate. Standing still must've been torturous for the creature, but he did so, looking up at me with wet glossy-black eyes.

He was a bit leaner than the average verman – evidently the club owners didn't feed their employees as well as their guests – and he was missing half of his left ear. He didn't carry an order pad because vermen didn't

need to write things down. They never forgot the details of an order.

I shook my head and the verman bowed his head before shuffling off in search of someone else to serve. I
headed toward the bar to check in with Tavi when I felt
a hand on my shoulder. At first I thought the verman
had returned for some reason and was trying to get my
attention, but his kind never came in physical contact
with the clientele where they worked, perhaps because
they knew how revolting their touch was to most people. So since I didn't know who had laid a hand on me,
I reached into one of my pants pockets as I turned.
Nekropolis is a dangerous place at the best of times, and
along with a 9mm loaded with blessed silver bullets
currently resting in a shoulder holster concealed beneath my jacket and a squirt gun filled with a blend of
holy water and garlic juice tucked into my jacket
pocket, I always carry a number of useful trinkets with
me in case I run into any unpleasantness. I had my fingers on one such item, ready to pull it out and activate
it, as I turned to see who wanted my attention. In the
back of my mind I was thinking that Scream Queen's
would-be kidnapper had gotten wind that Devona and
the rest of us were on the job and for whatever reason
had decided to confront me. But when I saw who was
standing before me, I knew that wasn't the case.

"Matthew Richter! I'm so glad to finally catch up
with you!"

She wore a white floor-length gown that resembled a
toga, bodice cut low to display an impressive amount of

cleavage. She wasn't fat, but she was, shall we say, Rubenesque, and I wondered if she used some sort of spell to keep from spilling out of her dress. She wore a pair of dark wrap-around goggles to hide her eyes, something for which I was exceedingly grateful, considering she was a gorgon. Since I was a zombie, I had no idea whether her direct gaze could turn me into stone, but I didn't want to find out. Her hair, as you might imagine, was a nest of green serpents, although instead of heads, miniature video cameras sprouted from the snakes' necks. It's not uncommon for the denizens of Nekropolis to sport cybernetic or genetic enhancements, for their inhuman physiognomy is able to adapt to such drastic changes in ways that merely human bodies can't, but this was one of the stranger body modifications I'd seen since taking up residence in the city. Although, technically, this wasn't the first time I'd seen the woman's cyberserpents, just the first time up close and in person and I wasn't thrilled about it.

"I'm too busy to talk right now, Acantha!" I had to shout to make myself heard over the band.

The gorgon smiled, revealing a mouthful of slightly pointed pearl-white teeth. "No need to raise your voice, sweetie. My little pets can filter out any background noise, even when it's as loud as this. Just speak normally." Her smile widened. "And by the way, just so you know, we're on live right now."

I grimaced. *On the Scene with Acantha* was one of the most popular Mind's Eye programs in Nekropolis. Devona and I watched it now and again, more as a guilty pleasure than anything else. Acantha specialized in live, on-the-spot tabloid-style interviews with the city's famous and infamous, the up-and-comers and the downward-sliders. She came across as all sweetness and light at first, but it never took long for her true nature to reveal itself. She could be more vicious than a lyke suffering from a bad case of intestinal parasites and those who were unfortunate enough to get cornered by her rarely came across well during the interview, to put it mildly. I joked with Devona that the gorgon's program should be re-titled *Verbal Evisceration with Acantha*, so as you might imagine, I was eager to get away from the woman as fast as possible. Besides, I couldn't afford to be distracted while I was supposed to be watching for another abduction attempt on Scream Queen.

Before I could protest any further Acantha launched into her first question. "Are you on the job right now, Matthew? Trying to track down some nefarious villain, no doubt. I'm sure you can't tell us the whole story – detective/client confidentiality and all that – but perhaps you can give us one or two juicy tidbits to satisfy our curiosity?"

To be honest, I was a bit flattered. The dead aren't held in high regard by other Darkfolk and zombies are considered to be on the lowest rung of that particular ladder. I was used to people turning up their noses at me – especially when I'd gone a bit too long between applications of preservative spells to keep me from rotting – so the fact that Acantha at least appeared to be happy to see me was a nice change. And it occurred to me that doing an interview with Acantha might garner some good publicity for Devona's business. But I was working, and as tempting as it was to do the interview, the job came first.

"I'm afraid I don't have any tidbits to offer, juicy or otherwise. Like I said, I really don't have the time for this right now."

Muted light flashed behind the gorgon's dark goggles and her lips stretched into a hard, thin line. Translation: *Acantha Is Not Pleased.*

"I've wanted to get you on the show ever since you saved the city last Descension Day, but for some reason my calls to you weren't returned." Before I could respond she reached out and grabbed hold of my left hand and turned it palm up. "So the rumors are true!" she said, her tone triumphant, as if she'd caught me with my pants down and my undead zombie dick exposed for all the world to see.

I had no doubt that her serpentcameras were focusing on a close-up of my hand and the pattern of puckered scar tissue there that formed the letter *E*.

"You *are* a servant of Lord Edrigu!" the gorgon crowed.

Edrigu, Master of the Dead, is one of the five Darklords who rule Nekropolis.

I yanked my hand free of Acantha's grip. "One of Edrigu's servants did a favor for me and now I owe Edrigu a favor in return. That's the extent of our relationship."

That was true enough as far as it went, but I had no real idea just how much I owed Edrigu for the help Silent Jack had given my friends and me. I tried not to think about it too much. It's never a good idea to owe a Darklord anything and if I'd had any other choice at the time… Well, I hadn't and I'd made the deal with Silent Jack and one day I would have to pay for it. I just hoped that day was a while in coming.

I wasn't really paying much attention to Acantha at this point. I'd returned to scanning the crowd, keeping an eye out for anything or anyone that seemed out of the ordinary. Well, more out of the ordinary than usual for Nekropolis. While I knew that Scream Queen's would-be abductor had cloaked his or her true appearance with illusion spells during the two previous attempts to kidnap the singer, that didn't help much. Scream Queen's former guards had been able to describe the illusions well enough: a male vampire covered with synthticks, cybernetic insects that constantly filter and recycle their wearer's blood supply, adding various drug cocktails to it in the process, and a female demon who resembled a bipedal shark, complete with water-breathing apparatus and, according to the guards, a truly impressive pair of shark-skin-covered breasts. But it didn't matter what the abductor had looked like before. Assuming he or she stuck to the same MO a new illusion would be used next time and there was no way to predict what sort it might be.

Acantha spoke then, a sharp edge of impatience in her voice. It seemed she wasn't used to being ignored and the experience wasn't sitting well with her. "If you could try to *focus* here, Matthew. I only need a few minutes–"

I spun to face the gorgon. "I don't have a few minutes! I told you – I'm busy! And why are you even bothering to talk to me? I'm nobody special. I'm just a guy doing my job. There are dozens of people in here who are far more interesting than I am. Go pester some of them and let me get on with my work."

Acantha gritted her teeth and the light blazing behind her goggles was so intense now, I imagined that my normally stiff limbs felt a touch more rigid and heavy. Maybe it wasn't a good idea to irritate a gorgon, I thought. Still, she went doggedly on, speaking through her gritted teeth.

"Rumor has it that someone has tried to kidnap Scream Queen twice now. Is that the case you're working on?"

Back when I was alive, I'd worked as a homicide detective on Earth – in Cleveland, to be precise – and I'd had to deal with aggressive journalists on more than one occasion. But those reporters had been like playful little puppies compared to the pit bull that Acantha was. She'd sunk her teeth into me, metaphorically speaking, and I knew there was nothing I could say or do to get her to give up. She wouldn't be satisfied until she got what she wanted out of me and the sooner I delivered the sooner she'd move on and let me do my job. But by this point I'd begun to get irritated, too. I'm not exactly the go-along-with-the-program type. As my mother used to tell me, if you let people push you around they'll never stop,and in Nekropolis the last thing you need is a reputation as a push-over. Not if you plan to keep on living.

I still had my hand inside my pants pocket, my fingers wrapped around the object I'd planned to use to defend myself in case of attack. I withdrew the object, a small ball of white silk, and tossed it toward Acantha's face. It expanded rapidly upon contact with the air and by the time it struck the gorgon it had become a sticky white mass large enough to engulf her entire head, videoserpents included.

"Have a piece of Anansi's Web," I told her.

Out of reflex Acantha reached up to tear the webbing away from her face with her long black nails, but when her fingers came in contact with the sticky mess she realized her mistake. Anansi isn't just any arachnid: he's an African trickster god and his webbing is far stronger and more adhesive than simple spider silk. Acantha's fingers became stuck fast in the white mass covering her face and though she frantically tried to tear her hands free there was nothing she could do.

"Pretty nifty, huh?" I said. "Some clients pay with darkgems, while others prefer to pay in barter. I pick up all kinds of interesting toys that way. Don't worry about the webbing. It'll dissolve after an hour or so. In the meantime, I'd remain as still as possible if I were you. It can't be easy to breathe through that stuff and you don't want to asphyxiate while you're on the air, do you?"

I felt an admittedly petty sense of satisfaction as I turned away from the gorgon, who was now emitting muffled cries of indignation that I imagined were peppered with rather colorful language. I walked away, knowing I would end up paying for this one way or another, but at least now I could return my attention to where it belonged – keeping an eye out for Scream Queen's abductor.

Good thing, too, for at that moment I felt Devona's mind reaching out to mine.

Look stage left.

"Stage left" meant Scream Queen's left and the audience's right. I directed my gaze where Devona indicated and saw a female ghoul waving an autograph book in hope of getting the singer's attention. Ghouls are basically humanoid, hairless and ivory-fleshed, with thick reptilian lips and double rows of sharp teeth. They're voracious gluttons, but while the males tend to be obese, the females tend to be thin to the point of emaciation, though they eat just as much as their opposite gender. Different metabolisms, I guess. Neither male nor female ghouls were particularly pleasant to look at, especially considering they never wore a stitch of clothing.

Kakophonie's song built toward its climax and ended on a series of thunderous notes that made the floor vibrate dangerously. I wondered if Sinsation's architecture could stand up to the punishment or if the band would literally bring down the house before their set was over. Scream Queen shrieked one last time as the final note sounded and then she bowed to wild applause and cheers from the audience. The ghoul jumped up and down and thrust her autograph book toward the banshee singer, but I was already moving, as was Devona and the rest of the team. There was nothing about the ghoul's appearance to rouse suspicion, but I was certain Devona had gotten a psychic "hit" off the woman, marking her as a likely suspect, and we had to intercept her before she could make her move.

Which was far easier said than done, given how crowded the club was that night. I'd moved close to the bar, which meant that everyone on the dance floor was between me and the stage. I started shoving my way through the crowd, making liberal use of my elbows and shouting, "Security! Let me through!" but neither tactic helped me make much headway. Tavi had been sitting at the bar, so he had the crowd to contend with too, and while Scorch and Bogdan had been stationed on the dance floor, neither was all that close to the stage. Only Devona was near enough to reach the ghoul before she could get to Scream Queen and she headed toward the bald, naked autograph seeker, pushing people out of her way with surprising strength. Devona may only be half-vampire – and a petite half-vampire at that – but she's still plenty strong. And while she doesn't possess any telekinetic abilities, she was able to employ her telepathic powers to mentally urge the concert-goers to move aside and while many of them didn't get the message – or if they did, chose to ignore it – a good number did make room for her to pass, bewildered looks on their faces as if they weren't quite sure why they'd done so. I was impressed anew by how much Devona's psychic skills had improved since we'd first met. She'd worked hard to develop her powers over the last few months, and the results were paying off now.

But before Devona had gotten halfway to the ghoul, Scream Queen noticed the woman waving her auto-graph book and, gracious star that she was, reached down to take it and quickly scrawl a signature before the next song started. She handed the book back with a smile and then gave a nod for the band to launch into the next number. The ghoul gave a strange smile, al-most as if she were enjoying some private joke, before turning and beginning to head away from the stage. That struck me as strange. If you were a big enough fan to want an autograph, why would you leave after get-ting it, especially when you'd only gotten to hear one song? But Scream Queen looked unharmed as the band started in on another tune that had more in common with a ten car pile up than music and I began to wonder if Devona had been wrong about the ghoul. After all, she was heading away from Scream Queen, who was most decidedly *not* abducted, so she appeared to be no threat. Maybe her real interest in the autograph lay in its monetary value and she was eager to get on with the business of finding a buyer. As I said before, ghouls are gluttons and all the food they shovel down their gullets doesn't come free. But then Scream Queen opened her mouth to sing and I – along with everyone else in the club – realized that something was seriously wrong when no sound came out of her mouth.

Her fellow band members realized it too. They stopped playing and stared at Scream Queen with expressions of puzzlement that were rapidly edging toward outright alarm. The patrons in attendance were equally confused and shocked and the entire club fell quiet as everyone waited to see what would happen next.

Scream Queen drew in another breath and then opened her mouth once more. She squeezed her eyes shut and her neck muscles grew taut. She was clearly attempting to release a note with some real power behind it, but just as before, there was only silence. It seemed the Scream Queen had lost her voice. But that was OK: I knew where it had gone.

I started heading toward the ghoul.

TWO

I didn't get there first, though. Devona had telepathically broadcast her warning about the ghoul to the entire team and all of us were beginning to converge upon her. Scorch was faster than any of us with the exception of Tavi, but she was closer to the ghoul than the shapeshifter was. She became a blur as she wove swiftly through the crowd and she intercepted the ghoul before the creature was halfway across the dance floor.

Scorch said something to the ghoul, but I couldn't hear what. Even though Kakophonie wasn't playing right then, the confused audience were talking loudly amongst themselves, and even though I had a good view of Scorch and the ghoul, I couldn't read lips. Inwardly I was raging at Scorch for approaching the ghoul directly. We knew how dangerous Scream Queen's would-be abductor was and confronting her head-on was more than reckless – it was downright suicidal. And unlike Scream Queen's former bodyguards, Scorch only had one head to lose. But that was Scorch: she lived for

fun and as far as she was concerned danger was just another flavor of fun.

The ghoul was taller than Scorch by a good head and
a half and when she raised her right hand and displayed
her claws she looked like a most formidable figure, one
against whom a mere teenage girl wouldn't stand a
chance. But in Nekropolis judging by appearances is
never a good idea.

The ghoul pulled back her hand, no doubt intending
to slash out with her claws and lay open Scorch's throat,
but before she could move Scorch decided to show her
opponent how she'd gotten her name. Bright orange
flames erupted all across Scorch's body and the ghoul –
not to mention those audience members in the immediate vicinity – took a startled step backward. Scorch's
fire burned hotter and brighter, the flames completely
obscuring her form, but she didn't scream, didn't so
much as move a muscle. The fire expanded, the flames
stretching outward, rising upward, and then just as suddenly as they'd ignited, they extinguished, and where a
moment before a teenage girl had been standing, now
stood a seven-foot-tall, powerfully muscled, red-scaled
demon. Scorch's true form was that of an infernal monster from the old school: pointed ears, baleful yellow
eyes, mouthful of wicked-looking fangs, curling ram's
horns, a row of serrated scales trailing along her spine,
and a sinuous reptilian tail complete with an almost del-
icate little arrowhead shape at the tip.

The ghoul, who no longer had the advantage of
height over Scorch, quickly recovered and lashed out

with her claws anyway. Only now instead of having a throat covered with tender girl flesh, Scorch's throat was covered with shiny hard scales, and the ghoul's claws skittered off them without doing any damage. In response Scorch gave the ghoul a truly disturbing fang-filled grin and slapped her own clawed hands onto the ghoul's bony shoulders. As soon as the demon's flesh came in contact with the ghoul's Scorch released her flame and fire spread out from her palms to engulf the ghoul.

"No, dammit!" I shouted, not that I figured Scorch would hear me. Too many people were doing their best to get the hell away from Scorch and the ghoul and they weren't being particularly quiet about it. I knew that Scorch could control the intensity of her flame – as a fire demon that was her specialty – and she wouldn't kill the ghoul unless she had to. But I wasn't worried about our suspect getting fried; I was worried about the autograph book she still carried. We'd been assuming that the ghoul's plan had been to abduct Scream Queen, but now it looked as if she'd only been interested in stealing part of the singer: namely, her voice. I wasn't exactly sure how the ghoul had accomplished it, but it seemed clear that Scream Queen's signature in the autograph book had been an integral part of the spell. And if Scorch's flames reached the autograph book and turned Scream Queen's signature to ash, maybe the spell would be broken and the singer's voice would be restored to her – or if the signature was destroyed maybe Scream Queen's voice would be lost forever. While the latter prospect didn't strike me as much of a loss to Nekropolis's music scene, Scream Queen was my client – well, technically she was Devona's client – and I was determined to protect the banshee's voice by whatever means I could. Unfortunately it looked like there was nothing I could do to keep Scorch from incinerating the autograph book.

However, the ghoul – or whoever was masquerading as the ghoul – was prepared. As demonflame spread across her ivory-colored skin she appeared to reach *into* her side, sliding her long clawed fingers bloodlessly into her flesh and withdrawing a tiny figurine resembling a white ape. The ghoul spoke a single activating word and the ape's mouth opened, unleashing a torrent of frigid air at Scorch. Yeti's Breath was a powerful spell – with an accompanying stench so rank that it would make a carrion imp retch – and within seconds Scorch's flame had been extinguished and the demon was encased in a thick shell of ice. As strong as she was Scorch couldn't break free of her frozen prison and all she could do was stand there, literally frozen in place, as the ghoul grinned and started running toward the exit, the autograph book – which was singed around the edges a bit but otherwise undamaged – clutched in her hand.

I saw a blur of movement on my left and heard more than felt a rush of wind as something moved past me at a high rate of speed. Tavi was a mixblood, a shapeshifter who'd chosen to have his natural abilities augmented by genetic engineering at Doctor M's House of Pain. In his case the enhancement was rather clever:

the lyke was a hybrid of mongoose and cobra, though he steadfastly refused to tell anyone which wereform he'd been born with originally. Tavi still wore his Nehru jacket and pants, but his limbs had become lean and sinuous and his hands and face were covered with a mixture of mammal fur and reptilian scale. His head was shaped like that of a mongoose with a cobra's hood and fangs. The overall effect worked surprisingly well, far better than many mixbloods who look like something out of Darwin's worst nightmares. In his wereform Tavi moved with a liquid grace that was beautiful to see and which had no doubt served him extremely well in his former career as a thief.

Though much of the crowd had managed to get away from Scorch and the ghoul there were still enough audience members in the way that Tavi was forced to detour around them and while he did so with great velocity it slowed him down just enough to give the ghoul time to prepare for his attack. Once again she plunged her hand into her side, only this time she brought out a small black sphere and dashed it to the floor. The sphere was glass and shattered on impact, releasing a black liquid substance that rapidly spread into a thin coating about two feet wide and three feet long. Tavi was moving too fast to avoid the black liquid and he ran right into it. The instant Tavi's feet came in contact with the tar-like goo they stuck fast; unfortunately momentum carried the rest of his body forward. The sound of breaking bone cut through the air as Tavi's ankles snapped and the lyke screamed in agony as he pitched forward and slammed face-first into the floor. Lykes are tough and they heal damn fast, but they still feel pain and Tavi was suffering quite a bit of it then. Still, he raised his head, opened his mouth wide, and spat a stream of venom directly into the ghoul's eyes. I expected to hear the ghoul scream then, but all she did was reach up to wipe the venom from her eyes and then continued running toward the exit. Tavi tried to pull free of the black substance that had hold of him, but it was no use. He was stuck fast.

Two of our team were down and the ghoul – or whoever it was hiding behind a ghoul's guise – hadn't broken a sweat. The Midnight Watch hadn't exactly covered itself in glory so far.

I hadn't stopped moving toward the ghoul, but running isn't something my zombie body is good at. The best I can manage is a sprightly shuffle that, while more than a little embarrassing, manages to get me from point A to point B faster than walking. But the ghoul was running full out and she was running at an angle away from me. Devona was heading for her as well, but the ghoul was moving away from her too. Fortunately for our team the direction the ghoul had chosen led her directly toward Bogdan. The warlock's specialty was the materialization of physical objects and not just any object but precisely what he needed most at any given moment. When he'd first joined the Midnight Watch I asked him how he knew what objects he might need – and for that matter, where they came from – and with a smile and a wink he give me the same answer for both questions. "I don't know. I simply work my magic and trust in Providence."

Have you ever heard such crap?

Bogdan lost no time in appealing to Providence then. He gestured with his right hand and a metallic fan appeared in his fingers, each gleaming section sharp as a razor. With an unnecessarily theatrical flick of his hand Bogdan spread the fan out and then flung it toward the rapidly approaching ghoul. The sections of the fan separated as they flew toward the ghoul, becoming a dozen deadly missiles.

It was a neat trick and I might have applauded if the ghoul hadn't simply ducked and rolled beneath the blades. The ghoul came up onto her feet and continued running without breaking stride, leaving Bogdan's fan blades flying toward innocent bystanders. One of the blades flew in my general direction and I intended to ignore it until I saw that it was heading toward the verman server who'd spoken to me earlier, the one who was missing half of his left ear. Without thinking about it I flung myself forward and intercepted the blade. It thunked into my side just below my right armpit, slid neatly between a couple of ribs and stayed there. I felt nothing beyond a slight pressure – one of the advantages of being dead – and I managed to keep my balance and avoid falling, which was good. If I break any bones, it doesn't hurt, but it can impair my mobility and I needed to remain ambulatory if we were going to have any chance at stopping the ghoul from getting away with Scream Queen's voice.

The verman looked at me with an expression that seemed thoughtful, almost appraising in a way, but I didn't have time to deal with him right then. I had a ghoul to catch.

Bogdan had been thrown off by his miss and he'd stood gaping with horror as his fan blades struck several audience members. Given the fact that none of those wounded were human, the damage wasn't anything they couldn't heal sooner or later, so Bogdan was able to forget about them and refocus his attention on the ghoul. Unfortunately he wasn't able to do so in time to stop her from reaching him and delivering a solid punch to his throat. The warlock's eyes bulged, his face turned red, and his mouth opened wide but he wasn't able to breathe in. The blow had crushed his trachea. Gasping ineffectively, his red face already starting to shade toward purple, Bogdan fell to his knees and slapped his hands to his throat. He closed his eyes and his lips began to move soundlessly as he worked a healing spell. His specialty might be the conjuring of useful objects, but he knew enough basic magic to heal himself. But doing so meant he wasn't going to be anymore help in stopping the ghoul – not that he'd been much help as it was.

Sinsation's bouncer decided to enter the fray then and the monster surged through the crowd toward the ghoul, moving with a speed and grace that was shocking given his enormous size. His face sported a savage grin and there was cold delight in his eyes. He'd literally been born to bust heads and now he had another

chance to fulfill his life's purpose. For one of the repurposed dead it didn't get any better than this.

I'm not territorial. If Frankie Jr could get the job done,
more power to him. All I cared about was making sure
that the ghoul didn't get away with Scream Queen's voice.

The ghoul noted the monster's approach – no big
feat; considering his size, he was damned hard to miss
– and she reached into her body and pulled out a tiny
metal disk. With a quick flick of her wrist she sent the
object sailing toward the bouncer. The disk struck him
on the forehead, right on the scar line, and stuck to the
flesh as if covered with glue. Crackling tendrils of electricity shot forth from the disk's metal surface,
spreading outward to surround the monster's head in
a cage of miniature lightning.

The bouncer stopped running toward the ghoul, his
body spasmed several times, and then lines of smoke
curled forth from his nostrils. His eyes rolled over white
and for an instant the monster stood there, white-eyed
and stiff-legged, and then the giant collapsed to the
floor with a sound like a dozen bags of cement dropped
from a half-mile up.

Frankenstein monsters are born of electricity and if
you can overload the energy matrices of their central
nervous system it's like flipping their off switch, a fact
the ghoul was obviously all too aware of.

Four down and – since she's far faster than I am – it
was Devona's turn at the ghoul.

Half-vampires aren't as swift as their full-blooded rel-
atives, but they're a damn sight faster than humans, let

alone a shuffle-gaited zombie, and Devona managed to reach the ghoul when she was within a dozen feet of the exit. Devona's stronger than a human, but she's not trained in hand-to-hand combat, and physical confrontation doesn't suit her personality. What she *is* trained in, however, is security magic. And that meant she'd taken the precaution of having a special enchantment placed on all of Sinsation's exits earlier that day, an enchantment she now activated by speaking a phrase in a language I didn't understand, but which I recognized as the ancient tongue of the Bloodborn. The edges of the main entrance began to glow and a red mist rose from the floor in curling crimson tendrils, rapidly rising upward to completely block the doorway. The spell was simple: the red mist would prevent Scream Queen from passing through. To anyone else, the mist would be nothing more than that, easily passable, but to the banshee singer – or to anyone trying to force her physically through the doorway – the mist would feel solid as rock. How do you keep someone from abducting your client? Make sure she's physically incapable of leaving the premises. Of course, the ghoul wasn't carrying Scream Queen, just her voice, but I assumed the principle would be the same.

Evidently the ghoul made the same assumption – or maybe she simply assumed the red mist would do something nasty to her if she tried to go through it – for she came to a stop and spun around to face Devona.

Devona might prefer to fight with her mind instead of her fists, but that doesn't mean she can't brawl when she needs to. She continued running toward the ghoul, fangs bared, eyes wild and blazing with a feral yellow glow. I felt a wave of psychic pressure and I knew she was using her telepathic abilities to broadcast negative emotions at the ghoul, more in an effort to intimidate her and keep her off balance than to actually harm her. The ghoul, however, appeared to be completely calm as she once more reached into her side, this time drawing forth a small metal object. I recognized the object the instant I saw it and I started to shout a warning to Devona, but the ghoul moved too fast. With a flick of her wrist she sent the small silver cross flying toward Devona. The four tips of the cross were sharp as needles and the holy shuriken struck Devona in the left shoulder, biting through her leather outfit and sinking deep into her flesh.

Devona gasped in pain, stumbled, and fell to the floor. She clutched at her wounded shoulder, trying to grab hold of the cross and pull it free, but it had already sunk too deep. Holy objects and silver don't affect half-vampires as strongly as they do full-blooded vampires, but that just means their poisonous and corrosive effects are slower. Devona wasn't in danger of suffering any long-term damage from the cross, provided she could get it removed within the next half-hour or so, but the pain was excruciating and there was no way she would be able to continue battling the ghoul. It was all she could do to hold on to consciousness. This also meant there was no way she could concentrate effectively to use her telepathic powers against her assailant.

But wounding Devona wasn't enough for the ghoul. She plunged her hand into her side – right in the spot where I estimated a shoulder holster would be – and pulled out a 9mm handgun. She stepped forward, her ghoul disguise wavering as she did so and, by the time she knelt next to Devona and placed the gun barrel against her forehead, the ghoul illusion was completely gone. The voicenapper was revealed to be a humanoid of indeterminate gender and species encased in black body armor, just as had been reported.

"You have five seconds to remove the spell on the exit. If you don't, I'll put a blessed silver-jacketed bullet through your skull. You'll have a hell of a time healing from that."

The kidnapper wore a hooded mask and black goggles, but the muffled voice that came through was unmistakably that of a woman. And that gave me an idea of who we might be dealing with.

I'd finally reached Devona and I stopped a couple yards away so as not to make the kidnapper too nervous. There's a reason someone coined the phrase "itchy trigger finger" and I didn't want to put the kidnapper's combat cool to the test.

"You might as well give it up, Overkill. There's no way you're leaving with Scream Queen's voice."

The woman turned to look at me, but she didn't remove the gun from Devona's head. She was a consummate professional.

"What are you going to do, zombie? Drop flakes of dead skin on me?"

"So you *are* Overkill."

A slight hesitation. "I didn't say that."

"But you didn't deny it, either. No one would be stupid enough to pretend to be Overkill or even allow anyone to think she's Overkill. If the real Overkill ever found out, she'd hunt them down and make them pay for using her name in vain."

The woman seemed to consider that for a moment. "True." She tucked the autograph book under her arm and then, with her free hand reached up, pulled off her goggles and face mask and tossed them to the floor. She was an attractive woman in her twenties, with brown hair, brown eyes, who stood five-eight and weighed around a hundred and forty pounds. She looked normal enough, but everyone in Nekropolis knows that looks are deceiving. If something appears dangerous it's probably ten times worse and if something appears harmless you'd best turn and run screaming in the other direction as fast as your feet will carry you. I'd never met this woman before, but despite her appearance, I knew I was standing face to face with one of the most feared mercenaries in the city.

"You gave it your best shot, but you're not going to get away with the voice, Overkill. You know that. The best thing for you to do is put the autograph book down, take the gun away from Devona's head, and leave."

She smiled. "I don't know anything of the sort. I'm the one holding the gun against your girlfriend's forehead. You know I'm not bluffing when I say I'll fire if she doesn't dispel the enchantment on the doorway."

I did know it. Overkill was one of the deadliest fighters in the city. She was a human who wanted to show the monsters that ruled Nekropolis that not only could she be their equal, she could surpass them, becoming a bigger, badder monster than any of them could ever hope to be. To this end she employed weapons both mundane and mystical in her work, usually to quite deadly effect, but she accepted no enhancements to her body, magical, cybernetic, or genetic. She was one hundred percent homo sapiens and two hundred percent bugfuck crazy. She took on only the most difficult of jobs – the more suicidal, the better – and while rumor had it that she was obscenely well paid for what she did, money meant nothing to her. As Dr. Scott says in *Rocky Horror*, Overkill lives solely for "ze thrills".

"So you have a gun. I do too." I slowly opened my jacket to show her the 9mm resting in my shoulder holster, a souvenir from my days as a human cop.

Her smile took on a mocking edge. "Even if you were alive, there's no way you could move fast enough to draw your weapon before I pulled the trigger on mine. And as a zombie, your reflexes are way too slow to even think about it."

I didn't take any offense at what she said, mostly because she was right. "You're not the only one who carries magical toys. I have all kinds of surprises I can pull out of my bag of tricks."

"Maybe so, but that doesn't change anything. The second your hand so much as twitches in the direction of one of your pockets, my gun goes off and your lady love's half-undead brains will exit the back of her head suddenly, violently, and quite messily. There's no way she'll be able to repair that kind of damage on her own, and even a top-flight healer won't be able to help her. She won't have enough brains left to be resurrected as a zombie – not that she'd be intelligent like you. I suppose you can always hope she'll return as a ghost, but you can't ever predict who'll come back and who'll cross over to the next life, whatever that may be. So if you want her to live, you'll back off and let her remove the spell on the door for me."

So far I'd managed to keep Overkill talking, but I had no illusions that I might be able to make some sort of deal with her. She was verbally sparring with me only because it amused her. It wouldn't take her long to get tired of our little *tête-a-tête* and then she'd make good on her threat to kill Devona – an outcome I'd prefer to avoid, as you might imagine. Death isn't necessarily the end in Nekropolis, but it does seriously cut down on your options.

"There are a lot of heavy hitters in here," I pointed out, "and any number of them could give you a serious run for your money. If they teamed up..."

"Nice try, but if any of them were going to interfere, they'd have done so by now." Her smile turned into a leer. "Maybe they're having too much fun watching."

Unfortunately she was probably right. Most Nekropolitans aren't big on altruism, mostly because sticking your nose into other people's business in this city is an excellent way to get yourself killed – and that's just for starters. There are worse things than death in this town and they're usually standing a few inches behind you, ready to reach out and grab you when you least expect it.

"What about this?" I raised my hand and showed her the scar-tissue *E* on my palm. "Do you really want to defy the agent of a Darklord?"

That seemed to give her pause. Her smile fell away and she seemed to consider the matter. Meanwhile, tears of blood streamed down Devona's face and her breathing was becoming more labored. I knew the cross's silver – not to mention the holy power of the blessing that had been laid upon it – was causing her system to break down. She needed to get that cross out of her as soon as possible.

"I'd heard rumors that you'd been marked by Edrigu," Overkill said, "but that doesn't make you one of his agents. Maybe it's simply a sign that you're in his debt."

I kept my face composed – a task easily accomplished for a dead man – but I swore inwardly. Overkill wouldn't have survived in her profession as long as she has if she was stupid, but I'd hoped my bluff would work. Since it hadn't, that left me with only one other option: bluff bigger.

I took a half step forward. Overkill didn't take her gaze off me, but her finger tightened on the trigger.

"You said you'd heard rumors about me," I began. "What have you heard about what happened last Descension Day?"

Overkill's eyes narrowed and she took a moment before answering. "Word on the street is that someone tried to interfere with the recharging of Umbriel and the city was almost destroyed. You prevented that from happening."

Umbriel the shadowsun is what provides the perpetual dusky half-light that illuminates Nekropolis, but it does much more than that. It also keeps the city stabilized in the dark dimension where it's located and what's more – and I'd only recently learned this – its power keeps the city safe from the native inhabitants of this dimension, who view the Nekropolitans as colonizing invaders.

I took another half step forward. "Anything else?"

Her eyes narrowed another fraction. "They say that your body decayed to dust in the battle to preserve Umbriel and that Father Dis himself restored your physical form."

Dis was once worshipped by the ancient Romans as a god of death, and he's the ultimate ruler of the city. It was Dis who several centuries ago led the Darkfolk to leave Earth and establish their own city in another dimension, where they'd be safe from a humanity grown too numerous and technologically advanced. There are other godlike beings in Nekropolis – most notably the five Darklords that rule the city's separate Dominions – but none are as powerful as Dis... or as feared.

"It's true," I said. "I'm not going to stand here and tell you I saved the city single-handedly, and I'm not going to claim that Dis and I are best buddies and I can ring him up whenever I feel like it. But if Dis went to all the trouble of putting me back together when all the king's men and all the king's horses couldn't, I'd say that means we have more than a casual relationship. How do you think he'll react when I tell him the love of my life was killed by a certain mercenary who's too stubborn to know when she's lost? You're tough, Overkill, one of the toughest in town. But do you really think you can stand up against Father Dis?"

Her brow furrowed and for a moment I thought she was actually calculating her chances.

"You're bullshitting me." She said the words forcefully enough, but there was a slight hint of doubt in her voice.

"Probably," I admitted, "but you have no way of knowing for sure. Look at it this way: if you find out for certain that I'm bluffing, think how much satisfaction you'll get hunting me down and making me pay for lying to you."

Overkill looked at me for a long moment before slowly breaking into a grin.

"Good point." She hesitated a second longer before removing the gun from Devona's forehead and replacing the weapon in her shoulder holster. Moving with a warrior's brisk, economical motions, she stood and tossed me the autograph book. "Well played, Matt. Hope to see you soon."

In other words, she couldn't wait for a rematch. If I had a working nervous system, the statement might've caused a chill to ripple down my spine.

She gave me a nod, one professional to another, before turning and striding briskly through the crimson mist still filling the doorway. Now that she no longer carried anything of Scream Queen on her, the spell allowed Overkill to pass without any ill effect. Once she was gone, the mist dissipated, the enchantment no longer needed.

I tucked the autograph book into my jacket and then knelt next to Devona and took her hand. Bloodtears continued to stream down her cheeks and she grimaced in pain.

"I guess I don't need to ask how you're feeling," I said.

Devona spoke through gritted teeth. "You realize you just made an enemy, don't you?"

"I'll add her name to the list."

Devona kept a steel bladed knife in a sheath on her right boot. With my free hand I reached down and pulled the knife free. "This is going to hurt," I warned her.

"It already hurts," she snapped.

"Then this is going to hurt worse. Ready?"

She squeezed her eyes shut, gripped my hand, and nodded.

Though technically I didn't need to I took a deep breath and then I started cutting.

THREE

"How's the shoulder?"

"Like new." Devona's leather outfit had a tear over the shoulder, the edges crusted with dried blood, but the exposed skin was once more smooth and healthy. "Thanks, Bogdan."

The warlock shrugged in what I thought was a blatantly insincere attempt to appear modest. "Healing magic doesn't always work with Bloodborn – they are, after all, undead – but as you're half-human, I thought I'd make the attempt. I'm glad my spell was successful."

As for my own injury I'd removed Overkill's blade from between my ribs and aside from a new hole I'd need to get sewn up the next time I visited my houngan, I was no worse for the wear. Papa Chatha is able to use his voodoo magic to keep me from rotting away to nothing, but when it comes to torn skin, broken bones and the like, instead of invoking the Loa, Papa tends to rely on thread, staples and superglue.

Devona and I – along with the rest of the team – had returned to the Midnight Watch building and now lounged in the great room. When Devona had first bought the building the stone fireplace was cracked and filled with cobwebs, musty old paintings hung on the walls, and the wooden beams overhead were rotten and falling apart. Devona had spent a significant amount of money to renovate the building's interior and the great room now had all new leather furniture, abstract holo art hanging on the walls – not really my taste, but hey, it's Devona's business, not mine – and an illusory fire flickering in a brazier set in the fireplace, providing plenty of light but no heat. Zombie flesh tends to be on the dry side, especially when I'm due for a new batch of preservative spells, and I try to stay away from fire whenever possible. Devona, considerate partner that she is, had the magical brazier installed just for me.

"She could've healed herself simply by chugging a mug or two of the red stuff before we left Sinsation," I said, trying not to sound irritated with Bogdan and failing miserably.

Devona scowled at me. "You know how I feel about drinking blood in bars, Matt."

Many of Nekropolis's denizens require blood as a major part of their diet and supplying that need is one of the city's major industries. The real thing, as you might imagine, is difficult to come by and the artificial substitute aqua sanguis – while providing a certain amount of nourishment – mostly just takes the edge off the thirst. Vampires often get blood from their shadows, human followers who serve their undead masters in the hope of one day joining their dark ranks, and over at the Foundry, Victor Baron produces blood by the gallons from an army of cloned human bodies that lack higher brain functions, primarily because, as rumor has it, they don't possess any heads. But all of those sources still aren't enough to meet the demand and there's a brisk black market trade in blood – and the sellers aren't too picky about how they come by their supply or who they have to kill to obtain it. According to the law in Nekropolis humans who choose to live in the city are not inferior beings to be exploited, save by their own choice, but they are fair game as prey, as is every other being in the city.

During the decades Devona served her father she lived in the Cathedral and gave little thought to where her food came from. In the stronghold of the Darklord Galm blood flows freely from a large marble fountain that never runs dry. If a member of the household or one of the staff wishes to slake his or her thirst they need only dip a goblet into the fountain and drink their fill. But during the few months since Devona had abandoned her sheltered existence and come to live with me, she'd learned a great deal about what life is like outside the walls of her father's home and she'd developed a social conscience. She refused to take part in exploiting humans – after all, her mother was human – and if she wasn't absolutely sure where blood came from, she wouldn't drink it, like humans back on Earth refusing to eat tuna from companies whose indiscriminate fishing practices result in the death of dolphins. And bars were among the worst offenders when it came to selling black market blood. As a former human myself, I normally admired Devona's attitude, but it bugged me that night... mostly because it had led to Bogdan getting to use his magic to heal her.

Are you getting the idea that I wasn't the warlock's biggest fan?

Devona sat on a couch near the fireplace and she'd just finished arranging five piles of darkgems in front of her on a crystal coffee table. She looked up at everyone and smiled.

"Scream Queen was very happy with our work tonight," she said. "So much so that she gave us each a bonus of ten darkgems." She gestured at the money. "Go ahead. You earned it."

Bogdan, Scorch and Tavi – the latter two once again wearing human form – stood on the other side of the coffee table. I stood next to the fireplace, learning against the wall, arms crossed, a scowl on my face. Normally I enjoyed standing close to the coldfire since I liked to gaze into its flickering flames and I knew they couldn't do any damage to me. But that night I stood there mostly out of habit. I wasn't enjoying myself in the least.

Despite Devona's invitation to collect their pay the three members of the Midnight Watch didn't step forward. Instead they exchanged uneasy glances and remained standing where they were.

Devona frowned. "What's wrong?"

Bogdan spoke for the trio. "Scorch, Tavi and I are reluctant to take a full share of tonight's profits. We don't feel as if we earned it."

"We were hired to protect Scream Queen," Devona said, "and we stopped Overkill from stealing her voice. She was pleased with the service we provided and she paid us. *All* of us." She looked at Bogdan. "And you were able to cast a spell that returned her voice to her."

Bogdan shrugged. "It was a simple matter. An Arcane child could've done it."

My scowl deepened. You're a modest son of a bitch, aren't you? I thought.

"And all of you—" Devona took in Scorch and Tavi with her gaze now – "participated in the fight against Overkill."

"For all the good we did," Scorch said in a pouty voice, sounding like the preteen she appeared to be. "The three of us got our butts kicked."

"We *were* up against Overkill," Tavi pointed out. "We're lucky to still be alive." He turned to glance at me. "Uh, sorry, Matt. I didn't mean–"

"Don't worry about it," I said. "Living or dead, I'm still ambulatory and that's all that matters."

"Look, everyone," Devona said in what I'd come to think of as her boss voice. "We all shared the risk, so we all share in the profit."

Bogdan, Scorch and Tavi all glanced at me then as if to see whether I had anything to say about the issue. While none of them seemed to have bought into any of that 'savior of the city' crap that folks like Acantha wanted to saddle me with they did seek my opinion every now and again – though I felt Bogdan did so more to keep up appearances with his fellow employees than because he really cared what I thought about anything.

When I didn't answer right away Devona said, "Well, Matt? What *do* you think?"

When you're part of a couple there are times when you know your significant other is asking you a question to which there is only One Right Answer. I recognized this as one of those times. Unfortunately I had no idea what the correct response was. So I did what I usually do in situations like that. I gambled.

I shrugged and tried to sound as casual as I could as I replied: "It's your business, so it's your call."

I knew my gamble had been a spectacular failure when Devona gave me a scowl that said *We'll talk about this later*. Then she returned her attention to her employees.

"So it's settled then."

The three exchanged glances one last time before finally stepping forward and collecting their share of the night's earnings.

"So…" Bogdan said. "When are we going to discuss what happened tonight? I have some ideas on ways we might improve our performance next time."

I'll just bet you do, I thought. And from the way the warlock looked at Devona as he spoke I had the feeling that when he said *we* he wasn't talking about all five of us sitting down for a chat.

Scorch groaned. "Really, Bogdan, why do you always have to be such a worker bee? It's getting late and I have a pile of newly acquired darkgems burning a hole in my pocket. I say we head on back to Sinsation and see what other kinds of trouble we can get into tonight."

Bogdan frowned at the demon, but Devona cut him off before he could reply. "Was there anything we could've done differently to deal with Overkill? Of course. There's always room for improvement, but that's not important right now. What matters is we got the job done and that's enough for one night. Let's save the post mortem for another time, shall we?"

She gave Bogdan a smile to take the sting out of her words and the warlock responded with a courtly half bow that, if I still had a gag reflex, would've made me want to vomit on the spot.

"Of course, Devona," he said. "It's probably a good idea that you don't work anymore tonight anyway. After the injury you sustained you could use some rest. Magical healing can only do so much you know." The warlock then gave her a wink and Devona actually blushed a little. Considering how pale she is even a mild blush looked like fiery explosions beneath her skin.

I ground my teeth so hard I thought I might have to visit a zombie dentist.

Bogdan begged off accompanying Scorch back to Sinsation. Tavi tried to escape as well, but Scorch wasn't about to be denied twice. She hooked her arm in his and, since she was far stronger than the shapeshifter even while wearing the guise of a preteen girl, he had no choice but to allow her to drag him off in search of further excitement. Given the sort of activities a demon considers fun I hoped the lyke survived the night.

That left Bogdan, Devona and me – and you know what they say about three being a crowd? Well, evidently Bogdan had never heard of the phrase for he sat down on the couch next to Devona, laying his arm across the back, almost but not quite putting it around her. At that point I was a very unhappy dead man.

"You were really the star tonight," Bogdan said to Devona. "It was the security spell you placed on the club's entrance that prevented Overkill from simply waltzing out of there with Scream Queen's voice. It was extremely sophisticated spellcraft, worthy of one of my own people. Very few non-Arcane can work magic of that level. It was most impressive."

The warlock scooted an inch closer to Devona. If she noticed, she didn't react. Maybe, I told myself, she didn't react because she liked the idea of Bogdan – a living man – getting closer to her.

Don't be an idiot, I told myself. You know how Devona feels about you.

Still, there are a lot of disadvantages to being dead and one of them is that I'm not exactly fully functional in certain key areas, if you get my drift. And despite the fact that I disliked Bogdan quite a bit at that moment – actually, *loathed* might be a more accurate description of my feelings toward him – I had to admit that he was handsome enough, in a sleazy kind of way. And as sheltered as Devona had been for most of her life she hadn't had a lot of experience with men and might not realize just what a superficial, shallow and manipulative jerk he was. Yeah, *loathed* is definitely the right word.

"Thank you, Bogdan," she said. "That means a lot, coming from a warlock as accomplished as you are."

I'd had enough. Beneath my breath, I whispered, "Sic 'em, Rover."

At first nothing happened, but then Bogdan's red hair began to stir as if tousled by a sourceless breeze. A second later a miniature windstorm erupted in the great room centered, strangely enough, on the couch where Devona and Bogdan sat. They squeezed their eyes shut against the wind and Devona shouted something, but her voice was muffled by the storm's howling. Devona and Bogdan tried to stand, no doubt intending to get away from the couch and the winds that buffeted them, but the small-scale gale was too powerful, and every time they managed to rise off the couch so much as an inch, a fresh gust of air would shove them back down.

I let this go on for a minute or so before whispering, "That's enough, Rover. Heel."

The mini windstorm gave a final howl that sounded almost disappointed before finally dissipating. Both Devona and Bogdan's hair was mussed – revealing the beginnings of a bald spot atop the warlock's head I noted with petty satisfaction – and though Devona's leather outfit had weathered the storm just fine, Bogdan's clothes were now rumpled and in dire need of a good pressing.

"I'm so sorry about that, Bogdan!" Devona said. "I've been working on housebreaking Rover, but as you can see, he still acts up from time to time." She shot me a look then and in an icy tone added, "Doesn't he, Matt?"

"He does have his high-spirited moments," I said, doing my best to keep my tone neutral.

When Devona first purchased the Midnight Watch building we'd discovered that the original owner – a powerful warlock named Leander Crosswise who specialized in security magic – had created a guardian creature for his establishment by granting a level of sentience to a wardspell. Unfortunately for Crosswise when he decided to retire and sell the business the guardian had decided that the warlock had become a threat to the place it was supposed to protect and it killed its creator. The building gained a reputation for being haunted after that, especially since the guardian attacked anyone who considered purchasing the place, and the Midnight Watch building remained empty for decades. The creature had attacked Devona and I when we inspected the property and we'd barely managed to figure out what was happening before the creature destroyed us. We made friends with it, after a fashion, and in a strange way it had become something of a pet to us, hence the name Rover. I'd never been much on having pets when I was alive, but for whatever reason Rover and I seemed to get along pretty well and I could usually count on him to listen to me – especially if I encouraged him to misbehave. In many ways he was just a big puppy. A big disembodied puppy formed of mystic energy that had killed his first master and any number of potential buyers that had been foolish enough to inspect the property he guarded over the years, but hey, nobody's perfect. At least he doesn't piddle on the carpet.

If Bogdan suspected I'd had anything to do with Rover's sudden burst of playfulness he gave no indication. But he didn't look in my direction, either.

"No need to apologize," he said, reaching out and patting her hand. Earlier that week a street vendor hawking second hand cybernetic implants had tried to sell me a pair of laser emitting eyes. At that moment I wished I'd taken him up on the offer. If I had I'd have focused my ocular energy beams on the warlock's hand and severed it at the wrist. Bogdan went on. "The fact that you've been able to tame the creature to the extent you have is only further testament to your skill with spellcraft."

I'd had just about all the Bogdan I could take for one evening.

"I hate to give you the bum's rush, Bogdan, but as you said, Devona should get some rest."

It was a damned broad hint and I was pleased the warlock didn't miss it. "Of course. Forgive me for prattling on." He rose from the couch then turned to Devona. "Should I return tomorrow at the usual time? I know we don't have another job lined up at the moment, but if you want to get together to discuss our performance this evening…"

Devona gave me a quick frown before standing and giving Bogdan a smile. "That sounds good. I'll give you,

Scorch and Tavi a call tomorrow and we'll set up a meeting time."

Bogdan had been smiling, but now his smile faltered a bit, as if he were less than thrilled at the prospect of having his fellow employees invited to his meeting with Devona, but his tone remained pleasant enough as he said, "I'll look forward to it. I hope you enjoy the rest of your evening."

With that the warlock turned and exited the great room, giving me a curt nod of farewell as he passed.

Devona waited until she heard the front door open and close before speaking.

"What was *that* all about?"

Now that Bogdan was gone I was beginning to regret my childish actions toward him and even though I knew I deserved the chewing out Devona was about to give me I still wanted to put it off as long as possible. So I decided to try and change the subject.

"I've been thinking. Maybe we should continue guarding Scream Queen a while longer. Overkill isn't exactly the type to gracefully accept defeat. There's a chance she might make another attempt to snatch Scream Queen's voice."

Devona shook her head. "Now that Overkill has failed three times and been exposed as the kidnapper – voicenapper? – she won't try again. Whoever hired her won't risk employing her any longer. What if next time she's captured and forced by the Adjudicators to reveal her employer's identity? No, after tonight Overkill's become a bad risk. Unfortunately that means the only way for her to regain face is to confront the person who forced her to stand down without so much as raising a hand against her."

"Which would be me."

Devona nodded. "If anyone needs guarding it's you, Matt. Not Scream Queen. But you know this. You're just trying to avoid talking about your problem with Bogdan."

Since distraction hadn't worked, I figured I'd give denial a shot.

"I don't have a problem with Bogdan. As far as I'm concerned he's no better or worse than the others." As soon as the words were out of my mouth I knew I'd screwed up royally.

Devona had been frowning at me, but now her frown deepened into a truly serious scowl. "What do you mean by that?"

I was sorely tempted to try summoning Rover again and see if he might blow up another windstorm to distract Devona and allow me to beat a hasty retreat, but I knew she'd never fall for that.

"This is your business, Devona, and they're your employees. It doesn't matter what I think about them."

While we'd been talking Devona had remained standing next to the couch, no doubt keeping her distance from me because she was irritated. But her irritation now edged toward anger – I could feel it through our telepathic link – and she walked over to the fireplace where I was standing and fixed me with a look that said I'd better stop jerking her around.

"It matters to me," she said.

"Uh, could we go back to how I'm an idiot for being jealous of Bogdan?"

Devona just kept looking at me, and since it was clear that I wasn't going to get out of this, I decided to give it to her straight.

"You've been running the Midnight Watch for over a month now and you've done a great job. Word that the Watch is open for business again has gotten around the city and people are starting to hire you for some high profile gigs – like tonight."

"And…?"

"And so far, so good. When you re-opened the Watch you hired the best employees that you could afford and they did well enough when all you had to do was inspect a business's current security set up and recommend updates or investigate a case of employee theft at a warehouse. But now that you're landing bigger jobs the work is getting more dangerous. And I'm afraid Bogdan, Scorch and Tavi just aren't up to the challenge. Not only did Overkill almost get away tonight the three of them could've easily gotten killed. Sure, they survived, but what about the next time? And what about any innocents who might get hurt because your employees can't do their jobs?"

As I talked Devona's skin tone had become increasingly darker, changing from a pale white to a faint pink. On a fully human Caucasian woman the new color would've looked natural, but for Devona it was a sure sign that she was getting furious. When she opened her mouth to speak, instead of yelling, she spoke with a cold control. When you grow up in the house of a Darklord you learn to keep a tight rein on your emotions when you speak or else you might not live to reach the end of your sentence.

"I'll grant you that Bogdan, Tavi and Scorch need more training, but Overkill got the best of me tonight too, Matt. Are you suggesting that I'm not up to the challenge either?"

At this point I'd have rather gone a few more rounds with Overkill than continue with this conversation and I was desperately searching for an exit strategy.

"Of course not. Like I said you've done a fantastic job getting the Midnight Watch up and running again. I guess what I'm trying to say is maybe you should think about moving more slowly and not taking on jobs that are too dangerous until your team is ready for them."

I thought I'd done a decent job of sounding reasonably supportive while trying to climb out of the hole I'd managed to dig for myself. But I realized I'd failed when Devona said, "*Our* team."

"Huh?"

"It's *our* team, Matt. You and I run the Midnight Watch together." Her eyes narrowed and I could feel her probing my mind through our telepathic link. "Don't we?"

Normally I like being linked mind to mind with Devona. It allows us to experience a closeness that I've never known in a relationship before and that closeness allows us to have a physical relationship – simulated on the psychic plane – that would normally be impossible given my biological limitations. But right then I'd have happily severed the link if I'd known how.

"Devona, you know I'm proud of everything you've accomplished with the Midnight Watch so far and I'll support you in every way I can as you continue to grow the business. But the Watch is yours, Devona. Not mine. I'm happy to help out whenever I can, but I have my own work." I shrugged. "I guess I'm just used to being my own man – or zombie."

I'd tried to make a joke, but it went over like an explosive burst of flatulence at a funeral. Not only didn't Devona smile, she averted her gaze and I knew that my words had hurt her.

"Back on Earth you didn't work alone," she said. "You had a partner."

Dale Ramsey had been my partner when I'd worked homicide in Cleveland. We'd been a team for years until we investigated a series of murders that led us to Nekropolis. Both Dale and I were killed during the investigation, but unfortunately for my partner he didn't rise from the dead afterward like I did. Then again, I sometimes wonder if Dale wasn't the luckier of the two of us.

"Well, yeah. But… you know. He died." I sensed that Devona was trying to get at something, but telepathic link or not, the message wasn't coming through.

"Yes. But I thought that…" She trailed off and looked at the flickering coldfire flames.

"What?" I prompted.

She continued gazing into the fire a moment more before looking up at me and smiling.

"Nothing. You made a good point about the training we need if we're going to take on more risky jobs. I'll see what I can set up. In the meantime, I've got some work to finish up here, but it's nothing I need you for. It shouldn't take me more than an hour. Why don't you head on home and relax a bit? As busy as we've been lately, you could use the rest."

As a zombie I don't tire and I don't need to sleep, but periodic rest slows my body's rate of decay and helps me put off my next dose of preservative spells, which is a good thing considering how expensive they are. I'd seen Papa Chatha within the last week so I was still pretty fresh, but my skin was starting to get that tell-tale grayish tinge and I knew Devona's advice was sound. I couldn't help feeling that she'd been about to say something important and had changed her mind at the last minute, but I decided not to pursue the matter any further just then. It was getting late and I wanted to avoid a fight. We could always resume the conversation at a later date and if she decided not to bring the issue up again, that was OK too.

Feeling more than a little like a coward I gave Devona a kiss, said goodnight to Rover – who ruffled my hair with a tiny breeze of farewell – and left the building.

The large oak door closed with a sonorous *thud* behind me and I stepped out into the dusky half light of Umbriel's perpetual gloom. I heard the sounds of various locks – magical, mechanical and electronic – engaging behind me, and though I didn't possess the skill with magic to sense it, numerous wardspells also kicked in. The stone building didn't just house a security business – it was one of the most secure places in the city.

A metal plaque on the door read THE MIDNIGHT WATCH: SAFEGUARDING ALL WORKHOUSES AND INSTITUTIONS AGAINST INTRUDERS AND MEDDLING. SAVAGE BEASTS EMPLOYED. It was, as you might tell from the phrasing, the original sign put up by the Watch's founder several centuries ago and Devona had decided to keep it. Not only to maintain continuity, but because after decades of safeguarding her father's collection of rare objects, she had an appreciation for historical artifacts. The sign seemed a bit stuffy to me, but I had to admit it suited the place.

Devona and I lived only a few blocks west of there. This was a relatively sedate part of the Sprawl – one of the reasons why I'd chosen to rent an apartment here – but the emphasis was most definitely on *relatively*. The Sprawl is the Dominion of the Demon Queen Varvara and she believes in absolute freedom. It's rumored that the old Beast, Aleister Crowley, stole his infamous satanic commandant from her: *Do as Thou Wilt*. I wouldn't be surprised. If the Sprawl doesn't exist in a state of total anarchy, it'll do until the real thing shows up. But, like I said, this neighborhood was quiet enough, with pedestrians going about their business searching for prey or trying to avoid becoming prey – often at the same time – and vehicles of various makes, models and degrees of sentience rolling, crawling and scuttling down the street.

Some of the vehicles were imports from Earth: sports cars, SUVs, Hummers and so on. The Darkfolk may have relocated to another dimension, but they maintain ties with the world of their origin, mostly so that they can get their greedy little talons on the latest toys the human race invents. But there were plenty of home grown vehicles racing along the street as well. Carapacers – vehicles created from the hollowed-out animated husks of giant insects – drove alongside Meatrunners: leprous constructions of sinew, muscle and bone that didn't so much roll as lurch spasmodically forward on disjointed legs, diseased lungs expelling rancid exhaust as their drivers hurried toward whatever dark destinations awaited them. The latter monstrosities, like so much of the city's organic tech, sprang from the feverish and ever fertile imagination of Victor Baron, the original Frankenstein monster, who was something like Nekropolis's version of Thomas Edison – or maybe Bill Gates would be a more apt comparison. Everywhere you go you encounter one of his fleshy machines, each of them tattooed with the slogan *Another Victor Baron Creation*. Baron isn't a Darklord, but in his own way he's as powerful as any of them and certainly he's as rich. The city would grind to a halt without the monstrous tech his Foundry produces.

To the right of the Watch building was a misfortuneteller's establishment and on the left was a head shop (new and used, all species, original size and shrunken). Not exactly the most glamorous of neighbors, but they were, if not normal, harmless enough at least. Both businesses were closed – doors shut, windows dark – and I started walking west past the head shop in the direction of my apartment. Nekropolis follows a standard twenty-four hour Earth day, but because so many of its citizens don't need sleep, shop owners keep their own hours and many businesses stay open all the time. Not the Midnight Watch's neighbors, though, and given my current mood, that suited me just fine. The last thing I wanted was to have a bored shopkeeper stroll out onto the sidewalk and attempt to strike up a conversation with me. I wanted to be left alone with my thoughts.

The Sprawl contains a bizarre mix of earthly architectural styles – Victorian, gothic, baroque, postmodern, American colonial, classical, neoclassical, Spanish and more – along with structures that look like something straight out of a fever dream. Buildings that resemble giant insect hives resting next to structures formed of light and mist. Many of the buildings were formed from material resembling bone and the streetlights were made of the same stuff, making them resemble skeletal arms holding globes of greenish light. As I walked through the crazy quilt of Varvara's Dominion on my way home, I brooded and kept an eye out for danger. In Nekropolis, not paying attention to your surroundings is an excellent way to commit unintentional suicide. Viscous blue pseudopods extruded from sewer grates as the Azure Slime quested for bits of detritus to feed upon, but as long as I didn't step too close to the curb and tempt the creature, I'd be fine. Building fronts were covered with leech vine, a parasitic plant that grabs hold of its prey and feeds upon its blood. As a zombie my blood had long since turned to dry dust in my veins and the vine ignored me as I passed. Devona has to be more careful around the stuff, though. Leech vine loves vampire blood best of all – even half vampire blood. It's like the finest of wines to the plant. I find it poetic justice that one of the city's greatest predators has a blood thirsty nemesis that desires to feed on its liquid life essence, but the vampires don't see it that way. That's why the best leech vine exterminators in the city are Bloodborn.

I passed a number of nightclubs as I walked down the street and a majority of them had Frankenstein bouncers standing outside their entrances who resembled the bouncer at Sinsation – a few of them resembled him so much, in fact, that it was obvious they'd rolled off the same assembly line. More of Victor Baron's handiwork. 'Making life to make life better', as another of his slogans went.

I was halfway home, reviewing my conversation with Devona and mentally kicking myself for acting like such a jerk, when I passed by an alley. Out of the corner of my eye I saw movement in the shadows and an instant later something obstructed my vision. I realized a cloth hood had been dropped over my head, but before I could do anything about it, I felt a razor thin sharpness bite into my neck. A garroting wire, I guessed. It didn't hurt, but I could feel the pressure as the wire was pulled backward, slicing through my bloodless flesh. When the garrote hit my neck bone, the wire began to vibrate with a soft humming sound, as if it were some sort of mechanical device, and it cut the rest of the way through my neck with the ease of a laser bisecting a stick of butter. All of this happened in mere seconds, far faster than my undead reflexes could react, and the next thing I felt was a sudden dizzying lurch as I fell, hit the ground, and bounced a couple of times before coming to a stop. At the same moment, I heard the sound of something large landing next to me with a muffled thud. This was followed by shuffling footsteps, rustling cloth and grunts of exertion. More footsteps then, quickly fading away. After that, there was only silence and darkness.

I already had a good idea what had happened to me, but I had to check. I tried to reach up and remove the hood from my head, but my arm refused to obey me. I then attempted to sit up, but once again my body failed to cooperate. The reason for this was distressingly simple: I no longer had a body. Or at least, it wasn't currently attached to my head.

This was not good. And a moment later, it got even worse.

I heard something moving – *lots* of somethings. Tiny claws scraping against stone, little high-pitched voices muttering, drawing closer as they spoke.

"What is it?"

"Something in a bag."

"Just more trash."

"No, no. Take a whiff!"

Soft snuffling sounds.

"Meat!"

"Starting to go bad."

"Starting to go *good*, you mean!"

Dark laughter then, with a hungry edge to it.

Inside the hood I couldn't see what was coming for me, but I already knew: carrion imps, some of the nastiest little scavengers in the city. Normally the miniature versions of ghouls aren't much of a threat, but I no longer had a body with which to defend myself. Now I was just a hunk of discarded meat, an unexpected but quite welcome feast for the little bastards, and once they picked my skull clean not all the magic in Nekropolis could resurrect me again.

All in all it was turning out to be a pretty shitty night.

FOUR

I may have only been a decapitated head, but I still had my brain, so the first thing I did was send out a telepathic SOS to Devona. I'd never tried to communicate with her through our psychic link at such a great distance before, but even if she did receive my message I knew there was no way she could reach me in time to prevent the carrion imps from chowing down on me – both sections of me.

I'd heard my body fall at the same time as my head struck the ground, so presumably my other half was lying close by. I wondered then who'd done this to me, sliced me in two and left me lying on the street for scavengers to snack on. I had any number of enemies, but there was only one person I'd seriously pissed off that evening: Overkill. Devona's words came back to me then.

The only way for her to regain face is to confront the person who forced her to stand down without so much as raising a hand against her.

Well, I certainly couldn't raise a hand now – or any other body part, for that matter. But I had a hard time believing Overkill was responsible for my current state. She was certainly capable of ambushing me and slicing off my head before I could react, no doubt about that. But my attacker hadn't said a single word to me and Overkill would have definitely wanted me to know she was the one who'd taken me out. But I didn't have time to worry about that now. I needed to survive long enough for Devona to reach me – assuming she'd received my psychic call for help and was on her way. If she hadn't… I thrust the thought aside and focused on not becoming imp food.

They approached cautiously, clawed feet scratching against the pavement, breath softly hissing in and out of their nostrils as they scented the air.

"You really don't want to do this." My voice came out as a rough croak, but it seemed I still possessed enough of my throat to speak. How I managed to do so without a pair of lungs to move air over my vocal cords, I'm not sure. I decided to put it down to zombie magic. A severed head is much scarier if it can talk, right?

The scuffling stopped and was replaced by a tense silence. I pictured a crowd of carrion imps gathered around my hooded head, standing frozen, eyes agape as they realized what they'd taken for a hunk of discarded meat was, in fact, alive – or a reasonable facsimile thereof.

A few seconds passed and then one of the braver imps spoke. "Yeah? Why not?"

His words were tough enough, but his voice quavered. Individually carrion imps are cowards. They're only truly dangerous when gathered together in packs. If I could keep them off balance and play on their fearful nature I might be able to prevent them from swarming me. It wasn't much of a plan, I admit, but it was all I had.

"Because I'm lying in wait for prey, and while I'd rather feed on something more tasty than imp, I'll settle for you if I have to."

A few more moments of silence and then the imps began whispering among themselves. I couldn't make out what they were saying, but I had a good idea. Eventually the brave one spoke again.

"What sort of creature are you that lies in wait for prey concealed by a piece of cloth?"

Damn good question, I thought. "I'm a... a sharp-sting," I said, thinking fast. "I'm waiting for some curious passerby to reach into the hood. When they do, I'll sting them and implant an egg in their body. The egg will carry my consciousness, so I'll leave my current body and take up residence in my new host. Once my egg hatches I'll begin to slowly devour the host from the inside over the course of several months and when the host dies I'll leave the hollowed out corpse in search of a new home."

I was impressed with myself for coming up with such a good bluff on the fly. But then the imps – all of them – began talking.

"You fill up that hood pretty good. Big as you are, you don't seem like you'd be a very effective ambush predator. I think–"

"Would a creature like you need to be sentient at all, let alone possess the power of speech? How does thinking and talking help you find new hosts? It's not–"

"Wven if you are what you say you are, why should we be afraid of you?"

"Yeah, you can only lay an egg in *one* of us."

"That's right. The rest of us will eat the body you leave behind and then kill your new host – and then we'll devour him too."

"Seems like a win–win scenario for us."

"Besides, 'sharpsting' is a *stupid* name," one of the imps concluded and there were murmurs of agreement all round.

I'd known carrion imps could talk, but because they were scavengers, I'd assumed they weren't too bright. I'd assumed wrong and it looked like it was going to result in my skull being picked clean by the smart little bastards.

I heard claws scratch pavement as the imps started toward me again. I tried to turn my head from side to side in the hope that the movement might frighten them, but I couldn't do it. The most movement I could manage was to open and close my eyes and mouth and wiggle my tongue. Not exactly the most intimidating of actions.

I felt tiny hands grab hold of the hood's cloth and begin searching for an opening, as if I were some kind of treat the imps were trying to unwrap. This would be an excellent time for Devona to get here, I thought, with more than a hint of desperation.

That's when I heard the first imp scream. It was quickly followed by a second scream, then a third, and then dozens of imps were shrieking in terror and I heard them scuttle away en masse as they fled into the alley. I felt a tug on the hood and I allowed myself to hope that help had arrived.

"Devona? Is that you?"

No reply, just another tug on the hood. Then I felt myself being dragged slowly across the pavement away from the alley, which meant I was being dragged toward the street. I wasn't currently connected to my body, so technically I couldn't feel a sinking sensation in the pit of my stomach, but that's exactly what I did feel when I realized what was happening. The Azure Slime had hold of my head and was pulling me toward the nearest sewer grate. This was worse than being eaten by carrion imps. At least they would've left my skull behind. Once the Azure Slime was done digesting me there'd be nothing left but a memory.

No one knows for certain what the Slime is or where it came from. Some believe it migrated from Earth with the other Darkfolk when they first came to Nekropolis, while others believe Varvara created the amoeba-like monstrosity to keep the streets of her Dominion clean, while still others believe the Slime evolved from all the nasty stuff that's been dumped into the Sprawl's sewer system over the centuries. Whatever the truth is, while the Azure Slime mostly confines itself to feeding on trash left in the Sprawl's streets and gutters, if anything remains on the sidewalks too long, the Slime will try to grab hold of it and drag it down into the sewers where the main mass of its body can begin the digestion process – and that includes pedestrians, which as you might guess, tends to discourage loitering. When the imps had decided to check me out, they'd ventured too close to the mouth of the alley and lingered there too long. They'd drawn the Slime's attention and, from the way it had sounded, a number of them had been snatched by the Slime before the rest had managed to escape. Unfortunately for me the Slime had discovered my head and was now retracting its pseudopod, pulling me hood and all toward the main mass of its body where I would be absorbed and then digested. Since I don't feel pain I wasn't worried that being digested would hurt, but I did wonder how long it would take before enough of my brain was destroyed for me to lose consciousness. If I managed to retain consciousness long enough there was a chance that Devona might be able to find me, even down in the sewers, trapped inside the Slime's viscous blue goo. But that all depended on how fast the Slime took to metabolize the goodies it scavenged and I had no idea how long that was.

Now would be an even more excellent time for Devona to get here, I thought.

I felt a sharp tug on the hood, pulling me in the opposite direction from the street. The Slime tugged back and I heard a soft grunt as someone yanked harder.

"Let go, damn it!"

Swaddled within the hood's darkness, I smiled.

"Your timing is as impeccable as ever, my love."

Devona gave one last tug before the Slime finally gave up and released me. Devona shifted me around in her hands to get a better grip and then pulled the hood off of me. I glanced to the side and caught a glimpse of the Azure Slime's pseudopod illuminated by the greenish glow of a streetlight as it slithered back into the sewer.

"Better luck next time," I muttered. Then I looked up at Devona. "Guess you heard me calling."

"Good thing, too. You were about to become an appetizer for that thing." Devona was working to keep her tone light, but I could hear the worry in her voice. Even in Nekropolis it's more than a bit disconcerting to find yourself having a conversation with your lover's decapitated head. "What happened?" she asked.

I gave Devona a quick rundown.

When I was finished she frowned. "Do you think Overkill's responsible?"

I tried to shrug, but considering I currently lacked shoulders, I settled for answering her verbally. "Maybe. It doesn't seem like her style, though. Not public enough."

"True. But we can worry about whodunnit later. Right now we need to get your head reattached to your body."

"Papa's not going to be happy when we come knocking on his door." Papa Chatha had done a number of various repairs on me over the years – reattaching body parts from ears all the way up to arms. But I'd never asked him to reattach something as complicated as my head before. I feared it might be beyond the houngan's skill, but he was someplace to start. "Do you think you can manage to carry my body by yourself?" Devona may be petite but her half Bloodborn physiology makes her stronger than an ordinary human and I'd learned not to underestimate what she was physically capable of.

"Maybe," she said. "If you'll just tell me where it's at, I'll give it a try."

I blinked in surprise. "Excuse me?"

"Your body. It's not here. Just tell me where to find it and we can…" She broke off. "Why are you looking at me like that?"

I thought of the sounds I'd heard after my head had been cut off: shuffling footsteps, rustling cloth, grunts of exertion… There was a good reason my body wasn't anywhere in sight.

It had been stolen.

"I've heard of body snatchers before," Papa Chatha said, "but this is a new one on me."

Papa is a dignified, handsome black man in his early sixties with a tattoo of a blue butterfly spread across his smooth shaven face. At times the edges of the butterfly's wings seem to ripple, but it's probably just a trick of the light. He sat on a simple wooden stool, tapping his bare toes on the wooden floor as he considered my predicament, Devona sitting across from him on a second stool, my head cradled in her lap.

While Papa thought, I scanned the shelves in his workroom, taking in the multitude of materials that a professional voodoo practitioner needs to perform his art: wax-sealed vials filled with ground herbs and dried chemicals, jars containing desiccated bits of animals – rooster claws, lizard tails, raven wings – candles of all sizes and colors, varying lengths of rope tied in complicated patterns of knots, small dolls made of corn shucks and horsehair, books and scrolls piled on tabletops next to rattles and tambourines of various sizes, along with pouches of tobacco, chocolate bars, and bottles of rum. Papa says he uses the latter three substances to make offerings to the Loa, the voodoo spirits, and while I have no reason to doubt him, I've noticed that he tends to run out of rum before anything else.

Papa frowned, smoothed his loose white pants which matched his pullover shirt, and then sighed.

"I suppose the first thing we need to do is find out where your body is," he said. "Assuming that it hasn't been destroyed already. Or eaten." He rose from his stool and walked over to one of his worktables and began rummaging through the bits and pieces of voodoo paraphernalia scattered across its surface.

"You really need to work on your bedside manner, Papa," I said.

He replied without turning around to look at me. "You want a reassuring bedside manner, go visit the Fever House. You want someone who can sling a little goofer dust for you, I'm your man."

"What I don't understand is why someone would want a zombie's body," Devona said. I couldn't turn my head to show her the withering look that was on my face, but she must've realized how her words sounded, because she immediately added, "Sorry, Matt."

"A corpse is a useful ingredient in any number of spells," Papa said. He picked up an object that resembled an inside-out geode covered with chicken beaks, considered it for a moment, then shook his head and put it back down on the table. "A man who's been resurrected from the dead has even more uses, and considering how rare Matt is..." Papa shrugged. "I don't fully understand the magic that animates him, but I understand enough to know that he's one of a kind. And the more unique an object is, the more power it has."

I died destroying something called the Overmind, a psychic weapon created from the combined brains of powerful psychics, and I'd used a magical device called the Death Watch to do it. I died the precise instant the energies of both the Overmind and the Death Watch were released and somehow they'd combined to resurrect me as a fully intelligent, self-willed zombie. I was no drooling mindless thing shambling about on an endless quest for fresh brains to devour, nor was I the undead slave of a sorcerer. I was my own man, albeit a dead one. The Overmind had been, you'll pardon the expression, the brainchild of the Darklord Talaith, ruler of the Arcane, and I'd been on the top of her shit list ever since. And that gave me another suspect to consider in my bodynapping.

"Maybe Talaith is responsible," I ventured, but I immediately realized my mistake. "No. Even if for some reason she wanted to decapitate me, she'd never take my body and leave my head behind. Revenge is personal with her and she'd want my head if for no other reason than to rub my nose in the fact that she's finally gotten even with me."

"Probably," Papa said. "Then again, Talaith's crazy. Who knows what she might do, or why?"

"You know, Papa, you may be a good houngan, but it's your optimistic worldview that keeps me coming back," I said.

Papa grinned as he glanced over his shoulder at Devona and me. "All part of the service." He continued speaking as he turned back to his worktable and resumed rummaging through its junk. "By the way, Matt, I caught your interview with Acantha on the Mind's Eye tonight. You have a real knack for dealing with the media."

"You know me," I said. "Always gracious and cooperative during an interview."

I considered the possibility that Acantha might have been the one who attacked me – or at least arranged for the attack to be carried out. I'd embarrassed her on her own show in front of thousands of viewers and there was no way the gorgon would ever forgive that. But as with Talaith I had a hard time seeing Acantha carrying out her revenge anonymously. Not only would she want me to know she was making me pay for humiliating her on the air, she'd want to broadcast her payback for the whole city to see. The more I thought about it the more unlikely a suspect Acantha seemed. Still, I couldn't rule her out, just as I couldn't rule out

Overkill or Talaith or several dozen others who'd I'd managed to piss off since I'd arrived in Nekropolis. You know the old saying about how you can judge a man's success by how many enemies he has? Well, right then I felt like the most successful dead man in Nekropolis.

"Aha! I thought I had one of these lying around somewhere." Papa turned back around to face us once more, holding out his hand to show us the round flat object resting on his palm.

"It's a compass," Devona said.

"Yes, indeed," Papa confirmed. "And when I'm finished with it, it'll lead you to Matt's body."

I gazed doubtfully upon the compass. "It doesn't have a needle," I pointed out. "And even if it did it wouldn't work in Nekropolis, would it?" When the Darkfolk decided to leave Earth they'd chosen to build their new city in a dimension of darkness called the Null Plains. I'm not sure the place is even a planet… not like Earth, anyway. But from what I understood the Null Plains didn't have magnetic poles, so a compass wouldn't function.

"It's not that kind of compass," Papa said. "Instead of magnetism it employs sympathetic magic. In particular, the Law of Contagion."

"What's that?" I asked, but it was Devona who answered.

"'Once connected, always connected,'" she said, sounding as if she were reciting from memory. "It means that once two things have been in contact they're forever after bound on a magical level. The longer they've been in contact the stronger that connection will be."

Papa nodded. "We're lucky. Since your head was left behind we can use it to locate the rest of you."

I glanced at the compass. "I hate to break this to you but my head's too big to fit inside there."

"We don't need your whole head. Just part of it." Papa grinned as he showed me what he held in his other hand: a pair of pliers.

"Head east, Lazlo."

"You got it, Devona." Lazlo hit the gas and his cab swerved alarmingly as he rounded a corner.

"Take it easy on the curves, OK?" My voice was stronger now, louder and clearer, thanks to some of Papa's hocus pocus.

"Relax, Matt," Lazlo said. "No need to lose your head." He guffawed, a sound something like a cross between a shotgun blast and a whoopee cushion's fart.

Lazlo's a demon cabbie who works the Sprawl, though he'll drive you to other Dominions if the fare's right. In my case the ride was always gratis because Lazlo refused to take any darkgems from me after I'd helped him out of a jam not long after I'd first become zombiefied. Whenever I needed a ride Lazlo would appear as if by magic and ferry me to my destination. Once when I'd asked him how he knew whenever I needed a lift, he just shrugged – at least, I think that's what he did. Lazlo looks something like a cross between a mandrill and a ferret, with a little carp around the edges, and with his inhuman physiognomy it's sometimes hard to read his gestures. "I keep a close eye on you, pal," is what he told me.

His answer might be a bit on the stalkerish side but Lazlo's always been there when I needed him, so I did my best to ignore the creepiness factor.

Lazlo's cab is a patchwork monstrosity cobbled together from metal and swaths of what I hope is animal hide and I've seen the vehicle open its hood to reveal a very large mouthful of sharp teeth. I'm careful to avoid walking too near the front of the cab just in case it isn't too picky about what it eats.

Given the bizarre nature of Lazlo's ride I wasn't sure it had anything resembling a suspension but, if it did, it was in dire need of new shock absorbers. I felt every little dip and bump in the road as if they were major seismic events and if Devona hadn't been holding me in her lap and steadying me by keeping her hand on top of my head, I'd have been bouncing around the cab's interior like a giant pinball covered in rotting meat. In her other hand Devona held the compass Papa Chatha had given us. In place of its missing needle it now had one of my back teeth. As we navigated the twisting, winding streets of the Sprawl the tooth spun slowly around as it tried to get a fix on my missing body.

I thought back to Papa's extraction of the tooth. It had taken him several minutes to pry the thing loose from my jaw and the entire time I was giving thanks to whatever deity might be listening that the nerve endings in my mouth were as dead as the rest of me.

We weren't simply relying on the tooth compass to locate my body, though. Papa had also promised to put the word out on the street that someone had stolen my body. I might've made my fair share of enemies over the years but I've made plenty of friends, too, and Papa would make sure they were all keeping their ears to the ground for any word of what might've happened to my body or who might be responsible.

"Magic's all well and good," he'd said. "But sometimes friends are more help than the most powerful spell."

Devona – always security-conscious – had worried that putting the word out about my current condition would let my enemies know that I was vulnerable to attack, but Papa had promised he'd be discreet about who he spoke to and we decided to leave it at that.

Lazlo glanced in the rearview mirror at us, an action which never failed to alarm me. The way Lazlo drives it's never a good idea for him to take his gaze off the road.

"What's the range on that thing?" he asked.

"Papa wasn't definite," I told him. "A couple miles, give or take, was his best guess. We'll just have to drive around until the compass gets a hit."

"No prob. I'm at your service for as long as it takes. We may have to stop and refuel, but maybe we'll get lucky and my cab'll find something to snack on along the way."

"I hope you're joking," I said.

Lazlo burst out with another of his deafening laughs.

"You're a funny guy, Matt!"

Thankfully I was spared from having to learn anything more about his vehicle's dietary needs when Lazlo turned on the radio. A DJ's voice full of exaggerated enthusiasm blared from the tinny speakers.

"You're tuned to Bedlam 66.6, Nekropolis's hit machine! Coming up this hour we'll have tunes from Hard Rock Zombies, The Crypt Kicker Five, and Jude's Hammer, but first here's a blast from the past from Kakophonie, in honor of Scream Queen *not* losing her voice tonight. Better luck next time, Overkill!"

I groaned as the band's so called music blasted through the cab. Sometimes Nekropolis is more like a gossipy small town than a large city and word about any scandal – the juicier the better – travels more swiftly than a flock of vampire bats equipped with jet packs.

"I hope Overkill didn't hear that," Devona said. "She'll be more determined than ever to get back at you." She paused. "That is, if she isn't the one who stole your body in the first place."

It was true. As pissed off as Overkill undoubtedly was at me, the last thing I needed was for people to start gossiping about how I'd stopped her. The bad publicity would only turn her already fiery fury to a white-hot incandescence.

"I'll worry about that later," I said. "First, I have to find my other half."

"I thought *I* was your other half," Devona said.

"No, you're my *better* half."

Devona gently ruffled my hair. "You're sweet. Hopefully we'll be able to locate your body soon. But if we don't... well, things won't change between us. You know that, right?"

"Yes."

As I might have mentioned earlier I'm not anatomically functional in certain areas but, with Devona's ability to create a mindlink between us, I didn't need to be. We're able to join on the astral plane, merging spirits in a way that's more deep and profound than any physical lovemaking could ever be. As long as my mind was intact we'd still be able to bond psychically, although the prospect of Devona carting me around in a hatbox the rest of our lives didn't exactly appeal to me. I forced myself not to think about that. Back on Earth I'd never been the type to borrow trouble and my time in Nekropolis – where living, dead, or somewhere in between, existence is precarious at best and fleeting at worst – had only strengthened that trait.

Instead I turned my thoughts to the conversation Devona and I had before I'd left the Midnight Watch. I'd been telling myself that I kept apart from Devona's business so as not to interfere, but now I wondered if that wasn't just an excuse. Maybe I hadn't gotten to know her employees because I hadn't wanted to bother. Not long after we'd first met Devona told me that I'd died inside a long time before my physical body did. Her observation had hurt at the time, all the more so because she was right. I'd been trying to be more emotionally available – as a therapist might put it – ever since, but I still wasn't very good at it. The next time any of the Midnight Watch team invited me out for a drink after work maybe I should accept, I thought. Unless it was Bogdan.

"Devona, about the things I said earlier…"

I felt her hand atop my head tense.

"Don't worry about that now, Matt," she said, just a little too quickly. "For now, let's concentrate on finding your body."

Her words were delivered in a calm, rational tone, but through our link I could feel how much she was still hurting. As strong and intelligent as she was I still sometimes forgot how much she depended on my support and tonight I'd failed to give it – or at least, it seemed that way to her, and that was all that mattered.

But she didn't want to talk about it right then and I had to respect that. And truthfully, I was grateful to postpone what promised to be an uncomfortable conversation a little while longer. So I tried to send a psychic message through our link, a combination of *I'm sorry* and *I love you*. I didn't know if she received it or not, but she patted my head and even though it made me feel a bit like a cute pet sitting on his owner's lap, it reassured me.

Lazlo drove on and Devona and I continued to watch the tooth compass, waiting for it to indicate where my body was.

It was well after midnight but the Sprawl is always open for business. The streets were thick with traffic and Lazlo wove erratically in and out of lanes with disturbing regularity, earning a multitude of raised middle fingers – many with claws on the tip – horn blasts and snarls from the more feral drivers. At one point he nearly sideswiped the Headless Horseman and ended up with splattered pumpkin smeared across his rear window. I was just glad the Horseman hadn't glanced into the cab and seen me or else the specter might've been tempted to replace his missing head with mine. Then again, if he had, at least I'd experienced a smoother ride on the back of his ghostly steed than I would've in the backseat of Lazlo's nightmare conglomeration of a cab.

We crisscrossed the Sprawl, cruising the main drag of Sybarite Street and passing such well-known landmarks as the Freakatorium and the Grotesquerie, as well as the House of Dark Delights and Pandemonia. We even circled the high rise of Demon's Roost, the seat of Varvara's power. But no matter where we went my tooth continued its slow rotation around the compass's face, never once indicating my body might be near.

We drove past the crystalline pyramid that was the Eidolon Building where the city's major media outlets were housed. The *Daily Tome*, Bedlam 66.6 and Mind's Eye Theatre all have offices there and I wondered if even then Acantha was inside, seething over how I'd humiliated her on the air and planning revenge – assuming she hadn't already taken it by stealing my body, that is. But if she had orchestrated the theft of my body it wasn't located anywhere near the Eidolon Building, according to the compass.

Our drive continued like this for several hours and I'd just about resigned myself to living the rest of my unlife as a talking head when the tooth finally swiveled to point northeast of our current location.

Devona told Lazlo and I followed up by ordering him to step on it.

I immediately regretted my words as the cab shot forward as if suddenly rocket propelled. Devona lost her grip on me and I tumbled to the floor and bounced around a bit before she managed to get hold of me again and settle me back onto her lap. The severed head routine, to use a metaphor that technically didn't apply at that moment, was becoming a real pain in the ass.

Devona kept a close eye on the tooth compass and called out course corrections to Lazlo as he drove. Fifteen minutes and uncountable traffic violations later we found ourselves at the edge of the Sprawl, close to its border with the Wyldwood, the Dominion of the lykes. The businesses there tend to cater toward their shapeshifter neighbors, mostly restaurants that served hunks of raw meat and mugs of blood – few self-respecting lykes would go near a glass of aqua sanguis. They'd rather drink animal blood just as long as it was the real thing. Devona instructed Lazlo to pull up to a rundown shack of a restaurant called Tooth and Claw. He parked in front of the establishment, earning wrinkled noses and low throated growls of disapproval from a group of lykes on the sidewalk. But the cab just growled right back and the lykes suddenly remembered a pressing engagement elsewhere and departed.

"Keep the motor running, Lazlo," Devona said.

"No problem. Holler if you need help, though."

I promised we would, then Devona opened the door and, holding me tucked beneath her arm, climbed out of the cab. In her other hand she held the tooth compass and she kept her gaze fixed on it as she stepped onto the sidewalk.

"You think the restaurant owner stole my body because their scavenger customers have been craving filet of zombie?"

I was joking – mostly. But lykes came in all types, not just the typical werewolf kind. Werehyenas, werevultures... there were any number of lykes who preferred decayed meat to fresh.

"Let's hope not," Devona said, not taking her eyes off the compass. "Otherwise, while we might be able to get the bulk of your body back, we'll have to wait a while, and I don't think you'll appreciate the state it's in once we recover it."

"I didn't realize you possessed a crude streak, Ms. Kanti."

"Must be the bad influence of the company I've been keeping lately, Mr. Richter." She paused. "Bad news. The compass is pointing directly at the restaurant. Should we go in?"

I thought about it. Without my body I didn't have my jacket and that meant I didn't have any of the various toys I carry around for dealing with occasional annoyances, like a restaurant filled with territorial lykes who would be less than thrilled to have a half-vampire carrying a zombie head enter their establishment. Most lykes can't stand the smell of undead flesh, zombies in particular, so neither of us would receive a warm welcome if we went inside.

"Let's go around the back," I suggested. "Maybe we'll find a way to sneak in."

In lyke culture the strongest predators have the highest status and the lower ranking predators, along with the herbivores, serve them. So the kitchen staff would be composed of lower caste lykes, which meant they'd be easier to deal with than the alphas dining at the Tooth and Claw. At least, that's what I hoped.

Devona carried me down an alley alongside the ramshackle building. I had a few bad moments when we passed a group of carrion imps sifting through a pile of trash – I'll never look at the little bastards the same way again – but otherwise we made it to the other side of the alley without any trouble.

The rear of the Tooth and Claw looked like the back of any other restaurant: Dumpster alongside the aisle wall, back entrance lit by a single light overhead, a metal bucket lying on the ground next to the door to collect cigarette butts and gnawed clean bones left by staff during breaks.

I was trying to come up with some kind of story that we could use to tell the kitchen staff to get them to let us in and take a look around when Devona stopped walking.

"Uh, Matt? The tooth isn't pointing to the restaurant any more. It's pointing to the Dumpster."

I wondered then if my earlier joke hadn't proved prophetic, if maybe some lyke chef had carved the dead meat from my bones for his scavenger customers and then tossed my bones into the Dumpster. After all, the tooth compass was designed to locate my body – or what was left of it. There was no guarantee what state my body would be in when we found it.

The Dumpster lid was down, and fearing the worst, I told Devona to open it. She tucked the compass into a back pocket – though considering how tight her leather pants were, I have no idea how she managed to do it – and then reached up with her free hand, gripped the Dumpster lid, and threw it open. As short as she is she couldn't see into the Dumpster, so she gripped my hair and held me up as high as she could so I could take a look. There, lying atop a mound of animal bones and bloody rags, lay my body. The arms and legs were askew but they didn't appear to be broken and aside from the wound on my neck where my head had been attached, my body looked none the worse for our time apart.

My body wasn't the only thing in the Dumpster, though. Standing on my chest was a single carrion imp. The tiny creature ignored me as he cupped his hands to his mouth and shouted, "Hey, guys! You're not going to believe what I found!"

"Call Lazlo," I told Devona. "We need to get the rest of me out of there, pronto."

Devona shouted Lazlo's name and at the same time

a pack of eager carrion imps came racing out of the alley.

I hoped Lazlo was a fast runner.

FIVE

Devona and Lazlo managed to get my body into the back seat of the cab and then we all climbed in. Devona gave my body a quick examination and confirmed that it hadn't suffered any significant damage. We also learned that whoever had stolen my body hadn't removed any of the tricks I carried in the pockets of my suit jacket and he or she had left my 9mm in the shoulder holster.

Lazlo pulled away from the Tooth and Claw and Devona took out her handvox, called Papa Chatha, and then held the device to my face so I could talk with him. Handvoxes are the Nekropolis version of cell phones and they're yet another patented Victor Baron creation. They're made of flesh with an ear for you to speak into and a mouth that relays the voice of the person on the other end. If you hold a vox too close to your own ear you can sometimes feel the moving lips of the mouth against your skin, a sensation that, despite my dead nerve endings, never fails to make me a little queasy. Because of this, and so Devona could hear as well, I asked her to put Papa on speaker phone.

I quickly filled Papa in on what had happened since we left, and while Lazlo drove around this section of the Sprawl, Papa told me he'd been doing some more thinking about my situation.

"You know I'll do anything in my power to help you, Matt. You're not just one of my best customers, you're also my friend. But – and this is no false modesty on my part – while I can sew back on an ear or finger, even reattach an arm, there's no way in the Nine Hells that I'll be able to successfully reattach your head. You may be dead, but your nervous system still functions in its own fashion. I simply do not possess the necessary knowledge and skill to repair all the required connections between your brain and body. I'm sorry."

Papa went on before I could reply.

"Something else you need to be aware of is that an injury of this magnitude has severely damaged the integrity of your preservative spells. You'll need to get them reapplied as soon as possible. The longer your two… er, pieces remain separate, the more decay you'll experience. I can cast preservative spells on your head and body separately, but doing so will make it more difficult to rejoin them. It's hard to explain, but basically, by treating your two halves as separate objects, I'll be making them separate. So if at all possible, it would be better to wait until your head and body are reconnected before I apply any new preservative spells. No more than a couple days. Otherwise…"

He didn't need to spell out the alternative for me. Without preservative spells I'd rot away to nothing within a short time. Normal voodoo zombies decay more slowly because they're tied to their master's life-force, and as for the brain-munching zombies – well, nobody's exactly sure where they came from, but they tend to decay more slowly too. Not me, though. I decay at a fairly constant rate and it usually takes me a couple weeks to go from looking almost human to looking like boiled chicken sliding off the bone. But injuries to my body, while they don't hurt, speed up the process of decay. The more damage I take, the faster I rot. So even though I don't have to avoid serious injury to preserve my life the same way I did when I was human, in many ways, my current condition isn't all that different. Instead of seeing a physician, I see a voodoo priest, and his magic – along with his admittedly clumsy sewing skills – has kept me in a state of undead health for years.

"Well, if you can't put me back together, who can?"

"You could try the physicians at the Fever House," Papa said.

The Fever House is a hospital in Gothtown that provides the most advanced medical care in Nekropolis, in many ways more advanced than back on Earth. In order to preserve the quality of the human blood supply over the millennia vampires developed the medical arts and passed them along to human physicians. When the Darkfolk left Earth several centuries ago the Bloodborn established the Fever House and continued exporting

medical knowledge to Earth – which is more than a little disturbing when you stop to consider that the flu
shot you're getting is the result of a predator species
wanting to keep its food supply healthy. But at any rate,
the doctors at the Fever House might well possess the
knowledge necessary to reassemble me.

Devona spoke for the first time since I called Papa.
"The Fever House takes in patients of all species," she
said. "With one exception."

I sighed. "Let me guess: zombies."

She nodded. "You know Bloodborn view them as
nothing more than reanimated corpses. Never mind
that full-blooded vampires are too. It's the fact that
zombies don't have any blood that disgusts them."

"I hadn't thought of that," Papa said. "I suppose that
leaves only one alternative."

"And that would be?" I prompted.

"Who else deals on a regular basis with stitching dead
things together and bringing them back to life?" Papa
asked. "Or at least a semblance of life."

"Victor Baron," I said.

I thanked Papa for the suggestion, he wished me luck
and then he disconnected.

I told Devona what Papa had said. She called Information, got the number for the Foundry, and called. It
was close to three in the morning now but in a city of
perpetual dusk the citizens keep odd hours, so it was
worth a shot to give Victor Baron a call. If we had to
wait until morning it would be no great hardship. I
needed to be reconnected before Papa could reapply my

preservative spells, but I wouldn't rot away to dust in the next few hours. Still, the sooner I was whole again the better.

Devona had taken the vox off speaker phone and now held the device to her ear. I could hear a faint ringing from the other end and it went on long enough that I was beginning to think no one was going to answer, but then I heard a soft click followed by the sound of someone speaking, though I couldn't make out the words.

"It's a voice menu," Devona said. She listened for a moment and then pressed a button on the vox. She listened a few more seconds, frowned slightly, and made another selection. This went on for several more moments and I thought she was going to end up having to leave a message. Evidently Devona did too because she gave a start when someone actually answered.

"Oh, hello. Sorry to be calling so late but I'd like to make an appointment to see Mr. Baron. A friend of mine is a zombie and he, well, not to put too fine a point on it, someone cut off his head and–"

She stopped and listened for a moment.

"Yes, we have both his head and his body. No, the body isn't moving on its own." A pause as she listened again. "His name is Matthew Richter, and–"

Another interruption, another pause. When Devona started speaking again, she sounded pleased and surprised in equal measure.

"We're in the Sprawl right now, but we can come over right away. Thank you so much!"

She disconnected, closed the vox, and slipped it back into her pocket.

"Believe it or not, we have an appointment with Victor Baron. He'll be waiting for us whenever we get there."

I was pleased, of course, but an inherently suspicious nature is a prerequisite for a PI, and I couldn't bring myself to believe it had really been that easy.

"Who did you talk to?"

Devona shrugged. "An assistant of some sort, I assume. He said his name was–"

"Ygor," I guessed.

She frowned. "No. Henry. He told me not to worry about calling late. 'We never close here at the Foundry,' he said. He sounded blandly professional at first. You know, doing his job but not really interested in who I was or what my problem might be. But he became very interested when I told him your name."

"Why would that mean anything to him?"

From the front seat Lazlo said, "You helped save the city last Descension Day. You're famous." He thought for a moment. "Then again maybe he caught you on Acantha's show tonight." He chuckled, a sound like splintering bones. "I didn't realize you were so funny. You were a real sport to go along with her gags."

I sighed – which is a real trick when you're not attached to your lungs. "What can I say? You know how much I love a good joke."

Had everyone in the city seen that stupid program? I was really starting to regret my lack of restraint earlier in the evening. I considered sending Acantha a few hundred roses as a down payment on an apology, but as angry as the gorgon was, she'd probably just turn them to stone.

"All right, Lazlo," I said. "Let's head for the Foundry."

Lazlo pulled his cab onto the Obsidian Way and soon we were crossing the Bridge of Forgotten Pleasures, leaving the Sprawl and entering the Wyldwood. Nekropolis is shaped like a gigantic pentagram, its five Dominions separated by Phlegethon, a river of green fire that burns the spirit instead of the flesh. The only way to pass between Dominions is to use one of the bridges that connect them and the only way to cross in relative safety was to travel the Obsidian Way. The smooth glossy black road offers no magical protections for travelers, but the laws of Nekropolis state that travel between Dominions is not to be impeded for any reason – provided travelers keep to the Obsidian Way. If you venture from the road you're fair game for whoever, or whatever, might find you. Of course, as with a lot of laws in Nekropolis, it's really more of a strong suggestion than anything else, so traveling the Way is still dangerous. You need to keep your guard up and move as fast as you can and hope you don't attract any undue attention. And if you do you'd better hope you're stronger, faster or smarter than whatever is trying to catch you. Preferably all three.

The Wyldwood, as the name implies, is mostly forested, though there's a good amount of pastureland as well. There are villages located in the Dominion, though they tend to be few and far between. Those lykes who desire a more urban lifestyle tend to live in the Sprawl and while Lord Amon frowns on this, he doesn't forbid his subjects to leave the Wyldwood. Still, the vast majority of shapeshifters live there.

I'd traveled through a bit of the Wyldwood before, on foot, which is precisely as dangerous as it sounds. During that time, I'd stuck close to the Obsidian Way, but supposedly the interior of the Wyldwood changes its shapes just as lykes do. One day it might be a dark European forest, the next African grasslands, and the day after that, arctic tundra. I don't know if it's true but I've met Lord Amon, King of the Shapeshifters, and since he can change his form into that of any creature he desires, I've no trouble believing his Dominion is as metamorphic as he is. Sometimes I wonder if the only reason the land bordering the Obsidian Way remains stable in the Wyldwood is because Father Dis wants it that way to promote greater ease of travel. Then again, nice thick woods are much easier for predators to hide in and maybe that's the real reason the land around the Obsidian Way never changes. It makes for better hunting that way.

Whichever the case, the treeline on either side of the road varies little – huge, ancient trees with thick trunks and dense foliage kept us company as we drove. Although it wasn't long before we picked up new companions.

A dozen or so lykes appeared out of the woods and began running alongside the Obsidian Way, easily keeping pace with Lazlo's cab despite how swiftly we were traveling. They darted in and out of the woods on either side of the road, lithe forms moving with eerie silent grace. Some wore full animal forms, others appeared as human-beast hybrids, while still others were mostly human with only slight feral touches: pointed ears, sharp teeth, yellow eyes… But all the lykes moved with supernatural speed that was at once both terrifying and beautiful to behold. They were all predators of one kind or another, canine and feline, primarily. No mixbloods, though. Once a lyke has visited Dr. Moreau at the House of Pain for a genetic makeover, he or she isn't welcome back in the Wyldwood. A lot of mixbloods are lower caste lykes who've chosen to leave the Wyldwood rather than continue serving the alphas. Can't say as I blame them. I've always had a bit of a problem with authority myself.

The lykes pacing us on both sides of the road weren't simply out for a bit of exercise. The wrecked and abandoned vehicles we passed every few miles were testament to that. The lykes chased cars in the hope that they'd blow a tire or throw a rod and be forced to pull over, in which case it was snack time. Of course, few people are foolish enough to travel the Obsidian Way unless their vehicles are in tiptop shape and they're well armed. Which means that the lykes need to take matters in their own claws. The law forbids them from stepping onto the Obsidian Way to attack a vehicle, but if a driver just happens to encounter an obstacle…

Lazlo gazed out the windshield. "Aw, dammit! I hate lykes!"

"What's wrong?" I couldn't see, so Devona lifted me up and propped me on the back of Lazlo's seat so I could look over his shoulder and out the windshield.

"Spike strip," Lazlo said. "A lyke just tossed one onto the road ahead of us. Hold on."

I'd just managed to catch a glimpse of the gleaming metal of the spike strip illuminated in the wash of the cab's headlights when the vehicle suddenly lurched upward. I almost fell, but Devona grabbed hold of my head with both hands to steady me, though my body slumped over against her. We would've strapped my headless form in when we first put it in the cab but Lazlo doesn't believe in seatbelts. He says they show a serious lack of faith in a driver.

I have no idea how something that at least outwardly resembled an earthly cab managed to jump into the air, but that's exactly what Lazlo's vehicle did, sailing over the spike strip and landing on the other side with a jarring impact. No damage was done, though – or at least, none the cab couldn't contend with – and we kept going. The lykes keeping pace with us snarled with frustration, eyes wild, tongues lolling, jaws flecked with froth, but they continued flanking us, no doubt looking forward to their next attempt to force us to stop.

The snarls and growls gave way to full-fledged howls, and Lazlo grimaced. "I've had enough of this shit." He thumbed a switch on the dash and in response the cab's hood retracted into the main body of the vehicle with a moist sliding sound. A mottled discolored organ rose forth from the vehicle's cavity, flesh coated with slimy mucus and shot through with swollen purple veins. I recognized the cab's tongue, but as I watched it thickened and swelled, lengthened and extended, until it had assumed a very different shape, one reminiscent of a mounted machine gun. The fleshy weapon began firing – or perhaps spitting is a more appropriate term – swiveling back and forth, spraying silvery gobs of organic material as if they were bullets with accompanying *chuff-chuff-chuff* sounds. The silver sputum hit the lykes on both sides of the road as we passed and the werebeasts howled and screamed in agony as the ammunition struck them. From the severity of their reaction I knew that the mucusbullets Lazlo's cab produced somehow contained actual silver. A dozen lykes fell to the barrage from the flesh-gun, while the others decided that this night discretion really be the better part of valor and fled, slipping silently away into the shadowy woods.

Once the lykes were driven off the fleshgun stopped firing, descended into the vehicle's cavity – returning to its normal tongue shape in the process – and the hood slid back into place.

Lazlo then turned to look over his shoulder and gave us a grin.

"Nothing like a few hundred rounds of silver to make a lyke think twice, eh?"

The cab swerved alarmingly to the right while Lazlo said this and both Devona and I shouted for the demon to turn back around before his haphazard driving accomplished what the lykes couldn't and caused us to wreck. Lazlo faced forward again, seemingly unconcerned that we were heading straight for a huge oak tree, and he managed to bring the cab back under control in time to avoid a collision.

Lazlo continued driving and Devona and I were silent for several moments while we adjusted to the fact that we'd barely just avoided becoming weremonster kibble. When I had my nerves under control, I said, "That's a new feature, Lazlo. When did you have it installed?"

"What do you mean?"

I was used to Lazlo being, shall we say, of generally vague disposition, but I had a hard time believing he didn't understand my question.

"The gun. I saw you hit the switch to activate it."

"Switch?" Then Lazlo laughed. "Naw, I was just trying to turn up the radio to drown out the sound of the lykes. All that howling and snarling is like fingernails on a chalkboard to me."

"But the gun..." I insisted.

"I have no idea where that came from," Lazlo said. "My little baby is just full of surprises, isn't she?"

He patted the dash lovingly and the cab's engine made a noise that sounded surprisingly like a purr.

Evidently word that Lazlo's cab spit silver had preceded us for we saw no further sign of lykes as we passed through the rest of the Wyldwood. As we approached the Dominion's border we saw the green light cast by the flames of Phlegethon flickering against the grayish-black sky and soon we crossed the Bridge of Silent Screams and entered the Boneyard. The Dominion of the Darklord Edrigu, the Boneyard is the realm of the dead, and it fit the part perfectly. The buildings were rundown and always on the verge of collapse. Stone pitted and chipped, wood warped, glass smudged and cracked, mold and mildew clinging to every surface as if they were varieties of paint. Sounds are muffled in the Boneyard and refuse to travel as if the air itself is dead. And while I don't breathe and thus can't personally attest to it I'm told the air smells of must and slow decay, like an ancient tomb that's been sealed for a thousand years or more.

Here Lazlo's insane kamikaze driving was less of a hazard than usual. Few living people had reason to visit the Boneyard and those who did pass through stuck to the Obsidian Way. So the streets were deserted, giving Lazlo fewer targets to hit. The sidewalks were deserted too, but if you stare long enough and allowed your eyes to go out of focus, you begin to see ghostly images of pedestrians garbed in fashions spanning the course of human history, and you get the sense that, far from being deserted, the Boneyard is as full as any major metropolitan area on Earth, and in its own macabre way just as alive. As someone with more than one foot in the grave myself I'm able to see more of the Boneyard's true nature than most, but even I sometimes feel that I'm only catching a glimpse of a larger and more complex picture.

The longer we drove the more we began to see the suggestion of ghostly vehicles sharing the road with us. As with the spectral pedestrians, various ages were represented by the traffic – horse-drawn carriages, model Ts, stagecoaches, Roman chariots, ultra-modern sports cars... For the most part the insubstantial vehicles gave us a wide berth, but every now and then one would pass right through us, and even I felt a cold chill of ectoplasm as for the briefest of instants we shared the same space.

"Lousy ghost drivers," Lazlo muttered after a spectral double decker bus drove through us. "Where's a ghost cop when you need one?"

The drivers never acknowledged our existence, didn't so much as shoot us a single glance. They just stared forward, faces expressionless as they drove. I wondered if they were even aware we were present or if, having crossed all the way from one state of existence to the other, they were no longer interested in having anything to do with a mundane corporeal world that was now beneath their notice.

"You're a dead guy, Matt," Lazlo said. "Maybe you can help me understand something I've always wondered about."

He took a hand off the steering wheel – never a confidence building move considering how he drove – and gestured at the ghostly traffic surging silently around us.

"Where do all these ghosts come from? They can't all have migrated here during the Descension. That was almost four hundred years ago and many of these ghosts are more modern than that. Some of them are probably ghosts of people who died in other Dominions and eventually drifted to the Boneyard, but they can't account for this many spirits. I mean, there must be thousands of them."

"Just because I'm a zombie doesn't mean I'm an expert on everything to do with life after death," I told him, "but as I understand it, when the Darkfolk left Earth for Nekropolis, Lord Edrigu gathered up the world's ghosts – those spirits who for whatever reason remained earthbound after their death – and brought them with him, just as the other Darklords brought their subjects with them. Galm brought the vampires, Amon brought the shapeshifters, and so on. But Edrigu knew that people would keep dying on Earth, creating new ghosts, so he left servants behind whose job it is to scour the world, find earthbound spirits, capture them and then bring them to Nekropolis to live in the Boneyard."

"Kind of like a wildlife preserve for the dead, eh?" Lazlo said thoughtfully. "So that's it? The ghosts just stay here, going about their ghostly business, for the rest of eternity?"

Devona jumped into the conversation then. "Yes, although there are rumors that Lord Edrigu's dark mirror doesn't only open a portal to Earth. Supposedly it can open a doorway into... well, whatever comes next. After life, I mean."

Each of the city's five Darklords – as well as Father Dis – possesses a magic mirror that allows them to create a passageway to and from Earth whenever they wish. To be technical, the Lords possess two mirrors: a personal one and a second, much larger one that can be used to transport large object such as freight-laden vehicles back and forth between dimensions. The Darklords need some way of importing necessary materials and supplies. After all, Nekropolis couldn't function if it was an entirely closed system.

Lazlo drove in silence for several moments as he digested what we'd just told him. Eventually, he said, "What about you, Matt?"

"What do you mean?"

"You ever been tempted to go through Edrigu's mirror? I mean, you *are* dead, so you could pass through if you wanted to, right?"

"I don't know."

The thought had never occurred to me. I may be dead but I don't think of myself as a ghost. I still have a physical body after all. But physical objects can pass through a Darklord's mirror. That's how I originally came to Nekropolis. But I'd never thought that I might be able to physically pass from Nekropolis's dimension to... what? Heaven? Nirvana? Or maybe what lay on the other side of Edrigu's mirror was a hellish place worse than Nekropolis. Or – and in some ways this was an even more frightening thought to me – what if there was nothing on the other side? What if a spirit simply ceased to exist once it entered the mirror and instead of another world all that waited for those unfortunate spirits was final, everlasting oblivion?

Devona stroked the back of my head. "You know, Matt, if you ever want to…" She allowed the thought to trail off, unfinished.

"Thanks," I said, "but I'm content with remaining a living dead man in a city of monsters." I glanced toward my headless body propped on the seat next to us. "At least I will be if we can manage to make me whole again."

At that moment we entered a section of the Bone-yard that looked as if it had been bombed into rubble. The buildings here lay in ruins and the streets were strewn with rubble. Lazlo was forced to slow down and detour around the chunks of stone, brick and mortar in the road and the lack of intact buildings around us provided an unobstructed view for miles. In fact we could see all the way to the far east of the Dominion where Edrigu's stronghold lay, situated precisely on his point of the pentagram that formed the city's borders. Edrigu's home was called the Reliquary and it lay housed deep inside a gigantic prehistoric burial mound that looked something like a gently rounded mountain off in the distance. I'd never been there before – this was the first clear view I'd ever had of the place, as a matter of fact – but I had to admit it was something to see. I've visited other Darklord strongholds, and while each is impressive in its own way, there's an ancient grandeur to Edrigu's home, a primal simplicity as if it had been physically shaped from bygone millennia and set in place to stand for all eternity, as basic and uncompromising as Death itself.

Lazlo glanced out the window at the ruins surrounding us. "Man, Edrigu really isn't into urban renewal, is he?"

"He's the King of the Dead, not the King of Architecture," I said. I wondered if the ruined condition of this neighborhood wasn't the reason Victor Baron had chosen to locate the Foundry here. Baron began his life as the original Frankenstein monster, a creature made from the assembled parts of dead bodies and for this reason it made sense that he lived and worked in the Boneyard, a realm of the dead, and this unnamed blight of a neighborhood was among the most desolate of locations in this Dominion. Perfect for a being who was, essentially, a scientific version of a zombie.

Because it was the only intact structure for several miles in all directions, the Foundry loomed large against the surrounding landscape, a dark mass of gray stone that resembled a cross between a medieval keep and a factory built during the height of the Industrial Revolution. Towering smokestacks rose into the sky, fouling the air with black clouds of pollutants. But considering the inhabitants of this Dominion were already dead, the environmental impact was negligible. Perhaps another reason Baron had set up shop here: no need to worry about where and how he dumped his plant's waste products. Rising from the roof of the Foundry and stretching between the smokestacks was an intricate metal lattice containing thick tangled coils of rubber coated cable. Blue-white bolts of electrical energy coruscated across the lattice in a constant ebb and flow like ocean waves. I couldn't smell the sharp tang of ozone in the air, but Devona later told me it permeated the whole area, but even through the cab's closed windows I could hear the constant crackle, pop and hiss of the lattice's electrical discharge, as well as the deep thrumming sound of power so massive it could barely be contained, like the perpetual rushing of a huge waterfall.

Now that I was this close to the Foundry I wondered if Lord Edrigu – or maybe even Father Dis – had insisted Baron build his factory here because of the desolation, since it wouldn't matter if Baron's facility experienced an "industrial accident" that might affect the surrounding area. This was immediately followed by a more disturbing thought: considering that the Foundry had been there for over two centuries maybe Baron's facility had somehow been the cause of the surrounding devastation.

As you might imagine this thought did little to inspire confidence in the man's ability to help me get my head on straight, so to speak.

As we drew closer to the Foundry we began seeing vehicles in the road – not ghost vehicles, but physical, three dimensional ones. Dark semi trucks with the stylized VB of the Victor Baron logo on their trailers passed by, hulking creatures with patchwork faces behind the wheel, carrying the latest shipments of Baron's creations to customers throughout the city. Vehicles resembling hearses glided through the street as well, also bearing Baron's logo on their doors. They belonged to the Bonegetters, employees of Baron's who traveled throughout Nekropolis on an endless quest to locate dead bodies – or cast-off body parts – and bring them to the Foundry to be used as raw material for Baron's work. Considering the savage nature of the Darkfolk, violence occurs on an all-too-regular basis, and when deadly mayhem results, the Bonegetters do their best to make sure they're on the scene to recover any useful bits and pieces when the bloodshed is over.

The Foundry grounds were surrounded by a twenty-five foot wrought iron fence and Lazlo sniffed when he saw it.

"That thing might look impressive to tourists," he said, "but it wouldn't keep out a fly, let alone a…"

Lazlo trailed off as a large black gorecrow approached the fence. The bird flew high enough to pass over the bars, but the instant it crossed the fence's perimeter, there was a blue flash and the bird burst into flames and plummeted to the ground.

"Like I said, Baron's got himself a hell of a security system," Lazlo said, his voice sounding a bit weak. "Good thing we're expected."

"A force field of some kind," Devona said. "Impressive. I wonder if it only prevents physical objects from entering or if it can stop magical intrusions as well."

"If we don't get flashfried trying to get inside, you can ask Baron yourself," I said.

"I'd love to pick his brain," Devona said. "No pun intended. Along with everything else his factory produces, Baron manufactures a number of security products. Reanimated guards, both canine and humanoid, as well as living, organic alarm systems. The Midnight Watch is just small potatoes to someone like him, but if we can learn something from him, or better yet, enter into some kind of partnership, even if only on a small scale…"

Even though I knew it was childish of me, I was irritated by Devona's words.

"We didn't come here to network. We came to get me put back together, remember?"

Devona's eyes narrowed, an expression I knew meant she was struggling to contain her anger.

"Of course," she said, trying to sound as if she weren't upset and succeeding for the most part. "I was just thinking out loud."

If my head had been attached to my body right then I'd have kicked myself for being such an idiot. What was it with me and Devona's business? I'd criticized her employees earlier in the evening and now I'd complained when she recognized a potential opportunity in talking with Victor Baron. Why was I finding it so hard to be supportive? I had no answer, and not wishing to make matters worse, for a change I did the smart thing and kept my mouth shut as Lazlo turned off the road and stopped before the Foundry's main gate.

A metallic skull with organic eyes was mounted on a pole to the left of the gate and it swiveled to look at us. Lazlo rolled his window down and leaned out, but before he could say anything, the skull spoke.

"Damn! You're hideous! No wonder you couldn't wait until morning to see Mr. Baron. But I have to warn you: he may be a genius, but I'm not sure even he's going to be able to pretty up that ugly mug of yours!"

"I'm not the one with the appointment," Lazlo growled. "It's my friend Matt. He's in the back."

The skull sentry turned to face the back window. Devona rolled it down and held me outside so the skull could get a good look at me. The sentry skull's living eyes moved back and forth as it regarded me and I knew there was a living brain encased in that metal cranium. If I'd ever had any doubts that Victor Baron was who and what he claimed to be, they vanished at that moment.

"Just a head, huh?" the skull said. "Believe me, I share your pain."

The gate began to open with a soft hum, and when it had opened wide enough, Lazlo drove slowly through.

The intensity of the power thrum increased the closer we got to the main entrance until I could feel my teeth vibrating. The sensation was merely annoying for me, but when I looked up at Devona, I saw that she was grimacing, jaw clenched tight, lips drawn back to reveal her fangs, which were more prominent than usual, and I knew she was in pain. I heard a low moaning sound then that I first took to be coming from Lazlo, although I'd never known the demon to suffer discomfort of any sort. But I quickly realized the moaning wasn't coming from the front seat; instead, it seemed to be coming from all around us. I understood then that the sounds of distress were emanating not from Lazlo, but rather from his cab.

Lazlo patted the dashboard. "Don't worry, sweetie. It'll be OK."

There was something about the softness in Lazlo's voice that for the first time made me think that maybe the cab was more than simply a vehicle to him and he more than a driver to it. I've become a lot more broad minded since moving to Nekropolis, but even so, the images that went through my mind at the thought of Lazlo and his cab as a couple were more than a little sickening. But lots of people react to Devona and me the same way, so I told myself to be more tolerant.

A light above the entrance flared to blue-white life as we approached a pair of huge iron doors. Lazlo pulled up and the doors started to swing open before he finished parking.

A being cloaked in a hooded brown robe and pushing a wheelchair stepped outside. The being's movements were slow and it lurched from side to side as it walked. One shoulder was higher than the other and the left arm was considerably longer than the right. The flesh of the hands appeared almost bone white in the fluorescent light, and the skin was covered with thick, ugly scars.

The figure opened Devona's door and gestured for her to step out. She did so, carrying me beneath her arm.

"Welcome to the Foundry, Ms. Kanti, Mr. Richter." The voice was a rough whisper and I had to strain to hear it over the loud thrumming issuing from the Foundry. Though it was difficult to tell, I thought it belonged to a man – or at least something that had once been a man. He went on. "I take it the body is still in the cab?"

"I got it," Lazlo said. He left the cab's engine running, walked around to the rear passenger side and retrieved my headless body. He carried it with ease as if it weighed no more than a straw filled scarecrow. He placed my body in the chair gently and the robed man secured it with leather straps around the chest, wrists and ankles. Despite his obvious deformities he performed this operation deftly and within moments my body was ready to travel again.

Devona turned so that I could face Lazlo.

"Thanks for the help," I said.

Lazlo grinned, a sight that would make even the most vicious serial killer wet himself in terror. "You never have to thank me, Matt. You know that. Still, you're welcome."

Just then the cab's hood opened a crack and a mournful wail came out. Lazlo placed his hand on the roof and gently rubbed its surface.

"I'm afraid we can't stay and wait for you," he said. "The sound's getting to her. But we'll stay in the neighborhood and come back to pick you up when you're finished, OK?"

I almost asked Lazlo how he'd know when Devona and I were done – I'd never known him to carry a vox – but there was no point. One way or another Lazlo always knew when I needed a ride.

"Sounds good," I said.

Lazlo gave us a parting wave before climbing back into his cab and roaring away from the main entrance as fast as possible. For an instant I thought he would ram the now closed gate on his way out, but the sentry skull was able to open it in time, if just barely, and Lazlo zoomed off into the darkness, the skull's obscenity-laded shouts of angry protest following him.

The robed man turned to us and for the first time I caught a glimpse of the face hidden within the hood's shadow. Its features were misshapen and twisted, like a wax figure that had melted partway before cooling and becoming solid once more.

"Let's go," he said. "Victor is expecting you."

He gripped the wheelchair's handles and began pushing my body toward the open entrance, walking with that strange lurching gait of his. Devona followed, carrying me, and we entered the lair of Victor Baron.

SIX

Once we were inside the metal doors swung shut of their own accord. Given their size, I expected them to slam closed with a heavy clang, but they made no sound as they shut. What's more, the moment they closed, the power thrum that had been so intense outside disappeared and it became almost eerily quiet.

As if reading my thoughts the brown robed man said, "The Foundry is completely sound-proofed on the inside."

I don't know what I'd expected the interior of the Foundry to be like, but it certainly didn't reflect its gothic-industrial exterior. The floor was covered with clay-colored tile and polished oak paneling covered the walls. Stylish lights hung from the ceiling at regular intervals, providing soft, warm, soothing illumination. Classical music played at a low volume from hidden speakers, completing an effect that Devona later told me was somewhat spoiled by the faint odor of formaldehyde in the air.

The brown robed man pushed my body down a long hallway, moving in a lurching side-to-side motion and Devona had to slow her pace to keep from outdistancing him. The robed man wasn't much for small talk, it seemed, and after a few moments of our walking in silence, Devona tried to draw him out.

"Thank you again for agreeing to see us despite the lateness of hour, Mr....?"

"You may call me Henry. And think nothing of it. We don't keep regular hours around her. Victor has no need for sleep and his supply of energy is inexhaustible." He let out a snuffling laugh. "A little joke, there. As you might guess, Victor can recharge himself from the Foundry's machines whenever necessary."

As if in response to Henry's words, the hall lights dimmed for a moment before returning to full strength.

"Pay no mind to that," he said. "Happens all the time around here."

It was hard to tell given the state of the man's voice, but I thought I detected a hint of an accent that I couldn't quite place. European, certainly. German or maybe Russian. But such accents are common in Nekropolis given the amount of Darkfolk who had made their home in Europe before the Descension and I thought no more of it.

"Victor would've come to meet you himself, but he's caught up in his latest project. He's something of a workaholic."

Henry's words were spoken plainly enough, but there was a slight edge to them, as if he were making a criticism of his employer that he intended to only partially conceal.

Devona and I exchanged a glance at this, but neither of us responded. Disgruntled employees are the same no matter what dimension you live in.

We passed a series of paintings on the walls depicting various scenes of a castle nestled among forestland with picturesque mountains in the background. The paintings weren't sinister at all. The sky was a gentle blue dotted with white clouds, the grass and trees were painted in mild greens, as if the sun was shining down brightly upon them.

Henry noticed Devona and I admiring the paintings.

"You like them? They depict Frankenstein Castle and the family's ancestral lands."

"They're beautiful," Devona said with more than a trace of wistfulness. Though her mother had come from Earth, Devona had been born and raised in Nekropolis and had never visited her mother's home. She'd had the chance once, but she'd given it up to remain in Nekropolis with me. She'd assured me that she didn't regret her decision, but at times like these I couldn't help wondering if on some level she wished she'd chosen differently.

"Have you read Mary Shelley's novel?" Henry asked. He went on before either of us could reply. "Some things she got right, other things she got wrong or simply invented." He nodded toward a painting of the castle. "That's the monst– I mean Victor's birthplace."

Devona and I caught his verbal slip of course, but as with his earlier comment, we let it go without remark. Besides, it's not as if *monster* is a pejorative term in Nekropolis.

The three of us – or four if you count my body on its own – reached the end of the hall. It branched off to the right and left and Henry turned in the latter direction. This hallway resembled a hospital corridor, everything white with bright fluorescent light panels in the ceiling. We passed a number of office doors with name plates on them: DR. X, DR. HEIDEGGER, RAPPACCINI, DR. PRETORIUS, ROSSUM, HERBERT WEST, ROTWANG, DR. GOLDFOOT...

"Victor keeps a number of the city's most prominent scientists on his payroll," Henry said. "He likes to maintain a healthy supply of high quality brains, you know." He chuckled at his own joke, which was good since neither Devona nor I were so inclined.

Henry escorted us deeper into the Foundry and before long we began encountering other employees. Some were merely odd – like the wild-haired, wild-eyed man in a white lab coat who kept telling a pop-eyed hunchback in a black cloak that his name was supposed to be pronounced "Fronk-en-steen," along with the handsome young man with curly black hair wearing a corset, fishnet stockings, 70s glam-rock boots, and far too much make-up.

"A distant family cousin," Henry explained about the latter. "To be honest he's a mediocre scientist, but he's great fun at office parties."

Others were downright bizarre, even for Nekropolis, such as the fly headed man garbed in a stained lab coat who carried a tiny human headed fly perched on his shoulder. The tiny creature kept saying, "Help meeeee!" in a plaintive, high-pitched voice. Henry told us to ignore him.

"The lazy thing's always trying to con someone else into doing his work." He shouted after the departing duo, "You get paid for a full day's work, and we expect a full day's work!"

The fly lifted a foreleg that terminated in a miniature human hand and flipped Henry the bird.

And of course there were the monsters. Frankenstein ones, I mean. What Victor Baron's publicity refers to as the "repurposed dead." Some seemed benign enough, like the slightly silly and bumbling creature carrying a box of lab supplies who, when he attempted to wave hello to us, dropped the box to the floor with a shattering crash.

"That's going to come out of your salary, Herman," Henry said as we passed. "As usual."

Herman just sighed deeply and bent down to clean up his mess.

Other monsters were decidedly more sinister like the shambling mass of arms and legs that didn't appear to have a face and which left a slime trail behind as it traveled or the pack of upside-down human heads that scuttled past on what looked like crab legs growing out of their skulls.

"You know," Devona said thoughtfully, "if Baron isn't able to reattach you to your body…"

"Don't even think it," I said.

"One of Victor's more innovative designs," Henry said. "He's always trying to develop new uses for left-over parts."

Eventually Henry brought us to a set of double doors labeled LABORATORY 17. A sign above the door warned AUTHORIZED PERSONNEL ONLY.

"Victor should be waiting for us inside," Henry said.

There was a hand scanner on the wall and Henry pressed his right palm flat against it. The scanner hummed, a line of reddish light passed over Henry's hand, and a moment later the door swung inward.

"That seems like an easy enough security feature to bypass in a place like this," Devona said. "All someone would have to do is cut off your hand and hold it to the scanner."

I thought the comment sounded a little on the ghoul-ish side for Devona, but then I remembered where we were. Cutting off body parts was business as usual at the Foundry.

"Wouldn't work," Henry said. "The scanner is designed to check hypermetabolic energy rates on both the atomic and subatomic levels, as well as search for evidence of ge-netic tampering. Around here, when the sign says 'authorized personnel only,' it means it." He grinned, scarred, leathery lips drawing back to reveal a mouthful of twisted, discolored teeth. "After all, if you want to open a locked door, you need the correct key, right?"

Without waiting for us to respond Henry wheeled my body into the lab and Devona and I followed.

I'd never met Victor Baron before, but I'd seen him around town a few times, and I'd watched a profile of him and his business on Mind's Eye once. "Adonis-like" is one of the descriptions most commonly applied to him and for good reason. Physically Baron appears to be the epitome of human perfection. Mid-thirties, tall, handsome, body trim and fit, hair chestnut-brown, facial features any male model would envy, piercing blue-ice eyes that radiated both high intelligence and emotional depth. His lightly tanned skin was flawless – no signs of scarring or stitching. He wore a white lab coat over a white shirt, both of which were splotched with brownish-red stains, black pants and black shoes. He looked like a male model or perhaps a movie star who'd decided to chuck his career and take up mad science for a living.

As we entered, Baron turned and flashed us a smile so white and perfect it would have made an orthodontist weep with joy.

Baron's laboratory contained a bizarre hodge-podge of technologies which only made sense given that its owner was an amalgamation of parts taken from different bodies. Much of the assembled equipment consisted of hi-tech top-of-the-line imports from Earth – sophisticated computers, medical diagnostic machines and the like – but some of it would've been better suited to a display of antique technology: Van Der Graaf generators that sparked and sputtered and machine banks covered with rows of glowing-hot vacuum tubes. A half dozen worktables were situated around the room, containing rows of chemicals and powders stored in thick glass vials, along with spread out surgical instruments of various kinds, each longer, sharper and nastier-looking than the last. The instruments' stainless steel gleamed in the lab's fluorescent light and I was mildly surprised that the blades weren't coated with dried blood.

Victor Baron's own fleshtech was represented in the room as well. One of the computers had a woman's head attached to it instead of a monitor screen and a number of the cables that connected machines and which lay strewn about the floor resembled extended spinal columns. But most impressive – or perhaps I should say disturbing – of all was the operating table located in the center of the lab. An intertwined column of spines descended from the ceiling above the table, supporting a fleshy mass shot through with pulsating swollen veins. Extended outward from the bottom of the mass were a half dozen arms, a mix of male and female as well as various races, both human and non human. It appeared Baron was an equal opportunity vivisectionist.

"Sorry I didn't come to the door to greet you when you arrived, but I was trying to get caught up on one of my new projects. As you might imagine there's no end of work to be done around here and I feel like I'm eternally behind. Even with all the excellent help I have."

Baron's voice was a mellow tenor and he pronounced each word with the precision and ease of a skilled elocutionist. Listening to him speak was like listening to a master musician playing his instrument. As the story goes Baron hadn't been quite so godlike when he first came to Nekropolis, but he'd had over two centuries to become his own ultimate creation, the pinnacle of what the reanimatory arts could accomplish. Dr. Frankenstein might have given Victor Baron life, but by this point he was most definitely a self-made man.

Baron had approached us as he talked and he laid a perfectly manicured hand on Henry's shoulders. The assistant grimaced in response. Maybe the man was attempting to smile and didn't have enough control of his facial muscles to pull it off, but somehow I doubted it.

I glanced over at the table where Baron had been working. A large glass tank sat on the table's surface, filled with a thick clear liquid. Suspended in the viscous goo was a coiled mass of what looked like thin red tubing surrounding a trio of hearts that had been fused together. The hearts throbbed in unison and the tubing pulsed in time with each beat.

Baron must've noticed me looking. "It's an independently functioning circulatory system," he explained. "Something Lord Galm commissioned me to work on. There's a shortage of willing blood donors in the city and since aqua sanguis provides little actual nourishment for Bloodborn Galm would like me to create an alternative source of blood for his people. The Bloodborn would keep one of these creatures in their homes to feed off the blood it generates, something like a farmer getting fresh milk from a cow." Baron frowned then. "Unfortunately the creatures live only a few days at most, so they're hardly practical." His frown eased. "Still, we'll get it right eventually, won't we, Henry?"

"Yes, Victor. Eventually." There was a distinct lack of "go-team" enthusiasm in the man's voice, but Victor didn't seem to notice.

"I'm surprised my father hired you," Devona said. "He's not big on technology."

"Perhaps Galm's perspective is broadening as time goes on. The other Darklords make use of our products. Lady Varvara especially, considering the bulk of our customers live in the Sprawl, and of course Lord Edrigu finds many uses for our creations throughout the Bone-yard. But we have been known to do business in Gothtown–" he gestured toward his circulatory proto-type – "and even a bit in the Wyldwood. Not so much in Glamere, though. Lady Talaith forbids her people to have anything to do with modern technology. But even among the Arcane we've made a few inroads. Certain spells require toxic ingredients that are too risky even for the Arcane to handle. Here we can create assistants capable of withstanding all manner of dangerous sub-stances. But Talaith has permitted only a handful of our creations to enter her Dominion. Still, one step at a time, yes?"

"Speaking of Darklords, some refer to you as the Sixth Lord," I said. "There's even been rumors that some of your more influential clients have been lobby-ing Father Dis to make the designation official."

"That's very flattering, of course, and it speaks to how important the Foundry's products have become to the city. But when all is said and done, I'm an inventor and a businessman. I have no interest in acquiring political power." He paused, then shook his head and gave us a rueful smile. "Pardon my manners. I get too caught up in work at times. It's an honor to meet you, Mr. Richter. Though I must say I wish it had been under better circumstances. Henry told me about the attack on you earlier this evening. Horrid business, but that's the Sprawl for you. Violence is far too often a way of life there."

Baron leaned down to get a better look at me. I might've felt selfconscious about that, but given how tall Baron was, even if my head had been on my body, he still would've had to bend over to look at me.

"You know, Mr. Richter, I've been following your career with interest for some time now."

"You have?"

Baron reached out and gently prodded the edges of my neck wound with his index finger. "Of course! There are many varieties of reanimated dead in Nekropolis, but you're the only one of your kind. That makes you a unique specimen."

"Uh, thanks. I think."

Baron straightened then and reached out to shake Devona's hand. "Ms. Kanti, it's a distinct pleasure to meet you as well."

Devona had to tuck my head under her arm to free up a hand for Baron to shake. He held the grip a bit

longer than necessary, and though I couldn't see from
the angle I was at, I imagined Devona blushing a bit.
Baron is the handsomest man in the city, maybe the
handsomest who'd ever lived, whether in Nekropolis
or on Earth, and it was difficult for women not be affected by how attractive he was. Hell, I'm straight and
even I had trouble taking my gaze off him.

It was stupid of me but I couldn't help thinking that
if Baron had managed to perfect his physical form, then
all his organs – internal as well as external – would be
the epitome of anatomical perfection. In other words
he probably had an enormous and indefatigable
schwanzstucker.

What was it with me and being jealous lately? Devona loved me and our psychic bonding was as intimate
and satisfying as any physical lovemaking, maybe more
so. Still, I was glad when Baron finally released Devona's hand.

"Well, Mr. Richter, let's get you up on the table and
have a look at you."

Baron took my head from Devona and carried me to
the operating table. Over his shoulder he said, "Henry,
if you could bring Mr. Richter's body?"

Henry wheeled the rest of me over and between the
two of them they got the two halves of me onto the
table. Henry removed the clothes from my body while
Victor further examined my neck wound, all the while
asking me more detailed questions about how I got it.

"Interesting," Baron said. "Whoever attacked you
used something more elaborate than a simple garrote.

Your head was severed from your body with almost laser-like precision. And to judge by the swiftness of the attack the culprit was practiced in the use of the device."

Something about Baron's observation stirred a thought in me. There was something important there, but try as I might, I couldn't quite grasp hold of it. Baron continued.

"As to precisely what the tool was, I'm afraid I can't say. We have devices here at the Foundry that could do the job and there are any number of weapons available in the city that would serve the same purpose, at least to judge by the condition of some of the bodies my Bonegetters bring me." He smiled. "The good news is a clean cut like this makes for an easier repair."

"So you can fix him?" Devona asked. She'd joined Baron and Henry at the operating table, standing a little too close to the former for my liking.

Baron's expression became serious. "I didn't say that. While I normally work with dead bodies, my specialty is bringing them back to life, or at least a semblance thereof. But Mr. Richter is a zombie – he exists in a state between life and death. And he's not a typical zombie. He's a highly functional one whose body operates nearly as well as it did when he was alive. That makes his central nervous system more complex than a garden variety zombie. I can't simply sew his head back onto his neck and call it a day. I'm afraid it's going to be a bit more complicated than that.

He poked and prodded both sections of me some more, hmming and tsking as he worked. At one point he turned to Henry and asked, "What do you think?"

Henry scowled in thought. "Both sections are in a similar state of arrested decay. Typical of a zombie. Though the body's a bit worse off than the head. Probably because it's been inanimate for so long. Reconnection should be possible, if tricky." He paused. "If that's what Mr. Richter really wants."

Now it was my turn to scowl. "What do you mean?"

"We have all sorts of spare parts around here," Baron began, but then he stopped and frowned. "Speaking of which, I prefer to have a full complement of such when I operate, and none have been delivered yet. Henry, if you wouldn't mind? I seem to have forgotten my vox again."

"I swear you'd forget your head if it wasn't attached." Henry looked at me then. "No offense," he added before removing a hand vox from a robe pocket and turning away from the table to make a call.

"As I was saying," Baron continued, "I have numerous spare parts – including entire bodies. The mind, the personality, indeed the very *self* is contained solely within the brain, Mr. Richter. To put it simply you are your head and your body exists to move that head around. But you don't have to keep your old body if you don't want to. I can give you a new one: a living one."

The idea stunned me. Ever since Papa Chatha had suggested that Baron might be able to help me, I'd been thinking only in terms of his reattaching my head to my body. It had never occurred to me that Baron might be able to do better than that.

Baron went on. "Of course, there's no guarantee just how much physical perception your undead brain is capable of. You might not be able to experience the full range of physical sensations that a living body can. But then again, you might." He smiled. "In all modesty, I've been doing this for a very long time, and I've gotten awfully good at it."

Henry put his vox away and returned to the table.

"They're on their way," he said, and Baron nodded.

A living body... I'd long given up hope that I could ever be restored to life. There didn't seem to be any magic or science in Nekropolis capable of returning me to a fully human state. Even Father Dis had told me that it was beyond his capabilities. But now Baron was telling me he might be able to do it – if I was willing to let him experiment on me.

I looked at Devona, but before I could speak, she said, "Why would Matt want a different body? The one he has works just fine." Then she stopped and looked down at me. "I'm sorry, love. I shouldn't speak for you. It's your decision, of course."

If I'd been capable of doing so right then, I'd have taken Devona in my arms and kissed her.

I'd been dead for some time but I hadn't forgotten what it was like to have a body that could smell, taste and above all fully experience touch in all its forms. I've never told Devona but I sometimes have dreams in which I'm alive and do the most mundane things: drinking a soda, eating ice cream, inhaling the scent of autumn leaves, drying off after a long hot shower with a thick fuzzy towel. So I'd be lying if I said I wasn't tempted by Baron's offer. Tempted bad.

"Thanks anyway," I said. "But I'm happy enough the way I am. Besides, being a zombie detective is kind of my thing, you know? 'Zombie head on living body' detective just doesn't have the same ring to it."

"As you wish," Baron said. "But if at some future date you change your mind, feel free to drop by. There's always a spare body or two lying around here."

The lab doors opened then and a pair of men entered, one thin-faced like a weasel, the other with a round face sporting a pair of mutton chops. The men, who wore long black coats, caps and fingerless gloves, stood on either side of a large portable wheeled freezer, guiding it along by gripping handles bolted onto the sides.

"Where would you like it, Mr. Baron?" the round faced man said in an Irish accent.

"Over here close to the operating table, Burke. Within arm's reach."

"Righto. Glad to be of service."

The two men maneuvered the freezer close to the table, as Baron had asked. Now that the men were closer I could get a getter look at them and I saw that both had a bluish tint to their skin and thin scars around their throats and wrists. They appeared human enough, but it was obvious they'd had some work done by Baron.

The thin faced man spoke then, also in an Irish accent. "Anything else we can do for you, sir?"

"No, thank you, Hare," Baron said. "I believe we're all set."

"Best we be off then," Burke said. "Lot of work to be done."

"No rest for the wicked, eh?" Hare said.

Both men laughed at that, tipped their caps to Baron, and then turned and left.

When they were gone Baron said, "Two of our best Bonegetters. They have quite a knack for the work, don't they, Henry?"

"They're very reliable," Henry said noncommittally.

Baron clapped his hands together and rubbed them briskly. "Time to get to work then. Henry, if you'll help me get everything ready?"

"Of course," Henry said, sounding as if he'd just as soon have a hydrochloric acid enema. He lurched off to one of the work tables and began gathering surgical tools.

"Would you like me to step outside?" Devona asked Baron.

Baron answered while he donned a pair of black rubber gloves that looked as if they could use a good disinfecting, or better yet, a thorough going over with a blow torch.

"There's no need, Ms. Kanti. Since Mr. Richter's already dead, there's no risk of infection to him, and as he cannot experience physical pain, there's no need for anesthetics, so he'll be conscious and awake during the procedure. You're welcome to stay, as long as it's all right with you, Mr. Richter."

"Sure. Devona's seen me come apart before. She should get the chance to see me get put together for a change."

Devona smiled at me. "I'd hold your hand, but I know you can't feel it right now."

"Hold it anyway," I said. "For luck, if nothing else."

She nodded and took hold of one of my hands. Henry wheeled over a surgical cart containing a dozen different instruments that wouldn't have been out of place in Torquemada's playroom. One by one he held an instrument and the arms extending from the fleshy mass above me stretched down and grabbed hold of it.

I'd forgotten about the bizarre piece of fleshtech hanging down from the ceiling, but now I looked up at the hands gripping the surgical instruments and I saw that the mass was slowly descending toward me. When the hands were within reach of the table the mass stopped moving.

"Please tell me those things are just going to hold the instruments for you," I said to Baron.

He gave me a smile that did nothing at all to reassure me. "Don't worry. I'll be guiding them every step of the way."

And before I could say anything else Baron gave a command and one of the hands reached toward me.

The operation had begun.

At one point during the procedure Baron said, "Something just occurred to me, Mr. Richter. You're in a rather unique situation."

I tried to ignore the disembodied hands of the fleshtech device as they worked on restoring the connections between my brain and my central nervous system. "Considering that I'm a zombie having my head put back onto my body by the Frankenstein Monster, I'd say that was an understatement."

Baron chuckled. "Besides that, I mean. Tonight someone attacked you, cut off your head, stole your body, and later dumped it rather unceremoniously in the Sprawl. This puts you in a unique situation in that, since the beheading didn't kill you, you are in a sense able to investigate your own murder. How many private detectives can say the same?"

"I hadn't thought of it like that. I'll make sure to highlight it on my resume."

Baron was right about one thing. When the operation was finished my first order of business was to find out who'd done this to me and why. And once I did I intended to lay a serious hurt on them.

I gritted my teeth as the arms continued their work.

"Now stand on your right foot and touch your nose with your left index finger," Baron said.

"Is this really necessary?" I complained. "We've been at this for twenty minutes now. I've walked back and forth across the lab numerous times. I've clapped my hands and tapped my feet in various rhythms. I've written my name on a piece of paper a dozen times. If anything had gone wrong during the operation I think we'd know it by now."

Baron, Henry and Devona had been standing by the operating table watching me go through my paces ever since I'd climbed off the operating table and gotten dressed. And while I was happy to be in one undead piece again I was getting tired of being treated like a performing zombie monkey.

"Indulge me, please," Baron said. Despite my complaining the man didn't sound the least bit irritated. He had the calmest disposition of any monster I'd ever met.

I sighed, did as Baron asked, and promptly poked myself in the eye.

"I was afraid of that," Baron said. "The coordination is a bit off on your left side. If you'll just hop back onto the table, I'll take care of that."

The thought of lying on the operating table while those disembodied hands worked on me some more wasn't exactly appealing.

"I'm not sure that's necessary," I said. "In general, I'm more coordinated than I have been since I died. So I can't hop on one foot and touch my nose. It's not exactly a skill I use every day."

"Even so, Mr. Richter, it'll only take a few minor adjustments. I really–"

Henry interrupted. "The man seems satisfied enough, Victor. Remember, not everyone shares your drive for perfection."

"I suppose so," Baron agreed, but he didn't seem very happy about it.

"I think you should reconsider, Matt," Devona said. "Given the kind of work we – I mean you – do, you often end up in physical confrontations. The more co-ordinated your body is, the better."

"You're exaggerating," I said. "Yeah, I get in a fight

every now and then, but I hardly think–"

The entire time we'd been in the lab the woman's head attached to the computer had been silent, but now she shouted, "Mr. Baron! An intruder has just forced his way through the main entrance! And he's heading this way – fast!"

"Alert security, Elsa," Baron said as he headed toward the door.

"Where are you going?" Henry said. "This is why you built a security force – to take care of problems like this."

Baron spun back around to face Henry and for the first time since we arrived I saw him lose his composure. "This is my home and I will not allow others to defend it for me!"

Baron whirled around and shoved his way through the lab doors.

Henry shook his head. "He's as stubborn as the night is long." He turned to us. "Stay here. You should be safe enough."

Moving with his spastic, lurching gait, Henry went after his master. When he was gone Devona looked at me.

"What were you saying about how rarely you get into fights?"

"I have no idea what you're talking about. Let's go."

I took her hand, grateful that I could at least once again feel the pressure of her grip, and we hurried after Baron and Henry.

• • •

We found them standing in the hallway near the entrance, the one where the paintings of Frankenstein's homeland were displayed. A trio of hulking monsters – one male, one female and one which could've been either or both – stood battling a shadowy figure in a top hat and cape. The bodies of several other monsters lay behind them in the hall, heads and limbs severed from torsos, blood splattered on the floor and walls. The dark man held black knives in each hand, the blades of which seemed formed from solid shadow. The surviving security monsters attempted to grab hold of him but he avoided their hands with almost casual ease, deftly slicing out with his blades, their edges passing through flesh and bone as if they were no more substantial than air. The monsters roared in fury as they lost hands and arms and the dark man's attacks increased in speed, until he became a shadowy blur impossible to track, and when he once more grew still, the last three monsters had joined the others as bloody piles of severed body parts scattered across the floor.

I remembered something Baron had said: "There's always a spare body or two lying around here". If I'd been a living man, I'd have tossed the contents of my stomach right then. I consoled myself by remembering where we were. If anyone could put all those poor Humpty Dumptys together again, it was Victor Baron.

Despite the slaughter he'd just witnessed Baron stepped forward, hands clenched into fists at his sides, and the anger on his face was terrible to behold.

"Who are you and what do you want?" Baron demanded in a voice tight with fury.

The features of the cloaked man were shrouded in darkness, so his expression was impossible to read. It wasn't clear if he even *had* a face. But he seemed to be looking at me when he raised a black gloved hand and pointed one of his dripping knives.

I stepped forward to stand next to Baron and Devona came with me. Henry remained where he was, demonstrating more good sense than the rest of us, I thought.

"His name is Silent Jack," I said. "He's one of Lord Edrigu's servants. As for what he wants... well, I guess it's me."

Ever since Jack had marked my hand with Edrigu's sigil, I'd been waiting for the Lord of the Dead to summon me and It looked like the time had finally come.

"But why break into the Foundry?" Devona asked. "Why not just stay outside and wait for us to leave?"

"Maybe for some reason Jack couldn't wait," I said. "Or maybe it's just more fun for him this way."

Jack's some manner of spirit, but one who can be solid enough when he chooses, as Baron's unfortunate security monsters had discovered. But considering who he was reputed to have been during his mortal life on Earth, the bloodshed – while sickening – was hardly surprising. And Baron's monsters hadn't been about to let Jack enter the Foundry without challenge. So all appearances to the contrary, there might have been nothing especially sinister motivating Jack's appearance that night. But there was something in his stance, a cold anger radiating from him like an almost physical force that told me something was wrong here. And a moment later I had an idea what it was when a larger gray fleshed figure stomped around the corner and headed down the corridor toward us.

The creature stood eight feet tall and its naked body was roughly humanoid in shape, though its face was smooth and featureless, and it possessed no sexual organs. It was a Sentinel, one of the golems that served as Nekropolis's version of a police force, or as close to it as the city came. Sentinels were more like enforcers than cops, making sure that citizens obeyed the law – or else.

The Sentinel walked through the carnage Jack had wrought, not bothering to step over body parts, instead crushing them into bloody paste as it went. The golem stopped next to Silent Jack who, true to his name, spoke not a word as he continued pointing his black knife at me. The Sentinel stepped forward, grabbed hold of me with inhumanly powerful hands, and tucked me under its arm. It then turned and began carrying me back the way it had come.

After spending the better part of the night as a severed head, I was plenty sick of being hauled around like an infant. I squirmed, trying to break free from the Sentinel's grip, though I knew it was useless. I didn't know any creature that was stronger than a Sentinel. So I stopped struggling and allowed myself to go limp. As we passed, Silent Jack tucked his knives away somewhere in the dark folds of his midnight-black cloak, and turned to follow us.

Whatever was going on it looked like my long night was about to get even longer.

SEVEN

After capturing me, the Sentinel carried me outside to where Silent Jack's black rig waited. The Sentinel shoved me inside and Jack – who materialized in the driver's seat – cracked the reins and his two horses, Malice and Misery, reared up and let out ear-splitting cries that sounded uncomfortably close to human screams. As if the sound warped the fabric of reality, the world around us blurred, distorted and reformed, and instead of being parked outside the Foundry, we were now outside the black needle-like structure that was the Nightspire – center of the city and home to Father Dis. Another Sentinel stood waiting for us, or perhaps it was the same one, pulled along by the magic of Jack's supernatural rig. Since all Sentinels look alike it was impossible to tell and it really didn't matter for this one yanked me out of the rig with as much violent efficiency as another would've and marched me inside the obsidian tower. I glanced back over my shoulder just in time to see Jack tip his top hat to me before he and his rig faded away.

"Thanks for the ride," I muttered.

The Sentinel escorted me through the Nightspire's halls until we reached an area I'd heard about but had never visited. Most of the Nightspire is made out of black stone so highly polished it gleamed in the light cast by torches set into the walls. But here the stone, while still just as highly polished and reflective, was a deep crimson. This was the Sanctum, headquarters of the Cabal, Father Dis's personal servants. We passed a number of red robed men and women, all seemingly human, all completely hairless, including a lack of eyebrows and lashes. Whether they shaved and plucked their hair or it just didn't grow, I had no idea. None of the Cabal acknowledged us as we walked by. Either they were engrossed in conversation with one another or they stared straight ahead, lost in thought as they went about errands for their dark master.

Eventually the Sentinel brought me to an ivory door formed entirely of skulls stacked on top of one another. The skulls' eye sockets glowed briefly with crimson light as if they were examining us. The light faded and the skulls slid sideways into the walls – one row to the left, the next to the right and so on – until the doorway was open. The Sentinel forcibly removed my suit jacket, divesting me not only of my outer garment but also the various weapons and tricks I keep in its pockets. The Sentinel then removed my shoulder holster holding my 9mm. I'm not sure a gun would've been much use against any of Dis's servants, but it seemed the Sentinel didn't intend to take any chances. The golem didn't bother to check my pants pockets, though. I carry a few small items there, nothing very powerful, but at least I had a few weapons remaining to me. At that point I was happy to take whatever I could get.

The Sentinel then placed one of its large hands between my shoulder blades and shoved. I stumbled inside, only barely managing to keep from falling forward onto my face, and then the skulls slid back into place, closing me inside. The chamber was small – the bathroom in my apartment was smaller, but not by much – and it was empty. No furniture, nothing on the crimson walls or ceiling. There was no obvious source of light and yet the room was fully illuminated.

"Welcome to the Inquisitory."

The voice came from behind me, and though I was startled, I forced myself to turn around slowly. No need to let whoever it was know they'd gotten to me.

I found myself staring into the face of a Cabal member, a man who appeared to be in his seventies, with a long narrow face and patrician features. His eyes were an icy blue and his upper lip seemed curled in a permanent sneer.

"Let me guess," I said. "You're Brother Quillion, the First Adjudicator."

The skin over the man's right eye moved, as if he'd have raised an eyebrow if he'd had one.

"I see my reputation precedes me."

The cold sarcasm in his tone reminded me of Mr. Hedricks, my high school principal. The sadistic son of a bitch loved nothing better than to deal out discipline to troublemakers and the harsher that discipline was, the better he liked it.

"I've heard of you," I admitted. "I'm impressed. Whatever you people think I've done, it must be pretty damned bad for me to merit your personal attention."

Quillion's lips stretched into a bloodless smile. "And what makes you think you're accused of a crime, Matthew?"

I didn't like the overly familiar way he used my first name, but I decided to let it slide. After all I was technically the man's prisoner. Still, that didn't mean I was going to be all sunshine and daisies to him.

"You can cut the crap. I used to be a cop back on Earth. I've interrogated plenty of suspects in my time and I know how the game is played. I wouldn't be here unless you thought I'd done something to warrant it. So what was it?"

The Sentinels might serve as the city's police force but the Adjudicators were its judges – and executioners when necessary. I was in deep trouble and I knew it. But even so, I had no intention of going along with Quillion's program like a good little zombie. He might be one of the most powerful beings in the city, but I wasn't about to let him walk all over me. The only weapon I had to fight with right then was attitude and I intended to make full use of it.

Quillion was a pro, however, and he wasn't about to be thrown off his stride by a mouthy ex-cop.

"See for yourself." He made a languid gesture and the crimson walled room disappeared. We now stood in a much larger chamber formed entirely out of solid earth, the soil dark and rich. Jutting bits of bone stuck out from the walls and ceiling – arm and leg joints, half hidden skulls, both human and animal. Worms and black beetles crawled between the bones, small lives moving in the midst of so much death. Illumination was provided by flaming corpses that stood propped up against the walls at regular intervals around the room, and though their fires burned furiously, they did not consume the dead flesh they touched. The chamber itself was featureless, save for a raised mound of earth in the middle of the room, its soil dark as that comprising the rest of the chamber.

"We're not really here, are we?" I said. "This is some kind of illusion."

"It's a re-creation," Quillion said, sounding as if he took great satisfaction in correcting me. "Based on the evidence I've been able to gather so far."

So this wasn't the literal truth I was watching. Good to know.

Quillion went on. "This chamber is housed deep within Lord Edrigu's stronghold, and as you might surmise, it is well protected by many physical and magical defenses."

I was beginning to get an idea of what was going to happen next in Quillion's 're-creation,' but even so, I was surprised to see myself come walking into the chamber. As soon as I stepped into the room the flaming corpses stirred to life. They started running toward me, arms outstretched, obviously intending to grab hold of the intruder and immolate him. But before the first of the corpsetorches could reach me I held up the hand that contained Edrigu's mark. The sigil glowed and the burning corpses stopped, regarded it for a moment, and then turned and slowly headed back to their posts. When they were all once more safely back in position I lowered my hand and continued on into the chamber.

"When was this supposed to have happened?" I asked.

"Early this evening," Quillion said. "Now be quiet and watch."

I did as Quillion ordered and watched myself walk toward the mound in the center of the room. I stopped next to it, seemed to regard it for a moment, and then knelt down and began digging with both hands. It took several moments of work but eventually I uncovered the face of someone lying buried within the mound. I recognized Edrigu, Lord of the Dead. Watching the recreation of the scene with Quillion, I expected the Darklord's eyes to snap open now that his face had been uncovered, for I knew he wasn't dead but merely sleeping. But his eyes remained closed as I went about my work.

I reached for Edrigu's throat, and for a moment I thought I intended to strangle the sleeping Darklord, but instead of wrapping fingers around Edrigu's neck, my hand moved farther down his chest, pushing deeper into the mound. A few moments later I pulled my hand free and gripped in it was a slender cylindrical object

about ten inches in length. Black soil clung to its surface, but enough ivory color showed to tell me the
object was carved from bone and the holes drilled into
it told me that it was some kind of simplistic musical instrument: a pipe or flute. A tiny chain was attached at
one end and it was clear Edrigu had been wearing the
bone flute around his neck. My body gripped the chain
in both hands, yanked and it parted easily. Again, I expected Edrigu to awaken, but he kept on sleeping.

I brushed the dirt from the flute before tucking it into
the inner pocket of my suit jacket and leaving the way
I had come. The guardian corpses paid me no mind as
I left, carrying away one of their master's prized pos-
sessions.

When the scene was finished Quillion waved his
hand again and Edrigu's bed chamber vanished to be
replaced once more by featureless crimson walls.

"What do you have to say in your defense,
Matthew?"

"From the tone of your voice, it sounds like it doesn't
matter what I say. You've already made up your mind."
I'd have asked for a lawyer, but it wouldn't have done
any good. There aren't any in Nekropolis. As far as the
Darkfolk are concerned, lawyers just slow down the
swift course of justice. Besides, they're too scary, even
for Nekropolis.

"My recreation is based on evidence delivered to me
by Edrigu's servants. The theft triggered an alarm and
when they investigated they were able to draw forth an
image of your committing the robbery from the minds

of the chamber guardians. The servants then sent Silent Jack out to fetch you and informed me of the robbery. I promptly dispatched a Sentinel to accompany Jack. It took a while for them to find you. I must admit it was rather clever of you to hide inside the Foundry. Baron's defenses against industrial espionage prevented us from tracking you by magical means. Luckily Jack encountered the cabbie who dropped you off at the Foundry and was able to convince him to share what he knew about your whereabouts."

A wave of anger rushed through me. "If you hurt Lazlo…"

Quillion raised a hand to forestall me. "Relax. The demon is little the worse for wear. Besides, his kind heals swiftly. The main thing is that thanks to his grudging cooperation we were able to find you. And while Silent Jack was unable to materialize inside the Foundry, he is quite capable of relying on physical force when the need arises, and he was able to gain entrance that way. He's a very versatile creature, that Jack."

"Why didn't Edrigu himself come after me once he woke up? I thought Darklords prefer to handle affronts against them personally."

Quillion looked at me and for a moment I thought he wasn't going to answer. But finally he said, "Edrigu – like the other Darklords – expends a great deal of energy during the Renewal Ceremony. This year, because the ceremony was disrupted, the Lords were required to devote an extra measure of power to ensure Umbriel was recharged for another year. Because of this the

Darklords have been recuperating and are currently...
indisposed."

This was news to me. But now that I thought about
it I hadn't heard of any Darklords making appearances
in public since the last Renewal Ceremony.

"So they're... what? All sleeping, like Edrigu?"

"Basically. They must restore the energy they lost,
and while they sleep this deeply, they cannot be awakened. Usually they wake within a few weeks, but the
process is taking longer this year. And when none of
the Darklords are available to dispense justice in their
Dominions, that task falls to the First Adjudicator: me.
I have answered your questions, Matthew, because it's
not every day that we receive a... *guest* of your stature.
After all, you did help the Darklords and Father Dis
complete the Renewal Ceremony this year and your
service to the city was much appreciated. That's the
only reason we're having this conversation. If you were
anyone else your case would already have been decided. Now, I will ask you for the final time: what do
you have to say in your defense?"

I thought of Devona then. She'd surely guessed
where the Sentinel had intended to take me, if not why,
and she was probably on her way to the Nightspire.
Even now she might be standing at the entrance, trying
to convince the guards to let her in to see me. I tried to
reach out and connect to her through our psychic link,
but I didn't sense her presence. Either she was too far
away, or the Inquisitory was enchanted to prevent
magical and psychic energies from functioning inside it.

Either way, I wasn't able to reassure her that I was all right, which – given my situation – would've been a lie anyway.

At that point I decided to ditch my tough guy act and cooperate with Quillion. I told him everything that had happened to me that night in detail, up to the moment when the Sentinel took me into custody. I finished by showing him the seam on my neck as evidence that Victor Baron had recently reattached my head to my body.

When my story was done Quillion looked thoughtful. The walls became less solid looking as he considered, wavering as if formed from crimson liquid, and I realized the chamber was linked to his mind. It certainly made for a good interrogation room. Confronting suspects with scenes of them committing a crime was a great way to get them to confess. But I reminded myself that what I'd witnessed wasn't exactly the magical equivalent of video from a security camera. It was a recreation based on interpreted evidence and not proof by a long shot. Unfortunately an Adjudicator doesn't need proof. He or she just has to *believe* a suspect is guilty in order to pronounce a sentence. I just had to hope that my story, strange as it was, had sowed a seed of doubt in Quillion's mind about my guilt.

"You must admit that on the surface your story is quite outlandish," Quillion said after a time. "You expect me to believe that someone knew you carried Edrigu's mark, and what's more, that they knew it could be used to gain access to his collection. *And* that this someone stole your body, somehow animated it, and used it to steal the object?"

"I told you that Acantha asked me about Edrigu's mark and showed a close up of my hand on her program. Hundreds saw it, maybe thousands. One of them must've realized what the mark could be used for."

"Then why not just steal your hand?" Quillion asked.

I shrugged. "I'm no expert in Darklord magic. Maybe most of my body was needed for the mark to work properly. Maybe someone wanted to frame me and they wanted to make sure there was enough of 'me' present to be recorded by whatever security methods Edrigu had in place. Are you sure the chamber guardians saw me as complete? In other words, did I have a head?"

"Yes," Quillion said, but then he frowned. "I'll admit that the guardians' mental description lacked a certain amount of visual clarity, however. It's difficult to see through an aura of flame, you know. Their impressions of you were more mystically derived than visually. They know it was a zombie that entered the chamber, and they recognized the power inherent in Edrigu's mark. You are the only individual in the city who matches those criteria."

"So my headless body *might've* been used to commit the theft. Someone might have been controlling it from a distance, like a marionette with a very long set of strings."

"I suppose," Quillion said, but he sounded unconvinced.

I decided to try a different tack. "What was stolen?"

"An object of some importance to Edrigu, obviously, since he wore it on his person. Unfortunately none of his servants seem to know its purpose and since the Darklord himself is asleep and cannot be wakened to tell us more..." Quillion trailed off.

"Contact Victor Baron," I suggested. "He can back me up."

"Speaking with Baron would prove nothing. You could've committed the theft, perhaps at the behest of a client, and later cut off your own head and gone to the Foundry to have it reattached in an attempt to establish an alibi."

"I'm not a mercenary," I snapped. "I'm a private detective. There's a big difference."

"You do favors for people and they pay you in return," Quillion said with a shrug. "Perhaps this time the payment was enough to get you to suspend your moral code."

I wanted to tell Quillion he could shove my moral code up his hairless ass, but I knew it wouldn't help my case, so instead I said, "You could ask Devona. She–" I stopped myself. Quillion would just assume she'd lie to protect me. "We could ask Dis to verify my story. With his power..."

"Father Dis is a god," Quillion said stiffly. "He has far more important matters to attend to than deciding the fate of one zombie."

Quillion's dismissal of my idea had come a bit too quickly and was made too forcefully for me to take it at face value. A second later I realized what was really going on.

"You won't ask Dis to help me because you can't. He's resting just like the Darklords, isn't he?"

Quillion reluctantly nodded. "Dis normally uses far more energy than any of the Darklords during the Renewal Ceremony, but this year was especially taxing for him. He sleeps deeply, and like the Darklords, he cannot be awakened until he is restored to full strength."

This was bad for the city. With Dis and the Darklords temporarily out of commission Nekropolis was virtually unprotected. If a major crisis developed there would be no one available to deal with it. Hopefully, things would keep running smoothly enough until the Darklords awakened. If not… well, I didn't want to think about that.

"So what are we left with?" I asked. "We agree on the fact that my body was used to commit a crime, but there's no way I can prove to you that my consciousness wasn't in the driver's seat at the time the theft took place."

"That's not precisely true," Quillion said. "Because of your previous service to the city, I wanted to give you the opportunity to explain yourself. But since you are not able to do so adequately, I'm forced to rely on my usual methods of extracting information from those I question."

I didn't like the sound of that.

"I hate to break this to you, but I'm a zombie. Torture won't work on me. Whatever you do, I won't be able to feel it."

Quillion gave me a cold smile. "This is another thing that's not precisely true." As he spoke the crimson walls began to edge toward green and their hard smooth surface began to shimmer and flicker. "You know the flames which burn upon the surface of the river Phlegethon?"

This was sounding worse all the time.

"Yes. They're magical flames that burn the spirit instead of the flesh."

Quillion's smile widened.

"The Adjudicators created those flames."

He gestured and the walls of green fire, no illusion this time, came rushing inward toward us. For the first time since I'd died I felt pain – pain beyond anything I'd ever imagined was possible.

I screamed and I continued screaming for a very long time.

In the end I confessed. At least, I think I did. I don't have any memory of actually doing so, but Quillion made the green fire go away, and I lay on the floor of the Inquisitory, grateful that my dead body once more felt no sensation, though the echoes of agony still lingered in my soul, and I wondered if they always would.

He asked me more questions: who hired me, where was the bone flute now? But I just lay there, barely able to think, let alone answer. Besides, I knew it didn't matter what I said. Quillion believed me guilty, and that was the end of it.

"Very well," he said after a while, sounding irritated. "I suppose we'll sort out the rest of the details in due time. If nothing else, hopefully Edrigu will be able to track down the artifact once he awakens, and then we'll discover who hired you. For now, I pronounce you officially guilty of a crime against a Darklord and sentence you to be incarcerated in Tenebrus until the end of your days."

"You can't be serious!" I shouted. "This isn't about justice! It's about you having power and using it however it suits you! There's been no due process here, no real standards of evidence… I've spent my entire career in law enforcement one way or another, Quillion, and I can tell you that you wouldn't know justice if it walked up and bit you on your bald ass!"

Quillion's gaze became arctic cold. "Goodbye, Matthew, and may Father Dis have mercy on your soul."

Before I could summon up the energy to protest Quillion made a gesture and the floor beneath me disappeared and I found myself tumbling down into darkness.

EIGHT

I hadn't slept or lost consciousness since my resurrection, but I have no memory of my fall ending. One moment I was plunging through darkness, hands scrabbling to find some kind of purchase without success, and the next I was laying on a hard surface. I assumed I'd hit and not felt the impact – though I should've been aware of it at least – but when I sat up I discovered that none of my bones were broken. So either the fall hadn't been as long as it had seemed or some sort of magic was at work here. Whichever the case my body was still intact, and since I'd only recently gotten it back, I was glad I hadn't broken it.

I was surrounded by darkness and silence and part of me wanted to remain there, quiet and unmoving, in the hope that whoever or whatever inhabited this place might not notice me if I could avoid drawing attention to myself. But the passive approach has never sat well with me, even when it's the smart way to go. *Especially* then. So I stood up and called out into the darkness.

"This really isn't much of a welcome. You could do a little more to make a guy feel at home, you know."

No response.

I'd heard plenty of rumors about Tenebrus over the years, but I'd never spoken to anyone who'd actually been there. It was reputed to be a nightmarish place – even by Nekropolis's standards – and escape was impossible. Or so the stories went. I'd imagined it would be a more savage version of an earthly prison, but now that I was actually here, I began to wonder if this was it, if the darkness, silence and solitude were punishments in and of themselves. Was every inmate of Tenebrus in the same situation as I was, standing alone in the dark as minutes became hours then days, weeks, months, years… The thought was terrifying to me, a punishment far worse than anything I could've imagined. If this was to be my fate for a crime I didn't commit I wished Quillion had used his powers to destroy me back in the Inquisitory and been done with it.

But then I heard the first faint stirrings of sound, a soft grating of metal sliding against a hard surface. I started to turn toward the sound, steeling myself for the possibility of an attack. But before I could do anything to defend myself – and really, what could I have done? – I heard a loud jangling of chains and I sensed something streaking toward me out of the darkness. Metal clamped around my wrists and my arms were yanked over my head. I was pulled upward until my feet dangled in the air and then it stopped. Manacles on chains, I realized, hanging down from the ceiling. They'd been

lying coiled on the floor like a pair of iron snakes, waiting to lash out and grab hold of the newest inmate.

So not only was I destined to spend my time in Tenebrus swaddled in dark silence it seemed I wasn't going
to be permitted to move about either.

Great.

I don't know how long I hung there. Long enough
to regret the fact that I can't sleep and long enough to
give up any notion that I might be able to escape on my
own. I'd have happily chewed off my own hands to get
down, but since I couldn't reach them…

Eventually I became aware of a pair of flickering
glows ahead of me out in the darkness. Someone –
maybe a pair of someones – was approaching, carrying
a light of some kind. As whoever it was came nearer, I
began to be able to make out my surroundings. I was in
a cell whose bars were made of long lengths of bones,
detached arms clutching hold of each other with skeletal
fingers. The walls and ceiling curved around and above
me, formed from a grayish substance that looked more
like diseased flesh than stone. Rib-like protrusions extended from the walls, which were reinforced by long
curving spinal columns. The flesh walls expanded and
contracted as I watched, as if I were trapped inside the
pulsating organ of some gigantic beast. I also saw that I
wasn't alone in the cell. Hanging behind me were a pair
of skeletons, neither of them human, though I couldn't
guess their species from looking at them. Like me, they
hung from a pair of manacles on the ends of chains extending downward from the flesh ceiling. Unlike me,

they were far from recent arrivals, a fact which I freely admit took no great effort to deduce.

As I turned my attention back to whoever was approaching, a voice came from behind me.

"This isn't good."

A second voice added, "If that's who we think it is, you're going to wish you were left alone to rot in here with us."

I glanced back over my shoulder at the skeletal duo.

"Why didn't you two say anything when I called out earlier?" I was irritated. If I'd known I shared a cell with a couple talking skeletons I could've been pumping them for information the entire time instead of just hanging there, bored out of my mind.

"We didn't want to scare you," the first skeleton said.

"We figured we'd give you a few weeks to settle in before introducing ourselves. Give you a chance to acclimate a bit."

"Get your prison legs, so to speak," the second one added.

"Very considerate of you," I muttered.

"Thinking nothing of it," Skeleton Number One said, sounding pleased with itself.

I promptly forgot all about the ossified idiots as the light drew close enough for me to begin making out the features of the new arrivals. There were three of them, two men and a woman, the former walking on either side of the latter.

The males were of a type: eight feet tall, muscular and brown-skinned, naked save for small tan loincloths that left little doubt as to their gender. The most striking detail about the men was that each had a jackal's head resting atop his powerful broad shoulders. Their eyes shone with human intelligence, but as they approached my cell, canine lips drew back from sharp teeth in feral snarls. Both creatures held golden spears whose points glowed with warm yellow light – a combination weapon and torch. I wondered what would happen if that glowing spearpoint was thrust into my undead flesh and I made a mental note to myself to avoid pissing off the jackalheads if at all possible. But far more intimidating than the guards was the woman who walked between them. She was Keket, ancient Egyptian sorceress, demilord and overseer of Tenebrus.

Tall and slender she carried herself with regal bearing. Her body was wrapped in winding strips of grayish cloth and a long dark blue cape trailed behind her. Her face was concealed behind a golden mask of finely wrought feminine features and though the mask's eyes were made of solid metal, I had the impression that she could see through them – or perhaps somehow *with* them.

First Victor Baron, then Quillion, and now Keket. I was getting to meet a lot of dignitaries lately. I might've thought I was coming up in the world if my current situation hadn't demonstrated the exact opposite.

Keket and the guards stopped when they reached my cell door.

"Matthew Richter, welcome to Tenebrus."

Keket's voice was soft as the whisper of a snake sliding through grass, but I had no trouble making out every word.

I'd seen her once before, in the Nightspire during the last Renewal Ceremony, but it hadn't been an occasion for idle chat and we'd never spoken before.

"Do you always personally greet the new arrivals?" I asked. "Or am I just special?"

It was impossible to read Keket's expression behind her mask, but when she spoke, her tone was one of amusement.

"When Quillion informed me that the savior of Nekropolis would be joining us, I simply had to come welcome you in person. I do so enjoy seeing the high and mighty brought down low. It's one of my favorite parts of the job."

"Still bitter because Dis didn't choose you to be one of the five Darklords? You really ought to consider getting some therapy for that."

Again I couldn't see her expression but I could feel the anger rolling off of her as if it were a physical force. My skeletal cellmates must've felt it too for they let out frightened moans.

"I must say that I'm somewhat disappointed to see you," Keket said. "Guilty or innocent, anyone who was able to prevent the destruction of the entire city should be smart enough to avoid ending up here."

I sighed. "To be honest, I can't disagree with you."

Keket nodded to one of the jackalheads, and he stepped up to the cell door and removed an iron key ring from the leather belt holding up his loincloth. I say key ring, but instead of keys, it contained a number of skeletal fingers of various lengths and thicknesses. The guard stepped up to the cell door, selected a "key" and inserted it into a hole carved into one of the skeletal hands that formed the bars. The guard turned the key, was rewarded with a soft *snick*, and when he withdrew the key, the skeletal hands unclenched, releasing each other, and the bars withdrew into the ceiling and floor. The jackalhead then stepped into the cell, selected another key, and unlocked my manacles. He didn't bother to try and prevent me from falling to the ground, and though I tried to avoid it, I ended up falling onto my side. With a snarl the jackalhead bent down, grabbed hold of my shirt, and unceremoniously hauled me to my feet.

"Come with me," Keket said, and without waiting for me to reply, she started off down the hallway, her cloth wrapped feet making no sound as she went.

The guard who'd released me glared at me to make sure I understood I didn't have a choice in the matter and I walked out of the cell. He didn't relock it as we left, and given the state of my cellmates, I could see why he didn't bother.

"Good luck!" Skeleton One called out as I walked away.

"Whatever happens to you, we hope it won't be *too* hideously awful!" Number Two added.

I ignored them and followed after Keket, and the jackalheads walked beside me, keeping their gazes fixed on me and growling softly to let me know what they thought of me.

"Ever think about neutering these guys?" I asked Keket. "It might improve their disposition."

One of the guards snarled, whirled about, and rammed the butt end of his spear into my gut. The impact of the blow forced me to double over, though of course I felt nothing. It's a lot easier to act the part of a tough guy when you can't feel any pain.

I remembered then how Quillion had caused the green fire to blaze forth from the walls of the Inquisitory, and I shuddered.

Usually don't feel any pain, I amended.

Keket continued walking as if nothing had happened and the second guard prodded me in the back with his spear to get me moving again.

The four of us continued down a winding, curving hallway that was constructed from the same fleshy substance as the cell and similar bony protuberances stuck out from the walls and ceiling. We passed other cells as we walked, their doors formed from the same skeletal bars as mine was. The inmates represented every major race that inhabited Nekropolis – Bloodborn, Lyke, Arcane, Demonkin and the Dead – along with other creatures, some of whom belonged to nightmarish species that I'd never seen before. Many of them hung from manacles, as I had, but some were free to roam about their cells, presumably because they were better behaved than their fellow prisoners.

Keket spoke as we walked.

"Quillion informed me of the particulars of your case. A very interesting story. Personally, I would've investigated further before pronouncing sentence, but that's Quillion for you. He's rather single minded when it comes to matters of justice and punishment."

Keket's words were unexpected to me, but hardly unwelcome, and they filled me with new hope.

"Maybe you could talk to Quillion," I began.

"I said your story was interesting. I didn't say I intended to do anything to help you. It's the Adjudicators' task to judge. Mine is to incarcerate those individuals they send me. Matters of innocence or guilt mean nothing to me. Tenebrus is my Dominion, and once you are here, I am your ruler and you are my subject. End of story."

"I get it," I said. "You couldn't make it as a full-fledged Darklord, so you play god down here in the subterranean shithole you got stuck with."

One of the guards raised his spear as if to strike me down for my impertinence, but Keket turned around and raised a hand to stop him. The jackalhead snarled at me, foam dripping from his mouth, but he reluctantly obeyed his mistress and lowered his weapon.

Keket padded over to me, and though I couldn't tell, I had the impression she was smiling at me.

"You know what they say: it's better to rule in Tenebrus than serve in Nekropolis." She laughed then and turned back around and resumed walking.

The guards and I followed once more.

"Consider this talk your orientation to your new home," Keket said. "Tenebrus is actually a relatively simple system. It lies deep underground below the city and there are no entrances or exits. The only way in or out is by magic and only I and the Adjudicators possess the power to open passageways to and from Nekropolis. I'm sure you've been staying alert the entire time we've been walking, taking in everything and pondering possibilities for escape. But you needn't bother taxing your little zombie brain. There has never been an escape from Tenebrus because escape literally is not possible."

"Good to know," I said. "Now instead of wasting time trying to escape, I can devote my energies to my favorite pastime: mentally composing pornographic haiku."

Keket continued as if I hadn't spoken. "The prison is divided into three sections: maximum security, minimum security – which is where you were – and general population, which is where we're headed. Because of your service to the city, Quillion recommended that you be allowed to mingle freely with the general population. I think he may be underestimating how dangerous you are, but I've decided to follow his recommendation. After all, if Umbriel had been destroyed, everything – including Tenebrus – would've gone with it, so I owe you a debt of gratitude."

"You know, if you really want to repay me, you could always open a passageway back to the surface and look the other way while I scamper off."

Keket ignored me as she went on.

"Of course, should you cause too much trouble, you can always be returned to your cell – or if necessary, put in maximum security."

"Just out of curiosity's sake, what's maximum security like?"

"Are you familiar with humanity's various conceptions of hell?"

"In general."

"It's worse. So I recommend remaining on your best behavior."

We passed one cell where a gaunt Bloodborn male with long black hair and a thick mustache stood at the bars. He was dressed in formal attire, including a long silky black opera cape. When he saw me he stretched a clawed hand between the bars and contorted his long fingers into what I guessed was intended to be a mystical gesture, but which just looked silly. His eyes widened and glittered with a feral light.

"You are now under my power," the vampire said in a thick accent. "You will open the door and release me!"

"Not a chance, Vlad," Keket said.

We kept walking, and Vlad let out a blistering string of curses at the guard most unbefitting one of noble birth.

"Is that–"

"One of them," Keket said. "We have three and all of them say they're the real thing. That one's the least dangerous, which is why he's in minimum security."

We passed several more cells when I felt something wrap around my ankle, nearly tripping me. I looked down and saw that a tentacle had emerged from a cell and grabbed hold of me. Its surface was a spongy mottled green and was covered with large bloodshot eyes.

The interior of the cell was cloaked in darkness, so I couldn't quite make out what the owner of the tentacle looked like. Not that it really mattered.

Without missing a beat, I stomped on the tentacle as hard as I could, making sure I hit a couple of the eyes. The beast within the cell howled in pain, released its hold on me, and swiftly withdrew its wounded appendage back inside the cage. The creature than began making soft sobbing sounds.

"Stop whining," I said as I scuffed my shoes on the floor to get the viscous goo off them. "You've got plenty of spares."

One of the guards waved me on with his lightspear, and we started walking again.

"Starting fights on your first day?" Keket said.

"Look, anything that has eyes all over its body should know better than to attack someone. It's like wearing armor made out of your own testicles."

Keket grunted, but otherwise didn't comment.

We passed a number of other cells without incident, but then we came to one that had a water puddle in front of its door. Standing behind the bone bars was a young woman with long straight black hair hanging down in front of her face, concealing her features. She wore a white dress that was soaking wet and the flesh of her hands – the only parts of her body that were visible – were moist, blue-white and slightly puffy, like the flesh of a snail.

As we drew close the woman hissed Keket's name and her long back hair suddenly began to move. Ebony strands reached through the bars, rapidly extending in length as they streaked toward Keket.

The warden of Tenebrus didn't bother to acknowledge the threat. She merely continued walking as one of the guards pointed his glowing speartip at the thrashing mass of hair. Energy blasted forth from the spear, engulfing the hair which, despite being drenched, burst into flame. The young woman shrieked in a mixture of pain and fury, withdrew the smoldering remains of her hair back through the bars, and retreated farther into her cell, hissing angrily.

"Whoever that is, she doesn't have any love for you," I said to Keket.

"It's a long and not especially interesting story. But one thing I'll say: the woman can certainly hold a grudge."

We continued on and I was beginning to think Tenebrus wasn't half as bad as it was reputed to be. I mean, I wasn't thrilled at the idea of spending the rest of my existence here, but if what I'd seen so far was any indication, then I could handle this place, no problem.

As we walked we left the cell block behind and I began to become aware of a low level roar, almost like the constant rushing of a large waterfall. The corridor ended at a railing constructed from bone and Keket gestured for me to step forward and join her. I did so and found myself looking down upon a vast canyon formed from the same fleshy gray bone threaded substance as the rest of Tenebrus. The canyon floor was lit by large light spheres set atop pillars spread throughout the area, illuminating what I first took to be a writhing mass of crawling insects. But as I took a longer look I realized that I was seeing hundreds of people – inmates – circulating, talking, shouting, and in many cases, fighting. And when someone went down, huge scarab-like beetles scuttled forth from recessed spaces in the walls and floor, grabbed hold of the bodies, and pulled them back to their lairs, and judging from the screams, not everyone the scarabs collected was dead. Dozens of silvery round objects glided through the air above the prisoners, slowly criss-crossing the length of the canyon. I had no idea what they were or what purpose they served, but I guessed they were some manner of security or surveillance device. Jackalheads patrolled among the inmates, providing on the ground security. The canine headed guards were easy to spot because of their size and the glowing speartips of the weapons they carried.

With a sinking feeling I knew I was looking down at Tenebrus's general population and I no longer felt quite so confident about my ability to handle this place.

Keket turned to me and this time I could definitely hear the smile in her voice when she spoke.

"Quillion thought he was doing you a good turn by recommending you for the general population, but I know the truth. Down there are a number of criminals that you helped put away over the years, Matthew Richter. You can imagine how thrilled they'll be to learn that they will soon get a chance to become reacquainted with an old friend. Be sure to give them my regards."

Before I could react, Keket extended a cloth wrapped hand toward me and the bandages around her fingers uncurled and began moving toward me, lengthening as they came. Five strips of ancient Egyptian cerements took hold of me, encircling my neck, wrists and ankles, and then they lifted me off the floor as if I weighed nothing. Keket gestured and her cloth tentacles lifted me over the railing and held me out in the open air.

She gestured again and I began falling, still held tight by Keket's bandages. I plunged downward, feeling absurdly like a zombie yoyo, unable to do anything but watch as the canyon floor came rushing toward me. While most of the inmates below continued to go about their business without noticing my rapid approach, more than a few looked up, and the feral grins on their faces communicated their delight upon seeing that Keket was delivering fresh meat to them.

When I was within twenty feet of the canyon floor, the bandages jerked me to a stop and then lowered me the rest of the way more slowly. When I was within a couple yards of the ground, the bandages released me and streaked back up to return to their mistress, leaving me to fall the rest of the way. Luckily the inmates in the immediate vicinity had seen me coming and moved out of the way in time to prevent me landing on them. Unfortunately, that meant there was no one there to break my fall. I heard something snap when I hit – a rib or two, I guessed – but whatever it was that had broken, it didn't prevent me from quickly rising to my feet, so I decided not to worry about it.

I looked around at the faces staring at me. They belonged to different species and both genders – evidently Tenebrus was a co-ed facility – but they all had one thing in common. They all looked mean as hell. No one wore uniforms. Everyone had on street clothes, presumably whatever they'd been wearing when they'd been sentenced. And judging from the ragged, threadbare outfits of many of the inmates, they'd clearly been here for quite some time.

Keket's voice boomed from above, filling the canyon with sound.

"Ladies and gentlemen, I give you our latest arrival: Matthew Richter, knight errant and savior of the city who has, it should go without saying, suffered a recent reversal in fortune and is now joining us here at our happy little home. Won't you make him welcome, my children?"

Her last word echoed several times before finally dying away. I looked up at the railing where she'd been standing but Keket and her guards had already gone. Evidently I'd used up whatever amusement value I'd had and the demilord had left to attend to more important matters. That was good. I didn't feel like having an audience as I was torn apart by an angry mob of prisoners.

I brought my gaze back down to eye level and gave my best new-kid-on-the-block smile to my fellow prisoners.

"Anybody heard any good jokes lately?" I asked.

"I got one."

The voice sounded like two boulders grinding together and it was one I thought I recognized. A moment
later my guess was confirmed as a tall man dressed in a
black suit pushed his way through the crowd of prisoners gathered around me. His features were grotesquely
distorted – pronounced brow, bulbous nose, overlarge
ears, thick wormy lips and huge powerful hands that
constantly clenched and unclenched as if he couldn't
wait to wrap them around a neck and start squeezing.

"What do you call a zombie in jail?"

"I don't know, Rondo. What?"

Thick lips pulled back from large yellowed teeth as
he smiled.

"My bitch."

He raised those giant hands of his and started toward
me.

NINE

I'd encountered Rondo – known on the street as the Creeper – not long after I'd first come to Nekropolis. He'd begun his criminal career working as muscle for a veinburn manufacturer, but he didn't get enough opportunities to kill people working for drug pushers, so eventually he struck out on his own as a freelance assassin. Being a sociopath with a pair of insanely powerful hands designed to cause severe bodily damage, he excelled at the work and before long he was commanding quite a price for his services. One day he was hired by a vampire named Varney who'd had his blood bonded human lover, called a Shadow in Bloodborn parlance, stolen by another vampire. Rondo was hired to kill the Shadow and he succeeded in strangling the woman. But the woman's new lover, a Bloodborn named Camilla, was inconsolable at the Shadow's loss and she hired me to find the woman's killer. I eventually did, though Rondo had nearly managed to rip me apart with those hands of his before I turned him over

to a Sentinel. Both Varney and Camilla were minor no-
bility among the Bloodborn, so Varney got away scot
free. Rondo wasn't so fortunate. Camilla used her influence to make sure the Adjudicators sentenced Rondo
to Tenebrus and that was the last I'd heard of him –
until now.

Despite his ungainly appearance, Rondo could move
swift and silent when he wished – hence his nickname
Creeper – and he was nearly on me before I could react.
But after everything I'd been through since saving
Scream Queen's voice, I wasn't exactly in the mood to
dance with the ugly sonofabitch.

While I keep most of my weapons in my suit jacket,
I'm not dumb enough to keep all of them there. I was
grateful for Keket's sloppy security. Perhaps she'd assumed that Quillion's people had searched me
thoroughly and had removed any weapons I might be
carrying before sending me to her. If Devona had been
here she'd had given the undead sorceress a stern lec-
ture on basic security protocols. I reached into my pants
pocket and removed a small yellow sphere no larger
than a pill, but this medicine wasn't supposed to be
taken internally.

As Rondo came at me I threw the sphere to the
ground and it burst upon impact. A cloud of yellow gas
billowed upward, catching Rondo in the face. He stumbled to a stop and clapped those huge hands of his over
his mouth and nose to keep from breathing any of the
gas in, but it was too late. His already bulging eyes
bugged out even further as they began to water. He

took in two hitching breaths and then released a truly impressive sneeze that, if I hadn't braced myself, might've knocked me off my feet.

"As you've undoubtedly guessed by now, you've just inhaled a couple of lungfuls of the strongest sneezing powder in the city. There aren't many benefits to being dead, Rondo, but no longer having to breathe is one of them."

I'd picked up the powder at the same place where I get a lot of my toys – at Hop Frog's Delight, the best joke shop in Nekropolis. The dwarf who owns the place is an absolute genius when it comes to creating practical jokes and he handcrafts each one personally. But you have to be careful. As a joke on his customers, Hop Frog designed his jokes to randomly burst into flame upon activation – for some reason the jester has a thing about fire. Maybe they'll go off the first time you use them, maybe not until the seventh time. You never know, and for that reason, at Hop Frog's it's very much *caveat emptor.*

The cloud of itching powder was spreading and those inmates who were standing too close to Rondo and me quickly drew back to keep from inhaling any of the stuff. As for Rondo he was doubled over and sneezing so hard he could barely catch a breath. Hop Frog's jokes are extremely powerful and I wondered if Rondo was in danger of sneezing himself to death. Given the number of people who'd met their demises at the overlarge hands of the Creeper, the prospect of the man's death didn't exactly fill me with sorrow.

Rondo's super sized sneezing fit attracted the guards' attention and several of the jackalheaded musclemen were making their way toward us, plowing through the crowd of inmates, shouldering them aside and – if they didn't move fast enough – giving them a short blast of energy from their golden speartips. The guards weren't the only ones coming. Several of the silvery floating devices I'd seen from the overhead railing were heading in my direction, gliding soundlessly through the air. Now that I was closer I could see that the objects were levitating silver skulls about three times the size of a human skull. They reminded me of the skull sentry I'd encountered at the Foundry's main gate. These were more of Victor Baron's creations, I assumed, this type designed to provide additional security in Tenebrus. There were probably living brains housed within those metallic craniums that were even now sizing up the situation and deciding what to do about this disturbance in the general population. An instant later I got an inkling of what the flying skulls' response was going to be when their hollow eye sockets began to glow with ruby colored light.

I felt a tug on my elbow and a voice whispered urgently in my ear.

"Quick! Come with me if you want to live!"

I decided now wasn't the time to point out the irony in my newfound benefactor's statement and I allowed him to pull me away from Rondo, who was still sneezing so loud I figured it was even money that he would cough up at least one lung before any of the guards could reach him.

As I was led through the crowd of inmates I took a good look at the being who was pulling me along. It was a verman, although he was larger than usual, almost my height, and he was a true albino with white fur and red eyes. He wore a green frock coat with white ruffles at the sleeves and brass buttons down the front. I was surprised to see one of his species in Tenebrus. As mild and servile as vermen usually are they almost never cause any trouble, let alone commit crimes. I'd never seen a white furred verman before, nor had I ever seen one dressed so fancy. Something strange was going on here, but that didn't surprise me: something strange is always going on in Nekropolis. Weird is our stock in trade, after all.

The verman led me on a winding path across the canyon floor and while the inmates we passed glared at me none of them made a move to stop us. What's more none of them looked at the verman at all. They deliberately ignored him as if he were beneath their notice. At least that's what I thought at first, but as he continued to lead me, I saw that they made a point of getting out of his way. Most of them tried to appear casual about it, but it was obvious to me that they were showing deference to the verman, which was unheard of.

After a while we reached one of the canyon walls and the verman finally stopped. We stood close to a large semicircular opening which I recognized as a lair for one of the giant scarabs I'd seen earlier. I started to tell the verman that I didn't think this was the safest place to stand, but he put a finger to his mouth to shush me while he reached into a pocket with his other hand. He removed a large white cube and tossed it into the mouth of the entrance. Quick as a flash, a giant scarab darted forward, snatched up the cube in its mandibles, and scuttled backward into its lair. When the mammoth insect was gone, the albino verman visibly relaxed.

"It's safe to talk now. It won't bother us for a while." He gave a soft, snuffling laugh. "Those things are crazy for sugar."

This verman's manner was different from any of his kind I had ever encountered before. He stood up straight and looked me in the eye when he spoke and his tone contained no trace of servility. He talked to me as if we were equals and I knew this was no ordinary verman I was dealing with.

"My name is Gnasher," he said. "And you're Matthew Richter."

He held out his slender rodent hand for me to shake and I did so. When I let go he used his claws to rapidly scratch the fur under his chin and I saw several fleas fall to the ground.

"It's no wonder you know my name," I said, doing my best not to think about how many fleas Gnasher had remaining. "Keket made sure to announce my arrival loudly enough."

"True. The warden loves to stir up trouble down here. She gets off on watching the various little dramas that take place among the general population. Brawls, assassinations, gang wars... The bloodier the spectacle, the more she likes it." Gnasher pointed to one of the flying skulls floating off in the distance. "That's an Overwatcher. They're Keket's eyes and ears. Whatever they see and hear, she does too."

"I'm surprised we gave them the slip so easily, then," I said.

"There might not be many places to hide down here, but there are a lot of people. That helps. But I've got something that helps even more."

"What's that?"

Gnasher grinned, displaying a mouthful of long, narrow, flat-edged rat teeth. "A subcutaneous implant that renders me invisible to the Overwatchers' sensors. As long as you stay close to me, they won't be able to detect you either." He gave another of his snuffling laughs.

I frowned. "That kind of tech doesn't sound like standard issue for prisoners."

Gnasher's grin widened. "It's not, but then, I'm not a prisoner. And I knew who you were and that you were coming long before Keket made her announcement. In fact, I was waiting for you."

"Who are you? You don't act like any verman I've ever met. And why did you help me? Not that I'm ungrateful, but this doesn't strike me as the kind of place where altruism ranks high on the list of survival skills."

Another laugh. "*That's* an understatement! No altruism on my part. It's payback. You saved the life of one of our people at Sinsation, when Overkill failed to steal Scream Queen's voice."

I remembered the verman waiter who would've gotten skewered by one of Overkill's weapons if I hadn't stepped in and intercepted it.

Gnasher went on.

"Most people in the city wouldn't have bothered to save him, wouldn't have even seen him as someone worth saving. But not you. You saw his life as valuable enough to risk your own to protect it."

"Look, I was glad to keep the waiter from getting shish-kabobbed, but don't make me out to be something I'm not. I'm a zombie. I don't feel pain. It's no big deal for me to take a wound to protect someone."

"Maybe so but you still saved his life and for that we owe you. And we always pay our debts, Matthew. *Always*. Besides, Skully has spoken highly of you over the years and we trust his judgment."

Skully is a friend of mine, a bar owner with ties to the Dominari, Nekropolis's version of the Mafia. Despite being on different sides of the law we've always gotten along well and he's helped me out with cases on more than one occasion.

A suspicion was beginning to form in my mind.

"So you work for the Dominari too?"

Gnasher let out another snufflelaugh and scratched behind one of his ears. "*For* the Dominari! Don't you get it? We vermen *are* the Dominari!"

Gnasher went on to tell me more about the true nature of the Dominari, and while at first I found his story unbelievable, the more I thought about it all, the more sense it made. I'd lived and worked in Nekropolis for years and I dealt with the city's criminal element on a regular basis. But while I'd met plenty of people who one way or another worked for the Dominari, I'd never actually encountered a member of that criminal organization in person. The Dominari did its business in secret and kept the identities of its members well concealed. Not even Skully would tell me anything about the people he worked for. I'd always imagined the Dominari as a combination crime cartel and spy agency, with hidden headquarters located somewhere in the Sprawl. But the one thing I'd never considered was that the Dominari might be hiding in plain sight.

"My people came to Nekropolis during the Descension with the other Darkfolk, and as the city began to develop, we realized there was opportunity for us here. You see, my kind has always been pragmatic, willing to do things that others find distasteful in order to survive and thrive. Where others see mounds of trash, we see discarded resources to be recovered and made use of. Where others see nothing but rotting carrion, we see food going to waste. And when the Darkfolk began to build their city's infrastructure, complete with laws and legitimate businesses, we knew a shadow economy would inevitably develop. In this respect, the Darkfolk are no different than humans. Crime is a fact of life and if there was going to be crime in our new home my people decided not only would we take advantage of it, we'd run it. And so the Dominari was born. The Darkfolk already looked down upon us as lower lifeforms, so we used that as camouflage, acting docile and hiring ourselves out cheap as manual laborers and servants. We quickly infiltrated every level of society, allowing us access to all manner of information, for we made ourselves such a common part of everyday life – just another bit of background scenery – that few people noticed us, and even fewer guarded their tongues in our presence. Positioned as we were, we were able to take advantage of every business opportunity that came our way and over the years the Dominari grew strong. If there was a criminal enterprise in the city that we didn't own outright, we took a cut of the profits. We became rich as any Darklord – richer, even – and in our own way, just as powerful."

Gnasher's revelation completely changed my view of Nekropolis and as I struggled to process what he'd told me a thought occurred to me.

"Why haven't the Darklords done anything to stop you? Why hasn't Dis? Surely they must know the truth about you."

Gnasher grinned. "We've made ourselves such an integral part of how the city works, that if you destroyed us, Nekropolis's entire economy would collapse. Dis and the Darklords learned about us long ago, but they view us as a necessary evil and as long as we don't interfere with their personal business they leave us alone for the most part. From time to time they make token strikes at us to placate their subjects and make them think something is being done to curtail crime in the city, but afterward everything returns to normal."

I shook my head in amazement. Gnasher was right: in many the ways the Darkfolk aren't so different from humanity.

"So what are you doing here in Tenebrus?" I asked. "I'd think your people would've seen to it that you were never arrested, let alone convicted."

Gnashed snuffled again. "I'm not a prisoner. I am a Secundar, a high rank among my people. Only Primark is higher. I have the great honor of serving as the Dominari's liaison to Tenebrus. We can't prevent every captured criminal from being incarcerated, so we make sure to keep the lines of communication open between Tenebrus and the outside world. That way our associates' knowledge and skills don't go to waste. We *despise* waste."

It's no secret that organized crime figures and gang leaders back on Earth are still able to run their organizations from inside prison and it seemed the Dominari were doing the same here – only they'd moved one of their own into Tenebrus to do the job.

"I carry messages back and forth as well as delivering alcohol, cigarettes, drugs, pure blood and fresh meat for our people inside. No weapons, though. Keket is aware of my presence here, and while she allows me a great deal of freedom, she'd never permit me to bring in weapons that might be used against her guards – or more importantly, against her."

"Back and forth... You mean you can get out whenever you want? Keket told me that no one has ever escaped Tenebrus!"

Gnasher grinned. "I told you, I'm not a prisoner, so technically I can't escape. From time to time we're allowed to take some of our people out for a furlough, provided we return them. So again, no escapes."

For the first time since Quillion cast me down to Tenebrus, I began to feel a ray of hope.

"So you can get me out."

Gnasher spread his hands. "Maybe yes, maybe no. Intervening to keep you from getting torn apart by an old enemy is one thing. You save one of us and we owed you. And as long as you remain with me, you will be safe. No one in Tenebrus would dare touch anyone under my protection. But that's as much as we'll do to repay our debt to you. If you want more from us, we'll need to negotiate."

"I should have guessed as much. After all, everything is business with the Dominari, isn't it?"

Gnasher gave me a hungry smile. "Indeed."

The idea of dealing with the Dominari didn't sit well with me. Despite all of Gnasher's talk about his people filling an important niche in Nekropolis's society, the bottom line was that the Dominari were thieves and murderers, the very people I'd spent my entire adult life trying to get off the streets. Still, it didn't look as if I had much of a choice if I didn't want to live the remainder of my unlife trapped in Tenebrus, trying to avoid Rondo and the other prisoners I'd helped send here. I'd been framed for a crime I didn't commit and if I wanted to clear my name I'd need to return to the city proper to do it. Besides, I missed Devona and I was pretty sure Keket wouldn't permit conjugal visits.

"All right. What do you want from me?"

"Nothing, actually. When I said we need to negotiate, I meant the Dominari. Not you. Discussions are taking place even as we speak and if terms can be reached you will get your chance at freedom. If not…" He shrugged. "I suppose you can always work as my assistant."

I frowned. "If you're not going to negotiate with me, then who…" Then it hit me. "Devona."

"We contacted her as soon as we learned you'd been sent here."

Without thinking I grabbed Gnasher's coat by the lapels and gave the ratman a shake.

"If anything happens to her…"

Gnasher's eyes glittered dangerously and I felt the pressure of something poking my abdomen. I looked down and saw that the verman had drawn a black bladed dagger and held it pressed against my stomach.

Gnasher's voice was emotionless as he spoke. "I said I don't deliver weapons to prisoners. I didn't say I don't carry weapons of my own."

I stood very still. The black knife was a dire blade, one of the deadliest weapons in the city and a trademark of the Dominari. No one outside the Dominari, supposedly not even the Darklords, understood the magic that was used to create the foul things, but a dire blade could kill any supernatural creature with a single thrust, zombies included.

I very slowly released my hold on Gnasher's coat.

"Sorry," I said. "I appreciate everything you've done for me. I guess I'm just a little stressed out after everything that's happened to me over the last day or so."

Gnasher regarded me a moment longer before making the dagger disappear somewhere inside his jacket.

"Perfectly understandable, but a word of warning: if you touch me again, I'll gut you faster than you can blink."

Gnasher delivered the threat matter –of factly but the anger smoldering in his gaze told me he was deadly serious. He was, after all, Dominari.

"I get it."

Gnasher nodded curtly. "Good. We should go now. It's best to keep moving down here, and besides, one sugar cube only satisfies a scarab for so long. We keep talking here and we run the risk of becoming the insect's next treat."

He started walking away from the scarab's lair, and I followed.

"How long will your people's negotiations with Devona take?" I asked as we walked.

"It all depends on what she has to offer us and how swiftly we can come to terms. In the meantime, there's no reason to stand around doing nothing. Time is money, you know."

As Gnasher led me toward a group of prisoners I wondered what Devona could possibly have that the Dominari might want. I just hoped that whatever the price for my freedom might be it wouldn't prove too costly for her in the end. Despite Gnasher's last comment

I knew the Dominari wasn't solely interested in money. They had all sorts of ways to get their claws into you and the last thing I wanted Devona to do was make a deal with the Dominari that she would later regret. But I knew if our positions were reversed I'd do whatever it took to win her freedom. But there was nothing I could do right then except try not to worry and stay out of trouble while I accompanied Gnasher on his rounds.

I had a feeling that both would be much easier said than done.

I spent the next several hours tagging along with Gnasher. Sometimes the transactions he conducted were obvious, like when he delivered several vials of tangleglow to a porcine creature with a bushy red beard who looked like Porky Pig and Yosemite Sam's love child. The pig thing immediately opened one of the vials and snorted the contents while tucking the second away in a pocket. A few seconds later the creature's eyes began to shine with a kaleidoscopic light. Satisfied, he handed a bag of darkgems over to Gnasher and the ratman placed it into one of his own pockets. A jack-alheaded guard standing nearby kept his gaze averted during the transaction, giving no sign he was aware of us, let alone that he had any intention of interfering. When I later asked Gnasher about the guards he said, "They'd better look away. We pay them enough."

Other times the verman's errands were more enigmatic, like when he walked up to a naked woman whose body was covered in fish-like scales and whispered a series of seemingly random numbers in her ear. The woman nodded, whispered a different series of numbers back to Gnasher, and the verman thanked her and we departed.

Everywhere we went the guards ignored us and the Overwatchers gliding above seemed oblivious to our existence. The inmates still pretended not to be interested in Gnasher as they had when I first arrived – unless of course he had direct business to conduct with them – but now I knew the prisoners were well aware of him, and by extension, of me too. They maintained their distance, though, never approaching the verman, always waiting for him to come to them. I kept watch for Rondo, and while I didn't see him, I wasn't foolish enough to think he'd leave me alone just because I was in Gnasher's company. Wherever the Creeper was I knew he was plotting his next move against me.

I saw other criminals that I'd help put away – the Lotus Bleeder, Zack the Knife, Nightshadow, Carnality and more. All of them glared at me as if hoping the hatred in their gazes might reduce me to dust, but none made a move toward me, presumably out of respect for – or fear of – Gnasher. It's good to have friends in low places.

After a while I realized that Gnasher had been pulling more objects from his pockets than he should've had room for. I was sure there was some sort of magic at work and probably a high-level enchantment too. After all, the Dominari could afford the very best. Given that I rely on the contents of my own pockets in my work I was more than a little envious of Gnasher's jacket, but I didn't ask the verman for the name of his tailor. Whoever it was I knew I couldn't afford his services.

Gnasher was talking with a tall man in a black suit who'd been jailed for smuggling dead bodies between dimensions without proper authorization when a fanged being covered in crusty armor plates lumbered up and grabbed the verman from behind. The creature – a she, I guessed based on the configuration of her armored chest – got Gnasher in an arm lock and held him tight.

"What do you think you're doing?" the verman said in an indignant squeak that sounded more like Mickey Mouse's voice than that of a well connected mobster. "Don't you know who I am?"

"She knows," said a gravelly voice. "She just doesn't give a damn."

I turned to see Rondo approaching, a grin splitting his distorted face. The Tall Man decided he was suddenly needed elsewhere and rapidly moved off on those long legs of his.

I nodded toward the vaguely lobsterish looking She Creature. "I'm surprised you found someone to help you. I didn't think scum like you had any friends."

Gnasher struggled in the She Creature's clawed grip, but she was too powerful and he couldn't break free.

Rondo stopped a dozen feet from me, evidently having learned to keep his distance after our last encounter. He might look like a slender Neanderthal but that didn't mean he was stupid.

"I don't need friends," Rondo said. "Not when there are lots of people here who hate your guts almost as much as I do. You don't know her –" he nodded toward the She-Creature – "but her brother was a gill man you had a run-in with once."

"I remember. The fishface kidnapped a selkie and was holding her captive as his sex slave. Her parents hired me to get her back, which I did, but I needed a dehydra's help to do it." I turned to face the She Creature, who was glaring at me, long ropey strands of saliva dripping from her fangs. "You ever see a dehydra at work? Those creatures can suck all the moisture out of a person in seconds. They're like water vampires. Your brother went from gill man to bipedal prune in less than five seconds."

The She Creature snarled and started to loosen her grip on Gnasher, clearly tempted to let him go so she would be free to attack me.

"Don't listen to him, Marla," Rondo warned. "He's just trying to goad you into making a stupid move."

The She Creature looked like she was still considering having a go at me, but in the end she tightened her grip on the verman once more.

Rondo gave me a triumphant grin and I shrugged.

"Can't blame a guy for trying. So... what's next? She's going to hold Gnasher while you and I fight? Do you really think that will help? I managed to kick your ass all by myself the last time we met and I only needed a little sneezing powder to do it. You're not nearly as tough as you think you are."

Rondo kept grinning, but his gaze turned deadly cold.

"Much as I hate to admit it, I agree. Which is why I've brought along another former friend of yours."

A crowd of prisoners had gathered as we talked, all of them looking excited at the prospect of witnessing some prison yard mayhem. But now they began whispering among themselves and looking back nervously over their shoulders. More than a few moved off, as if they decided they'd be better off watching the proceedings from a distance. A moment later I found out why when a husky man with shaggy brown hair came walking toward us. He wore a loose tan shirt and matching pants, but no shoes. His black eyebrows were just as thick as the hair on his head and they met in the middle, a sure sign that he was a lyke. But I already knew that because I'd encountered this shapeshifter before. I didn't know what his given name was, but I was all too familiar with his street name.

Lycanthropus Rex.

TEN

"Don't take this the wrong way, Rex, but I sincerely hoped I'd never see your butt ugly face again."

"I bet," Rex growled.

For reasons that were still unclear to me about a year earlier Lycanthropus Rex had gone on a rampage in the Sprawl one night when I happened to be working on a separate case. I was in the right place at the right time (or maybe wrong place, wrong time – take your pick) to stop him. When the dust settled, seventeen people were dead, thirty-two were injured and Papa Chatha had to reattach all four of my limbs. Rex had been taken away by the Sentinels and cast down into Tenebrus.

Rex walked up to join Rondo, and while I was gratified to see the lyke also kept his distance from me, the feeling was tempered by the knowledge of how much firepower he packed. I'd been lucky as hell during our last encounter and even then I'd barely defeated him. I didn't think much of my chances to win a rematch, let alone survive it.

"I never met Rondo before today," Rex said, "but he and I have something in common. We've both spent every minute since we were thrown into this shithole dreaming about someday getting a chance to tear you to fucking pieces. And you know something, zombie? That day's today." He grinned, displaying a mouthful of sharp canine teeth. "Who says dreams don't come true?"

Rondo began to step away from Rex then and I knew what was coming. Lycanthropus Rex was going to show his fellow inmates how he'd come by his name. A lyke's transformation from human to wild form is usually a rapid one, but with Rex it took a bit longer, I think because he got off on watching people's reactions when he changed. And I had to admit, the man put on a hell of a show.

There were two separate aspects to his change. First came the standard shift from humanoid to animalistic features and in Rex's case that animal was a wolf. Thick tufts of brown fur sprang forth from his skin, his fingernails darkened and lengthened into ebon claws, his ears became pointed and moved farther up on his skull and his mouth and nose blended into a canine snout. His already intimidating teeth became longer and razor sharp and his eyes – while still blazing with human intelligence – became a feral yellow. But as impressive as that change was, the second part of the transformation was what really made you want to drop a load in your shorts.

Rex began to grow. And when I say grow, I don't just mean Rex put on a few dozen extra pounds of monster muscle and another foot or two of scary height. This son of a bitch *grew*. He stood about 5'5" in human form but as he assumed werewolf shape he increased in size to seven feet tall, eight, nine, ten – and he kept on growing. His clothes had been loose on him when he'd started changing, but they soon grew tight, then split at the seams and fell away to become nothing more than torn rags lying on the ground.

Everyone in the vicinity was watching the spectacle of Lycanthropus Rex's transformation – everyone, that is, except Rondo. He was watching me and grinning like it was Christmas morning and Santa Claus had brought him a pair of gold-plated hand exercisers.

"You liking this, Richter?" he asked, grinning. "Because I'm loving it!"

Fifteen feet... twenty... twenty-five... and Rex's growth showed no signs of stopping.

One of the things about monsters is that they're so used to being well, monstrous. Like animals facing off in the wild, they often seek to intimidate one another with displays of size, strength and ferocity before attacking, partly because – like Rex – they enjoyed scaring their victims first. And if, also like Rex, you can scare other monsters... well, it just doesn't get any better than that. So while Rex was busy frightening the piss out of everyone within eyeshot, I had a few precious moments in which to act.

First I checked my pants pockets to see if I was carrying anything that might prove useful in combating a gargantuan wolfman. I usually carry all my best weapons in my suit jacket, though, and what I had left was even less deadly than the sneezing powder I'd used against Rondo. And even if the Sentinel hadn't taken my jacket and gun from me back at the Nightspire none of my weapons would've had much effect on Lycanthropus Rex. My 9mm was loaded with silver bullets that had been dipped in a solution of holy water and garlic along with a few other herbs and chemicals given to me by Papa Chatha that make them effective on just about any creature I might encounter in Nekropolis. The silver in my bullets might've killed Rex when he was normal sized, but now... But I didn't have my gun, so the matter was academic. What I needed was a weapon powerful enough to slay even a giant werewolf, preferably one I could get my hands on in the next several moments.

Something like Gnasher's dire blade.

I glanced at the verman and the She Creature who still held him in a tight grip. I couldn't just run over and try to grab hold of the dire blade, though. For one thing I didn't know where Gnasher kept it. In his jacket, I assumed, but since his pockets seemed bottomless, it was possible there were other enchantments on his frock coat that would prevent anyone else form locating the blade, let alone taking it off his person. But that wasn't what made me hesitate. I may be unique among Nekropolis's zombies, but there's one thing I share with my dead brothers and sisters: I'm slow. If I made a go for Gnasher's blade I'd move so slowly that both Rondo and the She Creature would guess what I was up to and one or both of them would stop me. If I wanted a chance at Gnasher's dire blade I'd have to use my head. Good thing Victor Baron had put it back on for me.

"You know, Rondo, you didn't have to go to all this trouble," I said. "If you want to destroy me, all you have to do is walk on over and give me a close-up look at your face. The shock would be so intense that I'd probably just collapse into a pile of dust on the spot."

Rondo's grin gave way to a truly impressive scowl.

"Laugh it up, Richter," he snarled. "That's the last joke you're ever going to make."

"No it's not. This is: when you were born, you were so ugly the doctor couldn't tell which end was your ass, so he slapped both ends just to make sure."

Rondo roared with fury and came racing toward me, ham-hands outstretched and ready to cause some serious damage.

I had to time this just right. When Rondo was almost upon me I sidestepped and angled my body so that instead of grabbing me his right hand struck me a glancing blow on the shoulder. I didn't feel the blow, of course, and I allowed the impact to spin me around, and I stumbled toward Gnasher and the She Creature, trying my best to make it look like an accident. As ungainly as I was I didn't have to try very hard.

The verman guessed what I was up to, for as I collided with him, he whispered, "Inside front pocket," and spoke a couple words in a language I was unfamiliar with. Some sort of mystic phrase I figured, designed to deactivate whatever enchantment protected

Gnasher's blade. Before the She Creature could react I reached into the jacket and I felt cloth part beneath my fingers as if it were a living thing willingly opening itself to me. I found the hilt of the dire blade, grabbed hold of it and pulled it free of Gnasher's jacket. I'd never touched a dire blade before and I was surprised to feel a sensation of intense cold as my fingers wrapped around the handle. The sudden feeling in my dead flesh was so startling to me that I almost dropped the weapon, but I managed to hold on to it.

I spun around, ready to wield the dire blade against Rondo with deadly efficiency. But before I could do anything Rondo grabbed my wrist with one of his giant hands and squeezed. I heard bones splinter and my now-useless fingers sprung open and the dire blade tumbled to the ground.

Rondo's grin was back.

"Nice try."

"I have to admit, I'd have preferred to kill the three of you myself," I said, "but I suppose I'll just have to be satisfied with letting Keket's people do it for me."

I pointed with my left hand and – still holding on to my broken wrist – Rondo turned to look. A half dozen jackalheads were rapidly approaching from different directions, as were a trio of silver skulled Overwatchers.

"You really didn't think Lycanthropus Rex could transform without drawing the guards' attention, did you?" I asked.

Rondo said nothing, but he continued to hold my crushed wrist as we both watched the jackal-heads go to work. When they were within twenty feet of Rex – who had by this time reached his full fifty-foot height – they stopped, leveled their golden spears and released blasts of energy at the giant wolfman. Rex roared more in anger than pain and lunged toward one of the guards, snatching him up in one gigantic paw with a single swift swipe. Rex squeezed and the guard let out a scream as the life was crushed out of him. Rex then hurled the body at another guard, taking him out with truly impressive aim.

One of the Overwatchers glided toward Rex from behind and twin beams of light lanced forth from its silvery sockets to strike the gargantuan wolfman directly between the shoulder blades. From Rex's bellow of agony it was clear that whatever energy the skull emitted it was more effective than that produced by the jackalheads' spears. But however powerful the energy blast was it didn't slow Rex down. He whirled about, snatched hold of the Overwatcher and hurled it to the ground. The metallic skull hit not far from where I was standing and I saw the device break open like a large silvery egg, spilling out electronic components, blood and bits of brain matter. Victor Baron built his creations to last, but even his genius hadn't anticipated the Overwatchers going up against a creature of Lycanthropus Rex's power. A second later the Overwatcher exploded in a spectacular flash of light and fire.

Seeing an Overwatcher brought down, the prisoners in the area let up a cheer and, emboldened by seeing how easily Rex had dealt with Keket's guards, they began to riot. Inmates turned to whoever happened to be standing close to them and began hitting, clawing and biting – sometimes all three at once. Jackalheads fired energy blasts and Overwatchers unleashed eye beams in all directions, hoping to quell the riot before it could spread too far, but they might as well have been trying to hold back a tsunami with a few sandbags and a whole lot of good intentions. Within moments the fighting had spread throughout the entire general pop- ulation as near as I could tell from where I stood and the canyon air was filled with the sounds of hundreds of beings beating hell out of each other. On impulse I glanced upward toward the balcony from which Keket had dropped me down to the canyon floor and I saw the mistress of Tenebrus standing there, gripping the railing with cloth wrapped fingers, face hidden behind her golden mask. I remembered what Gnasher had told me about how Keket was entertained by watching the inmates fight. If so, the undead sorceress was undoubt- edly ecstatic right then.

I was used to matters going from bad to worse – it's pretty much standard operating procedure for me – but this was bad even by my standards. I could've tried to slip away from Rondo and Rex in the confusion and lose myself among the rioters, but I didn't want to abandon Gnasher. He might have been Dominari but he'd taken care of me since I'd been tossed into the gen- eral population and I owed him. Besides, the thought of running from lowlifes like Rondo and Rex made my dead stomach turn. Still, I had no idea what I could do at this point. If I was faster I might've made a lunge for the dire blade lying on the ground, but if I so much as twitched in the weapon's direction the She Creature would snap Gnasher in half like a white furred twig.

I felt gentle fingers of thought brush my mind, the sensation both familiar and very welcome.

Don't worry, love. I know someone who specializes in fast.

I saw a blur of motion and felt the pressure of a breeze whip past and suddenly I was holding the dire blade in my left hand – which was good since Rondo still had hold of my broken right wrist and the hand attached to it was useless now.

Thanks, Tavi, I thought and swung the dire blade toward Rondo's chest. The Creeper's gaze was fixed on Lycanthropus Rex who was still battling jackalheads and Overwatchers and thus didn't see the strike coming. Not that it mattered. My arm swung wild and instead of driving the ebony blade deep into Rondo's chest it swept through empty air.

See? You should've let Victor Baron fix that when you had the chance!

I didn't respond to Devona, partially because I didn't have any time, but mostly because she was right, and it irritated me.

Rondo must've caught the motion of my failed strike out of the corner of his eye for he turned to face me and without hesitation rammed a fist into my face. I felt nothing, but given the force with which he struck, if I hadn't been dead already, I'm sure the blow would've killed me. As it was my nose was reduced to pulp and

I'm pretty sure my skull was fractured. Rondo had maintained his hold on my right wrist with his other hand and now he yanked me back toward him, intending to hit me again. But there was another blur as something whipped past us and a stream of liquid splashed into Rondo's eyes. Rondo screamed as Tavi's cobra venom did its job and the Creeper released his hold on my wrist so that he could use both hands to frantically try to clear the venom from his eyes.

With Rondo momentarily out of commission I turned to Gnasher and the She Creature. Seeing Rondo get injured – and more importantly, seeing me standing before her gripping a dire blade – she tightened her hold on Gnasher and the verman shrieked in pain.

"Stay where you're at, zombie, or the rat-man dies!" she said in a gurgly voice, as if she had a throat full of mouthwash.

"You know, it's a policy of mine never to listen when someone threatens me, but considering that a friend of mine is walking up behind you as we speak, I think I'll make exception this time."

The She Creature let out a laugh that sounded like a water balloon bursting. "You don't seriously expect me to fall for that old trick, do you?"

"It's no trick," I said, "and yes, I do expect you to fall – hard."

The She Creature frowned, perhaps realizing from my tone that something wasn't quite adding up here. A moment later she realized what it was when a scaly clawed hand clamped down on her shoulder and burst into flame. The She Creature screamed in agony at Scorch's fiery touch, and while the demon might not have been able to suck the moisture out of a water monster with the ruthless efficiency of a dehydra, she was no slouch in that department. The She Creature's armored plates quickly dried and tiny cracks fissured across their surfaces. She released Gnasher and the verman fled, moving with a swiftness that would've done Tavi proud, and disappeared into the crowd.

Once Gnasher was safely away, Scorch increased the intensity of her flames and the SheCreature became wreathed in fire. She screamed, flung herself to the ground and attempted to put the flames out by rolling, but it was too late. A few seconds later she lay still, while the flames continued to burn.

Scorch, in full-on scary demon mode, grinned at me.

"Looks like her fellow prisoners will be dining on fresh cooked lobster tonight," she said.

It's times like that which make it hard for me to remember that Scorch's normal form is that of a relatively innocent looking young girl.

"Good to see you again," I told the demon and meant it. "But where's Devona?"

"Right here."

Her voice came from right next to me, but when I turned I saw nothing. An instant later the air shimmered and Devona and Bogdan were standing there, the warlock holding on to her arm.

I felt a wave of jealousy until I realized Bogdan had been in physical contact with her in order to extend his invisibility spell around the both of them. That didn't mean I had to like it, though, and I was happy when the warlock let go of her.

Devona had undergone something of a makeover in the hours we'd been apart. Her normally blonde hair had been dyed midnight black and instead of her usual black leather catsuit she wore a tight white sweater, a short black skirt, black leggings and knee-high black boots. I wasn't sure why she'd changed clothes – she finds her regular outfit not only comfortable but it doesn't constrict her movements if she needs to fight. Maybe she'd decided that breaking her lover out of jail was such a special occasion that she needed to dress up. If so I wasn't complaining. She looked damned good, but then she could wear a burlap sack and she'd still look beautiful to me.

Devona ran over and hugged me and I hugged her back as best I could given the number of injuries I'd sustained since we'd last seen one another.

When we parted I looked at her and said, "What's with the new look? Here I am, stuck in Tenebrus, while you decide to pay a visit to your hair stylist?"

She smiled. "I'll explain later. Right now–"

She was interrupted by Rondo bellowing my name.

"Richter! I'm going to fucking tear you apart!"

The Creeper – eyes so red and swollen he could barely see – started toward me, killer hands raised and ready to do what they did best.

Bogdan gestured and a baseball bat suddenly appeared in his hand. He got a good grip on it with both hands, stepped forward, and swung as Rondo came at me. The bat splintered as it came in contact with Rondo's head and for an instant I thought the Creeper would shrug off the blow and keep coming. But he stopped, swayed on his feet back and forth a couple times, and then his eyes rolled white and he fell face first onto the ground.

Bogdan dropped the broken bat next to Rondo then came over to join Devona and me.

"Nice hit," I told him. "You ever get tired of magic, you might consider a career playing baseball on Earth."

Scorch walked over too and Tavi was suddenly there as well, having arrived so swiftly he might as well have magically appeared as Devona and Bogdan had done. The lyke was in his combination cobra–mongoose wild form and he looked just as intimidating as Scorch did in her full demon guise.

"I've never broken anyone out of jail before," Tavi said. "It's actually quite a lot of fun."

I was about to warn Tavi not to jinx us but I was too late. Lycanthropus Rex had fought off the jackalheads and Overwatchers and now reached for us with his giant clawed hands. He caught us by surprise, including Tavi who otherwise might've gotten away, and lifted us into the air, Scorch, Tavi and Bogdan in his left hand, Devona and I in his right. He brought us up to his mammoth grinning face and I was grateful that I couldn't smell his undoubtedly horrendous breath.

"Looks like you found some friends of your own, eh, Richter?" Rex said in a booming bestial voice. "They can't help you, you know. Not against me. I'm too strong."

I tried to keep my voice steady as I spoke, but in truth I was terrified. You don't have to confront a fifty-foot wolfman everyday, even in Nekropolis. "Right now Keket is having fun watching the chaos you and Rondo created, but she'll grow tired of the show and reestablish order soon enough, and you'll likely end up thrown into maximum security. From what she told me, it makes Hell look like a tropical resort."

"Maybe so," Rex growled. "But at least I'll get to crush you and your friends to a pulp first." He bared his teeth in a hideous parody of a grin. "Any last words, Richter?"

"Yes. You're about to feel a slight prick, and it's most definitely going to hurt."

I still had hold of Gnasher's dire blade, and while my arms were pressed tight against my body due to the pressure of Rex's grip, I was able to angle my hand so the knife point touched the flesh of the giant lyke's hand. I didn't need my full coordination to simply shove the dagger forward, and given how deadly its magic was, I didn't have to do more than break the skin for it to work.

The effect was as dramatic as it was instantaneous. Lycanthropus Rex's eyes glazed over, his body went limp and his fifty-foot frame plummeted to the ground like a felled tree. It was all I could do to resist yelling "Timber!" on the way down.

The impact was rough but most of us were hardier than normal humans and Tavi and Scorch used their bodies to protect Bogdan, so none of us received any serious injuries when we hit. Too bad I can't say the same for Rondo – the poor unconscious sonofabitch was directly beneath Rex when he fell.

Once Rex was done we pried ourselves free from his dead hands and started moving away from the body. Not because we were afraid of Rex coming back to life – which isn't unheard of in Nekropolis – but because a horde of excited scarabs came scuttling toward the downed giant from all directions. We managed to get clear just in time for the beetles to fall upon Rex's remains, and as we ran, we heard the sound of noisy, moist chewing as the insects tucked into the feast of their lifetimes, illustrating an important principle in Nekropolis: the bigger they are, the better they taste.

We didn't stick around to watch the grisly show. Numbers of jackalheads and Overwatchers were hauling ass in our direction and it looked like my great escape was in danger of being over before it had fully gotten under way. I had no idea what to do, but Devona grabbed hold of my hand and pulled me toward the nearest canyon wall, the others keeping pace with us. I soon realized she was leading me toward a scarab's lair – the same one Gnasher had taken me to before. The five of us hurried inside the cave and were swallowed by darkness. My night vision isn't any better than it was when I was alive but Devona led me on confidently and I continued to follow, trusting her.

We soon reached the rear of the cave, having to pick our way through the scattered skeletal remains of past

scarab meals, but instead of stopping we kept going. I
half expected to run face first into a wall, but we encountered no obstacles. We stepped from darkness into
light and it took my eyes a moment to adjust before I
was able to get a look at my surroundings.

We were standing inside a tunnel formed of the same
gray fleshy substance as Tenebrus. Behind us was a
solid wall, or at least what appeared to be a solid wall.
I reached out to touch it but my hand passed through
without resistance.

"Hologram," I said.

Devona nodded. "It's how Gnasher comes and goes
from Tenebrus. The passageway is too small for any of
the scarabs to get through, though."

"How come the big bugs don't eat him?" I wondered
aloud.

"Because I always make sure to carry extra sugar
cubes with me."

I turned toward the sound of Gnasher's voice and
saw him standing next to a tram made from bits and
pieces of junk. Sitting behind the wheel was a verman,
but this was a patchwork version cobbled together from
the parts of separate rodent bodies. It seemed Victor
Baron did work for the Dominari, too.

Looking at both the hodge-podge tram and the reanimated verman I remembered what Gnasher had told
me about his people: *We despise waste*. From the looks of
things it was a principle they took to heart.

The sole illumination in the tunnel was provided by
the tram's headlights, and they revealed the tunnel ex-

tended for some distance.

"Where are we?" I asked.

"This is the Underwalk," Gnasher said with more than a hint of pride. "Over the centuries the Dominari have created an intricate series of tunnels beneath the city. Not only does it help us get around more easily, we're able to do so without attracting unwanted attention."

I was impressed. The Darklords strictly control travel to and from their Dominions by monitoring traffic across the bridges that connect them. The only way a system of tunnels such as the Underwalk could exist was with the Darklords' tacit approval. The Dominari were even more powerful than I'd imagined, almost as powerful as Gnasher liked to make out.

I turned to Devona. "I take it you were able to reach a deal with the Dominari."

She nodded. "Once we did, they brought us down into the Underwalk, loaned us a tram and a driver, and he brought us to their secret entrance to Tenebrus. As soon as we were inside, we started looking for you. It seemed like we found you just in time."

"I had the situation well in hand before you four showed up," I said defensively. Then I looked down at my crushed wrist. "Poor choice of words," I admitted. "Thanks for coming." I looked to the other members of the Midnight Watch. "All of you."

They nodded, looking insufferably pleased with themselves. Still, there wasn't anything I could say about it since I suppose they had technically rescued me, though I like to think that I'd have found my own way out, given enough time.

I turned back to Gnasher. "I appreciate that your people are willing to do business with us but I have a hard time believing that you intend to trust us with so many of your secrets – the true nature of the Dominari, the existence of the Underwalk, that you have a direct pipeline in and out of Tenebrus..."

Gnasher grinned. "Trust is for fools. We believe in insurance."

"I'm afraid he's right, Matt." Devona reached into her skirt pocket and removed a small glass vial containing a tiny wriggling worm.

"What's that?"

"A tongue worm," she said. "You place it on your tongue, as its name suggests, and it sinks into the flesh. It lies dormant within, but if you ever try to tell anyone anything you know about the Dominari, the worm will explode, taking your head with it. All four of us accepted tongue worms before the Dominari would agree to help us. This one is for you."

I looked more closely at the worm inside the vial. It looked like a simple inch worm, nothing special about it, but I had no doubt it could do what Devona said. No wonder the Dominari were able to keep their secrets so well.

I looked to Devona's employees, trying to understand. They'd all taken quite a risk by accepting tongue worms, and while I had no problem believing Devona would do so for me – for I'd do the same for her in an instant – those three barely knew me, and I barely knew them. Hell, I didn't really like them, and I *hated* Bogdan. Why would they have taken such a risk for me?

I decided that was something for me to ponder later. If we were going to get out of here it was obvious what I needed to do first. I didn't even think about objecting; I had a pretty good idea what would happen to me if I refused to accept a tongue worm. I took the vial from Devona, grasping it as best I could in my right hand, and pulled the rubber stopper out with my left – though as uncoordinated as that hand now was, it took me a couple tries. Devona frowned but thankfully she kept silent and let me have my pride. Once the stopper was out I upended the vial over my tongue and the worm fell out. I felt nothing, but Devona said, "It's gone," and I knew the worm had merged with the flesh of my tongue and disappeared. I replaced the stopper and tucked the vial into my pocket – vermen aren't the only ones who don't like to waste things – and faced Devona once more.

"Now what?"

"Now we board the tram and get out of here before Keket realizes you've escaped. Just because the Dominari helped us is no reason she'll allow you to get away."

"True," Gnasher said. "And our deal was to provide a means for you to escape, which we have done. We will not interfere with any attempt to recapture you. We won't directly defy Keket since we need to stay on her good side in order to continue operating inside Tenebrus."

I almost told the verman that his concern for my well being was touching, but I said nothing. He was Dominari and there wasn't anything personal in his attitude. It was just business.

I still had hold of Gnasher's dire blade and now I handed it back to the verman.

"Thanks for the loan," I said.

Gnasher nodded and took the blade from me. It was still sticky with Rex's blood and Gnasher held the weapon gingerly by the hilt as he reached into one of his pockets. I thought he would pull out a handkerchief to clean the blade, but instead he took out a plastic storage bag, popped the dire blade inside, sealed it and tucked the bagged weapon into his inner jacket pocket. I had no idea what the Dominari might want with a sample of Lycanthropus Rex's blood, but I'm sure they'd find some use for it.

Despite the fact the dire blade had saved all us from Rex, I was glad to be rid of the damned thing. Some weapons are simply too awful to use and a dire blade is one of them.

"Thanks for all your help," I told the verman. "I might've made it without you, but I doubt I'd have done so in one piece."

Gnasher accepted my gratitude with a nod. "It was a pleasure doing business with you, Matt. And now that we've established a relationship, perhaps we'll be able to work together again in the future."

I felt a mixture of anger and disgust upon hearing the verman's words. I wasn't the kind of guy who worked with mobsters... at least, I wasn't before that day. I bit back whatever reply I might've made, knowing it was probably unwise to piss off a Dominari Secundar who'd just helped get me out of prison. Instead, I returned his nod and left it at that. Still, I couldn't help wondering how many more times I might have to bend, if not break, my personal moral code before I managed to claw my way out of the mess I'd somehow fallen into – assuming it was even possible to get out.

Sensing I was uncomfortable Devona laid a gentle hand on my arm. "Let's go."

The five of us climbed aboard the vehicle I'd come to think of as the Scrap Tram.

"Good luck to you, Matt!" Gnasher said. Then he grinned. "You are most definitely going to need it and in industrial sized quantities."

I sighed as I took a seat up front next to Devona. "Truer words were never spoken."

As soon as we were all seated the Frankenstein verman started the engine – which sounded remarkably smooth-running given the tram's ramshackle appearance – and we started rolling down the tunnel.

As we traveled we passed other vehicles of similar design, each driven by a Baron built verman and containing a variety of cargo. Sometimes passengers – often other vermen, but just as often members of other species – and sometimes wooden crates filled with unknown contents. The Underwalk was a bustling place, in its own way as busy as the streets above us. It was like an entirely different city existed beneath Nekropolis and I marveled anew at the size and complexity of the Dominari's organization.

"So what landed you in the hoosegow?" Scorch asked. Once we'd boarded the tram both she and Tavi assumed their human guises and now she looked like a teenage girl again, but she still had the demon's gruff attitude.

I told them all about my visit to the Nightspire, my interrogation by Quillion and what the First Adjudicator had shown me.

Devona was scowling long before I was finished and when I stopped speaking she continued scowling, lost in thought. Then she shook her head as if to clear it.

"First things first," she said. There was a duffle bag on the seat next to us and she reached over, opened it, and pulled out a smaller cloth bag. She opened the bag and removed a bracelet made of tiny bones from a lizard or maybe a rodent.

Good thing Gnasher isn't here to see this, I thought.

"I stopped by Papa Chatha's before we came to get you," Devona said.

She slipped the bracelet onto my broken wrist and within seconds I could feel the bones knitting themselves back together and I could feel my smashed nose resetting itself. After a couple minutes Devona removed the bracelet and put it back into the bag.

"That should do it," she said. "Papa placed a restorative spell on the bracelet to heal any damage you sustained in Tenebrus and he also added a preservative spell to make you look as fresh as possible." She leaned forward and examined my neck. "It even healed the seam on your neck where Victor Baron reattached your head. Excellent!" She leaned back, looking very pleased with herself.

I experimentally flexed my left hand but its coordination was still off. I guess there's only so much the magic of a voodoo priest can fix. Still, I wasn't complaining. Papa had more than done right by me.

"Let me guess: if I'm going to operate incognito, I need to look like a living man, so no tinge of gray to my skin, and no obvious injuries that apparently don't hurt me."

She nodded. "If we're going to attempt to clear your name, we're probably going to run into trouble."

I smiled. "Don't we always?"

She smiled back. "When we do – difficult as this may be for you – try to avoid getting beat up. And if you do get injured, pretend like it hurts. You're the only self-willed zombie in the city, and you'll need to do everything you can to act like a living man if you want to avoid being recognized."

Sounds easy enough, right? After all, I'd spent almost four decades alive before becoming a zombie. But after being dead for several years, I wasn't sure that I could fake being alive. The big things I could do just fine. After all, I could still think and talk, but I move more stiffly than I did when I was alive and I don't notice small things like temperature changes and strong smells. Passing for one of the living wouldn't be easy.

Devona reached into the small bag again and this time pulled out a necklace made from dried chicken feet strung on braided strands of black hair – dead man's hair, I guessed. Before I could ask about it she placed the ugly thing around my neck and I felt a strange sensation of warmth pass through me briefly and then it was gone.

"What was that?"

"I knew that once we got you out of Tenebrus, Keket would search for you and the Adjudicators would probably get involved too. We need to conceal you from any tracking magic they might use so Papa created a charm that temporarily binds your spirit with that of one of the lower ranking Loa. It'll only last a few days, but during that time it will block the effects of any spell used against you. While you wear it you will be undetectable by magic and anyone who runs a magical scan on you will only detect the voodoo spirit's presence."

Having a security expert for a lover is a wonderful thing sometimes.

"What about scientific scans?" I asked.

"The charm won't affect those, but that sort of tech is rare in the city, so you should be safe enough."

"What about my scent?" I asked. There are any number of creatures in Nekropolis with enhanced senses – vampire and lykes chief among them. They'd be able to smell that I was a zombie.

Tavi was sitting behind us and he leaned forward to answer my question.

"Since you're now fresh your scent has only the vaguest hint of decay to it. Bloodborn have a somewhat similar scent so if you remain close to Devona you shouldn't arouse any suspicion."

Tavi was a lyke so I figured that his advice was sound.

"Looks like you've covered most of the bases," I said to Devona. "I can't be tracked by magic and for the most part I look and smell human again. Now all I need is a disguise."

"I've got that covered, too." She reached into the duffle bag and pulled out a black great coat with a double row of ivory buttons down the front. She thrust it at me. "Put it on."

As I donned the coat she pulled a large black hat out of the duffle. It was flattened a bit and she quickly re-shaped it and plopped it on my head.

"There! Just the thing for an escaped convict on the run," she said.

She said this lightly, trying to make a joke of it, but for the first time I realized that I was a criminal now. I might have been sentenced to Tenebrus for a crime I hadn't committed but I had chosen to escape the prison. I'd rationalized my act by telling myself that I hadn't had a real trial, let alone a formal one, and the only way I could hope to clear my name was if I was free to investigate the theft of Lord Edrigu's bone flute by myself. And while both of those things might be true it was also true that I'd broken the law. I was used to bending the law in my line of work, and when I did, I always told myself that it was necessary to get the job done and that I was doing it to find some measure of justice for my clients. But this time I hadn't just bent a law – I'd shattered it, and I'd done so for myself and no one else. I was still trying to right a wrong, so that hadn't changed, but somehow that didn't help me feel any better.

The great coat fit well, and while it was a little too stylishly neo-noir for my tastes, I had to admit it looked kind of snazzy.

"This is nice," I told Devona. "Where did you get it?"

Bogdan answered instead. "It's just something I had hanging around in my closet, but I'm glad you like it, Matt."

Great. Not only was I an escaped criminal, I was going on the run wearing one of Bogdan's hand –me downs. This day just kept going from bad to worse.

At least now I understood why Devona had dyed her hair and changed her own outfit: to disguise herself as well. She and I were too recognizable as a couple around the city, especially in the Sprawl, where we lived and worked.

"Thanks for everything," I told her, sounding less than thrilled. "Looks like I'm all set."

She frowned then, looking at me as if trying to read my thoughts, though if she'd really been trying, I'd have felt her probing my mind.

What was my problem? I should've been grateful for Devona's preparations, and I suppose on one level I was, but I was also upset about them, though I wasn't sure why. I decided to chalk up my mixed feelings to stress. After all, I'd experienced more than my fair share lately and I told myself not to worry about it.

One thing I *was* worried about was the price Devona had paid to the Dominari for their help. I was dying to ask her, but I didn't want to do so in front of her employees. I had no idea whether they'd been privy to her negotiations with the vermen – though knowing my love, I guess she'd negotiated in private – and I didn't want to put Devona on the spot by asking her for details right then. I decided to wait until we were alone.

"So now what?" I said, thinking aloud. I hadn't really intended it as a question for anyone, but Devona answered anyway.

"We can't go to any of your usual haunts –" she grinned at the joke – "so to speak. Once Keket reports your escape to Quillion, Sentinels from all over the city will be looking for you. That means we'll have to start out in the one place in Nekropolis you'd never set foot in."

I didn't like where this was headed.

"You don't mean–"

Devona grinned wider.

"Yep. Get ready, cowboy. We're heading to Westerna's."

ELEVEN

Devona and I sat at a corner table, too close to a speaker that was currently blaring "Achy Breaky Heart" by Billy Ray Cyrus. On the dance floor rows of vampires along with a smattering of other creatures wearing country and western regalia line-danced to the less –than dulcet tones of Cyrus the Virus. It made me long for the ear-splitting din of Scream Queen and Kakophonie. Like a lot of clubs in the Sprawl there were large Mind's Eye projectors hanging on the walls, transmitting images of Billy Ray cavorting around the stage as he sung. If I hadn't already been deceased I would've begged for God – any god – to strike me dead and put me out of my misery.

I'd never set foot inside Westerna's before, but the place lived down to my expectations. The walls were red brick, the floor old stained wood and the round tables and chairs looked as if they'd been stolen off a set of an old Western movie. Almost everyone here – patrons as well as servers – dressed like they'd just arrived from Nashville. It was like *Urban Cowboy* meets *Mad Monster Party*. Luckily not every customer was done up in C&W drag, so Devona and I didn't stand out too much.

Like Sinsation, Westerna's had a Victor Baron built doorman, this one looking something like a greenish skinned John Wayne with scars crosscrossing his flesh. He'd even greeted us with, "Howdy, Pilgrims," as we'd entered. Our server was a Bloodborn woman with a mound of bleach blonde hair and a Dolly Parton-sized chest who insisted on calling us "Hon" and "Sugar." I'll leave you to guess which was which. We both ordered mugs of aqua sanguis and Countess Dolly brought them over right away, giving us a smile and a saucy wink as she departed.

"Don't get any ideas," Devona warned as she took a sip of synthetic blood.

"I won't," I assured her. "Breasts like that are dangerous. I might lose an eye or something. Besides, how do you know she was winking at *me*? She might've been flirting with you."

Devona frowned and I immediately regretted my comment.

"Are you going to start being jealous of everyone we meet from now on?"

"Sorry. It was just a joke." I raised my mug to my lips and pretended to drink. I can ingest liquid and food when I want, but since I can't digest it, I eventually have to throw it up, otherwise it'll spoil inside my stomach and the resultant bacteria would begin feeding on my insides – not to mention the horrendous smell it would produce. So I avoided eating and drinking unless I absolutely had to. Since I looked fairly fresh, was dressed in black, and was in the company of a half-vampire, Devona and I had decided it would be best for me to try to pass as one of the Bloodborn, hence my ordering aqua sanguis. But I wasn't going to actually drink it unless it became necessary to maintain my disguise.

The Dominari tram had brought us to a point beneath the Sprawl and we'd emerged in a warehouse owned by the vermen only a few blocks from Westerna's. It was there that we parted ways with Bogdan, Tavi and Scorch. The members of the Midnight Watch wanted to help me clear my name, but while I appreciated the gesture, I refused to accept their assistance. For one thing I was in a Lycanthropus Rex sized pile of trouble and I didn't want to drag the others into it anymore than they already were. And to be practical the more people Devona and I had tagging along the greater the odds that we'd be recognized. Devona and the Midnight Watch had been making a name for themselves over the last couple months, and while her employees weren't exactly household names throughout the city, they were well enough known – especially in the Sprawl – that their presence was a risk we couldn't afford. They were disappointed but they understood and they wished me luck as Devona and I left the warehouse and headed for Westerna's.

We sat there for a bit, sipping our drinks and watching people make fools of themselves on the dance floor, and eventually I decided that this would be a good time to broach the subject of Devona's deal with the Dominari. I decided to be subtle about it.

"So… what did you have to give the Dominari in exchange for their help?"

OK, so I stink at subtle. But I was concerned about the price Devona had been forced to pay – what it might mean for her… and for us.

She gazed straight ahead and answered in a toneless voice. "I had to swear eternal allegiance to them and become one of their operatives."

If I'd had a working heart it would've skipped a beat right then, but she turned to me with a grin and punched me on the shoulder.

"Gotcha! You should see the look on your face!"

"Very funny."

Over the months since we'd gotten together Devona's sense of humor had developed a cruel streak. I think I've been a corrupting influence on her.

"Seriously," she said, "they only wanted information."

"That's all?" I was suspicious. The Dominari had gone to a lot of trouble to assist in my jail break – including probably damaging their working relationship with Keket. I couldn't imagine them doing so without significant compensation in return.

Devona looked down at the tabletop then and I knew whatever she'd done to help me it was serious. The only time she has trouble meeting my gaze is when she's feeling guilty.

"They wanted me to provide details of the Cathedral's security set up – which I did. At least, as much as I was able to. I was only the curator of my father's collection and not actually part of his security staff. Still, the Dominari were satisfied with the information I was able to provide."

If I told you I was shocked that would only begin to describe how I felt right then. Despite the fact that Devona had helped me stop Lord Galm's Dawnstone from being used to destroy the city, the Lord of the Bloodborn had cast his half human daughter out of his home, making it clear that, as far as he was concerned, they were no longer father and daughter. Nevertheless Devona still cared for Galm – you can't exactly love a Darklord, even when you're related to him – and I couldn't imagine her betraying him like this, no matter how much the son of a bitch deserved it.

"It's not as bad as it sounds," she said, still not meeting my gaze. "The Cathedral's security procedures are routinely revised and updated, so everything I told the Dominari was no longer current. I think they knew this, but they were happy to get whatever inside information they could. I'm not sure what they think they can use the information for, but since it's old, it won't do them much good." She looked up then. "At least, that's what I've been telling myself."

I reached across the table, took hold of Devona's hand, and gave it what I hoped was a reassuring squeeze.

"I can't tell you how much I appreciate what you've done. The risk you've taken... If Galm ever finds out..."

She smiled weakly. "If Father learns what I did I won't have to worry about being sentenced to Tenebrus. He'll hunt me down and kill me himself."

It's one thing when a person tells you they love you. It's another when they stick it out with you even when times are tough. But it's what we're willing to do for one another – the chances we take, the sacrifices we make – that truly speak to the depth of our love. Before this I'd known that Devona loved me, but I realized I hadn't appreciated just how much, and I felt like a world class idiot for being jealous of Bogdan, for being jealous of anyone. At that moment I didn't feel worthy of Devona's love and I decided right then and there that I was going to spend the rest of my life trying to become worthy of it. Of course, to do that, I was going to have to get my name off Nekropolis's Most Wanted list somehow.

Just then I saw coils of gray smoke drifting our way. They stopped next to our table, grew larger and thicker, and took on a human shape. An instant later a young – or at least young-appearing – Bloodborn male stood there, wearing a black leather jacket, white T-shirt, jeans and running shoes, a lit cigarette dangling from the corner of his pale lips. He was also wearing a backpack and he slipped it off and handed it to Devona before pulling out a seat and joining us.

"Tell me something, Shrike," I said, "I get how vampires' clothing transforms with you whenever you assume your travel forms, but how do you manage to take extra stuff like that backpack with you?"

Shrike grinned. "Magic," he said simply, and I nodded. What else?

"Thanks for coming," I said.

"Devona filled me in on the basics of what happened when she called me," Shrike said. "I gotta tell you, you have some of the worst luck of anyone I know, living, dead, or in between."

I sighed. "Wish I could argue with you on that."

Devona opened the backpack and quickly checked the contents.

"This looks good. Thanks." She looked up and met Shrike's gaze. "Did you have any trouble getting into our apartment?"

"I didn't even try," Shrike said. He took a long drag on his cigarette, and while the end glowed, the cig didn't decrease in size. It never did, and as far as I know, Shrike always had the same endlessly burning butt in his mouth. When he exhaled smoke, his entire body grew faint until you could see through it, solidifying again a moment later. "There are Sentinels posted on the corner for blocks in all directions around your building. Real subtle, huh? But I managed to pick up some goodies here and there for you. Maybe not as good as your regular gear, but hopefully it'll do."

Like Lazlo, Shrike's an old friend, and Devona knew we could count on him in a pinch, which was why she'd contacted him before heading for Tenebrus to break me out. She knew we'd need weapons and Shrike was the only one we knew who could move about the city undetected, given the nature of his travel form.

Devona handed the backpack over to me and it was my turn to examine the contents. There were a number of minor magical items from Hop Frog's and I chose several and tucked them away in various pockets in my coat. That is, in *Bogdan's* coat. I left the remainder of the magic items for Devona to choose from. She usually doesn't carry weapons, preferring to rely on her formidable intelligence, supernatural strength and speed, as well as her psychic abilities. But considering our current situation, I figured she might want to stock up on some extra insurance.

Best of all was the gun Shrike had found for me. It was a .45 instead of the 9mm I usually carry, but escaped convicts can't be choosers. A 9mm carries more ammo and the velocity is better, and there's less recoil, which makes it easier for me, with my slower zombie reflexes, to use. Still, the .45 has better stopping power, which makes it a decent weapon on the streets of Nekropolis. I removed the weapon from the backpack and tucked it into my jacket along with the box of ammo Shrike had brought along.

"I don't suppose you managed to score silver bullets?"

"Sorry," Shrike said, "just the regular."

I nodded. It would have to do. I returned the pack to Devona and she took the rest of the contents for herself. My vox had been taken from me back at the Nightspire so Shrike gave me his and I slipped it into one of my pockets.

"I know I don't have to ask if you were followed," I said to Shrike, "but as I'm more paranoid than usual right now, I'm going to anyway. Were you?"

Shrike looked as if my question had deeply wounded him. "Matt, I'm surprised by your lack of faith in me. For Christ's sake–" He didn't get any farther, for upon speaking the holy name his mouth burst into flame.

Shrike cursed as he attempted to beat out the flames with both hands. I sighed and handed him my mug of aqua sanguis. He downed the contents in a single gulp, extinguishing the flames but leaving his tongue and lips burnt and blackened. He took another long drag with his cigarette and this time when his body re-solidified his mouth was healed.

"You really need to learn how to watch your language," I told him for perhaps the hundredth time since we met. He just grinned at me like he always does and not for the first time I wondered if Shrike "accidentally" spoke holy names as simply another aspect of an eccentric street persona. After all, the man was nothing if not theatrical in his presentation.

"Well, at least we're armed," I said. I'd felt naked without some sort of weaponry on my person, and even though what Shrike had procured for us wasn't top of the line by a long shot, it was a damn sight better than nothing, and I felt a lot better than I had upon first walking into Westerna's.

"So what's the word on the street?" I asked Shrike. "Is anyone aware that I'm a wanted zombie?"

Shrike shook his head. "I don't think so. You know how it works. When the Adjudicators pull someone off the street and toss them into Tenebrus, word may never get out. As far as their friends and family are concerned, they've just gone missing – and since there are any number of reasons why someone might end up with their face on a milk carton in this city–"

"No one's ever sure what happened to them," I finished. Good. Bad enough that the Sentinels were looking for me, but as long as no one else was aware that I'd been sentenced to Tenebrus and escaped, I could–

Westerna's Mind's Eye projectors were showing a video from a homegrown group called the Hunchback Forty, when all of a sudden they went black, taking the music with them. The club's patrons booed and hissed, and since more of them were vampires, they had hissing down to an art. But the bartender shouted for everyone to be quiet.

"Acantha's just come on the Mind's Eye with a special broadcast," he said. "I'm going to switch over to it."

There were murmurs of surprise and delight from the crowd, but Devona and I looked at each other and said the same thing: "Uh-oh."

The Mind's Eyes activated once more, this time showing Acantha's transmission. As usual, since the image was captured by the camerasnakes on her head, Acantha herself wasn't visible, but the voice came through loud and clear. The person her cameras were trained on was very familiar to me, as it had been less than a day since I'd seen him.

Quillion.

The voice, however, was Acantha's.

"Hello, Nekropolis! You're live on the scene with Acantha! I'm standing inside the Nightspire talking with Brother Quillion, the First Adjudicator. Thank you *so* much for granting me this exclusive interview, Quillion. I'm sure my viewers are aware of how rarely Adjudicators speak to the media."

Implied in that was a big screw you to the city's other media outlets: *The Tome*, the *Daily Atrocity*, Bedlam 66.6 and others – as Acantha publicly gloated over her "exclusive."

Quillion, looking stiff and uncomfortable on camera, nodded.

"You're welcome, Acantha."

"I know you're a busy man, so let's get right down to it. As I understand it, you have a message you wish to deliver to my viewers."

"That's right." Quillion's gaze shifted slightly upward, and he was now speaking directly to Acantha's camera-snakes, and thus to everyone in the city who was watching Acantha's unscheduled broadcast which, given the gorgon's popularity, was doubtless one hell of a lot of people.

I had a good idea what was coming next.

"Citizens of Nekropolis," Quillion began. "Many of you are no doubt familiar with Matthew Richter, a self-willed zombie, who for several years has worked in the Sprawl as a private investigator. During that time he was reputed to have served his clients well. In fact, Acantha recently featured a brief interview with him on her program."

"Yes, I did, Quillion," Acantha broke in, more because she loved being on a first name basis with an Adjudicator than out of any real need to confirm his statement.

Quillion went on.

"Whatever Mr. Richter's past deeds, he was recently found guilty of a very serious crime, the nature of which I am not at liberty to divulge at this time, and he was sentenced to Tenebrus. As impossible as it sounds, Mr. Richter somehow managed to escape and is believed to be at large. I've alerted every Sentinel in the city to be on the lookout for Mr. Richter, but I wish to bring him back into custody as swiftly as possible. For that reason, I'm offering a substantial reward to anyone who can capture Mr. Richter and bring to him the Nightspire…" He paused. "Relatively intact."

"When you say substantial…" Acantha said.

"Five hundred thousand darkgems," Quillion said, speaking the obscenely large number without so much as blinking.

I was impressed by the size of the reward Quillion was offering. I hadn't realized I was so dangerous. Evidently Acantha was impressed too for she let out a low whistle and the image of Quillion started shaking. I guessed her camerasnakes had become overly excited by the Adjudicator's news. Acantha made a few soothing sounds to calm her pets and the image steadied.

"You heard it here first, folks," the gorgon said, sounding far too pleased with herself. After the way I'd humiliated her at Sinsation she had to be absolutely loving this.

"And for those of you who need a reminder of what Matthew Richter looks like…"

Quillion's image faded from Westerna's Mind's Eyes to be replaced by a still image of me. It was one from my disastrous interview with Acantha, pulled from her memory, no doubt. She'd selected a moment toward the end of the interview, right before I'd hit her with Anansi's Web. I was scowling and my eyes blazed with anger. I looked like I was ready to kill her.

Shrike turned to me. "I think you should probably avoid speaking to reporters in the future." He glanced back at the frozen image of my face. "Seriously."

The picture changed again, this time to an image of Acantha herself. Off to the right the extended length of a camerasnake curving away from her head was visible and I guessed one of her pets had stretched itself out in front of her face so it could film her.

"Matthew Richter: once thought to be a hero, now a wanted fugitive," she said. "How long will he remain at large? With five hundred thousand darkgems as a reward for his capture, my guess is not very long." She gave her audience a cat-that-ate-the-canary smile. "This is Acantha, saying good night and good hunting."

The image went to black and several seconds later the Hunchback Forty returned to Westerna's Mind's Eyes.

Devona, Shrike and I sat for a moment, staring

silently at the closest Mind's Eye. After a bit Devona turned to me, her normally pale complexion ashen.

"This is bad," she said.

"Extremely," Shrike added.

I would've loved to disagree with them, but I couldn't.

"Given the size of the reward Quillion is offering, every professional bounty hunter and mercenary in the city will be out looking for you," Devona said.

"Not to mention all the amateurs who'll be tempted by that money," Shrike said. "Hell, if you weren't my friend, I'd try to collect the reward myself."

"I appreciate your self restraint," I said drily. But I knew they were both right. The whole damned city would be trying to find me – which is exactly what Quillion wanted, and Keket too, mostly likely.

"What are you going do?" Shrike asked.

"Try to clear my name. What else can I do? Not that I have the faintest idea where to start. We don't have any solid suspects and I have no idea what the object stolen from Edrigu is, let alone why someone would want it."

"It's obvious why they chose you," Devona said. "Or rather, why they chose your body. You carry the mark of Edrigu on your hand. Whoever stole your body and animated it knew that mark would not only gain you entrance into Edrigu's stronghold, but it would also allow you to enter his bedchamber – and more importantly, to leave it without being stopped by his guards."

Clearing my name wasn't the only reason I had for wanting to discover who had stolen Edrigu's bone flute. The thief had used my body to commit the crime, with *used* being the operative word. One of the things about being a zombie is that, bereft of the full range of physical sensations you enjoyed while alive, you can become detached and remote if you're not careful. More than that, you can start feeling that you're a thing, no more alive than a brick wall or a piece of furniture. An object instead of a person. And that's exactly how the thief had treated me – as an object, a tool, a means to an end. But I wasn't an object. I was Matthew Fucking Richter and when I found the son of a bitch who'd stolen my body and used it like a remote control toy I intended to make damn sure he or she knew who I truly was.

"The solution to all this seems simple enough to me," Shrike said. "You find yourself a good forensic sorcerer, someone skilled enough to use their magic to discover the identity of whoever hijacked your body. I mean, there have to be some magical traces of them clinging to your body, right? Then you..." He trailed off. "Never mind. It's a stupid idea. The bounty on your head is so large, any sorcerer you contact would likely just cast a stasis spell on you and hand you over to Quillion."

"Yep," I said. "And because so many bounty hunters will be out looking for me, I can't consult my usual sources." Waldemar at the Great Library, Skully, Arval the ghoul restaurant ownerand a dozen lesser but still valuable contacts – all of them would be watched by Sentinels and bounty hunters alike. If I went anywhere near them, I'd be captured for sure."

Thinking about bounty hunters reminded me about Overkill. Acantha hadn't been the only person I'd humiliated at Sinsation and – assuming she hadn't had anything to do with the theft of my body, something I hadn't entirely ruled out – she'd be after me like the rest of her mercenary minded brothers and sisters. If Acantha had taken great delight in delivering news of Quillion's reward, Overkill would be ecstatic at the thought of getting a rematch with me, especially one that held the extra incentive of such a large paycheck. She'd no doubt be disappointed by Quillion's desire I be delivered to him 'relatively intact', but for five hundred thousand darkgems I'm sure she'd find a way to live with it.

Given the seriousness of my dilemma I would've considered asking Varvara for help. The Demon Queen isn't exactly a friend of mine but she finds me amusing, which is more valuable in her mind than friendship anyway. She's been something of a patroness to me since I arrived in Nekropolis, but even so, I'm careful not to ask too many favors of her. It's never a good idea to become too indebted to a demon, let alone their queen. But I wouldn't get a chance to appeal to Varvara's generosity this time. If what Quillion had told me was true, Varvara – like the other four Darklords – was still sleeping, recharging her energy after the last Renewal Ceremony. So no help there.

I was starting to feel hopeless and Devona, likely sensing my emotions through our psychic link, reached over and gave my arm a squeeze. "You're a detective, Matt, and a damned good one. You'll figure something out."

"I wish I shared your confidence in me." Truth was I relied on my network of contacts far more than I liked to admit, even to myself. Without them I wasn't sure I'd be able to discover the identity of the thief who'd stolen Edrigu's bone flute and framed me for the crime – not with the entire city out hunting for me, that is.

I was so stuck on where to turn for help that I considered trying to contact the Dominari, but I didn't consider it for very long. For one thing I wanted as little to do with the mobsters as possible, and for another I didn't want to think about what sort of price they might charge for their assistance this time. But in the end the reason I decided against contacting the Dominari was a purely practical one: they'd be just as likely to want to collect the bounty on me as anyone else in the city. As I'd learned from Gnasher the Dominari was nothing if not all business and five hundred thousand darkgems would make a nice profit for simply – pardon the expression – ratting me out to Quillion.

What I needed was someone who not only was tuned in to what was happening in Nekropolis on a daily basis but who wasn't someone I consulted very often. Someone who kept a low profile – so low that no one would even realize he was an information source.

Then it came to me and a slow grin spread across my face. Maybe – just maybe – I wasn't beaten yet.

I grabbed Shrike's hand and gave it a quick shake.

"Thanks again for everything, but Devona and I have to get moving."

"You've got an idea," Devona said with a smile. It wasn't a question and she didn't seem surprised in the least. Is it any wonder I love her?

"I do. I think it's time we paid a visit to the House of Mysterious Secrets."

"This is some kind of joke, right?"

Devona stood on the sidewalk, hands on her hips, head cocked at an appraising angle. I stood next to her, hands in the pockets of my new (Bogdan's old) coat. When Devona had procured my disguise she'd had no idea what crime I'd been arrested for, so she hadn't brought me any gloves. But since Edrigu's mark on my hand was what we used to call a 'distinguishing feature' back when I was a cop, I figured I should keep that hand concealed as often as possible.

We stood outside a large manor house surrounded by a high wrought iron fence with nasty looking spikes on the tips of the bars. We were still in the Sprawl, not far from the Grotesquerie, and the gamey smell of zoo animals hung thick in the air. I could tell because Devona kept wrinkling her nose.

The manor was constructed entirely out of black wood and brick and its grounds were overgrown with weeds and decorative shrubs that had long ago been left to grow wild. The shutters – black, of course – hung askew on their hinges, the windows were dirt-smeared and cracked and the entire structure listed slightly to the right, as if the manor were perpetually on the verge of collapse. Ravens perched everywhere – on the chimney, the roof, the fence... twenty-nine at my count. A low lying fog-like mist clung to the ground, the whitish vapors roiling slowly as if they possessed some sort of sinister life.

"The only thing missing is a miniature storm cloud hanging overhead discharging the occasional lightning bolt," Devona added. "It's the stereotypical haunted house. It's more than a cliché – it's a cliché of a cliché!"

"That's the whole point," I said. "In Nekropolis a place like this is as unremarkable as a ranch house in a suburban neighborhood back on Earth. It's the perfect disguise."

"Disguise for what?" Devona asked suspiciously.

I just smiled. "You'll see."

I walked up to the main gate. It wasn't locked and it swung open easily at my touch. But even though the gate's motion was as smooth as if it had just been oiled, a creaking groan that sounded almost human filled the air. Once the gate was all open I turned to Devona and gave her a courtly bow, or at least a reasonable version thereof.

"After you, milady."

Devona gave me a look that said she wasn't in the mood to play and walked through. I followed and the gate swung shut behind us of its own accord. Devona didn't even bother looking back over her shoulder at it.

"Cute," she said sarcastically.

We disturbed the layer of ground mist as we walked, but it closed right up behind us, leaving no evidence of our passage. We found the front walk by accident more than anything else and we continued along it until we reached the porch. The ravens roosting on the property made no sound as we approached, but they kept their beady eyed gazes upon us as if they were trying to determine whether we were up to no good.

A quartet of cracked stone columns held up the roof over the porch and spiders had spun elaborate webs between them. Something was caught in one of the webs and I took a closer look.

"Help meeeeeee!" came a tiny voice.

I reached out and with a thumb and forefinger carefully plucked the human headed fly from the webbing.

"Get on back to the Foundry, you slacker," I said.

I flicked the human headed fly off my fingersand his wings began to buzz. He circled our heads a couple times before straightening his course and making a beeline – or rather a flyline – in the general direction of the Boneyard.

"A little guy like that needs to be extra careful when he decides to take a flight on the wild side," I said.

I stepped up to the large front door – black, naturally – took hold of the thick iron ring knocker, lifted it, and let it fall once, twice, three times, then I stepped back to wait.

"Let me guess," Devona said. "The door will creak open and a scary-looking butler will poke his head out and say, 'Good eve-hu-ning' in a sepulchral tone."

"Exactly what does a sepulchral tone sound like anyway?" I asked.

The door opened then, and true to Devona's guess, it did so with a creaking sound. But instead of a scary butler an ordinary human man stood there. He was tall, in his early to mid-thirties, with a round face, thinning straight black hair, glasses and a neatly trimmed black mustache. He wore a navy-blue polo shirt, jeans and running shoes.

"Can I help you?" he said, speaking in a pleasant deep voice that was sonorous rather than sepulchral. He paused, frowned as he gave me a closer look, then he smiled.

"Matt!" I didn't recognize you in your new get-up." He turned to Devona. "And you must be Devona." His frown returned. "Funny, I thought you had blonde hair."

"She normally does," I said. "We're traveling in disguise right now."

The man nodded. "Of course. I should've realized." He opened the door wider and stepped back. "Come on in. My House of Mysterious Secrets is your House of Mysterious Secrets."

He smiled as his joke while Devona and I walked past him. Once we were inside he closed the door and entered a code on an electronic keypad on the wall next to it. There was the sound of locks engaging and I knew

the manor's impressive security system was now activated.

Devona had of course seen the keypad and had no
doubt noticed how out of place it was with the manor's
outside appearance. But that was nothing compared to
the place's inside. We now stood within a pleasant looking foyer more suited to an upper middleclass house on
Earth than a haunted mansion in Nekropolis.

Devona turned to me with a questioning look.

"Allow me to introduce you to the master of this for-
bidding edifice," I said. "The enigmatic and eldritch
being known only by the sinister appellation of... *David
Zelasco*!"

David gave Devona a smile.

"Hi."

David led us through his tastefully furnished home to
a workroom toward the back of the manor. It was a
large room with long tables lining the walls, a dozen
computer monitors with keyboards resting on top of
them. With the exception of a half empty liter bottle
of soda and a crinkled bag of nacho chips near one of
the monitors, the tables were clear and free of clutter.
It looked like a normal enough office space, except
each of the monitors had a raven perching on top of
it, the birds standing motionless, connected to the
monitors by wires plugged into the backs of their
heads. Images flashed across the monitor screens in
fast-motion, scenes from all five of Nekropolis's Dominions.

A wheeled office chair sat in front of one of the monitors and David went over to it and sat down.

Devona stepped closer to one of the ravens and examined it more closely. "These things are some kind of machines, aren't they? And I bet the ones outside are too."

David nodded as he turned the chair around to face us and sat down. "They're partially robotic. They were specially designed for me by–"

Devona held up a hand to stop him. "Victor Baron, right?"

David smiled. "Who else? I've got about a hundred or so working at any given time. They fly all over the city, recording video and audio. When their memories are full, they fly back here and I download the information they've gathered into my mainframe. That's when the real work starts."

Devona reached out a finger to prod one of the ravens. The bird gave her an angry squawk, startling her. It seemed to glare at her, as if to say, *Do you mind?* and then became motionless again.

Devona turned to face David.

"Real work?"

He nodded again. "I go through the hours of video my ravens collect, looking for something useful."

Devona gave me a mildly frustrated look which I interpreted as meaning *Would somebody just tell me what's going on here?*

But before I could say anything, an electronic tone sounded from the monitor closest to him.

"Excuse me for a moment."

David swiveled around to face the monitor and typed a few strokes on the keyboard. The video download on the screen paused, David minimized it and brought up a new window. This one showed a man in his early sixties with straight black hair, glasses and a friendly looking if somewhat long and rectangular face. The display showed him from the mid-chest up, revealing that he was wearing a black Ramones T-shirt. When the man spoke, he did so in a mild New England accent.

"Hey, David, how you doing? My publisher's breathing down my neck about the new book and I need something to send him real soon. You got anything good for me?"

"I've put together a few things for you, Steve. I'll email them to you right now."

David typed a few more keystrokes and hit SEND. A couple of seconds passed and then the man on the other end – who obviously was sitting in front of his own computer – said, "Got it! Thanks, David!"

"No problem. Take a look at the files and see if anything strikes you as interesting. If not let me know and I'll see what else I can dig up for you."

"You got it. Thanks again, man. From now on I'm going to start calling you Wint-o-green, because you're a lifesaver!"

The display went black as the man disconnected, and with a few more keystrokes, David closed the video chat window and resumed downloading the raven's information.

"That call," Devona said. "You have a direct connection with Earth?"

"Not exactly," David said. "I have to go through Nekropolis's Aethernet to connect to Earth's Internet – which isn't as easy as it sounds. The first thing you have to do–"

David's something of a techhead and I knew if I didn't cut him off right away we'd end up learning far more about Nekropolis –to Earth communication than we wanted to.

"You've just witnessed David in action," I said. "Horror is a way of life here in Nekropolis but back on Earth it's big business. Books, movies, comics, videogames… The people who create them all need ideas, and when they run out, they get in touch with David."

Devona looked at the ravens with new understanding. "You go through all the video they collect, looking for ideas to pass on to your customers," she said to David.

He nodded. "The business has been in the family for a long time – almost since the founding of Nekropolis. Back then ideas had to be sent out by courier and carried to Earth through Varvara's mirror. But as you can see, we've updated quite a bit since then, which has made the whole operation a lot more efficient and has allowed us to expand a great deal." David smiled proudly. "These days, almost every horror professional on Earth uses our service."

"It's very impressive," Devona said, "but why all the secrecy? The faux haunted house, the robotic ravens…

Why not just advertise what you do? You'd get a lot more people coming in to tell you their stories that way."

"True," David said, "but I'd also get a lot of people who aren't comfortable with the idea of their secrets being sent to Earth so that artists can create entertainment for humans. More than one of my ancestors found that out the hard way and ended up having to accept forced retirement, if you know what I mean."

"Of course, David doesn't get all his information from his ravens," I said.

"That's right. People drop by now and again to tell me their stories and I pay them for their time. That's how I met Matt, as a matter of fact."

Devona looked at me and I shrugged. "It's an easy way to pick up some extra darkgems when the investigation business is slow."

"I just wish you'd let me use *your* story, Matt," David said. "I know any number of people who'd love to get their hands on it."

I shook my head firmly. "No way. You know I like to keep a low profile."

David gave me a wry smile.

"OK, I admit that's something I haven't done an especially good job of lately."

"That's putting it mildly," he said. "I caught Acantha's broadcast."

"You and everyone else within range of a Mind's Eye," I said.

"You have to fill me in on all the details. You've told me some good stories before, but I bet this one beats them all."

"I'll have to take a rain check on that. Besides, the story's not finished yet. That's why we're here. I was framed, and in order to prove it, I had to get out of Tenebrus. But now that I'm free–"

"You can't go to any of your usual sources because you're a wanted man," David said. "Got it. I'll do whatever I can to help."

I briefly explained the basics of how my head was stolen and my body used to steal an object from Lord Edrigu.

"I'm hoping that one of your ravens might've recorded footage of either the attack on me or of my body entering and leaving the Reliquary."

"It's possible, I suppose," David said, "but I only have so many birds out at a time and Nekropolis is a big place. The odds aren't great that they collected the footage you're looking for."

"I know, but it's the best shot I've got right now at learning who did this to me and why."

David looked thoughtful. "Since my business is gathering ideas I program my ravens to wander the city randomly for hours at a time. It's more like fishing than hunting. I send them out and hope they manage to bring back something I can use. They don't perform systematic searches of designated areas. So even if they managed to record the real thief, it'll take me some time to search through all the most recent video and find it.

Don't get me wrong: I'm happy to do it. After all, I have to review the video eventually anyway. I just want you to be aware of how long it might take – assuming I find anything at all."

"I understand and I appreciate it," I said. "In return I promise to come back and tell you everything that happened in as much detail as you can stand. Provided I survive, that is."

Devona swatted me on the arm. "Stop that kind of talk. It's defeatist."

"What you call defeatism, I call realism," I said.

In response she swatted me again.

"So what are you two going to do in the meantime?" David asked.

"I'm not sure," I confessed. "I need to find out as much as I can about the object that was stolen from Edrigu." I described the bone flute to David. "Does it sound familiar to you?"

He shook his head. "No, I'd suggest you pay Waldemar a visit at the Great Library, but that's probably out of the question right now."

"It's too bad my father and I aren't on speaking terms anymore," Devona said. "He's spent thousands of years collecting objects of power. There's a good chance he'd know what the flute is."

I started to reply but I paused as a new thought struck me. Could Galm be behind the bone flute's theft? There were all kinds of ways to build a collection, not all of them legitimate, and the Darklords were constantly plotting against each other one way or another. And

Galm had no love for me. Perhaps it had amused him to use my body to steal something from a rival Dark-lord. Or maybe it had been Talaith. She'd had run ins with Edrigu before and she absolutely loathed me. Maybe she'd decided to kill two birds with one stone and...

But then I derailed that particular train of thought. According to Quillion all the Darklords, along with Fa-ther Dis, were still sleeping off the after effects of the Renewal Ceremony. Unless either Galm or Talaith had woken up early, they couldn't be behind the theft.

"You could try asking someone else about the bone flute," David said. "After all, Galm's not the only col-lector in the city."

"You got someone else in mind?" I asked.

"Maybe. I hear a lot of things in my line of work. For a couple years now I've been hearing rumors about a Bloodborn who owns a used bookstore in the Sprawl – not far from where you two live, if I remember cor-rectly."

I nodded. "The store's called Nosferatomes. Devona and I've been there before. What have you heard about the owner?"

"Nothing concrete," David said. "Just hints, really. But supposedly the owner – his name's Orlock – collects more than just old books. A lot of people come to tell me their stories and some of them are well connected to the seamier side of Nekropolis – or at least they like to make out they are: mercenaries, thieves, self-styled adventurers of one sort or another..." He gave me a meaningful look at this point. "And some of them claim to have done work for Orlock. None of them told me what exactly they did for him, but it wasn't hard to read between the lines."

"You think they acquired items for his collection," I said.

"And if he's a collector then he might be able to identify the bone flute for us," Devona added.

David nodded. "But like I said it's only a suspicion. My ravens have captured video of some questionable characters going into Orlock's shop, but that doesn't prove anything."

"Maybe not," I said, "but it's a lead and it's more than we had when we came in here. Thanks, David."

"You're welcome. Let me know what you learn about Orlock. I might be able to use the information for one of my clients. In the meantime I'll start searching through my ravens' recent footage and see if I can't find any video of the attack on you. If I do, I'll give you a call."

I gave David the number of Shrike's vox, then we thanked him again and said our goodbyes. He offered to see us to the door but I told him to go ahead and get started reviewing the video. We'd show ourselves out.

As Devona and I stepped onto the front porch she said, "You know, those ravens of David's could have all kinds of security applications. You think he might be interested in doing some work for us on the side?"

"You mean for you," I said.

Devona frowned. "I don't understand."

We continued talking as we walked down the porch steps and headed across the mist enshrouded grounds toward the gate.

"The Midnight Watch is *your* business. I just help out from time to time."

Devona didn't respond right away, and I knew I'd said something wrong, though I wasn't exactly sure what.

"I thought it was *our* business, Matt. Something we did together."

Aw, crap, I thought. Out loud, I said, "Look, I didn't mean—"

She cut me off. "I understand that you're used to working alone… living alone, being alone. You lived like that for years after you became a zombie and probably for more years before that. But you're not alone anymore. I don't understand why it's so hard for you to get that."

Right then being alone sounded pretty good. When you're alone you don't have to deal with other people's expectations and feelings and you don't have to worry about saying or doing the wrong thing and hurting them. Being alone means freedom and no hassles. There's only one problem with it: it's damn lonely.

As we passed through the gate and onto the sidewalk, leaving the House of Mysterious Secrets behind, I struggled to come up with some kind of reply that might salve Devona's hurt feelings. But my poor zombie brain was coming up empty, so instead I started looking around for a cab. It would take about twenty minutes to walk to Nosferatomes from where we were, but given my current fugitive status I figured the less I was seen in public the better. Our disguises had worked well enough so far but I didn't want to push it. The traffic was relatively light just then and there were no cabs for hire around. No real surprise there, since cabbies tend to frequent Sybarite Street, where the best clubs and restaurants in the Sprawl are located. Still, I'd hoped there might be at least one cab around, maybe even Lazlo, roaring up to the curb in his ramshackle machine, as he so often does when I need a ride. Riding with him would be a calculated risk, since I'm known to do it so often, but at that point I figured it would be one worth taking. But there was no sign of the demon.

I remembered what Quillion had told me about a Sentinel "interviewing" Lazlo and I hoped he was simply busy driving another fare around town. I knew from first hand experience that Sentinels weren't exactly the most gentle of creatures and I feared my friend might be laid up somewhere, metaphorically – or who knows, maybe literally – licking his wounds as he recovered from the Sentinel's little chat with him.

I turned to Devona. "Looks like we're going to have to hoof it."

Her frown deepened into a scowl and I thought she wasn't going to let me get away with trying to change the subject, but then she looked past me and her eyes widened and I knew our discussion was about to be tabled.

I turned around and saw a man striding purposefully down the sidewalk toward us. He wore a long black trench coat open to reveal a chiseled bare chest and well defined abs. Black jeans and worn cowboy boots completed his outfit. He was a handsome black man with mahogany skin, a shaved head and piercing, almost startling green eyes. He appeared to be unarmed but I didn't need to frisk him to know he wasn't carrying any weapons. You don't need to when you *are* a weapon.

The first of the bounty hunters had found us.

TWELVE

The man stopped when he was within half a dozen feet of us and smiled.

"Hey, Matt. What's up? Nice coat. Good to see you finally got a little style going on."

His voice was deep and rich and though his tone was relaxed on the surface it held an underlying current of tension. I knew exactly how he felt.

"Hey yourself, Malik," I said, ignoring his comment about Bogdan's hand-me-down. "It's been a while."

"Since we tangled with the Incarnator, remember?"

"How could I forget? We had a hell of a time figuring out which body he was inhabiting. If he hadn't kept that habit of his regardless of which body he wore–"

Malik laughed. "Right! He always kept sniffing and swallowing, like he had sinus trouble no matter who he was possessing. How weird was that?"

"Weird but useful," I said. "We might never have caught him otherwise."

We'd kept our gazes locked on one another as we talked, only pretending to enjoy our little trip down memory lane. In truth we were gauging each other – opening feints that were merely a warm up for what was to come.

"Matt, who is this?" Devona asked.

I hadn't forgotten about her, but there was no way I was going to take my eyes off Malik. I continued to keep my gaze trained on him as I answered.

"This gentleman goes by the street name of Crossbreed but his friends just call him Malik. We've worked together a couple times when we had jobs that ended up overlapping. As you might've gathered we took down the Incarnator together."

"And we recovered the Lost Shroud of Glorian, don't forget that," Malik said.

"Neither of us got paid on that one."

"Only because you insisted on destroying the shroud when you learned what it could do." Malik's tone took on a colder edge as he said this.

"What can I say? I have a thing about handing over deadly magical artifacts to psychopaths, which both of our clients happened to be."

"Maybe so, but their money would've spent as good as any sane man's."

"Money can't buy self-respect."

"You can't eat, drink, or screw self respect." Malik had continued smiling as we'd talked but now his smile fell away. "Speaking of money there's a pretty hefty price on your head these days, Matt. You've always had a

knack for getting in trouble, but *damn, son!* Five hundred
thousand darkgems' worth is serious even for you!"

I felt Devona's mind reaching for mine.

I can see that you two aren't exactly friends. Just how dangerous is he?

Let's just say you wouldn't want to go up against him
in a dark alley. Or a lit one. Or anywhere else for that
matter.

Aloud, I said, "And you've come to collect."

He shrugged. "Someone has to cash in. Might as well
be me. No offense."

"None taken. How did you figure you'd find me
here?"

Malik's smile returned. "Everyone else is watching
your usual hangouts, but they're idiots. We may have
only worked together a couple times but I know you
well enough. Anyone else in your situation would've
had the good sense to go into hiding, but not you. I
knew you'd try to find a way out of the mess you're in
and that means you need information. Since you can't
make use of your regular sources, I guessed you'd go to
David." His smile widened into a grin. "Looks like I
guessed right."

I suppose I should've expected this. With the number
of people out looking for me someone was bound to
have figured out where I'd go.

"Congratulations. I'm sure this'll get you a nomination for mercenary of the year."

Malik's body spasmed from head to toe as his bones,
muscles and flesh went through a rapid transformation.

His green eyes turned a glowing crimson, his teeth became sharp and long, his hands sprouted deadly looking ebon claws and his skin sprouted scaled armor.

"Now you see why Malik calls himself Crossbreed," I said to Devona. "You know how Overkill has worked to make herself the ultimate human? Well, Malik has made himself into the ultimate monster, courtesy of the genetic expertise of the good Doctor Moreau."

Just looking at Malik you could pick out vampire, demon and lyke in him and I'm sure there's more than a few other less obvious monster genes in the mix as well.

Devona frowned. "I didn't think it was possible to combine the DNA of Darkfolk like that."

Malik bared his mouthful of fangs in a savage grin and when he spoke his voice was rough and guttural.

"It's not – for anyone else, that is. Dr. M told me that every time he tried it before the subject died. But the procedure worked for me." His smile grew wider, making him look something like a shark in humanoid form. "Guess I'm just that tough. So, Matt… what's it going to be? You going to make this easy and come with me peacefully, or are you going to give me trouble? Please say it's the latter. It'll be more fun that way."

"You know, Malik, finding me isn't the same thing as catching me."

I can't draw a gun as fast as I could when I was alive, but what I now lack in speed I make up in technique. I had my .45 out and aimed at Malik's chest before he could react. At least, that's what I told myself. But then he laughed and I knew the only reason he hadn't attacked was because he didn't consider my weapon a threat.

"You can't hurt me with that thing," he said, sounding half amused, half insulted.

"You know the kind of ammo I pack is tailormade to put a hurt on just about any creature walking, stalking or sliming its way through the streets – and that includes you."

"Ordinarily that would be true. But you're carrying a .45 instead of your usual 9mm. My guess is your regular piece – along with your homemade ammo – was taken away before you were tossed into Tenebrus and what you got there is a replacement. Besides, you forget who you're talking to." He sniffed the air a couple times. "I can smell that the bullets are normal."

"Oh, well. Can't blame a guy for bluffing." I raised my gun barrel several inches and fired, emptying the contents of my weapon into Malik's face.

Greenish-black blood splattered into the air and Malik staggered backward, though he didn't fall and he didn't cry out, though the injuries he suffered had to hurt like hell. I aimed for his head because brain tissue is complex and takes more time to regenerate. It would be a few moments before Malik regrew enough of his brain to get his shit together and attack, giving Devona and me a few precious seconds in which to act.

As Malik leaned over, hands on his face to hold as much of it together as possible while he healed, blood streaming onto the sidewalk, I quickly glanced at the oncoming traffic and saw what we needed. I sent a mental image to Devona of what I wanted her to do and she stepped forward and grabbed hold of one of Malik's arms. Devona may be short and slender, but she packs a lot of muscle into her small frame and she hurled Malik into the street as if he weighed no more than a child.

As I said earlier, traffic was light that night, but "light" doesn't mean "nonexistent," and Malik landed directly in the path of a silver Volkswagen Beetle covered with long sharp spikes. He still hadn't recovered enough from the gunshot wounds to his face to think clearly, and instead of getting out of the car's path, he rose to his feet and just stood there bleeding onto the street, and the VW slammed into him at full speed. Malik let out a – pardon the pun – piercing shriek of agony as he was impaled on the VW's hood spikes. The impact caused the car to swerve, but it didn't stop. The driver – who was completely hidden from view due to the spikes – managed to straighten the VW out and zoomed off with Malik still pinned screaming to its hood. One thing Nekropolitans can always be counted on for – wherever they're going, they're in a hurry to get there and they don't let anything slow them down. Certainly nothing as inconsequential as a body stuck to their car.

I started to reload my gun while we watched the VW speed away, carrying Malik with it.

"Nice throw," I said to Devona.

"Nice shooting," she said. "That won't stop him for long, you know."

"He won't be able to heal fully until he pulls himself off those spikes. We'll be long gone by then."

"He's not going to be too thrilled with you when he does finally get free."

I sighed. "At this point, what's it matter if I make one more mortal enemy?"

"True," she said.

Just then a vehicle came swerving erratically down the street toward us and Devona and I automatically stepped back from the curb. When we saw the vehicle was Lazlo's cab we stepped back a couple feet farther, just to be cautious. Good thing, too, because when Lazlo pulled up he parked halfway on the sidewalk. The cab's windows were rolled down and he leaned out to speak to us.

"Sorry I'm late. You wouldn't believe how many people have been tailing me since Quillion announced the bounty on you. Even with all my considerable driving skills it took me a while to shake them."

Lazlo might have had an easier time of it if his cab wasn't one of the most recognizable vehicles in the city. But I didn't want to hurt his feelings, so I didn't say anything.

"You're sure you managed to shake them?" I looked up and down the street, but since no vehicles roared up to the curb, bounty hunters hanging out of open windows with their guns blazing, I figured we were safe enough for the moment.

I turned to Devona. "What do you think?"

"I think we're going to have people gunning for us whether we walk or ride. Riding's faster."

"Good point."

Devona and I climbed into the back of Lazlo's cab and I told him to take us to Nosferatomes. I'd barely gotten the words out of my mouth when Lazlo tromped on the gas and his vehicle surged away from the curb. The sudden acceleration threw Devona and me against the back seat.

"I'm all for speed right now, but can you take it a *bit* easier?" I complained.

"Sorry about that," Lazlo said. "My cab's kind of jittery after playing tag with so many other vehicles tonight – Dread Rider, the Chopper, Velocicide... It's a wonder she hasn't had a nervous breakdown by now." Lazlo patted the dash and the cab's engine – which up to this point had been running at a high-pitched whine – began to purr and the vehicle slowed to a slightly less than lethal speed.

"Some heavy hitters there," Devona said, sounding worried for the first time since breaking me out of Tenebrus. I wanted to reassure her that everything was going to be all right, but as I was starting to have major doubts myself, the best I could do was take her hand and give it a squeeze. It wasn't much but she gave me a grateful smile anyway.

Lazlo glanced at us in his rearview mirror. "I like what you've done with your hair, Devona. And Matt, I *love* the new coat! You finally look like a real PI, you know what I'm saying?"

Right then I vowed that I was going to find a way out of this mess no matter what, if only so I could celebrate by burning that goddamned coat to ashes.

Lazlo went on. "I saw you tangling with someone when I drove up. Who was it?"

"Crossbreed," I said.

Lazlo let out a low whistle. "He's a tough customer. Looked like you managed to get the drop on him, though."

"We were lucky," I said with no false modesty. I didn't like relying on luck, but I figured I was going to need a few tons more of it before everything was over.

"Speaking of lucky," Lazlo said, "I was sitting in Skully's when Acantha's surprise broadcast came on. Everyone in the bar immediately started making bets on how long it'll be before you're recaptured. Most people figured you'll be back in Tenebrus within twenty-four hours."

"Their confidence in me is underwhelming." I changed the subject. "I'm glad to see you hale and hearty. Quillion led me to believe one of his Sentinels worked you over."

Lazlo didn't say anything to that. He just kept driving. After leaving the House of Mysterious Secrets he drove us to Sybarite Street, the Sprawl's main drag, and we headed toward the west side of the Dominion, where Nosferatomes was located. When he eventually spoke again his tone was subdued.

"A Sentinel did question me and it… wasn't gentle. I healed OK. I mean, I *am* a demon, right? But it hurt so much that I…"

I knew what Lazlo was trying to say. He'd told the Sentinel I was at the Foundry, which was how Silent Jack had been able to hunt me down.

"Don't worry about it," I said. "They'd have found me eventually no matter what. I'm just sorry you had to go through that on my account. I'm glad no permanent damage was done, though."

Lazlo said his next words so softly I wasn't certain I'd heard them at all. But it sounded like he said, "Not to my body anyway."

Lazlo looks so monstrous that it's sometimes too easy to forget that he has feelings like anyone else. He might be a demon but that didn't mean he wasn't human too – at least, in the ways that mattered most. I wanted to say something to make him feel better, but before I could think of anything the ratcheting sound of automatic weapons fire cut through the cab, followed by a metallic pinging as rounds struck the outside of the vehicle.

Lazlo's cab screamed then, and of all the horrible sounds I've heard since coming to Nekropolis, that's one I hope to never hear again.

The cab swerved wildly and Lazlo fought to maintain control of his vehicle.

"We're under attack!" Devona shouted.

That part I'd figured out for myself. What I didn't know yet was by who. I turned to look out the rear window and saw a midnight-black Cadillac with glowing red headlights and a hood mounted machine gun riding our tail.

"Damn it, it's Carnage!" I shouted.

Lazlo's cab made a noise that sounded a lot like a terrified whine. I knew exactly how she felt.

There are any number of possessed, haunted or living vehicles traveling the streets of Nekropolis – Lazlo's
cab among them. So many that once a year the
Screaming Wheels tournament is held, a cross-Domin-
ion road race whose course traverses the entire city.
But of all the supernaturally animated cars, motorcy-
cles and trucks, none are as powerful or deadly as
Carnage. As legend has it the Caddy's owner died behind the wheel of his vehicle and his spirit – instead of
going on to its final reward – merged with the car,
bringing the vehicle to malevolent life. Standard stuff,
really, but what made Carnage different to the average
possessed car is that it – he? – didn't want to exist as a
haunted vehicle and so over the years he had consulted any number of magicusers and exorcists in the
hope that one of them would be able to remove the
spirit from the Cadillac and set it free. But for some unknown reason no one had ever been able to draw the
human spirit forth from the vehicle. Even Papa Chatha
had taken a crack at it and failed. But Carnage was determined to find some way to become free of his cursed
existence. Rumor had it that Carnage had attempted
suicide numerous times, but as is so often the case with
supernatural vehicles, all damage it suffered was magically repaired. So that left Carnage with one option:
keep trying to find a magicuser powerful enough and
skilled enough to set him free.

Trouble was magic doesn't come cheap in Nekropolis
and Carnage needed money in order to continue hiring
witches and warlocks and so the living vehicle had be-

come a mercenary, taking on high risk, high reward jobs to make enough darkgems to afford the cost of exorcism spells. And if a job was so dangerous that Carnage was finally destroyed during it, well, that was OK too. Just as long as the spirit trapped within the Caddy's metal body was free in the end. Of course, in order to do his work more effectively, Carnage had used some of his profits on upgrades like a high performance engine, a steel reinforced suspension system and his oh-so-useful machine gun. After all, as the saying goes, you have to spend money to make money.

What all this added up to was an insanely dangerous self repairing haunted car with nothing to lose and at that moment the damned thing was hot on our trail.

I knew that Lazlo's cab could heal a certain amount of superficial damage on its own, but anything more than that would require extensive repairs. The cab was a tough little car, but I knew it couldn't withstand a full out attack by Carnage.

"Try and lose him!" I shouted to Lazlo.

"Lose him?" the demon shouted back. "I'll be lucky if I can keep us on the road!"

"Just do your best!"

I started rifling through my pockets, searching among the magic items Shrike had brought me, hoping that there was something I might be able to use to at least slow Carnage down. Devona did the same, and while we searched, Carnage unleashed another burst of gunfire.

Devona and I ducked as the rear window shattered. Lazlo's cab screamed in pain and swerved violently to the left, right into the path of oncoming traffic. I caught a momentary glimpse of a large semi truck with a grinning green goblin face on the cab coming straight at us. I thought the truck was going to slam into us and deprive Carnage of his bounty, but Lazlo managed to yank the cab's steering wheel to the right in time to avoid colliding with the truck and the goblin face seemed to laugh at us as the huge vehicle roared past.

I noticed the cab was slowing down and the engine began to make unsettling sputtering noises. I assumed some of that last burst of gunfire had done more to the cab than simply break some glass and I wasn't sure how much longer Lazlo's vehicle would be able to keep going before it would be forced to pull over. Not long, I guessed.

Devona and I were still searching among our paltry supply of weaponry but in the back of my mind I was already considering giving myself up. Carnage wouldn't hurt me. He needed me more or less intact in order to collect the bounty on me. But when the possessed Caddy was on a mission it wasn't particular about who got hurt in the crossfire, hence his name. If this kept up there was an excellent chance that Devona and Lazlo would end up seriously injured, maybe even dead, and I wasn't about to let that happen simply to save my own slowly rotting hide.

I was about to tell Lazlo to pull over when Devona held up what appeared to be a ball made of woven black twigs.

"Got it!" she said, grinning.

It was one of the items I'd passed on when we'd looked through them in Westerna's, primarily because I hadn't recognized it and didn't know what it did. But before I could ask Devona what she had she turned around and chucked the object out the now open back window. The ebon twigball flew through the air toward Carnage's windshield. The ball looked solid enough, but when it hit the glass it flattened like liquid and expanded to cover the entire windshield. It then seemed to sink into the glass as if the Caddy was absorbing the black substance and then it was gone and the windshield was clear once more.

The effect was instantaneous. The machine gun's barrel drooped and Carnage began to slow down, swaying gently from side to side.

"What was that?" I asked.

Devona was still grinning. "Caligari's Sleep. It's a common spell used by Bloodborn who either haven't developed their hypnotic abilities or are simply too lazy to use them. The spell makes its victim sleepy and open to suggestion."

"Kind of like a daterape drug," I said. "Classy." Still, I couldn't argue with the effect it was having on Carnage. The car didn't have a flesh-and-blood body, but the spell must've been designed to affect a victim's psyche regardless of what form that psyche resided in, because it was clearly working. But the question was for how long.

Despite its name, Caligari's Sleep didn't render Carnage unconscious, just really, really sleepy. The deadly vehicle might not have been shooting at us anymore but neither had it broken off its pursuit. Carnage's glowing red headlights had dimmed and the vehicle was moving more slowly and swerving back and forth, but it was still managing to keep up with us. It didn't help that Lazlo's cab wasn't moving very fast at that moment either. Vehicles began passing us, drivers honking angrily and making obscene gestures as they flashed by. Several made mystic passes with their hands as if trying to lay a curse on us for pissing them off. They needn't have bothered. Given the way things had been going for me lately, I figured I'd already exceeded my bad luck quota for the next several decades at least.

Right then I wished that Shrike had brought me a bazooka instead of a .45 and I was amusing myself by imagining firing one at Carnage through the open back window when Lazlo said, "Great, that's all we need!"

Devona and I looked forward to see what he was talking about. Before us in the middle of the street was a massive misshapen being that resembled a small mountain formed entirely of flesh. Hundreds of legs – some human, most not – stuck out from its bottom to support its weight and provide locomotion, while the rest of the creature's surface was covered with other body parts: hands, arms, chests, abdomens, genitals, buttocks and worst of all, heads. Gazes blank, mouths gaping wide, tongues lolling, drool streaming past their lips. This was one of the strangest creatures in Nekropolis and probably the single most annoying one.

The Conglomeration.

No one knows where it came from, what it wants, or for that matter, exactly what the damned thing is. What it does is wander randomly through the city, absorbing anyone unlucky enough or stupid enough not to get out of its way in time. Mostly, the Darklords tolerate the Conglomeration's presence since in many ways it's like evolution in action, absorbing both the slow of foot and slow of mind. But whenever it gets too large – and it certainly appeared to be on the verge of that now – the physicians at the Fever House are alerted and they dispatch a specially designed ambulance to capture the Conglomeration and bring it to the facility where they begin the painstaking and laborious process of separating the people that had been absorbed. The story goes that when the doctors finally finish there's never anything left over that's wholly and completely the Conglomeration. It's like the creature doesn't exist in and of itself. But a few days later, it – or a replacement – is back on the street, absorbing bodies again.

"Can you go around it?" Devona asked.

"Yeah," Lazlo said. "It's not that big yet, but it's blocking enough of the road to cause a real slowdown." He glanced up at the rearview. "I'm afraid it'll give Carnage a chance to catch up to us."

"Which would be bad," I said. "Especially when it manages to shake off Caligari's Sleep." Something I feared would happen sooner rather than later.

A thought occurred to me then. Carnage wasn't alive in the strictest sense of the word, but then concepts like life and death are more than a little fuzzy in Nekropolis.

Carnage had a soul and could think and act independently. In many ways, the vehicle wasn't all that different from me. I was kind of alive, wasn't I? And *I* didn't want to get absorbed by the Conglomeration. And hadn't Devona told me that the recipients of Caligari's Sleep were highly suggestible?

I didn't waste anymore time thinking about it, primarily because we didn't have anymore time. The traffic ahead of us had slowed considerably and it would only be a few moments more before Carnage, sleepy though he was, caught up to us.

I turned around in my seat and leaned out the open back window. Before Devona could ask me what I was doing, I shouted, "Hey, Carnage! Don't tell anyone, but I'm hiding inside the Conglomeration!"

The crimson glow within the possessed Caddy's headlights had almost gone out by then but now it flared back to full blazing strength. The vehicle's engine roared and Carnage surged past us, swerving around slower-moving cars as it aimed straight for the Conglomeration. Carnage's hood mounted machine gun raised into firing position and began blasting the Conglomeration with rounds of ammo. At first the gigantic fleshy mass of body parts didn't seem to notice it was under attack, but then the eyes of all its heads came into focus and turned to look at the vehicle firing upon it. Faces contorted in anger and cries of rage issued from all its mouths. Undeterred Carnage continued forward, gun blazing away. Alarmed motorists in the immediate vicinity began trying to pull their vehicles out of the line of fire and if they found their way blocked by other cars and trucks they simply bailed out and ran for it. Lazlo lifted his foot off the gas and allowed his cab to slow down, which turned out to be an extremely wise move when a furious Conglomeration threw itself forward and fell down on top of Carnage.

The impact was tremendous, bouncing Devona and I out of our seats and fissuring the street with cracks. Bits of the Azure Slime oozed forth through the cracks as if curious to see what was going on above it, but a second later the Slime retreated, most likely having decided to leave the Conglomeration alone, perhaps as a courtesy from one absorbing monster to another.

Lazlo had slammed on the brakes when the Conglomeration fell and now we – along with dozens of other drivers and sidewalk gawkers along both sides of Sybarite Street – watched and waited to see what would happen next.

At first the Conglomeration just lay there in the street and I had the horrible feeling that any second we'd see Carnage come bursting out of the flesh mass, headlights shining with fury over having been tricked, gun ratcheting death as the Caddy came toward us. But instead the Conglomeration rose with slow, ponderous movements and we could see the undercarriage of a midnight-black Cadillac now embedded in its side. The Conglomeration just stood there for a moment, as if pondering the new addition to its body, and then it resumed its course, heading slowly down Sybarite Street.

"I have no idea if the Conglomeration has anything even remotely resembling a digestive tract," I said, "but one way or another, I'll bet it's in for a serious case of heartburn after that."

Devona smiled at me and I took her hand. To Lazlo, I said, "Can your cab make it to Nosferatomes or should we get out and walk?"

Lazlo patted the dash. "What do you say, sweetie? Can you do a few more blocks before taking a rest?"

The vehicle gave a weak bleat on its horn in response.

"That's my girl!" Lazlo said.

I almost felt like patting the back seat in thanks, but I resisted. After all, I have a reputation as a tough guy to maintain.

As soon as he could Lazlo turned off onto a side street to get away from the Conglomeration and we continued on our way, the cab driving slowly but steadily toward Nosferatomes.

We had Lazlo drop us off a block away from the bookstore, just in case anyone was lying in wait for us outside. Lazlo wanted to stay but once Devona and I were out of the cab we could see how extensive the damage caused by Carnage was. The cab's chassis was riddled with bullet holes that leaked an oily brown ichor as if the vehicle was bleeding. I supposed in a sense it was. The engine was still running but it sounded weak and it knocked and pinged in a way that suggested it was on the verge of collapse.

"Better get her to a mechanic," I told Lazlo. "Devona and I will be fine on our own." I knew no such thing, of course, but I couldn't allow Lazlo to continue helping us, not if it was going to cost his cab whatever version of life it possessed.

Lazlo was torn and it took a bit more convincing on my part, but in the end he agreed.

"Well, if you say so. She is sounding kind of punky. You two take care of yourselves, all right?"

We promised we would and Lazlo put his cab in gear and drove slowly down the street, the engine protesting all the way. When he was gone we approached the bookstore on foot. After encountering both Crossbreed and Carnage in such a short span of time I was seriously paranoid but none of the pedestrians we passed paid any attention to us and by the time we reached Nosferatomes I was relatively confident there were no bounty hunters in the immediate vicinity, but I didn't allow myself to fully relax. In Nekropolis the moment you let your guard down is the moment you risk becoming someone's snack.

Nosferatomes was housed in a nondescript two storey building constructed of gray brick with black roof tiles and shutters. A wooden sign hung above the door displaying the shop's name in stylized gothic letters. Aside from its name it could've been any used bookstore on Earth. A pair of other businesses flanked the shop: on the right, a Hemlocks, and on the left a restaurant called Matango. Hemlocks was a chain of coffee houses with locations spread throughout all five

Dominions, though the majority of them are located in the Sprawl. They don't just serve regular coffee anymore than their earthly counterparts did. Blood clottes, marrowchinos and spinal fluid smoothees are only a few of their nauseating offerings. Every time I walk past one it makes me grateful that my taste buds are as dead as the rest of me.

I'd never been to Matango before. It was a Japanese restaurant of a sort that specialized in mushroom dishes, a fact advertised by the various types of the fungi growing on the restaurant's stone walls. Supposedly the food there is so good it's addictive, but frequent diners need to be careful lest they find their skin taking on strange colors and textures. After all, there's a reason Matango's slogan is *You are what you eat.*

As we drew near the bookstore, a woman carrying a tray loaded with tiny cardboard cups came walking toward us. Devona and I instantly tensed in case this was yet another bounty hunter, but Devona quickly relaxed.

I sense no hostility from her, Devona thought to me. *In fact, I don't sense much of anything going on inside her.*

Why that was became apparent once the woman reached us. She had long straight black hair that fell to her waist, a prominent scar line circling her neck just below a pair of metal electrodes. She wore a black polo shirt and black slacks, along with a white apron with the stylized *H* of the Hemlocks logo stitched onto the fabric. She was another of Victor Baron's creations – Baristastein, I supposed.

"Would you like a free sample of our latest offering?" she asked, tone flat and face expressionless. I wondered if there was something wrong with her brain or if Baron had simply had trouble correctly hooking up her voice box and facial muscles. "It's espresso with a shot of bile. We call it a Sprawlicano."

I eyed the brackish liquid in the cup with more than a little suspicion. "More like spewicano," I said. "No thanks."

The woman took no offense at my comment, but then my words didn't seem to register with her at all. She simply moved on to accost another pedestrian. But a small crowd had gathered on the sidewalk outside Hemlocks to sip their drinks and chat in the open air. Some of them had overheard what I said and they chuckled in agreement. But one – a large minotaur with muscles on his muscles who wore a T-shirt bearing the intellectually provocative phrase *Horny is as horny does* came stomping over to us on hoofed feet.

"You disrespecting my girlfriend?" he said in a gruff, bestial voice.

"Not at all," I replied. "I was disrespecting the crap she tried to serve me."

The minotaur snorted angrily and grabbed hold of my jacket with both hands and lifted me onto my tip-toes.

"Think you're funny, huh?"

"I'm curious what you two see in each other." I glanced in Baristastein's direction and saw she was still trying to push her samples onto passersby without any sign she was aware of her boyfriend's confrontation with me. "Is it a case of opposites attract? I mean, she's the coldest of cold fishes and you've obviously got some anger management issues…"

Ferdinand roared in my face then and I just looked calmly back at him. I can be a pretty cold fish myself when I need to be.

I reached into one of my pockets and wrapped my fingers around one of the magic objects Shrike had brought me: a flea bomb. Judging by how thick the minotaur's fur was his coat would be a perfect home for a few thousand bloodthirsty insects. But before I could withdraw the bomb, I heard Devona's thoughtvoice, the tone slightly frantic.

He's three times your size, Matt! If you were alive, you'd be afraid of him. That's what he's used to and what he's looking for – for you to show some fear!

Not my style, I thought back as I stared into the minotaur's eyes. I gripped the flea bomb tighter.

That's the whole point, Devona thought to me. *You're supposed to be pretending to be someone else, remember?*

Oh, right. The whole fugitive-in-disguise thing… I released my hold on the flea bomb and prepared to put on a show.

It had been a long time since I'd felt physically threatened and I wasn't sure if I remembered how to do it. I started by turning my head to the side as if I was afraid Ferdinand was going to haul off and punch me any second. Then I lowered my gaze so I wasn't looking directly into his eyes. The minotaur didn't release me but his breathing eased a bit and I knew my act was working.

"You know what you're gonna do now?" he asked. "You're gonna apologize to Sandy." He paused and then his bovine face broke into a grin. "Wait – I got a better idea!"

He called for Baristastein to join us and she walked over, face still devoid of expression. The minotaur let go of me with one hand but kept hold of me with the other. He then reached out and took one of the sample cups from his girlfriend's tray and his grin took on a nasty edge.

"You're gonna try one of these and then you're gonna tell Sandy how much you like it." He looked at me expectantly and I realized he was hoping that the prospect of being forced to down the swill would provoke some kind of response in me.

"I'd, uh, really rather not," I said.

Way to sound terrified, Devona thought. I ignored her.

"Too bad," Ferdinand said. He put the cup of steaming liquid to my lips and poured it in.

I could've swallowed it easily since I couldn't feel the heat or taste the flavor but that wasn't what a living man would do, so I sputtered and thrashed my head back and forth, causing some of the Sprawlicano to spill down my chin. The minotaur continued to grin as he poured the rest of the cup's contents down my throat, then he let go of me and I allowed myself to fall back on my ass, making sure to let out a *whoof!* of air as if I felt the impact.

As I rose slowly to my feet I doubled over and made a face as if I was going to throw up the noxious brew, but Ferdinand said, "You barf and I'll make you drink two more."

I made a show of fighting to keep the Sprawlicano down and Ferdinand nodded, satisfied. "Now tell Sandy how good it was."

I tried to speak, coughed once, then tried again.

"Smooth," I croaked.

The minotaur turned to his girlfriend. "There you go, baby. He'll think twice before giving you anymore attitude."

Baristastein ignored the minotaur as she looked at me, as blank eyed and expressionless as ever.

"Thank you and come again," she said and then went off in search of someone else to serve.

The minotaur watched her go, his gaze softening.

"Isn't she something?" he said.

I wisely kept any opinions I had about that to myself and Ferdinand wandered off to rejoin the group of people he'd been talking with before Devona and I arrived. There was laughter and congratulatory backslaps from his friends and I found myself reaching for the flea bomb again.

Devona put a hand on my arm to restrain me. "Forget him. We have work to do."

I looked at the minotaur for a moment longer before nodding and letting Devona lead me toward Nosferatomes.

"What did you think of my performance?" I asked her.

She smiled gently. "Let's just say it's a good thing you chose a career in criminal justice."

"Everyone's a critic," I muttered.

Devona and I walked up to Nosferatomes' front door, keeping an eye out for possible attack the entire time and staying in low level telepathic contact. We couldn't read one another's minds this way but we could sense the other's feelings. If one of us spotted danger, the other would be instantly aware of it. But again, there was no sign of any bounty hunters, and we entered the store.

THIRTEEN

A bell tinkled as we opened the door and again when we closed it. The front room was filled with wooden shelves crammed with books, signs hanging down from the ceiling with section names painted on them to direct customers to the areas they were interested in. Self Help was directly next to Self Mutilation, and Dark Arts was followed by Darker, Darkest and Pitch Black Arts. As we walked up to the counter some of the titles that leaped out at me were *The Complete Idiot's Guide to the Necronomicon, Stabbing for Dummies, The Beginner's Book of Bodysnatching, A Child's Garden of Curses, Shapeshifting for Fun and Profit,* and *Death: A Life.*

There were a couple customers browsing the stacks. One was an elderly Arcane woman who, judging by the pile of books in her arms, was big into the culinary arts, especially cooking with children. The other was a small rotund man without eyelids who I recognized as the Insomnimaniac. I'd seen him in here before and out on the street a few times, but we'd never formally met, so

I wasn't too worried he'd recognize me, but I made sure to keep my face turned away from him as we walked by, just in case. I felt a certain kinship with the man. I hadn't slept since I died and I'd often come here to buy books to give me something to read to pass the time when I wasn't working.

The counter held an old fashioned cash register and a desk bell to ring for service. Behind the counter was a closed door leading to a back room of some sort. A stock room or maybe a private office, I guessed. Since no one manned the counterI tapped the bell, received a clear *ding* for my effort, and then Devona and I waited. It didn't take long.

Scuttling sounds came from numerous directions as small sleek black shapes rushed toward the counter from throughout the store. The rats – or rather pieces of darkness shaped like rats – scurried behind the counter and merged to form a single shadowy mass that grew as it reshaped itself into humanoid form. A second later a grotesque looking Bloodborn male stood before us. Cadaverously thin, bald, with pointed ears, narrow rat-like features and a pair of needlesharp incisors jutting down from his upper jaw. He was dressed in a black great coat that hung awkwardly on his spindly frame. He rested long talon-like fingers on top of the counter and gave us what I assumed was supposed to be a welcoming smile, but which looked more like a grimace of pain.

"How may I serve you?" His voice was little more than a whisper and his accent was thick. It was clearly

of eastern European origin, but it contained hints of
other regions I couldn't place. That wasn't uncommon
among the Bloodborn since so many of them were at
least centuries old and had lived in many countries on
Earth before relocating to Nekropolis, but there was
something about this vampire's voice that spoke of
great age, almost as if he were speaking with the voice
of Time itself.

As I said, Devona and I had both bought books here
before and we'd been waited on by Orlock every time.
If he had any employees I'd never seen them. But the
vampire gave no sign that he recognized us. He just
stood there behind the counter, smiling that unsettling
smile of his, patiently waiting for us to tell him what
we wanted.

"We're interested in learning about rare magical artifacts," I said.

"I see. I have a section on magic items that contains
a number of thorough examinations of the subject. If
you come with me, I'll be happy to take you there."

A shadowy cast came over Orlock's features and I
knew he was about to separate into the components of
his travel form to escort us to the section in question. I
held up a hand to stop him and the shadowy aspect
vanished, leaving his features clear once more.

"Is there something more?" he asked. His tone remained professionally pleasant, but his beady rat eyes
narrowed with the first hint of suspicion.

"We're not so much interested in reading about artifacts," I said, "as much as we are in selling them."

Orlock hesitated a few seconds before responding, his eyes narrowing even further, as if appraising us.

"I have several books in stock that deal with the basic fundamentals of buying and selling, but none that specifically focuses on trading in magical objects per se."

I held Orlock's gaze with my own as I spoke. "As I said we're not interested in *reading* about the subject."

Orlock arched a thin eyebrow at this.

"Pardon my presumptuousness," he said, "but why come to a bookstore if you're not interested in reading?"

I felt a pressure begin to build behind my eyes and I realized that Orlock was trying to probe my mind. I was surprised since usually half-vampires like Devona are the more psychically gifted among the Bloodborn. But almost as soon as it started I felt the pressure ease and I knew that Devona was running interference for me, blocking Orlock's mental probe with her own psychic powers.

Orlock realized it too, for his gaze flicked to Devona and he pursed his lips in irritation. He then turned his attention back to me.

"I'm sorry but I'm afraid I can't help you. Now if you'll excuse me, I have a great deal of cataloguing to do in the back room."

He began to go shadowy on us again and this time I reached across the counter and grabbed hold of his right wrist to stop him.

"Let's cut the crap, Orlock," I said softly, so none of the other customers would overhear. "We know what your real business is, and unless you agree to talk with us in private, we'll tell the Adjudicators everything we know."

Orlock looked at me for a long moment, and though I no longer possessed the sensory apparatus to feel temperature, I swear the room seemed to get colder by several degrees.

"An empty threat coming from someone the Adjudicators would dearly love to find," Orlock said through gritted teeth.

So the vampire *had* recognized me. I wasn't worried that he'd turn us over to the authorities, though. If what David had told us about Orlock was true he had his own reasons for not wanting anything to do with the Adjudicators.

Without another word Orlock gestured for us to come around the counter. Then he turned, removed a key from his coat pocket, unlocked the door and – moving with an awkward, jerking motions that put me in mind of a scuttling crab – he entered the room beyond.

Devona and I exchanged glances.

A trap? she asked telepathically.

In Nekropolis? What are the odds?

She grinned at me and we followed after Orlock. Once we were inside the vampire closed and locked the door behind us.

The back room turned out to be a private office and a cozy one at that. A trio of comfortable chairs, Persian rug over a wooden floor, round table with a teacup and saucer resting on top of it, though instead of tea, the cup held a bit of reddish liquid at the bottom. And bookshelves, of course, though these were made of highly polished oak and contained one leather bound volume after another. Orlock's private stock, I assumed.

Orlock sat at the table and gestured for Devona and I to sit in the two remaining chairs. I preferred to stand – easier to fight that way – but Bloodborn, especially older ones, can be rigid when it comes to matters of etiquette, so we did as Orlock wanted and sat.

At first Orlock didn't say anything. He just folded his spiderish fingers together over his skeletally thin chest and looked at us. When he did finally speak his voice held a hint of amusement.

"Did you really think your pathetic disguises would fool me? Even if you weren't a well known personality around town, I'd have recognized you, Matthew Richter. You too, Devona Kanti. I remember the names and faces of everyone I've ever done business with, even if it was only a single transaction."

He reached out to pick up his teacup then and drained the remaining dregs of liquid.

Devona licked her lips as we watched Orlock finish his drink and I realized it had been a while since she'd fed on real blood instead of settling for aqua sanguis. I sometimes forget that while she's only half-vampire, that half needs nourishment the same as any other Bloodborn. I try not to let her dietary needs bother me, though. After all, we monsters need to stick together.

Orlock put his empty cup down on the saucer then sat back in his chair, hands once more interlocked on his chest.

"So tell me why you're here," he said. "I admit that I'm extremely curious why a fugitive from justice would choose to interrupt his flight from the authorities to visit a used bookstore."

"I suppose I could tell you that even fugitives need something to read, but the truth is I need your help. Are you aware of the reward the First Adjudicator is offering for my capture?"

Orlock looked at me as if I'd just insulted him.

I went on. "All right then. In that case, then you know the basics of the crime I was arrested for."

"Yes. You stole something from Lord Edrigu." He suddenly brightened. "Don't tell me you've come here looking to sell the object!"

"I'm not going to tell you that because I didn't steal it." I paused. "Well, my head didn't."

Orlock just looked at me.

"It's complicated. The point is I didn't steal the object, so I don't have it. The reason we've come to see you is that I intend to discover who actually committed the crime so I can clear my name. But to do that I need to know more about the object that was stolen from Lord Edrigu. It was a flute carved from bone that he wore around his neck."

Orlock's only reaction to the object's description was a slight narrowing of his gaze.

"Interesting," he said softly. But he added no more.

"We came to you because you have a reputation for being a collector," Devona said. "We know you sometimes hire people to acquire certain items for you.

Supposedly you're not too fussy about how you obtain them, either."

"And you believe I may be able to provide information on this flute for you?" Orlock asked. "Or is it more than that? Do you suspect me of engineering the theft?"

"The thought had occurred to me," I admitted. "But to be honest at this point we have no more reason to suspect you than anyone else in town. And since you're the only lead we have at the moment, I suppose we'll just have to trust that you had nothing to do with the theft."

"Because you have no choice," Orlock said.

"That's about the size of it."

The vampire looked thoughtful for a moment.

"I'm a businessman, not an altruist. If I agree to help you, how will I be compensated?"

"It depends," Devona said. "What would you want?"

Orlock considered. "Your services in the future, free of charge. There are a number of artifacts that I haven't been able to acquire over the years for one reason or another. The two of you might be able to succeed in obtaining them for me where others have failed."

"*One* artifact," I said. "And we'll reserve the right to choose which one we'll go after."

Orlock smiled. "Done!" He briskly rubbed his talons together in satisfaction. "Now, down to business." He grinned. "And I do mean *down*."

He reached beneath the table, pushed a hidden switch, and the floor began to descend. Devona and I gripped the arms of our chairs out of reflex but the descent was slow and smooth. A wooden panel slid into place above us to seal off Orlock's office and fluorescent lights affixed to its underside turned on to provide illumination as we continued dropping.

The floor descended about thirty feet before coming to a gentle stop. Devona and I looked around and saw only darkness. I remembered Devona's concern that we might be walking into some kind of trap and I steeled myself for an attack. But a moment later Orlock said, "Forgive me. I tend to forget that not all my visitors can see as well in the dark as I can."

He gestured with one of his clawed hands and more fluorescent light panels activated, revealing a corridor that extended off to the left.

"Please follow me."

Orlock rose and, moving with his crab-like walk, started down the corridor. Devona and I of course followed. It was why we'd come here, after all.

The corridor wasn't a long one and we soon found ourselves standing in a large open chamber I estimated to be at least the size of a football field, ceiling thirty feet above us, covered in fluorescent light panels that clearly illuminated every part of the chamber. Devona and I stood there for a moment, staring in amazement. For most of her adult life, Devona had served as caretaker of Lord Galm's collection of magical artifacts. I'd seen his collection and I'd been impressed, but Galm had nothing on Orlock. His chamber was packed full of items ranging in size from the three-masted sailing ship with the name *Flying Dutchman* painted on the side in faded letters to a round crystalline pedestal with a seemingly empty clear dome on top. A metal plate affixed to the pedestal proclaimed the dome as containing the Incredible Shrinking Man. There were hundreds of items surrounding us, from large to small, each more exotic and bizarre than the last. Rosemary's Baby's crib, the Darkwand of Manticore, Dr. Jekyll's first chemistry set, the Ark of Desecration, the Phantom of the Opera's original score for *Don Juan Triumphant*, two of the Headless Horseman's spare heads, a half dozen dried and preserved triffids and so many more.

While many of Orlock's displays were physical objects a number of his displays resembled exhibits that seemed more appropriate for a wax museum: men, women and creatures in frozen poses sealed within large domes of clear crystal, like that containing the Incredible Shrinking man, but on a larger scale. According to their plaques the domes nearest us contained the Seven Golden Vampires, Grendel and his mother, the Aztec Mummy, several devil bats and a pack of killer shrews. I knew without asking that these weren't wax recreations bur rather the real thing, held in stasis by some sort of enchantment or advanced technology and there were a lot of them in Orlock's collection and when I gave Devona a look and thought *We'd better watch ourselves*, she gave me a look back which said she agreed.

Devona turned to Orlock then, and though I knew like me she felt misgivings about the collection, she concealed them well as she said, "This is amazing! It puts my father's collection to shame! In fact, if all the Darklords' combined their separate collections, I'd doubt the result would rival yours."

Orlock bowed. "Your words do me great honor. Thank you."

As the ancient Bloodborn straightened, I said, "You know this makes you look even more like a suspect than you did before."

Orlock waved my comment aside. "If I was responsible for the theft of Edrigu's flute, I'd never have admitted the truth about what I do, let alone brought you both down here. Now let us have no more of such talk, yes?"

"What *do* you do exactly?" I asked. "I mean, we can see you collect things, but you seem to imply there's more to it than just that."

"There is," Orlock said. "But let us walk as we talk. I have guests so seldom and it gives me great pleasure to show off my displays."

Orlock began crabwalking deeper into the chamber and Devona and I followed. The floor was made of white marble and our footsteps echoed solidly as we walked. As we went we found our heads turning this way and that, trying to take everything in as Orlock spoke, but our efforts were doomed to failure. There were simply too many wonders surrounding us to fully comprehend, let alone appreciate them all, though we found the increasing number of beings frozen within domes to be more than a little disturbing.

"I am, as you might have gathered, incredibly ancient, even for my kind." Orlock glanced at Devona. "Old as your father, as a matter of fact. You might even say we're brothers, in a sense. When Dis began approaching the most powerful of the Darkfolk to explain his dream of creating a home for us where we would be separate and therefore safe from humanity, I was one of his first supporters. Even then humans outnumbered Darkfolk and I knew they would only continue to outbreed us as the years passed. If we were to survive as more than bits of legend and folklore hiding in the shadows, we had to build our own home. While Dis continued seeking support for his plan, he tasked me with a most important job. I was to scour the Earth and gather together scattered magical objects and creatures that didn't belong to a specific Darklord or demilord in preparation for the day when Nekropolis would be born and the Darkfolk would take up residence there.

"For the better part of a century I performed my duty, storing my finds in a system of caverns hidden beneath a mountain range in Europe. And when the day of the Descension arrived at last, everything I'd collected was brought to Nekropolis with us.

"Of course, I didn't get to keep what I'd collected. Once the Darklords were settled into their various strongholds, they paid me a visit and claimed what items and creatures they wished, leaving me to hold on to only those things none of them wanted."

"Your collection must've been massive beyond

imagination if they left you all this," Devona said, gesturing at the displays around us.

Orlock gave a soft hissing laugh. "My dear, what the Darklords left me wouldn't have filled a tenth of this chamber. What you see around you is what I've managed to gather in the centuries since the city's founding."

"What happened?" I asked. "Did you find yourself bitten by the collecting bug and couldn't shake the habit?"

Orlock smiled. "Not exactly. After the first hundred years of Nekropolis's existence, a citywide conflict broke out that would eventually come to be called the Blood Wars. When it was over much of the city lay in ruins and rebuilding took some time. It was during that period that I resumed my career as a collector, but now I viewed myself more as a preserver. You see, the Blood Wars made me realize that the Darkfolk can be just as shortsighted and foolish as humanity in their own way and I came to believe that one day, one way or another, Nekropolis would be destroyed and the survivors would be forced to move again and find a new place to settle. I'm collecting, preserving and storing items and creatures for that day, the same as I once did. I suppose that instead of being a simple bookseller, I'm actually in the insurance business."

He laughed at his own joke, but neither Devona nor I found it amusing. I doubted any of the beings frozen within stasis globes had volunteered to become part of Orlock's twisted version of Noah's Ark.

"Where did all these items come from?" Devona asked.

"Some are from my original collection that I've managed to reclaim over the years, one way or another," Orlock said. "Some are objects that were left behind on Earth during the Descension and which my operatives have located and managed to smuggle into Nekropolis for me. Oh, don't look so shocked. There are other ways in and out of the city besides the Darklords' mirrors. Not many, perhaps, but they exist. And still other objects were items ordinary Darkfolk brought with them to Nekropolis and which I've managed to obtain, along with new items that have been created since the Descension."

"What about the creatures?" I asked. "Not to mention the people." I tried to keep the disgust I felt out of my voice, but I wasn't entirely successful. Still, Orlock didn't seem to notice.

"They are rare and interesting lifeforms that were either unique or endangered. They're preserved here until the day the Darkfolk once again relocate. They will be revived then."

"I see." I couldn't help sounding skeptical. If Orlock thought he was preserving everything in his collection for some future relocation – if such a thing ever took place – what guarantee would there be that Orlock would disperse his collection then and free his captives? Wouldn't he be just as likely to continue holding them against the possibility of yet another future relocation? There was a good chance the beings frozen within Orlock's stasis domes would never be free again.

Still, I decided not to say anything about it to Orlock. We still needed him to identify Edrigu's bone flute and I didn't want to risk offending him. After what we'd seen I didn't like the idea of one day helping him add another item to his collection as the price for his help, but a deal was a deal. But I'd make damn sure that we wouldn't bring him anything – or anyone – alive.

I was about to ask Orlock another question when the vox in my coat pocket said, "Someone's calling," repeating the phrase until I pulled out the phone and answered it.

"Excuse me for a moment," I said to Orlock and stepped away to take the call. It was David.

"We got lucky, Matt. I hooked ravens up to each monitor and kept going back and forth between them as the video downloaded. I haven't found any footage of the actual theft yet, but I did find some of the attack on you in the alley. It's not very clear and I can't make out the faces of the men who attacked you. I've tried enhancing the images, but so far I haven't been–"

I broke in. "Men? You mean there was more than one?"

"That's right. There were two. They attacked from behind. One put a cloth bag over your head while the other used some kind of garrote to slice through your neck. It wasn't an ordinary garrote, either, but some kind of hi-tech device that cut through both flesh and bone as if they were water."

I'd already guessed as much about the nature of the garrote, but up to that point I'd been assuming there'd only been one attacker. But now that I thought back on it the attack had occurred swiftly – too swiftly for one man to do the job himself. And when I went back over the sounds I'd heard then I realized that while in the confusion at the time I assumed the noises had been made by one assailant, in fact, the sounds had come from different directions and they'd overlapped. I had been attacked by two men and the evidence had been there all along. I just hadn't recognized it for what it was.

I asked David a few more questions about my attackers but his raven had been some distance away when it recorded the incident and he couldn't give me anymore details about the men other than they were both humanoid and wearing black coats. He couldn't even make a guess as to their exact species.

"Thanks for the info, David. It's a big help."

"No problem." David promised to continue downloading video and that he'd call me again if he found any footage of my body entering or leaving the Reliquary. I ended the call, tucked Shrike's vox back into my coat pocket and rejoined Devona and Orlock who'd been waiting patiently for me. Devona gave me a questioning look when I returned and I gave my head a slight shake to let her know I'd tell her about the call later. She nodded and we continued following Orlock through his vast collection.

After a few more minutes, I said, "Thanks for the tour and the history lesson but as you might imagine I'm more than a bit anxious to get on with clearing my name. Can you identify Edrigu's flute for us?"

Orlock stopped walking and Devona and I stopped too. We stood in an open area next to a display of a large metal framework holding a dozen amputated arms and legs, all human, all connected by thick copper cables to an old-fashioned handcrank generator resting on the floor. The flesh of the limbs was a mottled greenish-gray and their look was a familiar one. I knew why a moment later when I read the plaque identifying the display as one of Dr. Frankenstein's earliest experiments in reanimation technology. It didn't take a genius to figure out how the device worked. You turned the crank, activated the generator, and the resulting electric current caused the arms and legs to move. I imagined it would be great fun at parties.

"Of course I can," he said. "The flute was part of my original collection. Its name is Osseal and it was carved from a bone taken from the first true human to walk the Earth. When played properly it has the power to command the dead."

The news stunned me. It's bad enough that the Darklords have that kind of power, but at least Father Dis holds them in check. But for some unknown person to possess the ability to command the dead... command *me*, for as a zombie I belonged to the ranks of the dead, was seriously disturbing.

"I wonder what the thief – whoever it is – wants with such an object," Devona said.

"There's a lot of dead folk of one sort or another in the city," I answered. "An object like Osseal would give its user a tremendous amount of power."

"Yes, but for what purpose? Someone went to a hell of a lot of trouble to obtain Osseal. That means whoever stole it wanted it pretty badly."

I shrugged. "For some people the acquisition of power is an end in itself. Look at your father…" I almost added *and Orlock*.

"Maybe," Devona said. "Or maybe whoever it was wants to raise their own personal army."

The thought was a chilling one.

"I can see why Edrigu wore Osseal around his neck," I said. "An object of that kind of power–" I broke off when I felt Devona's mind touch mine.

Something's wrong here, Matt. Orlock didn't have to bring us down here to tell us about Osseal. He could've told us back in his office.

Before I could reply, Orlock said, "You needn't bother trying to communicate telepathically. I can hear you as clearly as if you were speaking aloud."

I turned toward the vampire, intending to demand that he explain what was going on, but then I saw where we'd stopped. Devona and I were standing in a thin, almost invisible circle etched into the marble floor. Orlock, not surprisingly, was standing outside the circle. Before Devona and I could react Orlock raised a hand and a clear dome like dozens of others we'd seen since entering the chamber sprung into existence around us. I started to reach for my .45, intending to see if the inside of the dome was bulletproof, but I found myself unable to move. I tried to look at Devona to see if she was similarly affected, but I couldn't even turn my head toward her. Instead, I reached out to her mentally.

Devona?

I can't move either, Matt. We're caught in some kind of stasis field. I don't know if it's magical or technological, but in either case my psychic powers have no effect on it.

The Loa necklace that Papa Chatha had made to protect me from tracking spells blocked all magic. So that meant Orlock's stasis dome was technological in origin. That, or it was magic of such a high order that the necklace couldn't nullify it – which, considering Orlock's vast age, experience and knowledge, was quite possible. Whatever the case, the stasis field worked and we were trapped.

Orlock spoke then, and though he was on the other side of the dome, we could hear him just fine.

"I apologize for this, but I hope you'll understand. You're a most unique specimen, Matthew. The only intelligent selfwilled zombie who's ever existed. And now, through no fault of your own, your existence has become endangered. Assuming you aren't destroyed in the process of being recaptured by the Adjudicators, it's doubtful you will survive a second term of incarceration in Tenebrus. And let's be realistic. The odds of you being able to discover who stole Osseal and framed you for the theft before you are captured are exceedingly slim. So you see, I'm really doing you a favor by preserving you here. And as for Devona…" He shrugged. "Well, I wouldn't want you to get lonely. And don't worry. You'll find that time within my domes passes pleasantly enough. I've seen to that."

He smiled and started to turn to leave, but then he paused. "You know, it is rather ironic that you're now part of my collection. After all, thanks to you, Overkill wasn't able to obtain Scream Queen's voice for me. But you and Devona make more than fitting replacements for it. Scream Queen has a truly remarkable voice – she has both banshee and siren blood in her ancestry, you know. But the way she uses her gift…" He shuddered. "If I don't manage to preserve her voice soon, she'll ruin it beyond repair. Ah well, That's no longer any concern of yours now, is it? Perhaps I'll hire Overkill to make another attempt to capture the voice. With the both of you out of action perhaps she'll succeed this time. Farewell, and I hope you enjoy your stay."

Orlock turned away then and departed. He was soon out of my view, and since I couldn't move my head to track him, I could only listen to his footsteps as they faded away. A bit later the chamber lights went out and I knew Orlock had returned to his bookstore and might well be on the vox to Overkill at that very moment.

Inside I was raging with fury at being trapped like this, but frozen as I was, there was damn all I could do about it. I reached out telepathically to Devona once more.

Still there?

Sorry I didn't take your warning about the possibility of this being a trap more seriously.

Don't worry about it. There was no way either of us could've anticipated this.

I might've been frozen and surrounded by darkness but Devona's mental presence was a comfort to me and I was grateful for it. Orlock's insane, you know.

No argument there. The longer Bloodborn live the more unstable their minds become if they aren't careful.

I thought about Devona's father and I couldn't disagree with her assessment.

So what now? I asked. Since your psychic powers have no effect on the stasis field, what do we do? Stand around frozen and wait for someone to rescue us?

I'm afraid we'll have a long wait ahead of us, Devona thought. *No one knows we're here, except David, and he has no reason to suspect Orlock has captured us. And even if he did, he has no way to get us out.*

He might get words to some of our friends and they might come for us. It was admittedly a thin hope, but right then it was all I had.

Maybe, Devona thought back, though from the tone of her mental voice, she didn't think much of her chances.

Speaking of David reminded me of his call and I filled Devona in on our conversation. We "talked" about the revelation that I'd been attacked by two men instead of one, but we came to no conclusion about it.

At least we won't starve, Devona thought. *Stasis fields put all biological functions on hold, so I'll have no need for food and you won't be in any danger of rotting, either. We'll remain preserved just as we are…*

Forever, I finished. I'm sorry you're trapped too. Orlock wanted to preserve me. He just stuck you in here to keep me company. Like I'm a goldfish in a bowl whose owner tossed in another fish to keep the first from getting lonely.

If I'm here with you, then I'm exactly where I want to be, she thought. *I love you.*

I love you, too. But if it's all the same to you, I'm going to keep trying to think of a way out of here.

There was a hint of amusement to her thoughtvoice. *I'll try not to take it personally.*

What do you think Orlock meant there at the end when he said that he made sure time inside the domes passes pleasantly enough?

I don't know, but it hasn't been a barrel of laughs so far.

No kidding. Maybe it was just another sign of Orlock's insanity. I–

A strange feeling came over me then, a dizzy, plummeting sensation as if my body was falling and spinning wildly out of control. I tried mentally calling for Devona but I received no answer. Eventually the sensation of vertigo began to ease and my eyes were filled with light and the sound of voices yelling came to my ears.

"Daddy, Daddy!'

FOURTEEN

I turned off the lawnmower and ran the back of my hand across my forehead to wipe away sweat, though all I managed to do was smear it around. God, it was hot out today.

I turned toward the pair of children running toward me across the half mown lawn, one boy, one girl, both eleven, both blond-haired like their mother. They came up to me in a flurry of child energy, skin tanned from being outside all summer, their hair bleached almost white from all the sun they'd gotten. They both wore T-shirts and shorts and both were barefoot. I always had a hell of a time getting them to wear shoes when it was warm out, and my first thought was that one of them had stepped on something sharp, a nail or a piece of broken glass. But the guilty expressions on their faces told me neither was injured and I relaxed a bit.

"What's up, kiddos?" I asked. My lower back gave a twinge and I winced. Devona had been after me to get

a riding mower for a while now, but I insisted on using
a push mower for the exercise. But this season my back
had been putting in its vote for a riding mower too and
I was seriously considering breaking down and getting
one. After all, I wasn't getting any younger.

"It's not our fault!" Lily said.

"You mean it's not *my* fault," Toby said, giving his sister a sideways glance.

Lily shot him a dark look that accused him of betraying her before turning her attention back to me. "Not
our fault," she insisted.

I sighed. You know how twins are supposed to be in-
separably close? Maybe that was true for identical
twins, but for fraternal ones – at least for my twins –
that wasn't always the case. Maybe they didn't fight
anymore than other siblings, but sometimes it sure
seemed like it.

"What happened? And don't both of you talk at the
same time. Lily first."

Toby pursed his lips in irritation. "Why does she get
to go first?"

Because she doesn't let her emotions get the better
of her, I thought. Out loud I said, "We're going in al-
phabetical order."

Lily gave her brother a triumphant smirk before
launching into her story.

"We were playing catch in the backyard near Mom's
garden…" she began.

I already didn't like the sound of this.

"… when Toby threw the baseball too hard–"

"I did not!" Toby's hands curled into fists and his cheeks flushed with a mix of anger and embarrassment.

"… and it flew right by me. I tried to catch it, Daddy, really I did!" She lowered her gaze. "But I missed."

"What happened?" I had a basic idea by that point, but I wanted them to tell me on their own.

Lily didn't answer and Toby looked at her. When he saw how upset she was, the anger drained out of him. he sighed – sounding too much like me – and said, "You know the Buddha statue Mom has in the garden?"

"Yes…"

"The ball hit the statue pretty hard –" he glanced at Lily but she was still looking at the ground – "and, well, the head got knocked off."

I imagined Buddha's decapitated head lying on the ground amidst Devona's petunias and sunflowers. Something about the image of a headless body struck a strange chord in me, but I didn't know why. I decided to put it out of my mind and I laid a hand on each of my children's shoulders and gave them what I hoped was a reassuring squeeze.

"It was an accident, guys. Don't worry about it."

Some of the tension left them then and Lily's head snapped up, her expression suddenly hopeful. "Do you think maybe we can glue the head back on?" she asked.

"*Before* Mom gets back?" Toby added.

I started to answer, but another image flashed through my mind then: I was lying on a table, a nightmarish machine hanging above me, arms protruding from it, each gripping a stainless steel surgical instrument in its hand. The image faded as quickly as it had come, but it was so disturbing that for a moment all I could do was stand there and stare at my children. Eventually, I gave my head a shake to clear it – and for some odd reason I was reassured that it remained solidly attached to my neck.

I forced a smile.

"We can give it a try," I said, "but I think we'll need a lot of glue."

My smile, weak though it was, seemed to reassure the twins further and they smiled back. Before any of us could say anything else, though, we heard the sound of a car approaching and we turned to see Devona driving down the road in her Prius. She honked the horn in greeting as she slowed and then pulled into the driveway. The twins left me and raced across the lawn to greet their mother – and no doubt shower her with love in the hope of ameliorating her reaction when she learned about the fate of her Buddha statue.

Devona got out of the car. She'd gone out to play tennis with a friend, and she wore a sleeveless white blouse and athletic shorts, and she looked damned good to me. She hadn't returned empty-handed, though. She held a cardboard drink carrier with four cups on it. The twins squealed in delight when she held the carrier out for them to select a pair of drinks, all thoughts of the decapitated Buddha forgotten. They grabbed two, along with a pair of straws, stuck them through the plastic lids, and sipped.

"Milkshakes!" Toby said.

"I got chocolate," Lily said, making a face.

"Mine's strawberry."

The twins switched cups, took another sip, and were both much happier.

Devona and I laughed and I started walking over to the car.

"Why don't you two go play in the backyard some more while I break the news to your mom." I paused. "And I do mean *break*."

The twins looked worried again, but I gave them a wink and a smile to let them know everything would be all right. Their own smiles returned and they ran around the side of the house, carrying their milkshakes with them.

"I decided to run through a drive-thru on my way home," Devona said. She held the drink carrier out to me. "What's your pleasure, Mr. Richter? Chocolate or strawberry?"

"*You're* my pleasure, Mrs. Richter."

I leaned forward and kissed her with a bit more passion than was perhaps decorous for suburbia on a Saturday afternoon out in the open, but what the hell?

When we parted, I took a chocolate shake, popped a straw in it, and took a long sip.

"That's good. Doesn't quite hit the spot like a cold beer would right now, but it's an acceptable substitute."

She grinned as she took a sip of her shake – strawberry, her favorite flavor. Which was of course why I'd taken the chocolate.

"They didn't have any beer-flavored shakes," she smiled. "Sorry."

She took another sip and a little spilled out of the corner of her mouth. But instead of being a light pink color, the liquid was a deep crimson.

"Something wrong?" she asked.

I realized then that I was staring at the thick red substance trailing down her chin. I touched my own chin to signal her what was wrong, and she reached up and caught some of the liquid with her finger. She frowned as she examined it.

"That's weird. Maybe they didn't mix it properly and there's a pocket of strawberry syrup at the bottom."

"Maybe." But that explanation didn't feel right and the substance on Devona's chin didn't look like strawberry syrup so much as it looked like... like... The word refused to come and I found my thoughts drifting back to the yard work that still lay before me.

Our home was a ranch house sitting at the end of a cul-de-sac bordering a small park. The kids loved the park's playground equipment and the small woods with a stream running through it. Devona loved the large oak trees and weeping willows. Me? I loved living next to a giant yard I didn't have to mow and trees whose leaves I didn't have to rake every autumn. Dealing with my own yard was enough work for me.

It wasn't quite lunchtime yet and I'd managed to get half the front yard done, but I still had to finish up here and then do the back before I could call it quits for the day. I glanced up at the blazing sun hanging in the summer sky. That is, if I could take the heat for that long. Then again, the Browns were playing this afternoon. Maybe I could finish the front now and put off doing the back until tomorrow.

Devona reached out with her tongue to lap up the crimson liquid on her chin then and I found the action to be at once both arousing and disturbing. She frowned.

"Funny. It doesn't taste like strawberry. It tastes different. Better." She smacked her lips thoughtfully. "Sweet, but it has a kick to it, almost like it contains caffeine. Just a little bit gave me a jolt of energy." She looked at me then. "Wait a minute, what were you saying a minute ago about having bad news to tell me?"

"The kids were messing around in the backyard and accidentally broke the head off your Buddha statue."

"Really? Oh, well. It's not like we can't get it fixed, right? We'll just run on over to the Foundry and…" She trailed off. "Why did I say that? What's the Foundry?"

"I don't know." But the truth was I did know. At least, it felt like I did, somewhere deep down inside me. Only I couldn't quite remember. I decided not to worry about it, realized I seemed to be deciding that a lot lately, then decided not to worry about that.

I took another sip of my shake and my mouth was filled with a taste so foul that I turned to spit the muck out on the grass.

"What's wrong?" Devona asked.

"Damned if I know. It suddenly tastes like shit. Literally. Like the kind of swill they serve at Hem–" I frowned, unable to finish the word, though for the life of me I didn't know why I couldn't finish.

An unusually cool breeze blew across the yard then, causing both Devona and I to shiver.

"Something's not right," she said, a note of fear in her voice.

I knew just how she felt but once more, I decided not to worry about it. No, not decided. I *couldn't* worry about it.

Devona held her shake in one hand and the empty drink carrier in the other, so I couldn't take hold of her. Instead I stepped forward and put my arm around her waist.

"Tell you what, Mrs. Richter. The kids are busy making more mischief in the backyard and you and I are both hot and sweaty – me from my Herculean efforts to tame this lawn, you from exercising your athletic prowess on the tennis court. Would you like to join me in a cool, soothing shower?"

Devona eyed the half-finished lawn. "It's not like you to leave a job undone."

I kissed her gently on the neck. Her sweat coated skin had the tang of salt. I found it to be erotic and I felt my body responding.

"Some sacrifices are worth making."

I leaned in to kiss her lips this time – trying not to think about how she'd lapped up the crimson liquid a moment ago – but before we could kiss, the sun dimmed as if suddenly blocked by clouds. The sky had been clear only a moment ago.

We both looked up and saw that there were no clouds. Instead, the sun had taken on a shadowy cast, and it now gave off a purple-tinted light, painting the world in strange dark hues. A word popped into my mind then, one I'd never heard before but which at the same time seemed so familiar. *Umbriel.*

The breeze returned then, even colder than before, and this time it didn't pass but continued blowing.

Devona dropped the drink carrier and her shake and put her arms around me. I slipped my own arms around her shoulders, noticing that the lid had sprung off her shake cup when it hit the ground. Thick red liquid that looked nothing like strawberry was soaking into the grass.

"Matt, I'm scared. What's happening?"

It's breaking down, I thought, though I wasn't sure what that meant.

Yes, Devona said. *It's our link. Or maybe it's Papa Chatha's necklace. Hell, maybe it's a combination of the two. Whichever the case, something is preventing the illusion from taking full hold of our minds.*

I realized then that Devona wasn't speaking. I'd felt her reply more than heard it, as if she were somehow speaking in my head.

"Illusion?" I said aloud. I had no idea what she was talking about. And yet... I did.

She frowned. "I don't know." She'd returned to speaking her words instead of thinking them to me. "It made sense a second ago, but my thoughts keep slipping away. I can't seem to hold on to them for very long."

I gripped her tighter as the world continued to darken around us. "I know what you mean. It almost feels like we're fighting on some level... resisting. But I don't know exactly what we're fighting."

Devona started to say something, but her reply was cut off by the sound of our children crying out in alarm from the backyard. Without thinking I dropped my shake and Devona and I started running. When we reached the backyard we saw the twins near their sandbox. They lay on the ground, bodies covered with long tendrils of some kind of strange weed growing out of the ground.

Leech vine, I thought. I didn't know what that was, but I instinctively knew it was something very bad.

The vine had burrowed into the children's skin at various place – face, neck, hands, back, belly – and it was pulsing rhythmically as if it was pumping something into them. No, I realized with horror. The plant was pumping something out of them: blood.

Devona and I stood there in shock for several seconds and during that time we watched the twins' suntanned skin begin to pale as the leech vine rapidly drained the life out of them.

Devona and I started forward. I didn't know if I would make things worse by tearing the vines away from the twins' flesh. I only knew I couldn't stand by and watch as my children succumbed to some sort of parasitic plant. But before either Devona or I could reach the twins, Lily held her hand out in a *stay back* gesture.

"Don't!" she said. Her voice was so much weaker than it had been only a few minutes ago in the front yard and hearing it broke my heart. I started forward again, but Toby repeated his sister's gesture.

"Listen to her!" he said, his voice just as weak as his twin's. "We know what's happening." His hand dropped then, as if it were too weak to hold it up any longer, and Lily's did the same.

"None of this is real," my daughter said, her voice now little more than a whisper. "We're not real, Toby and I, we're... *pretend*. This whole place is pretend."

Toby's head gave the slightest of nods, all that he could manage. His skin, like his sister's, was almost ivory-white now, eyes sunken in, lips blue-tinged.

"You and Mom are fighting. Trying... to break free. That's why all this is happening. Why we're..." He trailed off.

"Dying," Lily finished for him. "But it's OK, because we were never really..."

"Alive," Toby said.

I turned to Devona, and I saw she now possessed overlong incisors jutting down from her upper jaw. I looked at my hands and saw they were gray-tinged, the flesh dry and flaking.

"Pretend," Lily said. "Just... pretend."

Sorrow welled up strong inside me, along with anger. This family, my house, my *life* wasn't pretend. It couldn't be! I wouldn't let it be!"

A shimmering passed through the air, like ripples in a pond, and when it cleared, the sunshine had returned in full force and my children stood there, free of the leech vine, strong and healthy once more. Devona no longer had fangs, and my hands looked normal again. Everything was as it should be.

I was so relieved that I started toward the twins, wanting nothing more than to wrap my arms around the two of them and never let go. But the expressions on their faces – sadness, disappointment, regret – made me pause.

"Don't, Daddy," Lily said. "Don't use us as an excuse to hide."

"You've always faced the truth, no matter how hard it was," Toby said. He smiled then. "That's your job, right? To find out the truth."

"Find it now," Lily said. "For us, if for no other reason."

I turned to Devona, and I didn't know I was crying until she reached up and gently brushed the tears from my face. She was crying too, but her tears were tinged with red, and while that should've seemed strange to me, I somehow knew it was perfectly normal for her.

"It tears me up to say this, Matt, but they're right. I can feel it. And I know you can too."

I wanted to tell her that I didn't feel anything, that this was real, and I didn't want to hear another word about it. But instead I nodded. I took her in my arms and held her as tight as I could.

"This really sucks," I said softly.

"I know. Ready?"

I wanted to look at the kids one last time, but I knew I couldn't bear it. So I closed my eyes and said, "Ready."

I felt Devona's mind reaching for mine and I reached back. Vertigo took hold of me then and when the world stopped spinning I opened my eyes and found myself standing amidst dozens of bizarre displays – and I remembered.

I was no longer physically capable of crying, but if I had been I'd have broken down and sobbed right then.

It's all right, love, Devona thought. *It's over. We're back.*

I tried to move, but I still couldn't. Orlock's stasis field was still in effect and I knew that it had remained so the entire time.

What he said about time passing pleasantly… He created an illusory life for us to live while we were trapped here. Like filling an aquarium full of plastic plants and ceramic undersea ruins for the fish to swim around.

Yes, Devona thought. *But he didn't count on your necklace and our telepathic link. They reinforced what was real and fought against what wasn't. Because of that, the illusion couldn't sustain itself.*

I thought of all the other beings trapped within Orlock's stasis domes, all of them living virtual lives deep within their minds while their bodies remained frozen as the long years passed. It was like being trapped in a kind of hell, only one that you weren't aware of. Somehow that made it all the worse.

Then again, maybe it was worse to come out of the dream. I missed my children and grieved for their deaths, even though I knew they'd never been real.

And now Devona and I faced the prospect of spending our time in stasis without the comfort of Orlock's illusion to distract us. I wished my necklace had nullified the stasis field too, but either it was completely technological or its magic was too powerful for the necklace to handle on its own without the added help of Devona's and my telepathic link. For whatever reasons we'd broken the illusion but the stasis field remained intact.

Are you all right? I asked her.

Devona didn't answer right away. Finally she said, *Honestly, no. You?*

Working on it, I said, tying to sound braver than I felt at that moment. I'll tell you one thing, though. When we get out of this damned bubble, I'm going to find Orlock and... My thoughts trailed off as I realized something. The lights are on. They were off when the illusion took hold of our minds.

You're right, Devona thought. *Maybe Orlock's coming back. Maybe he wants to ask us more questions about Osseal, since he'd love to get his talons on it.*

Since Orlock's a vampire, he can see in the dark, I reminded her. He said he uses the lights only for his guests.

We heard footsteps coming toward us then and I could tell right away that they didn't belong to Orlock. The pace was too measured, the rhythm too steady for the crablike way he walked. My surmise turned out to be correct when a few moments later a woman approached our dome and stood regarding us, hands planted on her hips, head cocked at an angle, grin plastered on her face.

"Hello, Matt," Overkill said. "You're a damned hard man to find, you know that?"

My first impulse was to tell Overkill that she was a sight for sore eyes, but since I wasn't able to speak, I couldn't. Besides, I wasn't entirely sure her arrival was a good thing.

She was dressed the same way she was when I saw her last, only now she was better armed, with a P-90 submachine gun slung over her shoulder by a strap, and a weapons belt around her waist with a holster for a 9mm, sheaths for several lengths and types of knives – including, I was disturbed to see, a dire blade – and storage pouches that presumably held whatever the well-accessorized mercenary was carrying these days. Considering how often I have to root around in my pockets for my own toys, I wondered if I should invest in a belt like that, but I decided against it. I don't like my adversaries to know how well armed I am. I prefer to let them underestimate me. Besides, a belt like that would just look silly on me.

"First things first," Overkill said. "Let's get you two out of there."

She reached into one of her belt pouches and removed a small glass vial. She took a deep breath and held it before prying out the stopper and splashing the liquid contents onto the area of the dome directly in front of where Devona and I stood immobile. As we watched, the place where the liquid – which was a foul yellow color – had struck began to sizzle and steam.

Within moments the liquid had eaten a lopsided hold through the dome and once the structure's integrity had been compromised it shuddered violently and then popped out of existence as if it were nothing more than a giant soap bubble. Once the dome had vanished the stasis field ceased functioning and Devona and I were able to move and talk again.

"Whatever that stuff was, it's pretty handy," I said. "I may need to pick up a few gallons myself."

"It's demon piss," Overkill said as she replaced the stopper and put the empty vial back into its pouch. "Once it's exposed to air, it'll eat through anything – and you don't want to know what I had to do to get it."

"You got that right," I said.

From her belt pouch she next removed an amulet stamped with the image of a winding serpent. "This is a charm I picked up from an Obeah woman I know. It allows me to command any zombie to do my bidding." She grinned. "Including you, Matt. You're going to accompany me to the Nightspire so I can collect the bounty Quillion is offering for you."

I looked at her charm. It appeared genuine enough, but I felt no compulsion to do as she ordered.

"Sorry, but I don't think so," I said.

Overkill frowned at the charm and gave it a couple shakes, as if she might be able to force it to work. Little did she know that Papa Chatha's necklace was protecting me from the charm.

"Cheap piece of crap," she muttered. "Guess we'll do this the old-fashioned way." She dropped the charm to the ground, took hold of her P-90, racked the slide, and aimed it at me. "Don't try anything," she warned, gaze cold and expression deadly serious. "You don't need legs for me to take you to the Nightspire and it'll only take a few well aimed rounds from my weapon to cut them off."

She looked to Devona. "And my ammo has silver blended into it, so it's effective against both your human and Bloodborn halves."

"Let me guess what happened," I said. "Orlock called to tell you we were out of action and to urge you to go after Scream Queen's voice again. But you figured you'd rather collect the reward on me, and in the bargain get back at me for stopping you at Sinsation."

"That is, unless you organized all this in the first place," Devona said.

Overkill frowned. "What are you talking about?"

"After you left Sinsation, someone cut off my head, stole my body, and somehow used it to steal a magic object called Osseal from Lord Edrigu," I explained. "I managed to get my body back, and Victor Baron made me whole, but then I was arrested and sentenced to Tenebrus for the theft – which I didn't commit."

"Orlock told me as much," Overkill said. "But you don't really think I had anything to do with it, do you? I mean, I'm not big on elaborate planning. I'm more of a shoot first and never ask questions kind of gal. And if I had an object of power like Osseal, I could sell it for a whole lot more than five hundred thousand darkgems. And then I'd just let you stay frozen down here for eternity. I almost did anyway, but since I don't have Osseal and you did piss me off at Sinsation, I figured, what the hell?"

She could have been lying, but my instincts told me she was telling the truth. But I didn't have to rely on my instincts alone.

Devona?

I don't sense any subterfuge on her part, but she could be shielding her mind from me. She's certainly strong-willed enough on her own, and she could also be using some kind of magic object to help conceal her thoughts.

So Overkill might've moved to the bottom of my suspects lists, but she wasn't officially off it yet.

"How did you manage to get past Orlock?" I asked. "He doesn't strike me as the kind of guy who willingly give up something once he's collected it."

"He's not, but I have my ways." Overkill smiled grimly. "I'm carrying a magic object that temporarily traps Bloodborn in their travel forms. Right now Orlock is stuck as a dozen or so shadow rats scurrying around his bookstore, unable to put themselves back together."

I had to admit, the woman was good.

"He's not going to be too pleased with you once the spells wears off," Devona said.

"Maybe, but he's nothing if not pragmatic. Once I collect the reward on Matt, I'm going to start looking for Osseal. If I can find it and bring it to him, there's a good chance he'll forgive me for freeing you two. And if not…" She shrugged. "There are plenty of other people in the city willing to pay for my services."

"I don't suppose it matters to you that I'm innocent," I said.

"Maybe you are, maybe you aren't. Orlock seemed to think you are and he's usually right about things like that. But I don't care. Guilty or innocent, you're still worth five hundred thousand darkgems to me."

I was racking my brain, trying to come up with a way to convince Overkill to let us go or, failing that, a way that we could escape her, when Devona decided to take matters into her own hands.

She bared her fangs and hissed as she sprang toward Overkill. Devona is only half-vampire, but she's still fast as hell and she was almost on top of the mercenary before the woman could tighten her finger on the trigger of her P-90 and release a burst of gunfire. Devona managed to avoid being struck by any of the bullets, and they flew on, hitting various displays around us, taking chunks out of rare and valuable objects. Orlock would have a fit once he finally managed to pull himself together and come down here and saw the damage.

Devona wasn't fooling around. She fastened her teeth on Overkill's neck and bit down. The momentum of Devona's leap sent both women falling to the floor, and the impact caused Overkill to lose her grip on the P-90, and the strap slipped over her shoulder. The weapon skittered away from her, coming to stop over by the Frankenstein experiment display. I started toward it, doing the half-shuffle, half-run which is the fastest way I can make my dead body move.

As I went for the gun, Overkill hit Devona in the temple with a solid left cross, dislodging her teeth from Overkill's neck in a spray of blood. But Devona had a firm grip on Overkill's shoulders and she managed to hold on. Devona tried to bite Overkill again, but the mercenary brought up a forearm to block her. I saw Overkill reaching for her dire blade and I knew I had only seconds to reach the P-90. A single strike from a dire blade is fatal, as I'd demonstrated to Lycanthropus Rex in Tenebrus, and if Overkill managed to draw her blade, Devona was as good as dead.

I reached the P-90 and was bending down to pick it up when I became aware of movement. I looked at the metal framework containing the severed limbs of Dr. Frankenstein's early work and saw that every one of them had become fully animated and was thrashing about wildly. I glanced at the hand crank generator. No one had touched the crank and the machine wasn't active. No electricity was reaching the limbs, so how were they moving? What could make a bunch of dead arms and legs suddenly –

Then it hit me.

I turned to Devona and Overkill, who were still fighting on the floor. Devona had straddled the mercenary who'd managed to draw her dire blade. Devona had hold of the other woman's wrist, preventing her from using the dagger, and from the look of fury on Devona's face, I figured Overkill had only a few seconds before her wrist snapped like kindling.

"Ladies!" I shouted. Then again, louder. "Ladies!"

That time I got their attention. They stopped fighting, though Devona kept hold of Overkill's wrist. They focused their gazes on me and I pointed to the rack of thrashing limbs behind me.

"We've got a problem," I said. "I think someone just started playing Edrigu's flute."

FIFTEEN

Once Devona and Overkill stopped fighting, the mercenary applied first aid to her throat wound – a powerful anticoagulant to stop the bleeding and a patch of plaskin to seal the bite and begin the healing process. Both items were developed by the Bloodborn physicians at the Fever House, undisputed experts in treating injuries sustained during vampire attacks.

I hated to leave the others who were trapped in Orlock's stasis domes, but there wasn't time to free them all and besides, Overkill hadn't brought enough demon piss to do the job. But after what Devona and I had experienced in that bastard's virtual fishbowl, I was determined to return one day and free Orlock's prisoners, even if I had to kill the sonofabitch to do it.

The three of us then returned to Nosferatomes and walked outside, where we saw my worst fears confirmed.

Fighting had broken out in the street and not the usual sort of brawling that can happen anytime in the

Sprawl. This was a serious toe –to toe, tooth-and-claw struggle for survival, complete with shouts of alarm, screams of agony, and lots of the red stuff being spilled. At first it was hard to come to any specific conclusions about the combatants because the fighting was so fast and furious, but after a couple moments it became clear that they could be broken into two separate camps: the dead and the living. A huge Frankenstein creature wearing only ragged jeans – the better to show off the jagged scars covering his obscenely muscled body – stood outside Matango, strangling a ghoul with one hand while he tore the arm off a lyke with the other. I recognized the man as Jigsaw Jones, one of the most popular professional wrestlers in the city and the sport's current champion. From the bleeding cuts on his flesh and the restaurant's shattered front window, I guessed Jones had been dining there when he'd flipped out and started killing people. I pictured him killing several of his fellow diners before leaping through the window and attacking the first people unlucky enough to be in his way.

In front of Hemlocks, Baristastein stood in the midst of carnage, a half-dozen bodies in various states of dis-embowelment spread out around her on the sidewalk. She currently had both hands wrapped around the throat of a toad-faced demon with overlarge insect eyes and was slowly squeezing the life out of him. No longer was her face expressionless. Now her features were contorted in savage joy as she throttled the struggling demon.

Ferdinand approached her, confused sadness in his eyes.

"Sandy, something's happened to you – something bad. Please… let me help you!"

Baristastein snapped the toad demon's neck with a single quick shake and then tossed his body aside. She then started walking toward the minotaur, her gaze glittering with hungry anticipation.

Any thought I'd had about getting even with the bull man for making me drink the Sprawlicano vanished when I saw the danger he was in. "Get away from her!" I shouted.

But either Ferdinand didn't hear me or he was in too much shock to listen, for instead of turning away from the approaching Baristastein and running like hell in the opposite direction, he opened his arms wide to welcome her.

I didn't want to look, but I forced myself to watch as Baristastein rammed a hand into her boyfriend's chest and yanked out his still beating, bloody heart. Ferdinand bellowed in pain, and as the life quickly fled from his eyes, he looked upon the object of his adoration uncomprehendingly, and then his body went limp and he collapsed to the ground. Baristastein looked at the grisly object clutched in her hand for a moment as if she didn't quite understand what it was, then she hurled it aside, roared in fury, and stomped off in search of new victims.

I might have made a joke about how even in death Ferdinand had given his heart to his girl, but even though I can't experience nausea, I didn't have the stomach for such gallows humor right then. The minotaur might've been a jerk, but he hadn't deserved to die like that.

Up and down the street the same scene was played out again and again as the dead made violent, bloody war on the living. It was the same *in* the street as well. Vehicles that contained any part of Victor Baron's fleshtech, such as Agony DeLites and Meatrunners ignored their drivers' commands and crashed into other cars, running them off the road or into each other, engines roaring with bestial joy.

"This is most definitely not good," Overkill said.

"I didn't realize that understatement was one of your many skills," I said, unable to take my gaze off the chaos that surrounded us.

I heard Overkill rack the slide on her P-90 and when I turned to took at her I saw she had the weapon trained on me.

"So if all the deaders in the city have gone psycho, why haven't you?" she demanded.

I opened my coat to show her the Loa necklace Papa Chatha had given me.

"This makes me immune to magic. It's why your bargain basement Obeah charm failed. Its primary purpose is to prevent anyone from finding me with a tracking spell, but it blocks all magic – including that of Osseal, it seems."

"Maybe," Devona said, "but I'm not sure that's the only reason." She was still looking out into the street.

"Have you two noticed something about *which* dead are attacking?"

Overkill frowned, though she didn't lower her weapon. "What do you mean?"

I turned to look at the mayhem once more and this time I saw what Devona was talking about. It was so obvious that I felt stupid for not having realized it before.

"Only Victor Baron's creations are attacking," I said.

Overkill swept her gaze up and down the street as she more closely examined the fighting taking place.

"Maybe it just seems like that," she said. "There's more of Baron's flesh tech in the Sprawl than there are other types of dead." Still, she sounded doubtful.

"This may not be the Boneyard, but there are numerous ghosts, revenants, liches, reanimated skeletons, zombies and the like around," Devona said. "Do you see any out there?"

"No," Overkill admitted. "So if it's true, and only Baron's monsters have gone crazy, what does that mean?"

"It means that whoever stole Osseal is using it to control only Baron's creations, and he's making them attack," I said.

The thought would've chilled my blood if I had any running through my veins. Baron's fleshtech was everywhere in Nekropolis, and I thought of all the businesses that employed his monsters, all the vehicles that incorporated his technology – voxes, Mind's Eye projectors, the Overwatchers in Tenebrus, even David's ravens… I imagined the scenes of death we were witnessing being played out all over the city, in clubs, bars, restaurants and homes.

And then, as if my thoughts were a cue, a chorus of piercing shrieks filled the air around us, and we looked at each other as we tried to determine where the deafening noise originated from.

"It's our voxes!" Devona shouted, though I could barely understand what she said, so loud was the din issuing from our phones.

The three of us pulled out our voxes and flipped open their covers. Their mouths were wide open and screaming at top volume, but once they were exposed they began snapping and gnashing their teeth, as if desperate to bite us.

Without consulting one another, the three of us dashed our voxes to the ground and then stomped on them. The plastic cases broke and pieces of electronic components spilled out, along with copious amounts of blood. Voxes incorporate Victor Baron's fleshtech and it seemed they were just as susceptible to the influence of Osseal as any other reanimated creature.

"Who would want to make Baron's creatures riot?" Devona asked.

"Who else but Baron himself?" I said. "For years there's been talk of making him the sixth Darklord, but Father Dis has always refused. So Baron worked hard to spread his creations throughout Nekropolis, getting his army in place so that when the time was right, they could strike. Now with Dis and the Darklords still sleeping to recharge their energies after the last Renewal Ceremony, that time has finally come."

Overkill opened her mouth to say something, but at that moment Jigsaw Jones – who'd just finished snapping a witch's spine by slamming her against his knee – turned to look at me. He discarded the screaming witch and came striding toward us. His scarred flesh was splattered with blood from his victims and from the expression of violent lust on his face, he was looking to add even more gore to his collection. I wondered if Jigsaw Jones and the rest of Baron's creations were listening to a mystic melody that only they could hear, music that drove them to go forth and kill.

Overkill turned her P-90 away from me and trained it on the approaching wrestler.

"Hold on," I said. I drew my .45, aimed, and put a bullet through Jones' right eye. His head jerked back, blood sprayed the air, and he staggered backward. He didn't go down, though, so I sent a second bullet to follow the first through the same hole, and that did the trick. Jones hit the ground like a giant slab of scarred, bloodied beef.

I felt bad for having to put the big lug down. After all, I'd made more than a few darkgems betting on him over the years and I knew his homicidal rage wasn't his fault. Still, in Nekropolis, kill or be killed isn't just a saying. It's a way of life.

I turned to Overkill. "No point in wasting ammo we might need later."

"That was good shooting," she said.

"Being dead means my hands don't shake. Makes my aim steadier."

"Still, that was impressive," Overkill insisted. "I'm not sure I could've done it." She looked at me then, reappraisal in her gaze, as if she were somehow seeing me differently.

I wasn't sure how to take it, and it made me uncomfortable. Devona didn't like it either, for she gave Overkill a hard look as she stepped forward and took my hand.

"We can't keep standing out in the open like this," Devona said. "Come on."

Without waiting for either Overkill or me to reply, she started leading me around the side of Nosferatomes and into the alley between the bookstore and Matango. Overkill followed, frowning slightly, though I couldn't guess what she might be thinking. The alley was blessedly free of Victor Baron's creations eager to tear us apart, and if only for the moment, we were safe.

"I still have a hard time believing Baron's behind this," Overkill said. "I mean, he's already rich and powerful. What more could he want?"

"The operative word in your question is *more*," I said. "What else is left for someone like him to want? Power can be like a drug, Overkill, and its addicts need ever greater doses in order to get the high they crave."

"Christina," she said.

I frowned. "Excuse me?"

"My real name. It's Christina. Christina Butts, actually."

"Seriously?" Devona said.

Overkill's finger tightened on the trigger of her P-90. "You got a problem with that?"

"Not at all," Devona said in an overly sweet tone.

"Look, I don't know what's going on between you two, but can you at least put it on hold until we can figure out what the hell is happening out there?" I gestured toward the mouth of the alley where the sounds of violent mayhem continued to filter in from the street.

"Nothing is going on!" Devona and Overkill said in unison and then turned to glare at each other.

I sighed. "Let's get back to business. Baron is the perfect suspect. Who else has the know how to cut off my head, animate my body, and use it to steal Osseal from Edrigu?"

Devona gave Overkill a last dirty look before turning to me. "I get how he found out about the mark on your hand. He doubtless saw Acantha's interview with you at Sinsation. But how did he know it could get you – I mean your body – past Edrigu's security at the Reliquary?"

"And how did he find out about Osseal and what it could do?" Overkill put in, as if she were determined not to be left out of the conversation.

"Baron's a couple centuries old, and he's extremely intelligent and well connected," I said. "He might've found out about Osseal any number of ways. Maybe from research into different reanimation techniques or maybe from Edrigu himself. He told me that Edrigu is one of his best clients. However Baron learned about Osseal, he probably learned about Edrigu's mark the same way. He just needed to find someone who possessed the mark that he could use."

"And when he saw Acantha's interview, he knew he'd finally found what he'd been waiting for," Devona said.

"But Baron didn't do the job himself," I said. "After he saw the interview, he sent a pair of Bonegetters to track me down and collect my body. And they probably used one of Baron's hi-tech vivisection tools to sever my head from my body. That's how they did the job so swiftly. And I think I know who it was, too. Remember those two we saw at the Foundry? Burke and Hare? They seemed awfully smirky to me, as if they were sharing a private joke. Now I know why. They were having a laugh at my expense, knowing I had no idea they were the ones who'd cut off my head."

"It all makes sense," Overkill said. "More or less. But one thing I don't get. From what I gather, you went to Victor Baron to have your head reattached. Why didn't he just have his men dispose of your body when he was finished with it?"

"They tried." I told her how we'd found my body in a Dumpster behind the Tooth and Claw restaurant.

"Why not just incinerate your body at the Foundry?" she asked. "Seems like that would've been easier."

"Baron didn't want any evidence at his place," I said. "A good forensic sorcerer would've been able to find traces of my body's ashes. It's doubtful anyone would've even thought to check the Foundry for such evidence – especially if Baron's coup succeeded – but he's too smart to leave anything to chance. That's why he agreed to reattach my head to my body when we called. He didn't want to arouse any suspicion. Better to just go along and fix me. Besides, that way there was someone else to take the fall for the theft. And since Baron helped put me back together, that further deflected suspicion from him."

"Seems like Baron thought of everything," Overkill said. "Except how good a detective you are."

She gave me that look again, and Devona scowled. I decided to start talking again before they could resume arguing.

"I'm not sure knowing the truth makes any difference," I said. "Who can we tell? Dis and the Darklords are still sleeping, and while I'm guessing their servants are right now trying desperately to wake them, there's no guarantee they'll succeed. Edrigu didn't wake up when Baron had my body steal Osseal from around his neck. If Edrigu slept through that, I doubt someone shaking him by the shoulders and shouting in his ear will do the trick. Same for the other lords."

"We could try to tell Quillion," Devona ventured.

"The Adjudicators and Sentinels probably have their hands full trying to deal with the rioting," I said. "I'd try to call Quillion, but our voxes are destroyed, and none of the others in the city are working, so that's out. We could try to tell him in person – assuming we could make it through the rioting monsters and reach the

Nightspire – but I fear Quillion would destroy me on the spot for escaping Tenebrus before I had a chance to get a single word out."

"To hell with Quillion," Overkill said. "Let's just go to the Foundry ourselves, kick Baron's ass, and take Osseal away from him. The rioting should stop then, yeah?"

"I suppose so," I said. "But since when did you become the hero type?"

"I'm not. What I am is a gal who likes her fun and right now the idea of fighting my way through a city of murderously insane Frankenstein monsters sounds like a blast!"

Devona regarded Overkill for a moment. "You really are a very strange woman. You know that, right?"

Overkill just grinned at her.

I considered Overkill's suggestion. Back when I was a cop on Earth, I once saw a piece of spray-painted graffiti on an alley wall that read *Justice = Just Us*. All too often, that was the way it worked in Nekropolis. Who else was there to deal with Baron? Besides, the sono-fabitch had used me like I was nothing more than a puppet, and I was determined to make him pay for it.

"It won't be easy," I said, thinking aloud. "The Foundry's as well protected as a military base – and I very much doubt we'll be able to get there on foot. Hell, I'm not sure we could get there by car, given how bad it is out there." I thought about Lazlo, but I doubted his cab had been repaired yet, and there was no way it could get us through a city of rioting monsters in the condition we'd last seen it in.

"We don't need to drive all the way to the Foundry," Devona said. "We could take the–" She winced, her face scrunching up as if she was experiencing a sudden, intense pain.

I understood. Devona had been about to say *Underwalk*, but the tongue worm the Dominari had given her had jolted her with a burst of pain to warn her not to speak the word.

"Take what?" Overkill asked, but we ignored her.

"Yes!" I said, but my enthusiasm for the idea quickly waned. "But we still need to get there." The only entrance we knew about lay in a warehouse on the other side of the Sprawl – and there were a lot of Baron's psychotic creations between us and there, every one of them eager to tear us into teeny-tiny pieces.

"I don't know what you two are talking about," Overkill said, "but if you need to get across the Sprawl, I can help you out." She grinned. "I've got a ride."

"You know, if someone had told me two days ago that I'd be riding shotgun inside Carnage with Overkill at the wheel, I'd have told them they were crazy."

"Funny how life works out sometimes," Overkill said.

From the back seat, Devona muttered, "Hilarious."

My love was obviously not thrilled to be stuck in back, especially since that left me sharing the front seat with Overkill, but we'd decided that each of us needed to be next to a window so we could fight if necessary, and there were only two windows on each side of the

car. Still, given the scowl that had etched itself onto Devona's face since we'd climbed into the car, maybe I
should've volunteered to sit in the back.

Only a few minutes earlier Overkill had led Devona
and me from the alley between Nosferatomes and
Matango to a spot a block away where Carnage was
parked. We encountered more than a little resistance
from Baron's mad monsters as we went, but between
the three of us, we managed to discourage them from
rending us limb from limb, and we made it to Carnage.
The car's black paint was bleached white in places, evidence of his time bonded with the Conglomeration,
but otherwise he looked little the worse for wear. We
all hopped in, and the possessed car roared away from
the curb like a Caddy out of Hell.

The streets of the Sprawl were clogged with wrecked
and abandoned vehicles, not to mention pedestrians
running for their lives from pursuing monsters. Carnage wove through the chaos with consummate skill
and we made our way toward the Dominari-owned
warehouse. As we traveled, Overkill explained how
she'd come to team up with Carnage.

"I was already out looking for you, like every other
hunter in the city, when one of my sources told me
you'd been spotted tangling with Carnage on Sybarite
Street. I hurried there and found Carnage stuck in the
Conglomeration – nice move, by the way. By that point
he'd almost extricated himself, and it didn't take much
help from me to get him the rest of the way free. I intended to pump him for information about his

encounter with you, maybe get a lead on where you were headed, when Orlock called. Once I knew he had you and Devona on ice, I wanted to get there as soon as possible, so I proposed that Carnage give me a ride and we'd split the bounty."

"More like Carnage overheard the call and threatened to kill you if you didn't cut him in," I said.

"That's one interpretation," Overkill allowed. "By the way, he still expects to be paid, and considering how you tricked him when you last met, he expects to be well paid."

"I suppose I should be grateful he's more mercenary than vindictive," I said. I had no idea where I was going to get my hands on the amount of darkgems Carnage would want, but I decided to worry about that later.

I'd never been close enough to Carnage to look inside it… him… whatever. The dashboard display was lit with the same crimson glow as his headlights and the interior was done entirely in black. The seats were leather and Devona later told me they felt slightly oily, as if they were living skin. She also said a faint odor of brimstone issued from the car's vents.

"Wait a minute," Devona said to Overkill. "You can talk to Carnage?"

"Sure," Overkill said. "There isn't a language in Nekropolis I can't speak, at least well enough to get by. Though I admit I'm not as fluent in possessed automobile as I'd like to be."

The more time I spent around Overkill, the more impressed I was by her. My feelings must've showed on my face, for Devona leaned forward and punched me none-too-gently on the shoulder.

"Keep you mind on the job," she said, her fangs fully extended.

Overkill glanced at Devona in the rearview mirror and just smiled.

Because Carnage was alive (in a sense) and intelligent, Overkill didn't actually have to drive. She rode behind the wheel, holding on to her P-90, which she'd reloaded as soon as we'd gotten into Carnage, gaze sweeping the street ahead for signs of trouble as we drove. She'd loaned Devona her 9mm, and I had my .45 and both of us had some magical items left over from what Shrike had brought us. We weren't exactly loaded for bear, but we weren't unarmed, either.

The scenes we saw as we made our way through the Sprawl were nightmarish even by Nekropolis's standards. Victor Baron built his creations to be tough and virtually unstoppable, and so far they'd lived up to their reputation. Buildings had their doors torn from their hinges, their windows shattered, and skeletal street-lights had been snapped in half. Cars – some that had been run off the road by Baron's vehicles, others that had been picked up by his monsters and hurled – were torn and twisted, lying wherever they'd come to rest. And there were bodies of course, more often than not ripped asunder, limbs and organs strewn about the streets like some sort of hellish decorations.

People were fighting back – this was Nekropolis, after all. Sentinels were out in force, the golems battling fiercely to quell the rioting, but while they were just as powerful as any of Baron's creations, they were seriously outnumbered, and we saw more than one Sentinel fall beneath a pile of savage monsters, never to rise again. I recognized some of the combatants that we passed. Outside Sinsation I saw the club's bouncer trying to get his hands on Eeriegami, but the latter kept folding and unfolding his body into different shapes, slipping out of the monster's grasp every time. In the street near Westerna's, I saw the Bloodborn waitress I thought of as Countess Dolly standing toe to toe with the Frankenstein monster decked out like John Wayne. Dolly clawed deep furrows into the monster's chest, but it didn't stop him from tearing off her head and throwing it as far as he could. Dolly's head flew right past my window and I saw the expression of fury on her face, and though I couldn't read her rapidly moving lips, I doubted she was singing her attacker's praises. As a recently decapitated head myself, I sympathized.

We even saw Shrike outside the Broken Cross, where he'd teamed up with a midget vampire called Anklebiter. The latter would run up to one of Baron's monsters and sink his teeth into the flesh of its leg. When the creature opened its mouth to howl in pain, Shrike transformed into smoke, flowed into the creature's mouth and down into its lungs, where he partially solidified, causing some serious damage. The monster would cough up copious amounts of blood and then fall to the ground, out of action. Shrike would then emerge and resolidify and he and Anklebiter would start looking around for another monster to tackle.

I had a lot of friends and acquaintances throughout the city, and I hoped that they'd have the good fortune – and good sense – to reach a hiding place where they'd be safe from the rampaging monsters, though I knew that most of them, like Shrike, were probably out in the thick of the chaos, fighting to protect their home. I found myself thinking of Tavi, Scorch and yes, even Bogdan, and wondering how they were faring right then. I'm sure they were on Devona's mind as well, but as neither of us had voxes at the moment, we couldn't call and check on them. As it was, all we could do was try our best to get to the Foundry, stop Victor Baron, and put an end to the violence ravaging the city as swiftly as possible.

Before long we drew close to the intersection where the Dominari warehouse was located, and it looked like we were going to reach it without further incident.

I should've known better.

As we rounded the corner, Carnage hit his brakes and came to a screeching stop. The street before us was filled with Baron's creatures – male and female, some battle damaged but still functional, all of them huge, grotesque and completely insane, thanks to the power of Osseal's song.

"We should've expected this," I said. "It looks like Baron has ordered his creations to join ranks and began an organized assault on the city."

"Maybe we can go around them," Devona said.

"Let's go through," Overkill said. She pushed a button on Carnage's dash and I expected to hear the ratcheting noise of his hood mounted machine gun activating. But instead a humming sound came from the rear of the vehicle, and I turned around to see a new weapon rising from the trunk. It had a long barrel like a gun, and a thick rubber hose extended from the back, connecting it to something in the trunk I couldn't see.

I turned to Overkill. "What's that?"

"Flamethrower," she said, grinning.

The weapon continued rising until it extended above Carnage's roof. The mass of monsters had continued to advance while Carnage had been deploying the flamethrower and now they were almost upon us. We didn't wait for Carnage to attack. The three of us leaned out and started firing our weapons. Overkill let loose with her P-90 and I fired my .45. Instead of using her borrowed 9mm, though, Devona selected one of the items Shrike had brought us – an explosive hawthorn ball. She hurled the device into the crowd of monsters and it burst apart in a shower of deadly sharp thorns. Devona immediately followed up by employing the 9mm.

None of our efforts produced any casualties, but the weapons fire gave the monsters pause, allowing Carnage to finish getting his flamethrower into position and activate it. A stream of flame shot into the creatures' ranks, and they bellowed in pain and anger as their clothes caught fire and their flesh blackened and burned. According to Devona, the stench was horrific. Carnage continued spraying fire at the monsters, swiveling the flamethrower back and forth to get as many as possible. Roaring, Baron's army backed up to get away from the deadly flames.

No one especially likes being hosed by fire – with the possible exception of Scorch – but Frankenstein monsters are especially susceptible to it (as am I, dry-fleshed thing that I am). In their case, there's something about the chemicals Baron uses as part of the reanimation process that react violently to fire, and as we watched, those monsters who were burning most furiously swelled up like balloons and exploded in showers of crispy black skin and steaming gore. Those explosions alarmed the surviving monsters even more, and they quickly moved out of our path.

Carnage started forward again, rolling slowly and spraying fire back and forth as we went, while Devona, Overkill and I continued to fire our weapons at any creature who took it into his or her head to risk the fire and come toward us. It was slow going, but we made it to the end of the block. Unfortunately Carnage's flamethrower was running out of fuel and the length and strength of the flame stream was severely diminished. The surviving monsters didn't fail to take note of this and they were beginning to mass together and approach again, making sure to stay just out of the flamethrower's newly limited range.

"That's the building we want!" I pointed to the warehouse, and Carnage zoomed over the curb and parked.

"This is our stop," I said to Overkill as I reached for my door handle. "Thanks for the help."

She grabbed hold of my arm to stop me. "I'm going with you. There's no way I'm going to miss out on the main event!"

"You don't understand. You *can't* come with us." I wanted to explain to her that Devona and I were both under a spell that wouldn't allow us to reveal the truth about where we were going and that our heads would explode if we ever tried. But of course, the tongue worm prevented me from doing even that much, and I felt a sudden stabbing pain in my mouth which, considering that I had no functioning nerves there, came as a shock to me.

Devona glanced out the car window.

"We don't have time for this," she said. "The monsters are coming." She leaned forward, grabbed Overkill by the shoulders, and turned the woman halfway around to face her. Devona's eyes flared red and she hissed a single word. "*Sleep!*"

Overkill tried to resist, but the psychic powers of a half-vampire are formidable, and Devona's had only gotten stronger since I'd met her. Overkill's eyes rolled up in her head, and she slumped over onto me, snoring softly. I gently pushed her off me and scooted over so she could lie flat on the seat.

"Carnage," Devona said, "as soon as we get out, take her away from here as fast as you can."

Carnage didn't respond at first, and Devona sighed. "Don't worry. If we make it through this, we'll see to it you get paid one way or another. You have our word on it."

Carnage might not be able to speak English, but the Caddy understood it well enough. He tooted his horn once, Devona and I climbed out, and he lost no time in peeling out of there, knocking aside several of Baron's creatures in the process. He didn't bother using his flamethrower, and I knew that the weapon was out of fuel. I hoped Carnage and Overkill would make it to safety. They might have been mercenaries, but we'd never have made it to the warehouse without their help. Of course, getting here was no guarantee that we'd survive to get inside. Without the threat of Carnage's flamethrower to keep them at bay, Baron's monsters were closing in on us fast.

We ran to the closest door and found it locked. Devona kicked it in and we ran inside, but at the threshold I paused. The nearest monster was almost within grabbing distance of me and I knew that we needed some kind of diversion to slow him and his buddies down long enough to get to the Underwalk entrance. I reached into my pocket, pulled out the first object that came to hand and threw it at the monster. The flea bomb – which I'd originally considered using against Ferdinand – was a smooth piece of amber inside of which was trapped a single insect. But when the amber struck the monster's chest, it burst open and hundreds of fleas poured forth, covering his body. Within seconds the fleas found their way beneath their new host's clothing and began biting. The monster roared in irritation and began slapping at his body, trying to crush the pests gnawing at him, but there were too many. He stood there, gyrating and contorting as he scratched and smacked himself, making a very effective door block that prevented his fellow monsters from getting past. And when they got too close some of the fleas leaped from his body to theirs. Within moments the entire mass of monsters was scratching frantically, trying to dislodge the fleas infesting their bodies. That's the beautiful thing about flea bombs: once activated, the number of fleas continues to magically increase until all host bodies in the area are infested. It's a diabolically nasty joke, one of Hop Frog's best, and I mentally thanked Shrike for picking it up for me before I turned and followed Devona into the warehouse.

SIXTEEN

Getting into the Underwalk was a simple matter of opening a hidden panel in the floor and climbing down a ladder. The panel was spelled so only people with tongue worms could open it and, though I didn't know for sure, I guessed there was a number of lethal security precautions in place in case someone without a tongue worm somehow managed to get into the tunnel.

Once we reached the bottom of the ladder a fluorescent light panel in the ceiling activated. Devona and I looked around, but we were alone and there were no Dominari trams in sight. Considering the latter were driven by vermen reanimated by Victor Baron, I decided that wasn't a bad thing.

Since there was no way the monsters pursuing us could get into the tunnel, I took a few moments to reload my .45. Devona, unfortunately, had no extra ammunition for her 9mm, and she tucked it into the back waistband of her skirt. I used up the last of my own ammo refilling the .45's clip, so I'd need to be stingy with my bullets from here on out since I wasn't likely to stumble across anymore boxes of ammo lying around in the Underwalk.

"Do you remember the way?" Devona asked.

"To Tenebrus, yes. But after that, your guess is as good as mine."

"Let's start heading in that direction," she said. "It'll at least get us halfway to the Foundry. After that, we'll play it by ear."

"Sounds like a plan," I said, and we started walking.

We hadn't walked for ten minutes before we saw the headlights of a tram heading toward us, the electric hum of the engine getting louder as it drew near.

"I think we may have just found ourselves a ride," I said.

I stepped into the middle of the tunnel, directly into the tram's path. Devona joined me, though I would've preferred her to keep close to the tunnel wall where it was safer. I didn't say anything, however. Devona is just as capable as I am in dangerous situations. Besides, I knew she wouldn't listen to me.

The light panels on the ceiling above the tram had trouble activating fast enough to illuminate the vehicle's progress and we could only catch glimpses of the vehicle and its driver as they moved from patches of light to patches of darkness, but those glimpses were enough to confirm that the tram was being driven my a reanimated verman and like all the other creations of Victor Baron's we'd seen, this one was caught in the grip of bloodlust.

The creature aimed the tram directly at me and from the bloodstains covering the vehicle's front I knew I wouldn't be the verman's first victim since Osseal began singing its song of death and destruction. But then, I didn't intend to just stand there and let the reanimated ratman run me down.

I still had a few surprises left, thanks to Shrike and I reached into my right side pocket with my left hand – I still held my .45 with my right – and removed a small red-skinned lizard. Its eyes were closed and it appeared dead, though its body wasn't stiff and there was no sign of decay. I held the lizard out in front of me, pointed it headfirst at the oncoming tram, and gave its belly a gentle squeeze. The lizard woke in my hand, opened its mouth and released a thin stream of fire at the tram. My left hand still wasn't fully coordinated, thanks to Baron's sloppy reconnection of my brain to my central nervous system, and my aim was slightly off, but then I wasn't trying to hit the verman.

The salamander's flame was nowhere near as powerful as that produced by Carnage's flamethrower, but it was enough to frighten the reanimated verman. The creature roared in fear and anger and turned the wheel to get away from the deadly fire. At the speed the tram was going, the sudden change in direction caused it to swerve. I tried to get out of the way, but I was too slow, and the tram clipped my leg. The impact spun me around and flung me to the ground. I watched the tram topple and slide on its side for a dozen feet before finally crashing into the tunnel wall and coming to a stop.

I'd stopped squeezing the salamander when I fell, though I'd managed to hold on to it. Its flame extinguished, it fell back to sleep, and it would remain that way until I woke it again. Small salamanders like this one are used in Nekropolis the same way lighters are on Earth, and while they don't produce all that much flame, I'd counted on the intense fear Baron's creatures had of fire to make up for the salamander's feeble stream, and my gamble had paid off.

I got to my feet and was relieved to find my leg wasn't broken – or at least not broken severely enough to keep me from walking. I limped toward the wrecked tram, intending to put a couple bullets in the reanimated verman's brain before he could extricate himself and resume trying to kill us. But Devona beat me to him. Moving with supernatural swiftness, she reached the tram in a blur of motion, knelt, grabbed hold of the verman's head and gave it a savage twist. The sound of snapping bone cut through the air and the verman's body fell limp. I knew the creature was dead (again), but I kept my .45 aimed at its head as I approached. In Nekropolis safe is always better than sorry. But the de-animated verman had the good grace to stay dead and Devona pulled his body free from the tram and left it lying next to the tunnel wall.

Together we righted the tram and quick examination revealed that while the vehicle was banged up pretty good, it was still functional. We climbed in, pushed a button to turn on the engine, and – with me driving – we headed down the tunnel in the direction of Tenebrus. Given my problems with my left hand, I would've preferred Devona drive, but since she was reared in Gothtown, the daughter of a Darklord, she'd always had drivers to take her wherever she wanted, so she'd never learned to drive herself. Since I needed both hands to drive, and since Devona's 9mm was out of ammo, I handed her my .45 and we both kept a sharp lookout for other reanimated vermen, whether on trams or on foot, as we drove. We came across a couple wrecked trams and the mutilated bodies of regular vermen which we maneuvered around, but we saw no sign of the Victor Baron variety. Presumably they were off causing mayhem elsewhere in the Underwalk.

"I'm not sure what your problem with Overkill was," I said after we'd been driving for a bit. "She did help us out."

Devona's face scrunched into a truly impressive scowl at the mention of Overkill's name. "It's not her that I have a problem with. It's the way she was flirting with you."

"Um… what?"

"Don't play coy. The way she was acting, I'm surprised she didn't jump your bones right there in Carnage's front seat."

I admit to not always being the fastest on the uptake when it comes to emotional stuff, but I really didn't believe Overkill was flirting with me. There might've been a certain amount of mutual appreciation of each other's skills going on, but flirting?

"That's ridiculous," I said. "And even if it was true – and I don't think it is – it doesn't matter. You have absolutely no reason to be jealous of her."

"And you don't have any reason to be jealous of Bogdan," Devona countered, "but that doesn't stop you from feeling that way, does it?"

"Touche," I said, feeling more than a little embarrassed. I decided to change the subject. "How are you doing after…" I struggled to find a way to express what I was trying to say. "Being trapped in Orlock's dome," I finally said. It didn't come close to communicating everything I wanted to say, but it was the best I could do.

"I'm managing," Devona said. She gave me a weak smile. "It helps that we're busy fighting to save the city again."

I smiled back. "Yeah, life-and-death battles have a wonderful way of distracting one from personal problems."

Her smile fell away. "How about you? How are you doing?"

"Coping," I said. "Even though I know it was all an illusion, it felt so real. You know?"

"Yes."

She put her hand on my leg and squeezed once and that was the last we spoke until we drew near the section of the Underwalk where I'd escaped from Tenebrus. I'd paid close attention at the time, so even though there were no markers of any sort to indicate our location, I was fairly confident we were in the right spot. But I knew it for certain when I saw Gnasher running down

the tunnel toward us, his red albino eyes wide with terror. An instant later I saw why. The silvery shape of an
Overwatcher glided through the air behind him, the
skull faced creature moving with silent, menacing grace,
like some manner of airborn shark. The Overwatcher's
eyesockets began to glow a bright crimson and I knew
the reanimated brain inside – driven insane by Osseal's
song – was powering up its optic energy blasters to take
out Gnasher.

Devona and I exchanged glances and in that same instant we telepathically came up with a plan. I worked
the tram's throttle and the engine whined as the vehicle
picked up speed.

"Gnasher, your dire blade!" I shouted. "Throw it
straight up into the air!"

The verman had no idea what we were planning, but
his people were quick witted and had even swifter reflexes. In a single smooth motion he drew the dire
blade, the same one I'd slain Lycanthropus Rex with,
and tossed it into the air. Devona dropped the .45 onto
the floor of the tram then sprang out of her seat, adding
the power of her half-vampire legs to the vehicle's forward momentum. As she sailed through the air, hands
outstretched, I swerved the tram to avoid hitting
Gnasher and gripped the wheel with my right hand
which reaching out to the verman with my left.
Gnasher reached back for me and I snagged his hand,
swung him into the tram and he scurried into the back
seat. At the same instant Devona's fingers wrapped
around the dire blade's hilt and momentum carried her

straight for the Overwatcher. She landed on the crea-ture's smooth metal back right behind its skull, straddling it backward. Petite though she is, the sudden addition of her weight caused the Overwatcher to dip slightly, and when it unleashed its eye beams, the twin bolts of ruby energy missed Gnasher and me, striking the tunnel floor and melting a section of the organic looking substance.

The tunnel shuddered then and a low tone reverber-ated through the air, almost like a moan. I thought of the organic nature of so much of Nekropolis – the Under-walk, Tenebrus, much of the strange architecture in the Sprawl – and for the first time since I'd come to the city, I found myself wondering if the Darkfolk hadn't con-structed their otherdimensional home so much as grown it. Was Nekropolis itself in some bizarre fashion alive?

As disturbing as the thought was I thankfully didn't have time to pursue it. I watched as Devona turned at the waist and slammed the dire blade into the Over-watcher's silver skull. Dire blades aren't just supernaturally deadly, they're supernaturally sharp as well. With Devona's strength to power it the blade easily pierced the Overwatcher's metallic hide and sank into the soft brain beneath. The effect was immediate. The crimson light in the Overwatcher's eyesockets winked out and the creature crashed to the tunnel floor. Devona managed to jump free in time, though she had to leave the dire blade embedded in the Overwatcher's skull. She landed with a fluid grace that I found incredibly sexy. I slowed down, intending to stop and pick her up, and she started running toward the downed Overwatcher in order to retrieve the dire blade, but Gnasher shouted, "Leave it! Those things are designed to explode once they're brought down!"

I gave the tram full power and it picked up speed again. Devona sprinted down the tunnel after us and managed to leap aboard just as the Overwatcher vanished in a burst of light and fire. I felt the pressure of the blast roll over us, though I didn't feel the heat. I turned back to look at Gnasher and Devona, and while both of them were a little singed around the edges, I knew they'd survive.

"Another of Keket's nasty little surprises," Gnasher said. "Any inmate who brings down an Overwatcher risks being destroyed."

"Always thinking, that woman," I said.

Devona climbed back into the front passenger seat and picked the .45 up off the floor where she'd left it.

"Nicely done, my love," I said.

"Why thank you, sir." She then grimaced and arched her back. "Though I think I might've pulled a muscle on that one."

"I have no idea what the two of you are doing here," Gnasher said, "but I am exceptionally glad to see you. It's total chaos inside Tenebrus." He paused. "Well. It's always chaos in there, but it's even worse now. Something's happened to the Overwatchers. They went mad and began firing energy blasts at everyone, including the guards. Keket herself came down into the general population to stop them, and the prisoners saw that as their chance to get revenge on her for using them as entertainment. They attacked her en masse, and even though she's a demilord, between the Overwatchers and the prisoners, she was having a hard time of it. I decided it might be prudent of me to take my leave until the current situation sorts itself out, but one of the Overwatchers followed me into the Underwalk. If you hadn't arrived when you did..." The verman shuddered as he trailed off.

"Our pleasure," I said. "And since we saved your snowy white hide, you owe us one. And your people always pay their debts."

Gnasher's eyes narrowed. "What do you want?"

"Not much," I said. "Just directions to the Foundry."

Gnasher guided us to a Dominari owned building in the Boneyard – a falling-down ruin not far from the Foundry. Before saying goodbye to us, he asked, "Are you going to try to stop whatever's happening?"

"That's the idea," I said.

He nodded. "Good. Too much death and destruction is bad for business."

I considered asking him how much was good, but instead Devona and I thanked him for his help, climbed the ladder, and emerged aboveground in what was left of a stone building whose original purpose I could only guess at.

"Why would the Dominari have entrances to the Underwalk in the Boneyard?" Devona asked. "It's not like there's a lot of profit to be made here."

I shrugged. "Who knows? Even the dead have needs. Maybe the Dominari figured out ways to meet them."

We moved cautiously out of the ruined building and into the street. The normally sparse traffic was nonexistent. The living had managed to get off the streets by now, and as for the dead... well, there was no sign of them, neither motorists nor pedestrians. It appeared that Devona and I had the street to ourselves.

We talked softly as we made our way to the Foundry, me limping on my injured leg but moving well enough not to slow us down too much.

"Where is everyone?" Devona asked.

"I don't know. I'm usually sensitive to the presence of other dead beings, but I don't sense any close by. It's almost like they're hiding... waiting for the trouble to blow over."

"Maybe they sense Osseal's power, and it scares them," Devona said. "Even if it's only being used to control Baron's creations."

"Maybe." That theory was better than anything I could come up with.

"Now that we're closer to the Foundry, can you feel Osseal's magic?"

I shook my head. "I don't feel a thing. Maybe it's because of Papa's spell blocking necklace, or maybe it's because Osseal is only being focused on Baron's monsters. Either way, I'm not sensing anything."

"Good," she said. "Now that we've made it this far, the last thing we need is for you to fall under the flute's power."

"That would well and truly suck, wouldn't it?"

We continued on in silence for several more minutes until we could see the Foundry up ahead. It looked the same as always – tower lattice crackling with electricity, smokestacks belching black into the sky, the heavy thrum of power filling the air. But as we got closer, we saw there was one thing new: behind the main gate stood several dozen of Baron's creatures. I recognized some of them from our last visit, but most of them were unknown to me. I had no doubt they were all equally dangerous, though.

Devona and stepped across the street and regarded the assembled monsters. Unlike the creatures we'd seen rampaging on the streets of the Sprawl, these displayed no sign of aggression whatsoever. They made no move to open the gate and attack us. In fact, they didn't react to our presence in any way.

"It's almost as if they've been waiting for us," Devona said.

"Waiting for *someone*. Baron's not the kind of man to leave anything to chance. He figured someone would realize he was behind the rioting and he commanded his monsters to guard the main gate in case someone showed up to try and stop him."

"Someone like us," Devona said.

"Yep."

We looked at Baron's monsters some more. Somehow they seemed ever larger and more intimidating than they had a few moments ago.

"We're not going to be able to fight our way inside," Devona said.

She'd returned my .45 to me when we'd stopped the tram, but it only had so many bullets left, and they weren't going to be enough. Same for the magic items we had left. None of them were particularly powerful, and with the exception of the salamander, I didn't see how they'd be of much use. And the salamander, small as it was, couldn't produce a strong enough flame to frighten all of the monsters gathered at Baron's gate.

"No, we are not," I agreed.

"So that only leaves us one option I can see."

I nodded. "The direct approach."

She sighed. "I hate the direct approach."

We headed across the street.

The monsters continued to show no reaction to our presence as we drew near, though it was obvious they were watching us closely. When we reached the gate, the skull sentry swiveled its organic eyes to regard us.

"You two have some serious *cojones* to show yourselves here, you know that?" the sentry said. "You do realize we're in the process of destroying the city, right?"

"We noticed," I said drily. "How about opening up and letting us in so we can tell your boss in person how much we admire his brilliant plan?"

"Seriously?" the sentry said. "Is that the best you can come up with?"

"I suppose I could've said 'Let us in so we can stop your boss,' but I thought that might be tipping our hand too much."

The sentry glared at me.

"Oh, I'll let you in all right, and when I do, my friends here will tear you into…" He trailed off, his gaze becoming unfocused as if he were listening to some inner voice. When his eyes refocused, he spoke in a monotone, as if mechanically repeating instructions he was being fed. "You've been granted safe passage. You'll be escorted to the Foundry. If you try anything even remotely suspicious, your escorts will kill you."

The gate swung slowly open and a pair of Baron's creatures – one male, one female – stepped forward. They continued to eye us dispassionately, but I had no doubt they'd do as the sentry warned if we didn't behave ourselves. Devona and I stepped inside, and with the monsters flanking us, we headed up the driveway to the Foundry. The sentry closed the gate behind us, and the other monsters continued their silent watch.

As we walked, I reached out to Devona's mind: Well, we're in.

Yeah, we have Baron right where he wants us.

I didn't have any witty rejoinder to that, especially since I was afraid she was right, so we continued the rest of the way to the Foundry in silence. The door opened as we approached to reveal a pair of men waiting for us.

"Didn't think we'd see you here again," Burke said.

"Took some slick detective work on his part to figure it out," Hare added.

"Too right," Burke agreed. "Guess he's got a good head on his shoulders, eh?"

"Has trouble keeping it attached, though," Hare said. He gave me a sly smile. "You really should pay more attention when you walk past dark alleys from now on."

"I'll keep that in mind," I said.

"Enough chit-chat," Burke said. He stepped back and motioned for us to enter. "His lordship is waiting."

We walked inside, our two monstrous escorts trailing along behind. I hooked a thumb over my shoulder toward them. "Don't you two think you can handle us by yourselves? Then again, it did take both of you to get my head. Guys like you probably need each other's help to wipe your asses."

Hare bared his teeth and took a step toward me, but Burke put a hand on his partner's shoulder to restrain him.

"Pay him no mind. He's just trying to rattle us." Burke smiled at me. "Shows that he's desperate is all."

I didn't reply, primarily because he was right.

Burke ordered the monsters to shut the door, one of them did, and we started down the corridor, Burke and Hare leading the way, Devona and I coming next, with our guard-monsters bringing up the rear. The halls of the Foundry were quiet and empty, the soundproofed corridors cutting out the omnipresent power hum that permeated the air outside the facility. We walked on in silence until we encountered a man coming toward us. I recognized him as one of the scientists Baron employed, the wild haired, wild eyed Dr. Fronkensteen. Only now his eyes were blank and staring, his features slack, mouth hanging partway open. Around his head was a metal band with thin rods jutting out, and it didn't take a great leap of deductive reasoning on my part to guess the crown's purpose. I had no doubt the rest of the Foundry's scientists wore similar devices.

"Looks like some of your boss's employees need a bit of technological coaxing to get with the new program," I said as the man passed us without the slightest sign that he was aware of our existence.

"You know how it goes," Burke said. "A motivated employee is a happy employee."

Both men laughed and continued leading us deeper into the Foundry. We soon passed the lab where Baron had reattached my head and still we continued onward, taking one turn after another, until Burke and Hare brought us to a stop outside a pair of doors with ornate woodwork and polished brass knobs.

"Welcome to the nerve center of the Foundry," Burke said. He nodded to Hare and the other man gripped both knobs, turned them, and pushed the doors open. He then stepped aside, gave us a mocking bow, and gestured for us to enter. Wishing I had anything even remotely approximating a plan, I did so, Devona at my side. Burke, Hare, and the guard-monsters followed, closing the door behind us.

The room was huge, easily three stories high, and a couple hundred feet across. The floor was tiled, but the walls and ceiling were flesh-tech, moist pink and shot through with swollen, pulsing veins, and I knew that Burke hadn't been joking. This was literally the nerve center – or perhaps more appropriately the heart – of

Baron's factory. Flesh cables extended from the walls and stretched toward a high-backed fleshtech chair in the center of the room where they twined together to form a large cable bundle affixed to the chair back. Hanging down from the ceiling in front of the chair, dangling from a thick optic nerve, was a large Mind's Eye projector, the iris slate-gray, the white marred by threads of broken capillaries. The Mind's Eye was active, glowing with a sour yellow light, and before I could finish taking in the rest of the room, it snagged my attention. Images of monsters rioting in the streets of Nekropolis filled my head, and I heard Acantha's frantic voice.

"– can't begin to describe how devastating the attacks have been so far! Initial reports put the number of dead in the dozens, and that number is sure to rise if this situation isn't resolved soon! So far, there's been no sign of the Darklords, and all attempts to contact them have failed. I've personally been in contact with First Adjudicator Quillion, who says he's been attempting to get in touch with Victor Baron to discover what's caused his creations to go mad, but so far Quillion has had no luck reaching him. Meanwhile, the fighting in the streets continues unabated. Sentinels and citizens alike are doing what they can to combat the rampaging monsters, but there's simply too many to–"

Acantha broke off as a particularly hulking monster came stomping toward her. She screamed, turned to flee, and the transmission ended abruptly. I hoped her camera snakes had simply stopped filming in the confusion, but I feared the worst.

Now that the Mind's Eye was inactive, I could once more focus my attention on the chair in the center of the room. One person sat there, while a second stood by his side: Victor Baron and his assistant Henry. But something was wrong. Baron was the one standing, while Henry sat in the chair, still looking at the inactive Mind's Eye.

"Now that's what I call entertainment," Henry said. Smaller flesh cables extended from the chair near the head and at the arm rests, their ends attached to Henry's temples and wrists. They detached and retracted into the chair as he rose, moving with his characteristically stiff, spastic motions. He turned to look at us, and I saw that he'd thrown back the hood of his robe to fully reveal his misshapen features. The robe was also now open down the front, displaying Henry's bare chest. Embedded into the flesh, running vertically from the base of his throat to his belly button, was Osseal. The mouthpiece of the bone flute was covered with a flap of skin, and every time Henry breathed, a series of soft notes emerged from the ivory instrument.

Henry came toward us with his lurching walk, but Baron – dressed in his white lab coat and black pants – remained standing next to the chair. When Henry noticed, he paused and glanced back over his shoulder with an irritated expression.

"Heel, boy," he snarled.

Baron turned and walked over to join Henry, brow furrowed, jaw muscles tight, eyes blazing with anger, as if he were fighting an intense internal struggle. Once he reached Henry, the two of them continued walking toward us. Burke and Hare led Devona and me farther into the room, and we met Henry and Baron halfway.

"Believe it or not, I'm glad to see you," Henry said. "It's nice to have someone I can properly gloat in front of."

When he spoke, Osseal's song grew louder, and his words took on an almost musical lilt. The flute's tone was a sad, haunting one, and even though I was protected from its influence by the Loa necklace, this close I could feel a slight pull from the instrument, as if it were calling to me. I knew that Victor Baron heard its music clearly, and that meant he was under Henry's control.

Henry looked at Burke and Hare. "You two can go now – and take the creatures with you." He gestured at our monstrous escorts.

Burke frowned. "You sure?"

Henry smiled. "Your concern for my safety is appreciated, but as formidable of opponents as Mr. Richter and Ms. Kanti may be, I believe I can handle them. Besides, I have Victor to protect me." He patted Baron on the shoulder, and while Baron's mouth tightened in anger, he gave no other reaction to Henry's touch.

Henry went on. "I want you two outside to direct the creatures at the gate. It won't be long before Quillion sends his Sentinels to pay us a visit. We'll need to be ready for them."

"Righto," Burke said before turning to me. "Pleasure seeing you again," he said to me with a mocking grin.

"Likewise," Hare said. "Call us the next time you need a trim. We'll be glad to take a little off the top."

Laughing, the two men left the room, taking the guardmonsters with them.

"So," Henry said once the others had departed, "are you surprised to discover I'm the ultimate villain in this little drama? Please tell me you didn't guess it was me. I'd be *so* disappointed if you had."

"I can truthfully say we didn't see it coming," I said. "So Baron had absolutely nothing to do with Osseal's theft?"

"Depends on how you look at it," Henry said. "In one sense he's responsible for everything that's happened." His jovial mood vanished then, and his tone grew cold. "Do you know how he came by his name? Victor Baron? He decided to take the name of his father, Baron Victor Frankenstein. Of course, he was determined to be his own man, too." He turned to Baron. "Didn't want to live his life in Daddy's shadow, did you?"

Baron glared at Henry but otherwise didn't respond.

Henry continued. "So instead of taking the Frankenstein surname, he indulged in a bit of juvenile wordplay and become Victor *Baron*. Pathetic, really, and more than a bit disrespectful, don't you think?"

As I listened to Henry talk, a suspicion began to form in my mind. "When we first met, I thought you were Baron's assistant. But you're not, are you?"

Devona looked at me, puzzled. "What do you mean?"

"When Henry rose from the chair and I saw he'd surgically grafted Osseal to himself, my first thought was that he was simply a disgruntled employee who was tired of being number two and wanted to take over his boss's business for himself." I turned to Henry. "But it's more than that, isn't it? A lot more."

Henry gave me a look so cold that, if he'd been Acantha, I'd have turned to stone on the spot.

Devona's eyes widened in sudden realization.

"You're Dr. Frankenstein!" she said.

Henry inclined his head. "At your service."

"If that's true, then why go by the name Henry?"

"It's my middle name. And I wasn't about to call myself Victor anymore. Not after he took the name."

I thought back to the interactions I'd observed between Baron and Henry. Henry had been more than a bit snarky toward Baron, but the latter had tolerantly accepted the other's behavior. At the time, I'd thought Baron had been simply too caught up in his work to care, but now I recognized his tolerance as that of an adult child good-naturedly putting up with the irritating behavior of an older relative.

"Why the resentment toward Baron?" I asked. "He seemed to treat you well enough. More like a partner than an assistant."

"That's what he wanted everyone to believe," Henry said. "But in truth he regards me as an inferior intellect, barely fit to wash out his test tubes."

A sorrowful look came into Baron's eyes, but he remained standing still at Henry's side.

"Is that what Baron thinks or what you think?" Devona asked gently, but Henry ignored her.

"When we met I told you that Shelley's novel got some of our story right, though many of the specific details are different. Suffice it to say that I'd attempted to create a perfect man, only to realize I'd fallen far short of that too-lofty goal and instead created a monster. I attempted to rectify that mistake and destroy the beast I'd made, and he in turn tried to destroy me. In the end I died and my monster lived and I went into the darkness with the consolation of knowing I was at least free of the grotesque abomination I'd brought into the world. But do you know what he did? He refused to let me stay dead! He claimed he did it out of love, because he didn't want to lose the only family he had in the world. But I knew the truth. He did it out of spite – for vengeance's sake! He brought my body to my lab and using my notes and equipment, he went to work. The result? He succeeded in returning me to life, but trapped inside this twisted joke of a body. He apologized for the crudity of his work, saying said it was because this was his first attempt at the reanimatory arts. He promised to continue, experimenting and learning, until he'd obtained the knowledge and skill to fully restore me. What a laugh! As if he ever had any intention of doing so!"

"Judging by how he looks, I'd say he succeeded in mastering his craft," I said. "Has he never offered to operate on you again?"

"Numerous times," Henry said. "But do you think I'd ever allow him to come near me with surgical tools again after what he did to me?"

I thought to Devona, Sounds to me like what Henry needs isn't a medical doctor as much as a really good psychiatrist.

No kidding, she replied.

He's already more unstable than a house of cards in a hurricane. Let's see if we can't push him the rest of the way over the edge, maybe get him to make a mistake.

Maybe get him to kill us, you mean, Devona thought.

What's life without a little risk? I countered.

Easy for you to say – you're already dead!

I had to keep from smiling at that. Aloud, I said, "It must've eaten away at you, coming to Nekropolis and working alongside Baron all these years, watching him improve himself physically while he became increasingly successful."

Henry nodded emphatically. "So successful that people started calling him the Sixth Lord? Can you believe it? What hubris!"

"And all the different refinements and applications he came up with were based on your original work," Devona added.

"That's right! And what's tattooed on everything that leaves the Foundry, on the laborers, voxes, Mind's Eye sets? *Another Victor Baron Creation*. As if I'd never existed!"

"Worst of all, Baron succeeded where you failed," I said. "Thanks to his efforts to continually improve himself over the years, he did become the perfect man. Or at least as close to perfect as possible."

Henry had become more and more agitated as we'd talked and now his face was red with fury and spittle flew from his mouth as he spoke.

Henry whirled on me. "*Yes, damn you, yes!*" He practically screamed these words and beneath his voice Osseal's tone became a highpitched shrill.

Now! I thought to Devona.

With Henry's full attention focused on me, Devona seized the opportunity to make a lunge for Osseal. As strong as she was, if she could grab hold of the instrument and rip it free from Henry's chest –

SEVENTEEN

– but before she could reach the magical artifact, Victor Baron, who'd stood motionless while his creator ranted, now burst into sudden motion.

Moving with a speed that put Devona to shame, Baron caught her hand by the wrist before she could get a grip on Osseal. She tried to pull away, but Baron held her tight, his face showing his futile internal struggle to resist Osseal's commands. Under Henry's control the celebrated Sixth Lord had become nothing more than an organic machine, performing whatever tasks he was told to.

Henry became calm again, and when he spoke his voice was filled with so much satisfaction, he nearly purred. "Nice try," he said.

I blew it, Devona thought to me.

Stay sharp, I thought back. We may get another chance. Since no other course of action presented itself, I decided to keep Henry talking.

"If you hate Baron so much, why keep him alive? It's not like you need him to run the city, once your takeover is complete. Unless the job is more than you can handle on your own."

Henry chuckled. "It appears you're not as intelligent as I gave you credit for. I don't care about taking over the Foundry or ruling Nekropolis. My plan has but a single, simple aim." He looked at Baron with loathing in his eyes. "To ruin everything *he's* worked for. That's why I'm using Osseal to control only Victor's creations. I want the blame for the rioting to fall squarely on his shoulders. And after the events of this night, the name of Victor Baron will be reviled by the citizens of Nekropolis. The Foundry will be shut down and Victor will be hauled off to Tenebrus. He'll go quietly and he'll make a full confession as well." Henry grinned as he reached up to tap the bone flute embedded in his chest. "I'll make sure of it."

"Speaking of Osseal, how did you learn about it in the first place?" I asked.

"The same why I learned about the mark on your hand and what it can be used for," Henry said. "Research. Since my resurrection I've spent every spare moment I've had searching for ways to increase my knowledge of the reanimatory arts, hoping to find any scrap of lore that I might be able to use against *him*. Victor's business relationship with Lord Edrigu helped a great deal. I've accompanied Victor to the Reliquary on several occasions, which familiarized me with the layout of Edrigu's stronghold. And whatever information Edrigu didn't readily supply, I discovered on my own through one means or another."

"And you had your plan all worked out," I said. "Except for one little detail: you didn't have someone who possessed Edrigu's mark."

"That's right. Edrigu's mark is only given to the dead, and the majority of them exist in semi-insubstantial states that made them unsuitable to my purpose. But then I saw your interview with Acantha, and I realized that after all these long years I'd finally found what I'd been looking for. Someone dead, who possessed the mark, but whose form was solid enough for me to use."

"So you dispatched two of your best Bonegetters to cut off my head and bring my body to you here at the Foundry. Seems like a lot of trouble to go through to get the mark. Why not just have them steal my hand?"

"That would've been more convenient, wouldn't it?" Henry said. "Unfortunately, the mark's magic is what's required, and that suffuses the entire body of the mark's bearer." He smiled. "A precaution of Edrigu's to prevent anyone from simply cutting off some dead being's hand and using it to gain entrance to the Reliquary. Fortunately, the magic remains functional so long as the majority of the body is intact. After all, the physical dead are known for losing bits and pieces of themselves, so it's rare to find one that's completely whole."

"What did you do once you had my body?" I asked. "Stick some kind of control unit on it and work it remotely like some kind of machine?"

"Nothing so crude," Henry said. He pointed to a fresh looking scar on his neck. "We work wonders here at the Foundry, you know. With Burke and Hare following my expert guidance – and while Victor was preoccupied elsewhere with his latest pet project – I removed my head and my assistants transferred it to your body. They drove me to the Reliquary where I used the mark on your hand to gain entrance. I stole Osseal from around Edrigu's neck, departed and Burke and Hare brought me back here. They returned my head to my own body and then took yours to the Sprawl for disposal. I supposed I could've had them destroy it here, but I didn't want to risk there being any evidence at the Foundry that a forensic sorcerer might be able to discover."

He smiled. "You can't imagine how amused I was when Ms. Kanti called and asked if we could reattach your head. The irony was simply too delicious to deny you, and as extra amusement I got to watch Victor put you back together, all the while being completely unaware that it was your body which served as the instrument of his ultimate downfall. And having you restored provided a useful distraction. Your arrest, incarceration and subsequent escape from Tenebrus kept the authorities occupied while I implanted Osseal in my body and learned how to use it."

All the pieces had fallen into place, but there was still one thing I didn't – couldn't – understand.

"How can you resent Baron so much?" I asked. "Isn't it the hope of every parent that their children one day surpass their achievements? I'd think you'd be proud of him."

Henry's face clouded with anger and he leaned his face close to mine as he shouted, "This misbegotten piece of stitched together filth is *not my son!*"

Henry had moved in close in order to yell in my face, giving me a chance to grab Osseal. I managed to wrap my fingers around the bone instrument, but I didn't have anything close to Devona's strength, and when I pulled, the flute didn't tear free.

Realizing what I was up to, Henry snarled and shoved me back. He gave no obvious command to Baron, but the man lashed out with his free hand and struck me a solid blow. The impact sent me flying and I heard numerous bones snap as I hit. I immediately got to my feet, though my broken body didn't want to obey me, and once I was on my legs, they wobbled as they struggled to support my weight. My jaw felt loose, too, but I was still able to speak well enough.

"From where I stand, Frankenstein, the only piece of filth in this room is you."

Henry's face turned purple with rage, but when he spoke, his words were measured and precise. "Your amusement value has run out, I'm afraid, Mr. Richter. I'm going to use Osseal to force you to stand still while Victor rips you to pieces." He smiled coldly. "But I'll allow you to retain control of your mind, just as I have with Victor, so you'll be aware the entire time. After all, I wouldn't want you to miss your own dismemberment."

Osseal's song seemed to swell louder then, almost as if it was coming from *inside* my ears. I could feel its power pressing against me, but try as it might, it couldn't overcome the spirit of the Loa inhabiting Papa Chatha's necklace, and my body remained mine to command.

Henry frowned. "Something's not right." He shrugged. "Well, no matter. It's not as if you have anywhere to run, is it?" He turned to Baron, and when he spoke next, his voice was cold as arctic ice. "Tear him apart."

I hope Baron would let go of Devona in order to fulfill Henry's order, but instead he picked her up and hurled her toward the flesh wall. She flew across the room and slammed into the wall, but before she could bounce off, the veins in that section of the wall wrapped around her like swollen, throbbing tentacles and held her fast. I understood what had happened. The fleshtech in the room had been created from reanimated tissue, and was therefore just as susceptible to Osseal's influence as any of Baron's other creations, and it was under Henry's control.

Baron turned and started walking toward me. There was no hesitation in his motion, but his gaze was sorrowful, and I knew that what Henry had said was true. Baron was fully aware of what he was being made to do, and though he fought against Osseal's power, he had no choice but to obey Henry's commands. I felt sorry for Baron, but not so sorry that I intended to let him reduce me to zombie nuggets. I drew my .45, took aim at his head, and started firing.

I was hoping to do the same to him as I had to Jigsaw Jones, but Baron was far faster than the wrestler, and he brought his arms up in time to intercept the bullets and protect his head. The .45's rounds tore into the flesh of his arms, and while there was some blood, it was far less than it should've been. Over the last century and a half, Victor Baron had made himself into the pinnacle of what the reanimatory arts could accomplish, and that meant he was strong and tough as hell. He could take a handful of bullets without flinching, and they certainly didn't slow him down. He came at me so swiftly that even if I'd had the reflexes of a living man I wouldn't have been able to get out of the way. I dropped my .45, pulled the salamander out of my pocket, and gave its tiny belly a good squeeze.

Flame shot out of the creature's mouth and it struck Baron on the side of his perfect face. The flesh sizzled and blackened, but Baron kept coming. He reached out, wrapped his hand around my wrist, and squeezed, crushing the bones along with the salamander. He then grabbed hold of my wrist and tore my arm out of the socket.

"Dammit! I *hate* that!" I shouted. "Do you know how many times that's happened to me?"

On the bright side, Baron had also torn the sleeve off Bogdan's coat when he pulled the arm off, so it wasn't a total loss.

Baron came at me, still holding onto my arm, and I remembered the swill the recently deceased minotaur had forced me to drink outside Hemlocks. The Sprawlicano had been sloshing around in my stomach ever since, and since I'd have to get rid of the wretched stuff eventually, I figured now was an excellent time to heave ho.

I tensed my stomach muscles, opened my mouth as wide as I could and let Baron have it right in the face. Whatever nasty ingredients the Sprawlicano had originally been made from, their time pickling in my zombie stomach had taken them to a whole new level of putrefaction. A nauseating liquid stew of browns, greens and grays splashed into Baron's eyes and he roared in pain and staggered backward. I imagined the toxic mess burned like hell and probably stank worse than a ghoul's breath after a two week eating binge at the Roadkill Roadhouse. Baron wiped his swollen, reddened eyes with his free hand and I was mildly surprised – and a bit disappointed – to see that Sprawlicano ala Richter hadn't eaten away the man's eyeballs. My reguritory assault hadn't done more than make Baron pause and a second later, eyesight cleared, he came at me again.

Baron had managed to retain hold of my arm, and wielding it like a club, he slammed it into the side of my head so hard that I thought he was going to undo his own handiwork and decapitate me again. But though the blow sent me sprawling onto the floor, my head remained attached. Thank Dis for small favors.

Still gripping my arm, Baron came toward me. The sorrow in his eyes was palpable now, and along with it was an impotent rage. Baron was fighting Osseal's power with everything he had, but no matter how strong his will was, he couldn't resist the artifact's magic on his own. I sat up, determined not to meet my fate lying down, and as I moved, the pieces of Papa Chatha's Loa necklace rustled together.

Maybe Baron couldn't throw off the effects of Osseal by himself, but if he had a little help…

Devona had been fighting to escape from the vein-tentacles that held her, and when she saw Baron tear my arm off, she decided to quit fooling around. She bared her fangs and bit down into one of the veins, tearing out a great bloody chunk which she spit out. Ichor gushed from the wound, spraying the air and soaking her in crimson. She instantly became too slick for the other veins to hold on to her, and she wriggled out of their embrace and fell to the floor. She landed on her feet and started running toward Baron, and even though I loved her, at that moment, seeing her covered with blood, fangs bared, eyes blazing with feral fury, I was scared of her.

Just as Baron was about to hit me with my own arm again, Devona launched herself through the air and landed on his back. She bit into the side of his neck and ripped out a hunk of flesh. Blood flowed from the wound – but again, less than it should have – and though the injury should've hurt like blazes, Baron's face showed only his internal struggle against Osseal's magic. With his free hand he reached up and grabbed Devona by the top of the head and flung her forward off of him. She sailed overtop me and slammed into the opposite wall where more coils of vein ensnared her.

But she'd given me the distraction I needed.

I rose to my feet, staggered toward Baron, and concentrating to make my uncoordinated left hand obey me, I removed the Loa necklace from around my neck. I knew I had only one shot at this, so – remembering how my bad hand now worked – I aimed for a point several inches to the left of Baron's head and threw the necklace. It flew through the air and while its trajectory was a bit lopsided, it looped over Baron's head and settled around his bleeding neck.

Score!

The effect was immediate. Baron's features twisted with anger. He dropped my arm and turned to face Henry. Frankenstein had been watching the fight with glee, but now a look of alarm came onto his face.

"How could you do this?" Baron said, anguish in his voice. "We may have had our conflicts over the years, Father, but everything I've ever done, I did to make you proud of me, to prove myself worthy of the life you gave me! I can't believe that you hate me so much that you could harm so many people just to ruin me."

Baron continued to walk toward Henry as he spoke and now the two men stood facing one another, creation to creator, son to father. The fear in Frankenstein's face gave way to pure loathing.

"Believe it," he snarled.

Baron gave his father a last sorrowful look before ripping Osseal free from the scientist's chest. Henry cried out in pain as Baron tossed the now bloody flute aside and the song of Osseal which had accompanied Henry's breathing was silenced.

Frankenstein gave his creation a final defiant glare. "Go ahead. Do it."

Baron nodded sadly, took hold of his father's head in both hands with a surprisingly gentle touch, and then with a single swift motion tore Henry's head from his shoulders. Frankenstein's body fell to the ground, blood pumping from both neck and chest wounds, but Baron paid it no mind. He held Henry's head so he could look upon his father's face as the light dimmed in his eyes and finally went out, taking the hatred with it, leaving nothing but a dull emptiness. Then Baron clasped the head to his chest and began to cry.

EIGHTEEN

A day later, Devona and I sat on the couch in the great room of the Midnight Watch, illusory fire burning in the hearth, Rover moving around us as playful gusts of air, the ward spirit occasionally tousling our hair to get our attention. My right arm was back where it should be, thanks to Victor Baron, who'd also adjusted my left hand. The rest of the damage I'd sustained over the last couple days had been repaired by Papa Chatha. I sat with my arm around Devona, her head – blonde again – resting on my shoulder. It might not have been as cozy as a family room in a little ranch house back on Earth, but it would do.

I was dressed in my usual suit and tie. Bogdan's coat was sitting at a tailor's, waiting for the sleeve to be repaired. Though I hadn't admitted it to Devona, the coat had kind of grown on me, and I was reluctant to throw it away. Not that I'd ever wear it again, but I supposed I could find room for it in my closet somewhere.

"It was nice of everyone to drop by and congratulate me on being a free man again," I said.

"Even Bogdan?" Devona asked in a teasing voice.

"Even him," I said, and I almost sounded like I meant it. Who knows? Maybe I did. After all, he had helped Devona and the others break me out of Tenebrus, and he'd accepted a Dominari tongue worm to do so, just like everyone else. And he'd loaned me his old coat. It was hard to hate the guy after all that.

"I'm glad none of them was seriously injured in the rioting," she said.

"Me too."

Most of our friends – those who worked at the Midnight Watch and our other friends around town – had survived the attack of Baron's creatures relatively unscathed. Unfortunately, the same couldn't be said for hundreds of other citizens who'd been caught up in the violence.

"It's good of Baron to offer to repair and reanimate anyone who was injured in the riot, free of charge," Devona said. "Especially since the violence wasn't his fault."

"He's an honorable man," I said. "I'm sure he sees it as the least he can do. Besides, staying busy might help keep his mind off what happened." I thought about the way Baron had cried as he clutched his father's head. "At least a little," I added.

Devona snuggled close to me. "I feel sorry for him. I know what it's like to have a father who doesn't approve of you."

I tightened my arm around her shoulder. Devona changed the subject then and I pretended not to notice.

"I'm glad Quillion dismissed the charges against you when Victor Baron told him about Henry being the one who engineered the theft of Osseal. But I was surprised when he took Henry's body into custody."

Quillion had asked Baron to pack Henry's head and body in separate refrigeration units and then shipped them to Tenebrus where – so I'd heard – Keket had them placed in separate sections of maximum security far away from each other.

"Frankenstein's a genius when it comes to reanimating the dead," I said. "I guess Quillion didn't want to take any chances on his coming back."

"But if Henry's *that* dangerous – which I definitely believe he is – then why not destroy his body?"

"I don't know. Maybe Quillion wants to keep Frankenstein on ice in case his knowledge is needed again someday. You know the Darklords and their servants, always scheming. But to tell you the truth, I wouldn't be surprised if Baron asked Quillion to spare his old man."

"You're probably right," Devona said. "I just hope we all don't come to regret his mercy one day."

I'd been to Tenebrus and I wanted to tell Devona that there was nothing to worry about. But then again, I'd escaped, hadn't I? And given how devious Frankenstein was, it wasn't out of the realm of possibility that he'd foreseen his incarceration and taken steps to ensure his eventual freedom and resurrection. Burke and

Hare had disappeared after Henry's defeat, and while Quillion had put bounties on their heads, so far, there had been no sign of the bodysnatching duo.

I decided that was a problem for another day. I had one of my own to resolve just then.

"I've been thinking," I said. "About the business."

"Yes?" Devona said, her tone carefully neutral.

I paused to choose my words carefully. "I know you see the Midnight Watch as the first major project we took on together... as a couple, I mean. And I love you, Devona. It's just—"

"You like your freedom too much to commit to the Watch full time," she said.

"Yes, but that doesn't mean I don't want to commit to *you*. Do you see the difference?"

"I do now." She smiled. "It helps that I can read your mind, you know. You really aren't very good at talking about this kind of thing."

I hadn't realized how tense I'd been until I felt myself relax.

"Whatever works," I said.

"Maybe we should make that our new motto," she said.

"I can think of worse ones."

We sat there quietly for a time, watching the fire and feeling the breeze as Rover circled invisibly around us. After a time, Devona spoke again, her voice so soft I could barely hear her.

"Do you still think about what we experienced inside Orlock's stasis field?"

"Yes," I admitted. "They still feel real to me, even though I know they weren't."

I didn't have to say who *they* were.

A few more moments passed before Devona spoke again. She sat up and faced me and I knew whatever she wanted to tell me it was important.

"I know it's not physically possible for us to have children of our own. I'm half undead and you're all the way dead, but I was thinking maybe we could adopt. One day."

I was married once back on Earth, but my ex and I had never had kids. I'd grown used to the idea that fatherhood wasn't on the cards for me – especially once I became a zombie. But after what we'd experienced in Orlock's dome, I wasn't so sure what was and wasn't possible anymore.

"It would be a lot of responsibility," I said.

"A big commitment," she added. "Do you think you could handle it?" She looked at me hopefully.

My first impulse was to say yes just to please her, but this was too important. She deserved a serious answer. We'd only been together a few months, and we weren't even officially married yet. On the other hand, I'd never been with anyone like Devona before. We matched in a way I'd never thought possible and our ability to communicate psychically had bonded us deeply in a short period of time. But raising a child is tough under the best conditions, and doing so in Nekropolis? We had a hard enough time keeping ourselves alive sometimes. If we had a child to protect…

I started to give Devona my answer, but then I realized something was wrong. She'd stopped moving and her eyes weren't blinking. At first I feared she'd somehow succumbed to some sort of after effect of Orlock's stasis field, but then a worse thought hit me. What if we were still inside the stasis dome and everything we'd experienced since then had been nothing but another illusion?

"Don't worry," came a soft male voice. "Devona's fine. I just wanted a chance to speak with you in private."

I turned toward the sound of the voice and saw a man climb out of the fireplace. The flames hadn't touched him since they were illusory, but I knew that even if they'd been the real thing they still wouldn't have harmed him. It was Edrigu, Lord of the Dead.

I rose to my feet to meet the gray shrouded man as he strode into the room. A violent gust of wind blasted Edrigu and I knew that Rover was preparing to deal with what he saw as an intruder.

"Down boy," I told the ward spirit. "He's a friend."

I had no idea if this was a friendly visit or not, but Edrigu was so powerful he could destroy Rover in an eyeblink without exerting himself. It took Rover a few seconds to back down, but the wind died away. Rover didn't retreat, though. I could feel the ward spirit hanging close by in case he was needed.

"I see you've rejoined the world of the living," I said. "So to speak."

Edrigu smiled at me. "The events of the last couple days caused quite a disturbance in the city's psychic atmosphere, Enough to penetrate the Darklords' slumber and wake us." His voice was the sound of a breeze wafting through a deserted graveyard in the dead of night.

"Too bad your alarm didn't go off earlier," I said. "You missed all the fun."

"I believe that was Dr. Frankenstein's intention," Edrigu said.

I saw the chain around the Darklord's neck, though Osseal itself was hidden from sight beneath his shroud.

"Looks like you got your flute back."

"Yes. Quillion removed Osseal from the Foundry and held it until I awoke, at which time I reclaimed it. I've come to thank you for getting it back for me, and more importantly, for stopping Dr. Frankenstein from misusing it so grievously."

I'd interacted more with the other four Darklords than I had with Edrigu and I found his lack of megalomaniacal posturing to be refreshing.

"I have to admit that there was more than a little self-interest to my motives, but you're welcome. And not that you've come looking for my advice, but if I were you, I'd give some serious thought to revamping the Reliquary's security. All Frankenstein needed to gain entrance to your bedchamber was this mark."

I held up the hand with the scar tissue E on the palm.

"That mark is intended for quite a different purpose," Edrigu said. "It took someone of Dr. Frankenstein's uncommon intelligence, not to mention deviousness, to turn it to a criminal purpose. Still, your point is well taken, and I'll make certain my private chambers are secure from all intrusion in the future."

"Speaking of your mark, Silent Jack gave it to me without explaining its purpose. Which, considering his name, isn't all that surprising. But since you're here…"

Edrigu nodded. "It's the last I can do to repay you. Jack is one of my best servants and one of his most important tasks is to find the dead wherever they might be in the city and give them my mark. Once they possess it, they are free to enter the Reliquary whenever they wish, allowing them to access my mirror and – should they choose to step through – to what waits for them on the other side."

This realization stunned me and for a moment all I could do was look at Edrigu.

"You mean it doesn't mark me as one of your servants?" I asked.

Edrigu smiled. "No. I already have enough of those. But if you're interested…"

"Nothing personal, but no thanks." I was still struggling to come to terms with what Edrigu had told me. The mark on my hand would allow me to enter his stronghold and pass through his dark mirror to the afterlife – whatever that might be. "Why give me the mark and not tell me what it means?"

"Some of the dead instinctively understand what the mark signifies. Others take longer to work it out. It all depends on whether or not they're ready – or interested – in moving on to the next realm of existence. Each must find the way to my mirror in his or her own time, which is as it should be. But now that you know, you are free to pass through whenever you choose."

I looked at Devona. "I appreciate the free ticket to the afterlife, but I don't have any intention of leaving Nekropolis any time soon."

"As you wish. My mirror will be waiting for you if you ever change your mind."

"Tell me one thing, though," I said, curious. "What *is* on the other side of your mirror?"

Edrigu grinned, displaying small rounded teeth that looked like two rows of ivory gravestones. "Sorry. That would be cheating."

I thought that the Lord of the Dead would take his leave then, returning to the fireplace like some dark version of Santa Claus going back up the chimney. But instead he said, "I have something I wish to give you. A reward for the service you rendered to me, and indeed, to the entire city. Hold out your hand."

I did so and an instant later a coin appeared on my palm. I held it up to my face to examine it. The coin was copper, incredibly old, its features worn so smooth that I couldn't make them out.

I looked at Edrigu. "Don't tell me this is a tip."

Edrigu smiled. "Of a sort, I suppose. That is one of Charon's coins. In Greek mythology, the dead have to pay Charon the ferryman to take them across the River Styx to the land of the dead. But once the coins have been touched by Charon they can be used to purchase a single day of life. You have but to grip the coin tight, wish it, and you will be become a living, breathing man for a single twenty-four hour time period. But be warned: you can only use the coin once, and afterward, you can never use another."

I stared at the coin, unable to believe what Edrigu had told me. To be alive again, if only for one day...

"I will take my leave of you now," Edrigu said. "As you might imagine, many tasks have piled up while I've been asleep that I must attend to, and of course my fellow Lords will undoubtedly soon be returning to their endless intrigues, and I must prepare to deal with them." He started to go, then paused. "One thing more. Just before I appeared, I overheard part of your conversation with Devona. There are many things a man might accomplish with one day of life." He gave me a knowing smile. "Including siring a child."

The Lord of the Dead gave me a parting nod, turned, and walked back into the fireplace and was gone. I stared at the flickering flames for a moment and then I heard Devona say, "Well? Can you?"

I remembered the last words she'd spoken before Edrigu had frozen her.

A big commitment. Do you think you could handle it?

I turned to see her frowning.

"Weren't you just sitting next to me?" she asked.

I looked at Charon's coin one last time before tucking it into my pocket and rejoining Devona on the couch.

"To answer your question, my love, I think I can handle it just fine."

She gave me a look filled with love and we kissed.

You know something? I have a pretty good life for a dead guy. And thanks to Lord Edrigu – and the coin he'd given me – I had a feeling that it was soon going to get even better.

ABOUT THE AUTHOR

Tim Waggoner is an American novelist and college professor. His original novels include *Cross County*, *Darkness Wakes*, *Pandora Drive*, and *Like Death*. His tie-in novels include *The Lady Ruin* series and the *Blade of the Flame* trilogy, both for Wizards of the Coast. He's also written fiction based on *Stargate: SG-1*, *Doctor Who*, *A Nightmare on Elm Street*, the videogame *Defender*, *Xena the Warrior Princess*, and others. He's published over one hundred short stories, some of which are collected in *Broken Shadows* and *All Too Surreal*. His articles on writing have appeared in *Writer's Digest*, *Writers' Journal* and other publications.

He teaches composition and creative writing at Sinclair Community College in Dayton, Ohio, and is a faculty mentor in Seton Hill University's Master of Arts in Writing Popular Fiction program in Greensburg, Pennsylvania.

www.timwaggoner.com

*The next Matt Richter novel will
be called* Dark War. *While you are
waiting, here's another case for
Matt and Devona...*

THE MIDNIGHT WATCH
A Matt Richter investigation

"You're really thinking about doing this, aren't you?"

Devona didn't answer me right away, and I took that
as a bad sign. I knew she heard me. We'd only been together a couple of months, but in that time I'd learned
that not only was her half-vampire hearing sharp as
hell, she rarely missed anything that went on around
her. So if she wasn't answering me, it could only mean
one of two things: I'd asked the wrong question or she
was afraid I wasn't going to like her answer. This time,
it turned out to be both.

We were standing on the sidewalk in front of a squat
stone building that put me in mind of a giant toad that
had looked a gorgon straight in the eye. Thick tendrils
of leech vine covered most of the surface, and the stone
that we could see was pitted and cracked. I wouldn't
have been surprised if the damned vine was the only
thing holding the ancient structure together. The building was located in the Sprawl, not all that far from my
apartment... make that our apartment. Devona had
moved in not long after we met, but I still sometimes
had   trouble   wrapping   my
undead brain around the concept that I was part of a

couple again. I'd been married back on Earth, but that was a while ago. I'd long since divorced and traveled to the other-dimensional city of Nekropolis where I'd died and been resurrected as a self-willed zombie. After that, I figured my dating days were over. I mean, really, would you want to go out with someone who's perpetually decaying? But Devona was a broad-minded woman, even for Nekropolis, and I regularly visited my houngan for periodic applications of the preservative spells that prevented me from completely rotting away to dust.

I was fairly fresh that day, with only a slight grayish-green tinge to my flesh. I wore my usual gray suit and my tie displayed images of Dahli's famous melting clocks draped limply over tree branches. If you looked closely, you could see the fabric hands of the clocks move and hear the soft ticking of gears at work. Devona wore a form-fitting black leather outfit, as she often did, and it looked damned good on her. She was a petite blonde who appeared to be in her twenties, but in truth was in her seventies. She might have been only half-vampire, but that was enough to significantly slow down her aging process.

This was a relatively sedate part of the Sprawl – one of the reasons why I'd chosen to rent an apartment there – but the emphasis was most definitely on relatively. The Sprawl is the Dominion of the Demon Queen, Varvara, and she believes in absolute freedom. It's rumored that the old Beast Alistair Crowley stole his infamous satanic commandant from her: Do as Thou Wilt. I wouldn't be surprised. If the Sprawl doesn't exist in a state of total anarchy, it'll do until the real thing shows up. But like I said, this neighborhood was quiet enough, with pedestrians going about their business searching for prey or trying to avoid becoming prey – often at the same time – and vehicles of various makes, models, and degrees of sentience rolling, crawling, and scuttling down the street. To the right of the stone toad building was a misfortuneteller's establishment, and on the left was a head shop (new and used, all species, original size and shrunken). Not exactly the most glamorous of neighbors, but they seemed… well, not normal, but harmless enough.

Devona finally decided to respond to my question. "Not thinking…"

A sinking feeling hit me. "Please tell me you haven't bought the place. Sight unseen, no less."

She shrugged. "All right, I won't tell you."

I suppressed a sigh. Devona was the half-human daughter of the Darklord Galm, and she'd spent most of her life living in his stronghold and serving as the caretaker of his collection of rare and powerful artifacts. So while she was chronologically older than me by several decades, in terms of actual life experience, she could be a bit naïve at times. And, as I'd been learning over the last couple months, a trifle impulsive.

"We talked about how it's not a good idea to buy real estate without a thorough inspection first, remember?"

Devona turned to me, eyes narrowed and lips pursed. I'd seen that expression before. It meant Stop patronizing me, Matt. "I remember it quite well, and perhaps you'll recall that my main motivation for purchasing the building was to acquire the name of the business associated with it more than the actual structure itself." She smiled. "Of course, now that we're here, I suppose we should go in and take a look around."

This time I didn't bother to suppress my sigh. I don't need to breathe, but I have to take in air to talk, and while strictly speaking, I don't have to sigh, sometimes a sigh can communicate more than a dozen well-chosen words.

"Couldn't you have bought the name by itself?" I didn't ask why she wanted it so badly. That was another discussion we'd already had.

The Midnight Watch was the security firm back in its day, Devona had said. Long before your arrival in Nekropolis, Matt. If you wanted something or someone protected, you hired the Watch. Even the Darklords were known to employ its services from time to time. If I'm going to go into business on my own, that kind of name recognition will help get me established. Besides, I was caretaker of Father's collection for many years. I like things with a little history behind them.

I'd met Devona when she'd hired me to help her recover an artifact that had been stolen from Galm's collection. In the process, we'd not only found the artifact and saved the city from total annihilation, we'd also fallen in love. Makes for a great first date story, don't you think? Unfortunately, Galm cast out Devona for losing the artifact in the first place – even though another of his children had been responsible for the theft – and so jobless and homeless, she'd moved in with me. She'd been helping me with cases ever since, and I thought we made a good team, professionally as well as personally, but Devona eventually decided she wanted to work for herself.

Please don't take this the wrong way, Matt, she'd told me. I've loved working with you, but I served my father all my adult life… lived in his home, tended his property… I've never had anything of my own. Never had to make my own way in the world. I want to see if I can. I hope you'll understand.

Of course I did. You don't get to be the only private detective in a city full of monsters, demons, and witches without having a strong independent streak. I told her I loved her and admired her for wanting to start her own business – which was true, though I knew I'd miss her working with me. The mean streets of Nekropolis would seem a little lonelier without her by my side.

When I asked her what business she wanted to go into, she said, I was thinking security. A big part of my job for father consisted of overseeing the protections – both magical and mundane – on his collection. I could put that experience to good use in my own security firm. And if I advertise that I used to do security work for a Darklord…

I had to admit, it sounded like my love had a head for business. If things kept going this way, I might well end up working for her one day.

Devona turned back to examine the building once more. "I did check into buying the name. When the original owner died, the property defaulted into Varvara's hands, and when I asked her if I could simply purchase the name Midnight Watch, she told me the name went with the property, and I couldn't have one without the other."

"I don't suppose she gave you a reason."

Devona looked at me as if I'd just said something incredibly stupid, and on reflection, I didn't blame her. The Demon Queen did what she did solely for her own pleasure.

"All right, then tell me this: did she smile when she told you that?"

Devona's face is normally pale – she is half Bloodborn, after all – but it went chalk white as the implications of my question hit her.

"I was afraid of that." If Varvara finds something amusing, it's usually bad news – especially if what she finds amusing is you. "So there's something wrong with the building… probably very wrong. All right, let's go find out what it is."

I stuck my hands in my jacket pockets and started toward the building's entrance.

Devona put a hand on my shoulder to stop me, and stop me she did, dead – if you'll pardon the expression – in my tracks. She's petite, but her vampiric heritage gives her greater strength than a human. I couldn't have gone anywhere if I'd wanted to.

"No, Matt. If it's going to be dangerous–"

I turned back to look at her. "I appreciate the concern, but this is Nekropolis. Everything is dangerous here: the only question is how dangerous. Besides, if you really want to set yourself up in business as the revived Midnight Watch, you'll need to use this building, right?"

"That's very sweet of you."

She leaned forward and gave me a hard kiss on the lips. Devona knows I can only feel the pressure of her kisses, so she always makes sure there's enough for me to feel. When she pulled back, she gave me a wry smile.

"And this gallantry of yours has nothing to do with your irritation over the fact that Varvara knew you'd come here with me to check the place out and was amused at the notion of you tangling with whatever lies inside."

"Not in the goddamned slightest," I said. "C'mon, let's go."

As we walked toward the door, I warned Devona to stay clear of the leech vines. The bloodsucking vegetation wouldn't bother me – no blood – but Devona had plenty of the red stuff coursing through her veins, and it was half vampire. Leech vine loves vampire blood best of all. It's like the finest of wines to the plant. Me, I find it poetic justice that one of the city's greatest predators has a bloodthirsty nemesis that desires to feed on its liquid life essence, but the vampires don't see it that way. That's why the best leech vine exterminators in the city are Bloodborn.

The door was covered with leech vine, but since I'd known the building had been abandoned for years and had likely fallen prey to the vine, I'd come prepared. I took my right hand out of my jacket pocket and aimed the object I'd removed – a tiny figurine resembling a white ape – at the door. I spoke a single activating word and the ape's mouth opened, unleashing a torrent of frigid air. The leech vine covering the door instantly turned black and fell to the ground. When the figurine was finished, I tucked it back in my pocket.

"What in the nine hells was that?" Devona demanded. "The stench is awful!"

"Yeti's Breath," I said. "It's a great spell for killing leech vine." I smiled. "Especially when your sense of smell is as dead as the rest of you."

Devona looked as if she was desperately trying to keep the contents of her stomach where they belonged. "Give a girl some warning next time, all right?"

"Sorry." Embarrassed, I turned away from her. When you're dead, it's easy to forget the strong impact that sensory input can have on others. Maybe, I thought, it'll be better for Devona when she doesn't have to work with me anymore.

I examined the door. It was covered with frost that was already starting to melt, but beneath it I could make out a metal plaque with these words engraved upon it:

The Midnight Watch: Guarding All Workhouses and Institutions Against Intruders and Meddling. Savage Beasts Employed.

"Catchy," I said. I turned back to Devona. "Sense anything?"

In response, Devona closed her eyes and concentrated. Not only was she highly skilled at detecting wardspells, as a vampire-human hybrid, she possessed certain psychic abilities that most Bloodborn did not.

"Yes, I…" She broke off, frowning. Then she opened her eyes. "I thought I sensed something there for a moment, almost as if there was someone inside the building, but the feeling faded quickly. Most likely I was picking up psychic impressions from the businesses on either side."

"Maybe." But I didn't believe it. I'd lived – or maybe I should say *existed* – in Nekropolis too long. Besides, if Varvara was amused at the idea of the two of us entering the building, there was definitely something Bad inside.

I pointed to the door knob. "How about that?"

Devona waved her hand over the knob several times and then bent down and examined it visually. She straightened.

"Clean. No traps, mystical or otherwise."

I hmpfed. "For a security firm, it seems they weren't too concerned with folks breaking in."

"Wardspells are intricate to construct and require constant maintenance," Devona said. "It's been at least fifty years since the building's been occupied. Any wardspells on the door would've lost their potency and deactivated long ago."

"Fifty years, and no one's bought the building in all

that time? Or at least tried squatting in it? I find that hard to believe." And considering the kinds of things I'd had to learn to believe in since coming to Nekropolis, that was saying something. "This might not be the most prime location in the Sprawl, but real estate here is always in high demand. After all, it's sin central for the entire city, and that means there's a hell of a lot of darkgems to be made here. What would keep a building in the Sprawl vacant for so many years? Wait – let me guess. It's supposed to be haunted. And not just regular haunted, with a few ghosts flitting about the rooms to lend the place some gloomy atmosphere. It's haunted with a capital H, by some kind of unknown and incredibly deadly force that will shatter our minds, mutilate our bodies, and ravage our souls, right?"

"As a matter of fact…"

I didn't sigh this time. I was too depressed to bother.

"This probably isn't the time or place for this, Devona, but I think you and I really need to work on our communication skills."

I tried the knob and wasn't surprised in the slightest to find it unlocked. I turned it (far too easily, I might add), pushed the door open (it didn't even have the good grace to creak), and we went inside.

It was dark, of course. Any windows were completely covered by leech vine, but since Nekropolis is shrouded in the perpetual dusk created by Umbriel the Shadow-sun, it would've been dark inside even if the windows were clear and left wide open. Devona's hybrid eyes could see in the dark far better than my undead ones, so while I took a flashlight out of my jacket pocket, I didn't turn it on right away.

After several moments, she said, "We're in a foyer, but I don't see anything special. You might as well go ahead and turn your light on, Matt."

I flicked the flashlight's switch and played its beam around to get my bearings. It was just as Devona had said: a foyer with stone walls and ceiling and a marble tiled floor. Nice enough, in a cold, Spartan way, but nothing to e-mail home about. There were sconces on the walls where greenfire torches had undoubtedly once burned to light the place, but the mystic flames had died away decades ago, and without an Arcane torchlighter to rekindle them, it looked like we were stuck with my flashlight.

As we started slowly down the foyer, I said, "So, are you going to tell me why this place is supposed to be haunted?"

"The original owner and founder of the Midnight Watch was a warlock named Leander Crosswise. He was reputed to be a genius when it came to devising new and innovative wardspells and was also known for breeding some of the fiercest and most intelligent guard animals the city has ever seen. He ran the Midnight Watch very successfully for nearly a century before he finally decided to retire. But before he could, he was murdered, right here in the building, doors locked, wardspells in place. When one of his employees arrived for work the next day, Leander was found lying face-down on the floor of his office, a Dire Blade sticking out of his back."

Nasty things, Dire Blades. Obsidian daggers with mystic runes carved into the surface, absolutely deadly to supernatural creatures, the Arcane included. They're the favored weapons of the Dominari, Nekropolis' version of the Mafia, but other criminals use them as well, provided they can scrounge up enough darkgems to purchase one of the things. They're damned expensive, and a good thing, too, or else every low life in the city would have one.

By this time Devona and I had left the foyer and entered a large room that looked something like a den – dilapidated furniture, stone fireplace filled with cobwebs, musty old paintings on the walls, rotting wooden beams overhead. I assumed the room had been used as a place to meet clients and was likely impressive enough, in its time. There was no sign of anything out of place, and certainly no ghosts leaping out from behind the moldy couch or the cracked leather chairs, so Devona and I left to continue our exploration of the building. As we walked, I asked Devona some questions about the story she'd just told me.

"Was the murderer ever caught?"

"No. Leander was a prominent citizen in the Sprawl, so Varvara sent her best Inquisitors and Hellhounds to investigate, but they turned up nothing. She even asked Talaith to send some Arcane investigators, but their magic failed to locate a single clue, let alone reveal the identity of Leander's killer."

So the warlock's employees were cleared and, while it was possible, if not likely, that Crosswise had enemies or even disgruntled clients who wished him ill, it seemed none of them had been implicated either.

"Did the investigators have any luck tracing the Dire Blade?"

Devona and I were walking down a hallway now. When we came to a door, we'd stop, Devona would check for wardspells or booby traps, and when she gave the all-clear, I'd open the door and shine my flashlight inside. All we found was office furniture: desks, chairs, filing cabinets and the like. Nothing of interest. At least nothing had jumped out of the shadows and tried to devour our faces – yet.

"The Blade belonged to Leander. As you might imagine, he owned quite a few weapons, some mystical, some not. Some he'd purchased for the business, some he'd picked up on various jobs. The employees all testified that the Blade was Leander's."

"And no fingerprints or DNA – or the magical equivalent – was found on the weapon," I said. "Except for Crosswise's."

"That's right."

That didn't necessarily mean anything. Nekropolis is lousy with beings who can manipulate objects magically or with the power of their mind. And a really good magic user could destroy any traces that they'd handled the weapon. But then again, two Darklords had sent their best investigators to look into Crosswise's death, and even if a magic user had tried to remove any evidence they'd handled the weapon, investigators of that caliber would've found it.

"You said Crosswise was going to retire."

"That's right. He was killed on the night before he planned to officially retire, as a matter of fact."

"That's interesting."

"Why?"

We'd just finished checking our third office and were headed toward our fourth. I was beginning to think that Varvara had been so amused at the thought of our coming here because she'd known the place would end up boring us to death.

"It might speak to possible motive," I said. "Maybe someone resented Leander retiring. Was he planning on selling the business or giving it to a successor?"

"Neither," Devona said. "He planned to close the business and sell the building. He wanted the Midnight

Watch to end with him."

"Maybe someone didn't want him to sell."

"Is that really enough motive to kill someone?"

We reached the fourth door. None of them had any names on them, but this was nicer than the others, made of sturdy black oak that I imagined had once held a highly polished sheen. I had no doubt this was Crosswise's office.

"Back when I was homicide detective on Earth, I once arrested a man who killed his brother for changing the channel during his favorite sitcom. And it was a rerun."

"Point taken," Devona said as she waved her hands in the air over the door. I figured she'd find nothing and proceed to visually examining the lock, but instead she stopped her hand waving and frowned. "Something's strange here."

I can't get cold chills anymore, but if I could've, I would've then.

"What?"

"I'm getting that feeling again, like I did outside. As if there's something alive in the office, only... not. Something that's almost there but not quite."

"You know, you still haven't told me why people believe this building is haunted." Although right at that moment, standing in a dark hallway before an ominous black door, I wasn't sure I wanted to know.

"People have tried to enter the building since Leander's death. Some report a force like a strong wind shoving them back outside. Others..."

"Go on," I urged.

"Others have died in some particularly horrible ways. Bodies turned inside out, blood boiled in their veins, that sort of thing."

"Lovely. And what distinguished those poor unfortunates from the lucky ones who were simply evicted?"

"The ones who died..." Devona paused, and time seemed to slow to a crawl while I waited for her to finish her sentence. "Were those who intended to purchase the building."

"Once again, we *so* have to work on our communication skills! When were you planning on telling me this?"

"I don't know," she said. "I was still trying to figure out the best way to tell you I'd already gone ahead and bought the damned building."

The instant the words left her mouth, the door burst open and a roaring wind filled the hallway. The force slammed Devona into the opposite wall and held her there. The wind – or whatever it was – grabbed hold of me with insubstantial hands and started dragging me away from her. I fought it, tried to tear myself free of its grip, but there was nothing I could do. I could feel the force holding me, but when I tried to touch it, to grab hold and dislodge myself, I couldn't feel anything. I dropped the flashlight. It hit the floor, luckily without breaking, and rolled into a position where its beam illuminated Devona. Her face was contorted with agony and bright dots of red covered her skin. Whatever this unknown force was, it looked as if it was drawing the blood out of her body through her skin. Vampires – even half ones like Devona – can take a hell of a lot of punishment and heal, but one thing they can't recover from is the loss of their blood supply. Their power is in their blood, and if they're drained, they have no magic to draw upon in order to heal themselves. I knew if I didn't do something fast, Devona would die, and she wouldn't be coming back.

I'd brought some other toys with me, various spells and such, but none of them would prove effective against the strange force attacking us. And with each passing second, the wind was pulling me farther from Devona. I had only seconds in which to act, and I had no weapons that I could use. Except the one weapon which has always served me best, whether I was alive or dead. My mind.

I thought fast. What did I know about the Midnight Watch, Leander Crosswise, and how he died? Devona had told me he specialized in creating new and powerful wardspells, that he also developed new breeds of strong, intelligent guard animals, and he was killed on the eve of his retirement, after which he planned to close his business and sell the building. And he was killed by a Dire Blade that had apparently wielded itself. Or been wielded by something that didn't need a physical hand to hold it.

That's when it came to me.

I shouted to be heard over the roar of the wind. "She did buy the building, it's true, but she did so in order to resurrect the Midnight Watch!"

It might have been my imagination, but I thought I felt the wind's grip on me lessen, and it seemed I was no longer traveling so swiftly down the hallway away from Devona. Encouraged, I continued.

"Her name's Devona Kanti, and she hopes to start her own security business right here, in this very building, and she plans to use the name Midnight Watch! It's a proud, noble name, one she's honored to be associated with!"

Blood had begun trickling in rivulets from Devona's pores, and while she was obviously in pain, she still possessed enough presence of mind to pick up on what

I was doing.

"It's true! I love the history associated with this place, and all I want to do is make the name Midnight Watch mean something in the city again!"

The gale's roar subsided to a mere whisper, and I was no longer being dragged away from Devona. I started toward her just as she slumped to the floor. By the time I reached her, the wind had died away completely and the hallway was silent again, save for the sound of her pained breathing.

I knelt beside her and took her hand. "Are you going to be all right?"

"I... I think so. It hurt like hell, but I didn't lose too much blood." She managed a weak smile. "You're going to have to take me out for a big meal tonight, though."

"You've got it."

She tried to stand, but I encouraged her to sit for a few more moments to give her metabolism time to counter her blood loss.

"So, are you going to tell me what you figured out," she asked, "or are you going to make me guess?"

"Once the wind – or whatever it was – attacked us, it seemed obvious to me that it must've wielded the Dire Blade that killed Crosswise. And that it was the force responsible for killing anyone who tried to purchase the building in all the years following. This force was clearly here before Crosswise was killed, and since it's remained here, that means it's part of the structure. And if Crosswise was such a skilled warlock, I can't believe there was any mystical force attached to the Midnight Watch that he didn't know about. So the force was something he was aware of but thought he had no reason to fear. And evidently he didn't: until he decided to retire and sell the building. When you told me what his specialties were–"

Devona's face lit up with sudden understanding. "It's a wardspell, isn't it? A supremely sophisticated one that Leander created!"

I nodded. "But more than that. You said he also bred guard animals – highly intelligent ones. I think the force is both a wardspell and a guardian, and it's smarter than Crosswise gave it credit for. When he planned to retire and sell the building–"

"The ward creature would be sold to, for it's tied to the structure. In a way, it's the lifeforce of the building."

"Crosswise was going to sell the building, and it's my guess any new owners wouldn't want such a powerful being as part of their new property."

"So Leander planned to remove the spell, which meant the ward creature would cease to exist. So it was defending itself when it killed Leander."

"Yes, just as it believed it was doing every time a potential new owner entered the building. That's why it only evicted others. The creature didn't perceive them as threats. I hoped that if I could make it realize you weren't a threat, it would break off its attack. Luckily, I was right."

Devona smiled. While streaks of blood remained on her face, neck, and hands, her color was less pale, and she seemed stronger. I stood, reached down, and helped her to her feet.

"My hero."

She gave me another hard kiss on the lips, and though there was still a bit blood on her mouth, I didn't mind at all. You come to expect that sort of thing when you're in love with a vampire. She has it worse; she has to worry about whether one of my lips might fall off when we kiss.

She took my hand and we started down the hallway back toward the front door.

"So," I said, "does this uh, revelation alter your plans any?" I was trying to be careful with my words. I didn't want to rouse the ward creature's ire again.

Devona thought about it for a moment. "Well, I still want to run my business out of this building, and I think that with a little work, I'll be able to make friends with the ward creature, and it'll make a wonderful guardian for the place." She paused, long enough for it to be a Meaningful Pause. "I'm not sure you're aware of it, Matt, but we've taken an important step forward in our relationship today."

Like a lot of men, I'm not always as aware of relationship milestones as my partner, and I wracked my undead brain, trying to figure out what Devona was referring to.

"Uh, you mean because you've officially established your independence?"

She grinned and punched me on the arm.

"No, silly. Because now we have a pet together."

We continued on down the hallway, hand in hand.

TIM WAGGONER

Introducing
Matt Richter.

Private Eye.

Zombie.

Nekropolis

"An atmospheric and exciting mystery." – *SF Site*

"Rejoice! It's a Sam Spade for a new generation."
SF REVU

Psssst! Get advance intelligence on Angry Robot's nefarious plans for world domination. Also, free stuff. Sign up to our Robot Legion at angryrobotbooks.com/legion Always more.

ANGRY ROBOT